THE
SECRETS
OF
FLOWERS

After studying history at university, Sally moved to London to work in advertising. In her spare time she studied floristry at night school and eventually opened her own flower shop. Sally came to appreciate that flower shops offer a unique window into people's stories and she began to photograph and write about this floral life in a series of non-fiction books. Later, Sally continued her interest in writing when she founded her fountain pen company, PLOOMS.

Sally now lives in Dorset. Her eldest daughter, Alex, is a doctor and her youngest daughter is the author Libby Page.

Sally's debut novel, *The Keeper of Stories*, was a *Sunday Times* bestseller, has now sold over 500,000 copies and has been translated into 29 languages.

sallypage.com
@SallyPageBooks
/sallypageauthor
@bysallypage

Also by Sally Page

The Keeper of Stories
The Book of Beginnings

THE
SECRETS
OF
FLOWERS

SALLY
PAGE

HarperCollins*Publishers*

HarperCollins*Publishers* Ltd
1 London Bridge Street,
London SE1 9GF
www.harpercollins.co.uk

HarperCollins*Publishers*
Macken House,
39/40 Mayor Street Upper,
Dublin 1
D01 C9W8

First published by HarperCollins*Publishers* 2024
1

A catalogue record for this book is available from the British Library

ISBN: 978-0-00-861290-0 (PB)

Typeset in Berling LT Std by HarperCollins*Publishers* India

Printed and bound in the UK using 100% Renewable
Electricity at CPI Group (UK) Ltd

This book is produced from independently certified FSC paper to ensure
responsible forest management.
For more information visit: www.harpercollins.co.uk/green

Dedicated with my love and thanks to
Pippa & Peter Bell
who took me 'sailing' on
the Olympic, *the* Queen Mary *and the* Royal Yacht Britannia.
&
for florists everywhere.

Flowers are like friends,
they bring colour to your world.

Prologue

Oxford

The scent of the rain summons the memory. Uninvited. Unwanted.

She is in the garden. It is late December, seven months after Will's death. She is digging into the frozen ground. There is no order to the way she tackles the work. All she knows is that she wants to gouge her pain away.

Rain falls as she scrabbles in the earth. She has become used to waves of disorientating anger, but this is new. She thinks her rage will consume her.

When she spots some early snowdrops peeping through a pile of old leaves, she pulls at them, ripping them from the soil. The sight of the pure, hopeful flowers is more than she can bear.

As the earth runs to mud and soaks into her frozen skin, she rocks back and forward on her knees, the tiny flowers crushed in her hand.

Five months on, the rain on the partly open window is different – a May flurry making a blustery fuss before passing on. But something in the metallic fragrance lingers, conjuring the past. Emma looks at the blank laptop screen in front of her and wonders why she is finding this so difficult. It should be a simple enough thing to write: *I resign. I quit. I shall be leaving.* They are just words. It shouldn't be this hard.

There have been times when she has found exactly the right words. Experienced the satisfaction of hearing a phrase settle just where it should, like a child posting the right shaped brick into the exact shaped slot. In the main, she associates these moments of succinct expression with the clinical environment of the lab in which she works, where everything is measured and nothing is left to chance.

But outside of work, in a world untrammelled by lines of white tiles, she finds her words are more likely to twist out of shape, like a scarf caught in the wind, swirling mid-air to wrap themselves with unintended meaning around the recipient. Either that, or her words are lost, carried away to be trodden, unnoticed, underfoot. Fear of saying the wrong thing makes her falter, and in that hesitation, she feels the substance draining from her words until all that is left in her mouth is a whisper. Then the best she can hope for is a pause, and a 'Sorry, Emma, did you say something?'

Still, better that. Better to watch, helpless, as the phrases flap quietly away, than to be a person who holds words securely between a thumb and forefinger, ready to press them with precision into the softness of flesh, burying them with a persistent, thrusting thumb so that they will eventually take root. Not to grow outwards to the sun but to burrow deep into the heart of you.

Emma wonders why she has started thinking about her mother – a woman who can plant words in her flesh like a seasoned gardener.

Ten minutes later, Emma looks down at her brief words of resignation. She knows the time has come. She has just turned forty, and she wants a change. There will be more research to do on the degenerative condition they are studying, working with other universities around the world, but they will have to tackle it without her. She suspects her colleagues will miss her grasp of languages – she is fluent in Spanish, Italian and French – but will they miss *her*? She doubts it. And, apart from the languages, there are others who can take her place. The team's PhD student is clearly itching to step into her shoes, and there is no doubt that he could. Literally. Emma is exceptionally tall and has always had large feet. She long ago gave up wondering why such a shy person was given a body and hair (corkscrew curly and very red) that make her so glaringly obvious in any crowd. Neither her science nor her grandmother's God has ever provided a satisfactory answer to that one.

She wonders who she will tell about her decision. Her stomach and heart take the plunge down the well-worn track of those she wants to tell but can't – her husband and her dad –

and there is still, after all this time, the residual surprise that, once, *once*, she was happily married. She did find someone. And not just anyone.

This never fails to amaze her.

Suddenly, there is something she needs to find. She unearths it from under the bundle of clean washing that is piled at the end of the table – the local free paper. The pages are turned over to the small ads. What she is looking for is ringed in black.

She frowns as she reads. Her memories of her father are invariably linked to his garden. Is this why it had jumped out at her? Could this be the change she is looking for?

Wanted: Florist to work part-time in garden centre. Experience useful but not essential. Training can be given.
Own car helpful.
Must be friendly and good with people.

Emma re-reads the advert.
Well, at least she has her own car.

PART 1

Chapter 1

Emma

Chocolate Cosmos

Emma's favourite time in the garden centre is first thing in the morning before it opens. The banks of plants smell of rich, damp earth where the owner, Les, has been watering – he is always there before her, and she knows where he is by the yellow hose moving in jerky jumps along the path. She never follows the yellow snake, preferring to walk on her own and breathe in the beginning of the day: still air with the promise of heat hidden in the haze; or cool air stirring the leaves, the precursor to blustery showers; and sometimes, days that are so clear it looks like the window cleaner has just been. On these days Emma sits on the bench by the cosmos that smell of chocolate and watches the downs that rise above the allotments at the back of the centre. She lets her mind go blank as shadows from the clouds chase each other across the hills. At lunchtime, she often retreats to this bench, preferring to eat alone rather than join the other staff in the café.

Emma has been working in the garden centre for just over two months and is still surprised that the husband and wife team, Betty and Les, gave her the job. At the interview she had decided not to dwell on her university work as it hardly seemed relevant, so instead, she had talked of 'a time for a change', 'an abiding interest in flowers' and said she was 'keen to learn'. Afterwards, she recalled these clichés and the awkward pauses when she lost her nerve or her train of thought. But in the end, they had offered her the position – three days a week in the Flower Cabin, plus the odd Saturday. She can't help wondering sometimes if anyone else even applied for the job.

It was Betty's idea to offer a floristry service in the centre, making up bouquets, arrangements and the occasional funeral piece, in the hope of bringing in additional business. Les had happily constructed and painted a shed next to the water features and birdbaths, and the early weeks had seemed promising, but then a new ring road opened, and now less and less traffic flows through the gates. Last week, Emma heard Les muttering about turning the Flower Cabin into Santa's Grotto in the autumn.

Betty has taught Emma how to condition flowers and make up arrangements and bouquets. She would like to use herbs and grasses from the plant section, too, but Betty is a traditionalist and likes her bouquets big and formal, filled with long-lasting, vibrant chrysanthemums and carnations. Emma is too grateful for the job to suggest anything different and has learnt how to make big bows out of shiny ribbon, just the way Betty likes.

The area where Emma feels she is making a difference is in the funeral work, and she has been pleased to find that the local funeral director is now recommending them. This has not gone unnoticed by Betty and Les and, although they raise their eyebrows at some of her tributes, they leave her to it. Emma sometimes wonders if they know about Will – theirs is an unusual surname, and Will's death was covered by the local paper. When she sees Betty and Les exchanging concerned looks behind her back, she is almost sure they do.

Today, she is working on a large wreath for a funeral, to be made entirely of vegetables.

Betty pauses as she passes, glancing at it over the top of her glasses. 'A few sprigs of crysanth or gyp would look lovely with that. Surely the poor woman wants a few flowers?'

Emma remembers the grey woman who arrived in the Flower Cabin after a round of calls to the undertaker, vicar, printer and caterer. She knew the exhausted woman would have accepted anything she suggested, but she wanted the flowers to be something her husband would have liked – a tribute that would remind her of the man she loved in life, not in death.

'I did ask her, but she said he wasn't much of a one for flowers, although he loved his vegetable garden.' Emma wires a plump pea pod into her base next to some baby carrots. She looks up; she can tell that Betty is not convinced. 'You don't mind, do you?' she asks, anxiously.

'No, love. To each their own.'

This is one of Les's sayings. Betty peppers her conversation with them, and Emma has caught herself starting to use them. Les is a large, quiet man who never rushes into speech. Emma imagines him searching his mind for the right saying or proverb to suit his purpose. Sometimes Emma tries to match him, cliché for cliché. She always loses.

Les: 'Looks like we're in for a bit of rain.'

Emma, looking up at the sky: 'Umm, yes, I think this is the calm before the storm.'

Les: 'Well, the gardens can certainly do with it.'

Emma: 'You know what they say – no rain, no flowers.'

Les: 'Yes, every cloud has a silver lining.'

Emma: 'Er…'

Les (now gently smiling as if in quiet victory): 'Well, I'd better see to the cosmos – they won't re-pot themselves.'

Betty's conversation is either 'on' or 'off'. If she is in the mood for talking, which she often is, her chatter flows on like water over pebbles, even if no one is in earshot. Emma finds it soothing, rather like having the radio on in the background.

Emma wonders what their home life is like: Les, big and bearded, filling the space in their compact bungalow at the back of the garden centre; Betty, small and busy, dodging around him. Emma is reminded of a YouTube clip she once saw of a large dog, apparently living in harmony with a small tortoiseshell cat. They shared the same bed, and the St Bernard let the cat walk all over him – literally. He looked happy enough, but Emma noticed that the dog never took his eyes off the cat for a moment. Still, she thinks, it must work: Betty mentioned recently that they are about to celebrate their fortieth wedding anniversary. That was when, with a jolt, Emma had remembered it would have been her and Will's tenth anniversary this month.

Betty continues to study the vegetable wreath, a small crease between her brows. She smooths her bumblebee jumper down across her small, rounded stomach and crosses her arms. Betty is very fond of wildlife jumpers, especially those displaying woodland creatures. She likes to keep with the seasons and, despite it being a cool, grey day, this is July – the time for bumblebees and butterflies.

Just as Emma thinks Betty is about to say something more, the door to the Flower Cabin slams open and a large man in his forties, wearing a high-viz jacket, bundles his way in, carrying three large boxes on his shoulder.

'Ah, Tamas, come in,' Betty says, guiding the man towards a space by a row of empty buckets. She turns to Emma. 'You've not met Tamas before, have you, Emma?'

The man deposits the boxes with practised ease into the small space.

'Tamas is our flower man,' Betty continues. 'He brings our orders from the local market and from our Dutch wholesaler. I've changed his delivery days so you'll be in when the new flowers come. It'll help having the two of us to unpack them.'

The flower man turns his large frame towards her, holding out his hand. 'Ah, Emma, I have heard a lot about you.' He speaks with a thickish accent – Emma, the linguist, thinks it might be Dutch.

As he grasps her hand and shakes it furiously, he looks down at her, which makes a change, though she wishes he would let go of her hand.

'Ha! Betty said you were a tall girl. And just look at you.'

'Yes, and look at you,' Emma fires back, surprised into an instant response.

Tamas grins. 'Your legs, look at that – you have no ankles!'

Emma is finding it hard to order her thoughts. She knows she has terrible ankles – her mother was fond of reminding her that she didn't get her legs – but it seems very rude for this stranger to say so.

In the end, all she can think to say is, 'And you have no hair.'

At least this stops Tamas from grasping her hand. He runs two large hands over his enormous, bald head. 'This is true. I am bald as a duck.' He turns to Betty. 'Is that right, Betty? Bald as a duck?'

'As a coot,' Betty says faintly, gazing from one to the other.

'And you've got no neck,' Emma adds for good measure. She thinks she is beginning to get the hang of Tamas.

His laughter rings out, and he slaps his ample belly. 'This is also true.'

Then Emma catches the look on Betty's face: startled, blinking. She has gone too far – she has got it wrong. Again. She doesn't want Betty to think badly of her, but she has no idea what to say next.

She is saved by Tamas, who starts telling Betty what flowers he wasn't able to get at the market that morning and which varieties he has put in their stead.

With a feeling of relief and slightly trembling hands, Emma returns to adding cherry tomatoes to her funeral wreath.

When Tamas leaves, Emma busies herself unpacking the new delivery of flowers, keeping her head bent, trying not to catch Betty's eye. She can feel her watching her.

What Betty says next surprises her.

'Les and I were wondering if you would like to join us tonight, here in the café? Just a small group of people. It's the local History Society that Les is treasurer of. He's doing a short talk – between you and me, I think he's a bit nervous, so he could do with the support. The theme for this evening's meeting is "Secrets of the *Titanic*". You never know, love – you might find it interesting.'

What surprises Emma more than this invitation is that she looks up at Betty and replies, 'Yes, that would be lovely.'

She meant to say, 'Sorry, Betty, I'm busy.'

Chapter 2

Violet

Wildflowers

If she were to tell the story of her life, she would start among the flowers. That is where her memory began – picking wildflowers as she walked through the pale grasslands of the Argentine Pampas.

She suspects this is not the tale most people want to hear. Most would clamour to know about that one night, as they strain to imagine the low, grinding sound of ice against metal. She has come to realise that people want to sail close to the horror, skim the surface, feel the splash of icy water on their faces and then race on, unharmed.

Those who were there understand it cannot be like this. They know that the horror will reach up and pull you under. Her mother would tell those trying to sail closer and closer, to stay well away from the deep water.

She learnt early on in her life to heed her mother's advice, and

14

so she does not look into the cold, black depths if she can help it. She prefers to remember lives lived and oceans sailed.

The story she would wish to tell is about the small thread that was her life, and though her thread may have been thin – hold it to the light and you can barely make out its colour – when it was woven with other threads it made a cloth that stretched through time.

Somewhere within the weave would be her story of the Titanic, *but she likes to think the cloth she was part of could be flung out full over a table or laid wide and taught across a room. It would not be a piece of fabric snagged on one single night.*

She knows the pattern would be intricate, woven with flowers. Honeysuckle would be there – her mother would insist on that – and roses, lily of the valley and, of course, violets. She would like to stand back and admire how the sun catches the colours and textures within the cloth and say:

'I was part of that.'

Chapter 3

Emma

Foxgloves

Why did she say, 'Yes'?

Emma has never taken much interest in the *Titanic*. She did a school project on it when she was about eight or nine, and of course she saw the film. But the story of the *Titanic* was much more Will's kind of thing: documentaries, history, National Geographic. She recalls him once showing her some 3D imagery of the wreck of the *Titanic* – which, looking back, *had* been fascinating.

Was that it? Had she thought for a split second that Will would be keen to go, that in another world, another life, this was something they might do together?

Whatever the reason, here she is, make-up on, smartish navy jacket over her jeans (what do you wear to a History Society talk?), making her way from the car park to the garden centre.

From where she is standing by the entrance, she can see the broad window of the café facing her. She instinctively steps to her left, keeping a pillar hung with hanging baskets between her and the people gathering inside.

Les is there, wearing a smarter than normal fleece (it's a cool evening for July) and Betty has on a denim shirt that appears to be embroidered with some kind of flying thing. Emma squints. Is that a flying fish? Surely not. Maybe an exotic bird?

This meander into Betty's wildlife-wear calms her, but not enough to make her want to step out from her hiding place.

It seems most of the group is now assembled; her reluctance to come has made her late. She can see Betty chatting and ushering people to rows of chairs. They are mainly middle-aged and elderly. Women in summer dresses with jackets or cardigans. Men in chinos and one or two in shorts. They look like they could all be members of the National Trust.

Emma forces herself to move out from underneath the baskets of busy lizzies and petunias. She steps through the main door, heading towards the café. There is no one around; everyone else appears to be already seated. She can spy the rows of heads through the glass panel of the café door. None of the people are looking at her; they are all turned towards Les, who is standing in front of a large white screen, nervously and vigorously rubbing his palms together. Emma has a hand on the café door when the next thought descends.

They will all soon be looking at me.

She fast-forwards to her opening the door. She pictures the group turning to stare at her. She knows her muted outfit of anonymous navy will not shield her. Her height. That hair. Then later, there will be small talk, people gathered in tight, impenetrable groups. She swallows hard as her breathing quickens. It feels like something is stuck between her throat and her ribs. She knows her hand is clammy on the door handle and with this comes a dizzying nausea. Heat floods through her body and she cannot move. She wants to sink to her knees but they are locked and she is left staring at the rows of heads in front of her.

A black and white photograph flickers onto the screen behind Les: the *Titanic*. The image releases something within her. It is not too late. No one has seen her.

Round-shouldered, head ducked, heart hammering, Emma twists on her heel and stumbles in her rush for the car park. She may be trembling and drenched in shame – it feels pathetic to let Betty and Les down like this – but if she is on her own, no one will see; no one else will know. The bleak dead thing within her will stay submerged and hidden.

She finds herself running towards her car. As she starts the engine, her mind is filled with the image of the *Titanic* slowly tipping, then ripping apart and sinking.

Emma stands in her kitchen, jacket abandoned on the back of a chair, half-drunk glass of wine on the table. It is nearly dark but she notices the temperature has risen. The July night air that flows in at the open window feels like tepid water over her skin. The sickness and panic have passed; only the shame remains.

She moves closer to the window and watches a badger scuttle across the lawn, leaving a dark rut in the grass. She follows its waddling form, a ripple of white and silver, until it disappears into the flowerbed where the foxgloves once grew.

The foxgloves have never returned to the garden. She often looks for them, unsure whether they are the kind of flowers that reappear each year. Gardening had been something she believed she would come to later on in life. She had imagined working with Will in this garden. Now she is left staring into the inky depths of the flowerbeds where the foxgloves once bloomed.

They had been in the cottage for just over a year when Will died. They moved there from a tiny house in the centre of Oxford. Time, they had joked, for a grown-up home. Far enough away from the city to be in the country but still close enough to the university and the station – an easy commute to Will's law firm in London. Neither acknowledged the painful irony of being able to afford a family-sized house now they had accepted they would never have a family.

One of the things Emma and Will liked most about the property when they first saw it was the garden. It circles the house, stretching up behind the cottage to a small, raggedy field. Now, each morning, Emma takes her coffee up to the edge of this field and stands looking down over the broad, sweeping Oxfordshire countryside. She likes it best when mist settles in the hollows and the world is revealed, not as one broad expanse, but layer upon layer of field and woodland, like scenes from a theatre.

Some mornings, when the light is golden and the mist rises, masking the lower landscape, she can believe she is staring out across a sea of islands and the dark trees marking the horizon are ships. On days when her mind is fuzzy from lack of sleep, when thoughts of Will submerge all other feeling, she imagines boarding one of these ships and sailing away.

At the front of the cottage, the garden dips down to a small orchard bordered by a wall on one side and a shallow stream on the other. The lawn around the house now lies patchy, like a bad home-haircut, overlong in bits and razored in others where Emma has hacked a path through with the lawnmower. Behind long fringes of grass, the flowerbeds emerge chaotic and overgrown. Near the gate to the lane is a shed that Will claimed as his own and an ancient greenhouse where Emma once planned to bring on her favourite flowers: blush-coloured hollyhocks, magenta poppies and lupins the colour of ice-cream.

Some of the flowers planted by the previous owners still hold strong in the overgrown beds. In the last month, the pastel rambling roses of June have given way to the scarlet penstemon and feathery white euphorbia of full summer. Lavender bushes fizz with bees and black-eyed Susans warm their faces in the sun. As flowers bloom and fade, Emma often thinks about how transient life is – there one moment, gone the next.

She wonders how she knows the names of all these flowers. Sometimes in the Flower Cabin, she is caught, unsure what something is called, but if she waits, the name usually comes to her. She must have absorbed these from her father, who spent hours working in his garden. Perhaps she subconsciously learnt this language in the same way she picked up the Spanish that he spoke to his parents. Sometimes she thinks of the name of a flower in English and also in Spanish. Foxglove – *Dedalera*. Lavender – *Lavanda*.

Emma turns away from the window, sits down at the kitchen table and reaches for a notepad. Occasionally, when she cannot order her chaotic thoughts, she writes. A stream of words unleashed to lance the overwhelming pressure of her pain.

She writes her letter in Spanish.

> Dear Papa,
>
> I have just watched a badger disappear into the flowerbed where the foxgloves used to grow. I want to ask you if foxgloves are meant to come back each year? There are so many things I want to ask you. Maybe I'll write this letter and bury it in the garden, in the hope that it will somehow reach you.
>
> I don't know who else to talk to. Granny Maria was a good listener. I often think of her. And I think of you and the time we used to spend in the garden together. I know we didn't always talk much, and as I'm finding out now, I didn't really listen when you told me what to do in the garden. But I do remember the names of flowers.
>
> I wish I could see you, Papa. I want to sit on the tree stump by your shed and tell you how I struggle these days to do the simplest things. I tried to go to a talk this evening, but I just couldn't do it. Such a simple thing, really.
>
> I've left my job – did you know that? I'm beginning to

wonder why. I think I was a good scientist, Papa. In our research work, it was all about looking for new connections. I keep coming back to that – I thought this job would be a way for me to find new connections. But I don't know anymore.

I thought things were supposed to get easier. Time is supposed to heal. Isn't that what everyone says?

No, I can't talk about Will, Papa. Don't ask me to.

What do I really want to do?

Now there's a question.

I want to sit in the garden with you and drink coffee. I want to be ankle deep in purple and yellow crocuses as you plan what to add to the borders this year.

I know I could work on this garden instead. I keep looking at it, but I don't ever do anything. I just don't seem to know where to start.

Follow the flowers?

What does that even mean?

Emma looks down at her close-spaced handwriting. What is she doing? Writing an imaginary conversation with a man who died a decade ago?

She tears off the page, screws it up and drops it on the chair beside her. The journey to the bin, like most things in her life, seems just too much of an effort.

Chapter 4

Violet

Blanket Flowers
Argentina, 1893

She is six years old.

Her father is on the hill waving, his old brown hat making circles in the sky. She starts to run towards him, scattering the small group of sheep in front of her. One animal stumbles and as it falls forward onto its knees she is worried she may have hurt it. Each year there are fewer and fewer in the flock, and she knows her father cannot afford to lose even one animal. She pauses, hovering on the ball of her foot, fear pinning her balance. The sheep scrambles to its feet and is off running with the others – and so is she, her heart pounding with relief. As she gets closer to her father, she anxiously searches his face in case he has seen the animal stumble and is ready to scold her.

But he smiles at her and sweeps his hat in an enormous arc, gesturing for her to look down over the brow of the hill.

'The blanket flowers are back. Have you ever seen the like?'

The land opens up in front of her, a collage of green grass and grey dust with a splash of blue far off in the distance, like a sweep of bright paint. To her right, down the slope, it looks as if someone has spilt a jar of yellow buttons: tiny dots mark the scattering of flower heads. Even though the nuns have taught her her numbers and have told her parents she is a quick learner, she cannot begin to imagine counting all those flowers.

She reaches up for her father's hand. It is large and calloused and engulfs hers easily. He squeezes her small fingers momentarily and then he is off, striding down the slope, sweeping a path through the yellow buttons, his mind back on his flock. She knows he has forgotten her and he is searching the horizon for stragglers.

Sometimes, she wishes she too was a sheep.

Chapter 5

Emma

Clove Carnations

From her phone screen she can see it is 2.49 a.m. For a while she lies listening: no dawn chorus, no passing cars – instead, a ringing silence so high-pitched she suspects only she and dogs can hear it. She wonders if it is her guilt that has woken her. She should have gone in to the talk to support Les. It wasn't much to ask. The last thing she had done before going to bed was to bake a cake to take in for Betty and Les by way of an apology. But as she forgot to add the sugar, this gesture ended up in the bin.

She stretches out her hand to the empty side of the bed and feels the coolness of cotton under her fingertips. How many quilts hide a sheet that is crumpled on one side and yet is pristine and smooth on the other? Months on. For some people, years on. Still, your side of the bed. Still, their side of the bed.

Emma shuffles up until she is sitting, pillows stuffed behind her back. She knows she is not going to get back to sleep tonight. She reaches for her laptop which is down by the side of the bed and starts searching for something to watch on catch-up TV. As she browses the BBC's Science and Nature section, one title leaps out at her: *Disappearing Titanic: Revealing how the ocean is eroding the shipwreck of the Titanic.*

Well, at least she might have something to talk to Les about.

Forty minutes later, Emma watches as a floral wreath is flung out into the Atlantic to commemorate the sinking of the *Titanic*. The story of the erosion of the shipwreck had been poignant; the ocean slowly reclaiming the huge bulk that was once a ship. The metal hull, the captain's bath, the glossy blue-green tiles of the steam room – all slowly fading way. Possessions that had laid scattered on the ocean floor – shoes, hairbrushes, opera glasses, violins – had either been recovered or left to sink into their sandy grave.

As she watches the wreath of lilies tip lopsidedly beneath the grey waves, a new thought comes to her: what about the flowers on the *Titanic*? Who arranged those? Surely there must have been flowers: smart table centres for the restaurants; carnation buttonholes for evening jackets; and corsages for crepe and silk gowns.

As the credits roll over footage of a disintegrating marble fireplace, Emma imagines the mantelpiece with a crystal vase of ruby roses on it, cut-glass sparkling in light reflected from banks of mirrors. In the labyrinth below deck she pictures plump stewards in white uniforms rushing to deliver bouquets to first-class cabins.

Somewhere on the *Titanic*, someone must have arranged these flowers.

She leans back on her pillows and closes her laptop. She shuts her eyes, hovering between waking and drowsing.

The documentary said that it was April when the *Titanic* set sail from Southampton; the dawn must have been cold and dank as the final preparations were made. Did the florist arrive at the docks at first light as the flowers were being delivered onto the wharf? Did she dodge between wagons as she searched for the nurserymen's cart? Perhaps she had lingered in the shadow of a heavily laden dray as she watched cases of Cognac and Champagne being winched into the hold? Did she count the wooden boxes of flowers being unloaded for the ship? Perhaps she picked out a rose, checking it for bruising, and was unable to resist lifting it to her face to smell.

Emma stirs and reopens her laptop. She starts searching online for information about the crew of the *Titanic*. A myriad of sites immediately pop up, many listing those who had worked on board. She can't give Les and Betty a cake, but maybe she can find out this bit of information, something of interest to show she is not a rude and thoughtless woman – an offering from their trainee florist to lay alongside her apology.

By 5.25 a.m. Emma has searched the entire crew of the *Titanic* but cannot find a florist, and with frustration creeps in a feeling of unease. She rubs her forefinger over the rough patch of skin on the top of her right thumb. Surely there must have been one? They had everyone else on board. The staff is recorded in painstaking detail: plate stewards, linen stewards – every type of steward – including racquet, Turkish bath and glory hole. There are electricians, ice-men, coffee-men, lamp trimmers, plumbers, greasers, stokers, firemen, confectioners and Viennese pastry chefs. Everything the 'largest ship in the world' could possibly need: from gym instructors to clothes pressers, printers, barbers, window cleaners, interpreters, even buglers.

But still, however hard she looks, there is no mention of a florist.

In her hours of browsing and note making, she has discovered much more about those on board – and their fates. As she expected, the women fared a lot better than the men ('women and children first', after all); three quarters of the female passengers survived compared to a fifth of the men. She also knew there would be a disparity in the survival rates between classes – like millions, she had gone to see Kate and Leo in *Titanic* – but she is still horrified to read that sixty children drowned, almost all of them third-class passengers. It seems children didn't always come first.

However, she cannot kid herself; after hours of searching, she is no closer to finding a florist, and who's to say she didn't drown among the flowers? Emma wants to feel hopeful for her but she is no longer a woman who believes in happy endings. Besides, she knows the odds are stacked against her. One of the first notes she made is: *Crew, 908. Survived, 212.*

By 6.45 a.m., Emma is following an inconclusive message board about floral buttonholes, that may, or may not, have been given to first-class male passengers each evening. She clicks off the page and dismisses the doubters. Everything she has read so far claims that the White Star Line spared no expense for their passengers – surely they would have provided buttonholes. She imagines carnations – rich, clove carnations, burgundy petals pressed against the black silk of a lapel, their peppery fragrance mixing with the smell of cigar smoke.

Illuminated by the watery glow from her laptop, she tries to pin down how she is feeling. Tired? Certainly. Frustrated? Yes. But also intrigued. She has missed the feeling of piqued interest that punctuated her scientific research.

Emma stares into space as she rubs her fingers once more over the top of her right thumb, caressing a patch of skin made rough by stripping dozens of thorns off the stems of roses. Now it is a very different sort of question that has wheedled its way into her brain. And the question is, *was* there a florist on the *Titanic*?

Chapter 6

Violet

Sage Flowers

What would you like to be when you grow up?

She didn't know that there was such a question. It certainly isn't a thing she has ever been asked. But recently she overheard this query directed at a boy who lives on a different street to them, a street that is edged with paving stones that get washed each morning.

The borrowed question occupies her as she rushes through her chores. She does not think she would like to be a sheep farmer like her father. Or is he still a farmer now that the flock is so sparse the sheep are like flecks scattered on the grasslands? She peruses the occupations of the women she has met. She is a girl, and girls become servants, mothers, dressmakers, nuns. She knows she doesn't want to be a nun. She doesn't know exactly why she feels this with such certainty, but the thought is as solid beneath *her feet as the smart paving stones she is not allowed to walk on.*

Her mother, who can normally answer most questions, only laughs at her and tells her she will be a good-for-nothing if she spends her days with her head in the clouds. So instead (when the chores are done) she lies in the garden and talks to her doll, whose bed is on a bank of earth under the sage bush. She has made her a blanket from sacking and leaves from the bush. When the purple flowers come, she scatters those on her too.

Her doll tells her she can be a princess with a large garden full of the most beautiful flowers and that she too will be able to sleep in a bed made of petals.

This is good to imagine, but she thinks that it is not something she will tell her mother.

Chapter 7

Emma

Crushed Clematis

'Are you all right, love? Les and I were worried when you didn't turn up last night.' Betty and Les are waiting for her in the Flower Cabin, Les peering at her over his wife's head – a double-decker of concerned faces.

Emma was hoping to sneak into work unnoticed. Mind befuddled by lack of sleep, she cannot seem to articulate her apology or explain her attempts at research; the harshness of the morning light illuminating their inadequacies. Just behind the door, she catches a flash of a high-viz jacket.

Tamas's large face peers at her from around the back of the door. 'Les says you promised to come to his talk – I am sure it was very good. You must have been ill. This is what I was saying to Betty.'

'Decided on an early night, I expect,' Betty suggests. 'Perhaps you weren't feeling quite the thing.'

'Always better to be safe than sorry when it comes to your health,' Les adds, nodding, his beard brushing the top of Betty's curls.

'Yes, sleep is often the best medicine,' Betty says, and Emma wonders if they are back to swapping clichés, or is Betty throwing her a lifeline? She tries to read the look on Betty's face – concern, but is there sympathy, too?

'You do not look ill.' Tamas comes out from behind the door and stands with his head on one side. 'You look healthy and strong. Like my cow.'

She feels like a cow, a prize exhibit, framed by the door, for all to stare at. They are all waiting for her to speak. What can she say? That she was frightened of being in a room full of strangers? That this fear of people is getting worse? That she had hoped, here, among the flowers, she might be safe, be able to make new connections, but now she thinks she may have made a mistake? That she feels useless and ashamed?

Still they wait. And still, she has no words.

She hears Tamas take a deep breath – a precursor to speech. She knows *anything* is better than being hit by another of his sledgehammer comments, so she says, quickly, 'I just couldn't face it.'

Which of course is true, but she tries to hide the pain of this truth by making herself sound jolly – like it is all a bit of a joke. She means to add an apology, but she's stopped dead by Betty's startled blinking. And worse than this, Les looks hurt.

It is Les who reaches across the gap between them. 'Never mind. Next time, eh?'

And then the three people in front of her start to busy themselves with their work, and she can do nothing, say nothing. The idea of explaining her tentative research seems ludicrous. So, she steps through the door, takes off her jacket and joins them. She has nothing more to offer – not even a coffee cake that without sugar never stood a chance.

After a few minutes, Les leaves the Flower Cabin to work elsewhere in the garden centre, and Betty offers to fetch Emma and Tamas coffee from the café, adding, 'And do you fancy some cake? I made a Dorset apple cake last night after the talk.'

Emma mumbles her thanks and is left alone with her shame – and Tamas. He is silent for some minutes, unloading and sorting the boxes, before giving her the delivery note to sign.

Then he starts. 'I think Les really minded that you were not there. He was sad. Do you not find the *Titanic* a fascinating subject for a talk? I myself find it of enormous interest. Or is it that you do not like Les and Betty?'

To divert him, and herself, she asks, 'Where is it that your accent is from, Tamas? I can't quite tell.'

He stands up tall with his hands on his hips. 'You must guess.'

'Netherlands?'

'No!'

'Finland?'

'No!'

She still thinks it might be Scandinavia. 'Norway?'

'Ha! You are getting cold! But then Norway is a country full of snow,' and he gives a great laugh.

Before she can say any more, Betty has returned, carrying their coffee and cake. Emma knows her face is burning as she says, 'I'm really sorry about last night, Betty.'

She wants to add that when she said, 'she couldn't face it', 'it' meant the other people, the prospect of feeling conspicuous and terrified. It was not the thought of listening to Les's talk. She can't seem to form the sentences she wants and as it turns out, Tamas has the last word anyway.

'Look, now I see, you have such large feet! Your shoes, they look like boats! It is good. With those feet you will never fall down.'

At the end of the day, as Emma is bringing in the flowers that form the display in front of the Flower Cabin, Betty remarks, mildly, 'Love, there's no need to have cake if you don't fancy it. Or you could have given it to Tamas – I'm sure he'd have liked a second piece to eat in his van,' and Emma realises Betty must have found the discarded cake that she had surreptitiously hidden, uneaten, in the bin.

She starts to blurt, 'No, it's not that…' but gets no further. How can she explain that she threw the cake away because she didn't think she deserved it and she feared it might choke her?

So, she says nothing and turning to collect the next basket of flowers knocks over a bucket of pink clematis with her size-ten boats.

A fitting end to her day.

Chapter 8

Violet

Crushed Roses

The rose petals are crushed, but she thinks she can make them better. She can't kiss them better, as she once did her little brothers. They claim they are too old for kisses now anyway, even though they still have the plump softness and bounce of baby animals.

The roses need smoothing with a gentle hand and the old petals need to be removed. Once perfect, she will weave them into her mother's best straw hat. Her mother tells her she has a way with flowers.

The sun is warm and the wind gentle as her parents prepare for a trip out to a street-side café. They are celebrating a 'little bit of luck' – for once, the sheep market prices favouring her father. She can hear the unaccustomed laughter and the lightness in their voices as they get ready. It makes her smile as she sits on the steps of the house, swiftly weaving flowerheads around the crown of her mother's hat. The air smells of soapy water, earth and roses. She has already tied a yellow bow at the back of the hat, leaving the tails to hang down low over the brim.

Her mother appears beside her and accepts the hat with a smile, then drops a few words of warning into her lap. Her nine-year-old self is expected to keep her brothers fed and out of mischief. One of these tasks, she thinks, will be easier than the other. Her father places a hand on her shoulder and whispers in her ear, 'The postman has been.'

She waves goodbye and darts inside.

Her father started this back when he was out early on the Pampas and gone for days on end. Just a few words, scribbled in his thick, clumsy script, left under her bolster. Pillow post, he calls it. It is one of the few things that truly belongs to her alone – his firstborn. Everything else is shared or fought over.

Sometimes he will leave a flower pressed between a rough sheet of paper. He knows the tangled bodies lying in the bed beside her will not look under the pillow. Little boys too busy rushing outside to find buried treasure to realise there may be a precious secret lying under their noses.

Chapter 9

Emma

White Peonies

Emma closes the car door and carries her small amount of shopping to the house. Leaving the bags on the back step, she retreats down the drive to put the bins out. Will always insisted on sorting the recycling – he was surprisingly fussy about it. That and the order the dishwasher was loaded. She picks up an empty bottle of wine from the box for glass recycling and dumps it in the bin for household rubbish. Then she waits.

Silence.

Her father once told her he had taken up smoking again when his mother died because he knew how much it would have irritated her. He said it seemed like the only chance he had of hearing from her again. Emma could well believe that Granny Maria would not have been able to contain herself. She had died when Emma was nineteen, but she had been a strong and welcome presence in her childhood. Yes, Granny Maria would have had something to say about her son taking up smoking again.

Returning to the house, Emma unpacks her shopping, then she finds a jug for the peonies she has brought home from the Flower Cabin. Tamas said they were likely to be the last of the season.

She smooths the soft, blousy petals, breathing in their delicate, sherbet-y scent. Today, for some reason, she's been thinking about Will's funeral. Had she bought the peonies because of this?

She takes the jug to the kitchen table, clearing a place for it by pushing a jumper and several magazines onto a chair. One small part of her registers that her home now resembles a car boot sale, but she knows nothing short of a visit from her mother or an estate agent would bring the chaos into focus. As it is, her mother isn't coming to stay and she doesn't want to sell their home. She sits at the table and strokes the feathery petals and gazes down at her feet encased in navy 'boats'. The sides of her shoes are scuffed and worn.

Despite the distance that separates them, Emma can still sense her mother's disapproval. She can even hear her mother's voice. She always kept certain phrases to hand, ready-made. After all, she would need them again.

'If only you would make a bit more effort.' This covers a raft of things from the state of her shoes to her interactions with her mother's friends. Emma cannot remember her life without this particular phrase.

'If you can't get it right, at least keep it simple.' As a result of this stricture, usually about her clothes, Emma rarely wears anything other than navy. She would like to wear more colour, but the problem is, every time her eye is caught by the flash of something enticing on a clothes rail, her mother's words return and doubt descends like rain.

'There are academic brains and then there is common sense, which is actually of some use.'

Does her mother really mean what she says? Can she really be that heartless? Or is it a case of like mother, like daughter, and her mother's words simply come out wrong? Emma has struggled with this conundrum for as long as she can remember.

She blows out a breath and looks again at her shoes. Another of her mother's sayings comes to her: 'You can always tell a lot about a person by their shoes.'

Transferring her gaze to the peonies, Emma reflects that you can also tell a lot about a person by the flowers they send to a funeral.

Will's firm ordered a formal spray of lilies and lisianthus. Emma could imagine the practice manager: 'We'll go for 3C, in purple and white. He was one of our partners so we want it to be a large arrangement.' A display unequivocal in its precise proportions, perfectly sized to outshine everything but the family's tributes. The lawyer's flowers. A large contingent had attended from Will's firm, neat in their monochrome precision tailoring – suitable wear for office, court and as it turned out, a funeral. The only discordant note was the visible grief displayed by one of the associates.

The university sent a wreath on behalf of the research team: an arrangement of uniform, yellow roses – beautiful in its simple symmetry, a circle of interconnecting flowers. The scientist's flowers. A few of her colleagues attended, men and women she had enjoyed sharing a coffee with. They struggled to know what to say and Emma struggled to know how to answer them.

Will's widowed mother made her own tribute: a twisted wreath threaded with sweet William. The mother's flowers. Five months after her son's death, she had also died – quietly, with no fuss. A gentle woman, too worn out by grief to put up much of a struggle.

Emma was pleased to see that at the funeral, her brother, Guy, looked after her. Guy did not bring flowers, but he did come in person, and that was more than enough. He flew in the morning of the funeral from his home in Singapore, and she walked into his hug with a feeling of being able to lay down part of her burden.

She felt the same as soon as she saw the 'Glory Girls'. She can no longer recall how she and her two closest friends from university came to be the 'Glory Girls'. She vaguely remembers a television programme about the Piccadilly Glory Girls. Later, when they set up a WhatsApp group, 'Glory Girls' seemed the obvious, if ironic, choice. And they all agreed it was better than their first thought of, 'Geeky Girls'.

Still, her friends *are* 'Glory Girls' in their way. They have both become well-known in their particular field of science, working either side of the globe in Harvard and in

New South Wales. She has just never kept up with them, unable to quite decide if she wanted to be a scientist or a linguist, ending up as a junior scientist who could be sent to that conference in Paraguay no one else wanted to attend.

The 'Glory Girls' came to Will's funeral bearing white peonies, knowing they were her favourite flower.

Acquaintances from the village brought posies of bluebells and cowslips – empathetic flowers that spoke of an English countryside that they and Will loved. Emma's mother sent rare Madonna lilies that told a tale of exquisite taste and a passion for all things Parisian. She would have come to the funeral, 'of course', but Eurostar was encountering problems, and she never flew. Her mother had lived in France since the death of Emma's father from cancer ten years ago at the age of sixty-five. Emma remembers drinking in the heady fragrance like a thirsty child, as she held tight to Guy's hand, trying not to choke on the familiar and bitter aftertaste of disillusionment.

More than anything, Emma wanted her dad. He would not have said much but he would have been beside her, every step. His suit, his shirt (chosen by her mother) would have exuded a subtle and expensive fragrance (also chosen by her mother) but Emma knew the dry skin of his hand, as he touched her cheek, would have smelt of wood-smoke and the jasmine flowers from his greenhouse.

When she thinks of her father, she cannot recapture the essence of the expensive scent her mother liked him to wear. A sophisticated fragrance that Emma suspects her mother had hoped would mask the simple truth of the quiet, humble man.

That scent had quickly evaporated from her memory. Yet even after a decade without him, the smell of burning leaves or the smell of jasmine always brings her father back to her as surely as if he were standing beside her in the orchard at the bottom of the garden. She does not know what flowers her father would have brought for Will, but she knows that he would have grown and cut them himself.

The only flower choice that surprised her was her own.

Emma had chosen the flowers that lay on top of the coffin. She had picked all white flowers: roses, lilies and anything else the florist suggested. It had been the first image of funeral flowers the florist had pointed to on a page littered with coffin sprays and wreaths. Emma could not bear to look beyond the first one.

As she followed the coffin into the church, she pinned her eyes on the flowers, in the hope that if she didn't break eye contact, they would draw her on and ensure she kept putting one foot in front of the other. She wondered why on earth she had chosen these flowers. Will had loved colour.

Her steps stuttered. Maybe she was at the wrong funeral? A heartbeat of hope had made her halt altogether. Maybe he wasn't dead? Then she spotted a white foxglove nestling in between the ice-white lilies, and deep inside its petals she caught a glimpse of purple. It was a rebel among the sterile white, and she knew for certain she was burying her husband.

Emma pulls herself back to the present. The effort is almost physical and leaves part of her aching. She tries to focus, to take a scientific approach, to concentrate on what has been written on the subject of grief. God knows, she has read enough of it. Heard enough of it.

It gets easier.

Just give it time.

But these are lies. She knows people don't mean to lie. Like children who point chocolatey fingers and blurt, 'He ate it' – these are lies from those caught out in embarrassment.

If there is anything I can do just ring me.

She realises now that no one ever rings.

Work can be a lifesaver.

Maybe that. Maybe that could be true. Her research work? Going back to the lab helped, at first. Her work demanded her concentration until the growing sense of needing a change overtook her.

And now this. Despite what happened today – the blundering into speech and into buckets of flowers – she finds that being among the flowers helps her. And being with Betty and Les? Yes, maybe, work can help.

A stray thought slips in. Work can be a lifesaver. But not if you are the florist on the *Titanic*. Then work might very well kill you.

Chapter 10

Violet

Lemon Hibiscus

Her lashes close and she thinks of her father. She knows he cannot come to the hospital – her mother has said he needs to be away, to take on extra work – but maybe he is thinking of her. She drifts back from dreams of musty sheep and sun-dried grasses. Her skin is baking like cracked earth. Nothing moves but the heat pulsing in time with her breathing. She tries to think the sheets off her burning legs, keep their weight away from her body.

Words she cannot grasp float in the hot air above her. She wonders if they have been left there by the doctor who is always leaving things in her room: a pencil, a pebble, a snail's shell wrapped in a handkerchief. Now she supposes he has left his words behind, to be picked up and tidied away by the nurses that drift around her bed like ghosts.

She may still be a child – eleven next birthday – but she knows that the doctor likes the dark-haired nurse with the merry eyes. She watches them as they move around her bed, both unaware she is studying them through her lashes.

Now the doctor turns, speaking to the merry-eyed nurse at his side.

'Move her into the garden.'

A pause.

'Yes, the whole bed.'

She hears a murmur of surprise, and she wonders if they are going to plant her there like a flower.

Merry Eyes queries, worried, 'Will she be all right out there at night?'

Above the rasp of her own breath, she can just unravel the doctor's reply, and through half-closed eyes she sees him take the nurse's hand.

'There is no more we can do, and I have heard this little one loves flowers. Why not let her sleep among them?'

Her mind flits to her doll, still sleeping under the sage bush – if the cat hasn't got her by now.

The doctor sighs, 'It should be no trouble to move her. She weighs less than a small bird.'

She would like to fly into the air like a bird, away from the heat that presses in on her, to find a shaded pool and dip her wings in cool water.

She cannot fly, but the bed is travelling with her in it. The words that flutter over her head are drowned out by the rattle of wheels, squeaking and bumping over tiles.

When she opens her eyes, she is in the garden. Above her the trees drip with hibiscus the colour of lemon sherbet.

Chapter 11

Emma

Daffodils

Emma tells herself she's not really doing anything wrong. She should have handed her university ID in months ago, but there doesn't seem any harm in using it one more time, and the university does have exceptionally good libraries.

She has hit a blank wall, or rather, she is faced with a dichotomy – cognitive dissonance brought about by two opposing pieces of information. As she wanders between the closely stacked shelves of books, the old language of her previous life comes back to her and she breathes out.

'Can I help at all?'

A young woman approaches – probably a postgraduate earning some extra money by working in the library. The weekend shift was never popular with the regular staff.

'Yes, I'm looking for books on the *Titanic*.'

'*Really*?' The girl's surprise is palpable. She smiles. 'I'm sorry – it's just that I thought I recognised you from…' She names the research project Emma was part of when she worked here.

Emma doesn't know whether or not to be pleased. She is certainly proud of her contribution – or is it her appearance that made her noteworthy?

'My boyfriend is working on his PhD with the team. He always spoke very highly of you. He was sad to see you go and so sorry about…'

The girl can't finish and Emma doesn't want her to. She is just pleased that her former colleague had something good to say about her and feels guilty that she always thought the PhD student was a bit of an entitled plonker. She hopes he is worthy of this girl standing in front of her, so smiley and friendly.

'Yes, the *Titanic*. Everything you've got.'

This turns out to be quite a lot, and soon Emma is sitting at a long wooden table surrounded by open books. She has decided (like the scientist she is) to go back to first principles. She got sidetracked in the middle of the night with thoughts of a florist, had even started thinking of her as The Florist, a very specific person to be sought out. She reflected what a difference a simple pronoun made: 'The' rather than 'a' – not just any old person. Then she had brought herself up short: shouldn't she first establish whether there were flowers on board at all?

She has conducted quite a lot of online research at her

kitchen table. But then she hit her 'cognitive dissonance' and decided a change of scene and a good library were called for.

Every so often the assistant appears with more books, engaging her in easy conversation. Emma is filled with gratitude towards this smiley girl; it is good to be reminded that she *can* sometimes chat and interact like she used to be able to. At the garden centre, she talks to the customers in the Flower Cabin, doesn't she? All right, it's not exactly conversation, but she's doing okay.

The girl reappears at her side, interrupting her thoughts. 'Have you found anything more?' It seems she is now fascinated by the flowers on the *Titanic*, too.

Emma nods. 'I've got some more quotes.' She glances down at her notes. 'When asked about her memories of the ship, one passenger clearly recalled that "the *Titanic* was a ship full of flowers".' Emma frowns. 'What varieties of flowers is less clear. Roses are mentioned, as are daffodils, carnations and daisies.' She pulls another book towards her. 'And here it lists all the things that were brought on board in Southampton, and there is a note in the loading log of five hundred vases.'

'That's amazing,' the girl enthuses. 'So what exactly are you struggling with?'

Emma spins a number of books around so the girl can see them more easily. 'Look at these.' She points to the few interior shots of the *Titanic* that she has found, often repeated across other books. 'Not a flower in sight.'

The girl studies them. 'I see what you mean. So why all the vases?'

'It makes no sense,' Emma admits, which still leaves her with the unanswered question:

Was there ever a florist on board?

When Emma answers Guy's Skype call, it is the closest she has come to smiling in a long time. She is back home in the kitchen, her half-eaten supper abandoned by her open laptop.

'What are you so pleased about?' Guy demands.

Emma thinks he sounds relieved. Their conversations haven't always been easy. Disjointed calls. Guy wanting to help her. Emma sure of her brother's love and grateful for it, but unable to tell him how she really feels.

'I've just found the flower stores on the *Titanic*.'

'You've what?!'

'It's where they stored the flowers. Sorry, that sounds a bit random, but I've been doing some research about flowers on the *Titanic*. I was just looking at deck plans, and on B deck near the Café Parisien I found a flower store and then another on G deck. Did you know, the *Titanic* was a "ship full of flowers"?' There is a touch of triumph in her voice.

'Can't say I did.' Guy laughs, sitting back more easily in his chair and sipping his wine. 'You know me – only interested in history if it's about art.'

Guy runs a very successful gallery in Singapore and has always had a passion for art, ever since he was obsessed with comic book artists as a young boy.

'So what's with the *Titanic* and flowers? Is it your new floristry thing?'

Emma knows Guy doesn't really understand why she gave up on science and moved to her new job, but he did his best to sound enthusiastic when she told him, and he remembered, along with her, the hours she had spent with their father in the garden. He even admitted: 'Well, I suppose you *have* always loved flowers.'

Before Emma can answer his query about the *Titanic*, he adds, 'Will was always quite interested in that sort of history stuff, wasn't he?' And even with a computer screen between them, Emma can tell he quickly wishes this unsaid.

Emma hears a sharp, disapproving, 'Ttch!' in the background. This distracts her. 'Is Mei Lien there?'

Guy doesn't answer but swivels his laptop around so that Emma can see his wife sitting at the other end of the table to him, bent over her own laptop. Mei Lien is a hedge-fund manager, and Emma has rarely seen her when she is not glued to a computer or a phone. Mei Lien raises her hand in greeting and her eyes upwards, towards her husband, acknowledging Guy's lack of tact. Then her head is down again, fingers flying over the keyboard.

Guy returns his screen to its previous position. 'So, come on, what's with the *Titanic*?'

Emma explains what she has been researching, although not why. She doesn't think she could even explain that to herself. 'But in all the photos of the *Titanic* there aren't any flowers,' she concludes, having explained the conflicting evidence.

Guy looks thoughtful for a while. Eventually he asks, 'When was this, nineteen ... what?'

'1912.'

After another pause, he continues, 'Okay, how about this for a theory? You're talking early twentieth century. Photography wasn't really used that much. Advertising and publicity was geared towards illustration, right? Often really detailed. It's not my area of speciality but I know dealers who collect that early twentieth-century stuff. Also, photographs took time to be developed so they weren't used in the media like today…'

Emma interrupts him. 'I know they didn't let the press on board the *Titanic*.'

'There you go. I bet you the photos you are looking at were publicity shots taken weeks before the *Titanic* sailed. Maybe when the ship was completed and kitted out at the shipyard.'

'Brilliant!' Emma feels a huge rush of love for her brother. 'So obviously, no flowers.'

Guy stares intently at her. 'This is really interesting, sis. It kind of changes how I imagine what the *Titanic* was like inside. I mean, I know it was opulent, but "a ship full of flowers" – that would have been something. I mean the fragrance alone…' He turns his head suddenly towards where his wife is sitting. 'What?'

Emma can hear Mei Lien's voice but not her words.

'Good idea,' Guy responds before turning back to Emma, 'The boss says, try and find the flower supplier.'

Emma always knew her brother had married a smart woman. She tells him this before changing the subject and catching up on her brother's news.

That night, Emma dreams she is on board the *Titanic*, walking along the deck carrying a vase of white freesias. When she reaches the first-class restaurant, the tables are ready-laid with stiff linen, along with silver cutlery and glasses etched with the fluttering flag of the White Star Line. In the centre of each table is an arrangement of spring flowers: daffodil heads bobbing gently in time with the vibrations from the ship's engines.

The Florist has been there before her.

Chapter 12

Violet

Freesias

They smile at each other over her head, even as they ask her questions. Then each in turn looks at her, checking on her, making her more comfortable. Sometimes she wishes the comfort didn't come at such a painful price.

Only once do they both look at her at the same time, Merry Eyes now serious. 'Can she keep a secret?' she asks.

The doctor looks away first, staring out into the garden where until last week her bed had been. Now she is on the veranda, half in the garden and half out, as if no one is sure whether she is coming or going.

Merry Eyes keeps looking at her. Would she let her hide a letter for her friend, the doctor, in the drawer by her bed? He would collect it when he came to visit and then leave his reply in the same place. It would be a kind of game. . .

Her words trail off.

She looks at Merry Eyes and thinks of the grey nurse with hair like twisted wool, whose fingers search the drawers and cupboards at night.

'You could play pillow post,' she replies, not wanting the grey nurse to be scrabbling away at their secrets, spoiling their game.

Merry Eyes looks puzzled, eyebrows frowning.

Has she spoken in English rather than Spanish? Sometimes she mixes the words, loses track of who she is with. At home, or with her father among the sheep, she speaks English. Her teacher has tried to untangle the language and the land for her. Ireland was her parents' home, yet they speak their neighbours' language: English. Now they live in a new country and there is a different language. In the yard with the other children, words are thrown around like a ball, back and forward, up, up high and then swooping down. Spanish, her teacher says. The only way to join in the game is to learn to play with the words.

In the end, she explains pillow post both in Spanish and in English, just to make sure, and Merry Eyes smiles and nods.

Then the doctor turns back from studying the garden, and both are looking at her again.

'You like it here among the flowers?' he asks. She notices his eyes stray to the nurse.

'Of course she does. She is as lovely as any flower,' Merry Eyes replies – only her eyes aren't merry anymore: they are suddenly full of tears.

When the pain is bad, she wishes she could trace the edge of the envelope under her pillow with her finger, but that is too far for her heavy hand to travel, like the cart and train ride that brought her to the hospital.

Sometimes she wakes and finds the envelope gone, and all that is left is the smell of cotton mixing with the faint scent of freesias.

Chapter 13

Emma

Woodbine

Today Betty's sweatshirt is greeny-blue with frolicking otters on it. She pushes her glasses up into her hair and hums as she pots up a tray of woodbine. Emma likes that Betty and Les use the old-fashioned names for plants: love-in-the-mist rather than nigella; woodbine rather than common honeysuckle. Still, she thinks honeysuckle is a good name, too. She searches for the name in Spanish – *madreselva* – and smiles.

She glances again at Betty. Her air of absorbed contentment gives Emma confidence. Following Mei Lien's advice, she has spent the last couple of evenings searching online for the *Titanic*'s flower supplier and after a while, with a huge feeling of satisfaction (and silent thanks to her sister-in-law) she found them: F.G. Bealing & Son, who in 1912 had a nursery in Southampton. She was able to find some information about them via a museum in Southampton and then all trace of them disappeared.

Emma knows that she needs help.

'Betty, have you ever heard of a flower wholesaler or a nursery called F.G. Bealing & Son?'

Betty looks up in surprise.

'Not that I can remember. Bealing's, you say? We could ask Tamas when he comes in later. Why do you want to know?'

Emma busies herself re-potting a white campanula, pushing her hands deep into the compost. 'I've been reading up on the *Titanic*, and they were the company that provided the flowers, but I don't know if they still exist. I can't seem to find them anywhere.' She risks glancing up and sees Betty looking at her oddly. She is sure that if Les were here they would be exchanging puzzled glances behind her back.

'Well, that's a new one on me, love.' After a pause Betty ventures, 'The *Titanic*, you say?'

Emma detects the unspoken question hanging there: *If you're interested in the* Titanic, *why on earth didn't you come to Les's talk?*

'It's just some research I've been doing, I don't really know what I'm hoping to find out,' she lies. This makes her feel guilty all over again, so she adds, 'I'm sorry I didn't come the other night. Maybe Les might know something about Bealing's?'

Betty purses her lips and her glasses slip down and settle on her nose. She studies Emma before saying, 'Well that's not really his area, but we could ask him later. He's out seeing a new garden furniture supplier this morning.'

From her tone Emma can tell that something is bothering her. She wonders if Betty is still wary of her after her failure to attend the talk – or perhaps it's nothing to do with her at all. She has overheard Betty and Les discussing the downturn in business on more than one occasion.

'That was a lovely film, though,' Betty says, suddenly looking brighter. 'You know, *Titanic*. Les said it was three hours too long but when it finished I could have sat through it all over again. I'd say I've watched it six or seven times over the years. A good one for a rainy afternoon.'

Talk turns to Betty's favourite films, and soon she is revisiting her love of everything that Sandra Bullock is in. Tom Hanks comes in for some praise, as does Denzel Washington. Emma feels herself relax slightly.

As Betty talks, Emma wonders if Betty and Les have children. She thinks Betty would be a nice mum. She must be just a little younger than her own mother – early sixties, maybe? The contrast could not be greater. She tries to imagine her mother in an otter sweatshirt. She looks down to hide her smile – she doesn't want Betty to think she is laughing at her. She catches sight of her feet and her smile fades. Tamas is right: she doesn't have ankles. Her mother's ankles look like they have been sculpted from alabaster.

She is about to ask Betty about her family when she is interrupted by the creak of the door slowly opening. It inches forward, then, with a flourish, is pushed back on its hinges with a bang.

'I was trying to surprise you ladies! I see you from the window and I think, they will not expect Tamas to come in quietly like a mouse.' He stamps his feet on the wooden floorboards, boxes of flowers still balanced on his shoulder. 'But, me, I am an elephant. My wife, Berta, she says one day she will take me to the circus and leave me there. And on other days she is saying it is she who will run away with the circus, just so she does not have to hear me stomping about anymore. Ha ha ha!' With this, he swings the boxes off his shoulder and lands them in the corner of the shed.

Emma looks at Betty with a bemused smile, but Betty is not smiling; she is looking at Tamas as if she is worried for him. Or maybe she is worried for the unknown Berta.

'Estonia!' Emma shouts. She once knew a Berta from Estonia.

Betty jumps and so does Tamas, turning as he does so. He stands feet apart, slightly crouched and points both hands at Emma as if he were a cowboy holding guns.

'No!' he bellows.

'Lithuania?'

'No!' he says again, making a motion of firing a pistol at her.

'Latvia?'

'No,' he repeats firing off another 'gun', blowing into the top of his fingers.

Emma glances at Betty, who is watching them in amazement.

Betty slowly shakes her head and then, looking at Tamas, nods towards Emma. 'Now, Emma here is wanting to find out about a nursery. What was the name, love?'

'F.G. Bealing & Son.'

'Have you ever come across them?' Betty asks Tamas.

'Bealing's, you say?' Tamas scratches his head, and Emma is reminded of a cartoon of a man thinking from one of Guy's childhood comics.

The two women nod at him.

'It is not a name I hear, and I know many. They are not famous, I think.'

'Emma says they supplied the flowers for the *Titanic*.'

Tamas turns and beams at her. 'You have talked to Les. You have asked him about the *Titanic* and his talk. This is good.' He claps her on the shoulder, pitching her forward into a bag of compost on the bench.

'No, not yet, but I do want...'

Tamas does not let her finish. He thumps his chest with his huge fist. 'I will find out. As you ask me—' he looks from one to the other '—I, Tamas, will find out for you.' With that he hoists the empty boxes onto his shoulder and strides out the door.

'Tamas, he is...' Emma tries.

'Yes, he is,' Betty says.

'He's very...' Again, Emma can't finish.

'He is indeed,' Betty agrees. 'Since you arrived it has made quite a change for me.'

Emma shakes her head, uncomprehending.

'Oh, Tamas, used to have a lovely time telling me how small I was, how he'd like to put me in his pocket. He tried to pick me up once and put me on his shoulder.' Betty starts to laugh. 'Now, love, he just can't seem to get enough of you. And isn't it lovely that you look so strong and healthy. Just like his cow.'

63

For a split second, Emma wonders what the sound is. It reminds her of something heard long ago.

And then she realises that the sound is coming from her – a bit like a bark, a bit wheezy, but it is definitely her.

She is laughing.

Chapter 14

Violet

Honeysuckle

People come and visit her here, moving quietly over the grass towards the veranda. They stand around her, talking in hushed voices, and she would like to ask them if she is already dead. She cannot always tell who is who, like the card game when different heads are put on different bodies.

She does not see her usual doctor for some time, and she wonders if he has forgotten that he left her here, like the pencil and pebble that he used to leave in her hospital room. But when she asks the grey nurse with hair like twisted wool, she says the young doctor and Merry Eyes have both left the hospital.

She tries to imagine all the places they might have gone. She pictures the two of them riding an elephant decked out in ribbons and jewels, like in a book she once saw. She tries to find out more from the grey nurse and whispers to her of the jolly elephant.

The grey nurse's laugh is like the harsh sound of a rake being dragged over stone. She says that HE, no doubt, will be working in a great hospital, but as for HER… She does not finish the words, but ends with a pat of her twisted wool hair.

After this, she asks no more questions. She slips her hand under the pillow that once hid envelopes to be collected by a nurse with merry eyes, who had pretty, shiny hair and who smelt of freesias.

She closes her eyes. She can no longer see the flowers but she can smell them on the warm air flowing over her skin. The heat no longer troubles her but a great weight still presses down on her chest, making each breath a journey. Her younger brothers once sat on her all at once, but it wasn't like this. She squirmed and pushed and kicked and got away. She can't get away now. Maybe her mother and father are on top, too. And sitting on the very top of them all, she imagines a small bird singing.

A noise bounds into the garden and scatters the birdsong. It rolls across the grass towards her. The weight when it comes topples the great imaginary pile off her chest and she pictures her brothers and her father flying through the air. All that is left is the weight of her mother. And the scent of honeysuckle. She can smell great wafts of it, as though a blanket of petals has been spread over her. She imagines her mother's worn, red hands tucking the blanket in around her and thinks of her doll. She cannot smile, although she wants to.

But she can open her eyes.

From that day on, her mother always says it is the honeysuckle that saved her. Once she has an audience, she starts, 'Weren't you lying there in the hospital garden, tucked up in that big bed – you were such a small thing. You looked like death itself. They swore nothing could save you and that the infection had finally won. But I leant over you with that big bunch of honeysuckle. I knew they were your favourite so I carried them for half a day to get them to you. The doctors had done their best, God bless them, but didn't the smell of those flowers bring you back to us. It was a miracle.'

She will never tell her mother that honeysuckle is not her favourite flower.

Chapter 15

Emma

Delphiniums & Lupins

Emma's head aches, and she wonders if she is going down with something. Or maybe it's because there is a missed call from her mother and a message asking her to call back.

From the field above the cottage, Emma looks down over the countryside, nursing her first coffee of the day. The morning is grey and the sky hangs heavy, seeming to squash the colour out of the scene around her. There are days when the woodlands and valleys are so distinct they seem in touching distance; on others – like today – they elude her, shifting on a backwards step to avoid her touch, her gaze. She understands this. After all, she grew up with it.

She thinks of her mother and searches beyond the horizon, looking into the distance that separates them: she imagines the valleys that run down to the sea; the channel full of boats;

the wide open kilometres in France; and the years that have passed since the days of her childhood. Surely all this should be enough to protect her from her mother?

She looks down on the garden and thinks of Les. He has taken to providing her with plants for her garden: delphiniums and lupins. He says the plants are damaged so will only go to waste (which she doesn't believe) and issues clear instructions for bedding them in and how to keep them pest-free. She must ask him if there are some weeds with roots that grow so deep you can never really hope to shift them.

With relief she heads down from the field to collect her things for her day in the garden centre. She will ring her mother later. Much later.

Once in the car, her thoughts turn to Will as naturally as water flows to the gravitational pull of the earth. She thinks Will would have made a good gardener. In fact, she is sure of it. He was methodical and physically strong. She knows he would also have been fascinated (and surprised) by her interest in the *Titanic*. Is that why she feels so suddenly committed to it – a link back to the man she loved?

They met in London through mutual university friends when Emma was twenty-seven. Emma remembers sitting down beside Will at supper, catching the slight scent of sandalwood and thinking it an unexpected and old-fashioned fragrance. She had been feeling worn out (her PhD research had hit a problem), set up (she had thought she was just meeting her friends) and then discouraged and unattractive when she noticed Will's thighs were so much thinner than hers. He exuded the physical wellbeing and confidence of a long-distance runner, and compounded this by saying he worked for a well-known law firm. Emma felt her insecurities surface and had sunk to meet them.

But by the end of the evening she had discovered three things: Will had been teasing her with a gentleness and skill that drew her admiration and genuine laughter; he had a voice she thought she would never tire of listening to; and in addition, she discovered she had a fondness for the scent of sandalwood.

There was also the way he looked at her. He gazed at her like he had never seen anything like her before in his life, like she was something gorgeous, magnificent. By the end of the evening, she was sitting straight on the uncomfortable kitchen chair, not caring that she was a good head taller than him.

At the time, Will had just started working as a senior associate for his law firm but what spare time he had he began to spend with her. Each time they met, she was sure his look of admiration would turn into one of bemusement – what had he been thinking? But instead it morphed into naked lust and then over time – she could no longer hide from it – into love.

Looking back on that time, she is sure her expression must have stayed the same throughout: sheer amazement. And love. She knew she loved Will the moment he made her laugh. She had just not expected him to love her back.

When she got her doctorate and then her research position, they moved together to Oxford. A newly married couple, a new city – for her, a new start. Later, when their hoped-for baby never came, they were both devastated. She rarely lets herself think about that time now; revisiting it feels like slicing into a wound that will never really heal. Once they knew for certain she couldn't have children – and there was no doubt in the end that the biological fault lay with her – Will had been unusually quiet for days. They discussed adoption, but both felt, based on friends' experiences, that it wasn't a simple answer. Then Will had taken his road bike out on one of the worst days they'd had for months and cycled a 100km route over the downs.

When he got back, he made it clear that it was nobody's fault; she, they, the two of them, were enough for him. Emma has never underestimated what that took.

By the time she reaches the Flower Cabin, the rain is hammering down. Betty and Les have taken shelter there to drink their morning coffee.

'Tamas has been asking at the market about Bealing's,' Betty starts. 'He's not got anywhere yet, but he's promised to keep going.'

Emma nods.

Betty turns casually towards Les. 'Emma's been doing some research on the *Titanic*. I'm sure she'd like to hear about the talk you gave the other night, Les.'

'The *Titanic*, you say?' Les replies, on cue.

Emma doesn't believe for one moment that this is news to Les. She steps back quickly to stop them glancing at each other behind her.

'Yes, I'm – I'm writing a book.'

This does look like it is news to Les. Emma is not surprised;

it's news to her, too. Where did that come from?

'About the *Titanic*?' Les frowns at Betty, and Emma can hear his thoughts as clearly as if he has spoken them out loud: *You didn't tell me that. What am I supposed to say now?*

'A book, you say?' Les queries, rubbing his beard.

Betty is the first to recover. 'A book – how interesting,' she says, forcefully offering him a biscuit from a packet of chocolate digestives.

'Ah, a book about the *Titanic*?' Les repeats, doubtfully, directing his question at Emma, but his eyes flicking to Betty.

'Oh, I don't know. I had this idea… It may come to nothing.' Les's confusion is contagious. Emma has no florist, Tamas can't find the nursery that provided the flowers. What was she thinking? And *why* a book?

In the silence that follows, Emma looks down, embarrassed. Then she looks up quickly; she just needs to get a grip. She is not a child. 'I'd like to hear about the talk you gave, Les. I'm sorry I didn't get there the other night. Sometimes I find groups of people a bit intimidating.' She shrugs her shoulders and looks slowly down at herself as if acknowledging that based on the size of her, this may be hard to believe. It occurs to her that these three sentences may be the most she has ever said to Betty and Les all in one go.

Les glances at Betty, and Emma cannot interpret the look that passes between them. Satisfaction? A bet won?

'You know, the *Titanic* is a fascinating subject.' Les leans back against the counter, coffee forgotten. 'Did you know there was a fire on board when they left the Harland and Wolff works in Belfast?' He doesn't pause for an answer. 'The fire was in the coal bunker behind the ship's boiler. It was a huge fuel store, three decks high. No one could get at the fire to put it out and there was no way they were going to delay the sailing date.' Les studies his wife for a moment, and Emma recalls Betty once saying that Les was a great one for the Discovery Channel. 'But this was just the tip of the iceberg, so to speak. Fires like that weren't uncommon, but this one was burning away against the hull. Scientists worked out this caused *Titanic*'s steel plates to become brittle. The straw that broke the camel's back, you could say.' Les nods slowly. 'Experiments showed this could have reduced the hull's strength by as much as ... oh ... I believe it was seventy-five per cent. Well, the result of that would have been catastrophic when they hit the iceberg.'

Betty starts to speak, but Les hasn't finished. He waves a large, stubby finger in the air. 'The stokers who survived were warned by the head of the White Star Line not to mention the fire at the enquiry. I think that speaks for itself – tells its own tale.' He takes a big slurp from his coffee, then looks round, his eyes momentarily widening, as if startled that he has found so much to say without his notes.

Betty takes her glasses out of the pocket of her bumblebee cardigan and starts to polish them. 'Look, Les and I were—'

But her husband interrupts. 'And that is why I called the talk, "Secrets of the *Titanic*". I don't think many people realise that it might have been the main reason for the disaster.'

'That's really interesting, Les. I wonder—' Emma starts.

This time it is Betty who interrupts. Emma can't help feeling there is something Betty is desperate to get out.

'Les and I have been meaning to say to you, Emma,' she says, turning her attention to the packet of chocolate digestives, and pulling one slowly from the pack. 'Well, we wanted to say, love, that we – well, we know about your husband, and we are very sorry. We know things must be difficult. Our accountant recognised your surname on the payroll and he was in the same running club as your husband. I don't want you to think we were prying...' She is looking increasingly uncomfortable. 'But if there is anything we can do...'

Emma's stomach lurches. She can fill in the blanks. *Just ring us. Just ask.*

But Betty wrong-foots her: '... to help you with your research... or the book, or whatever, we would be happy to. Les is very interested in history, as you know, and has done a bit of research himself in his time. And I, well, I...' Betty doesn't finish but looks up at Emma, frowning slightly. 'We thought if you needed time off, needed to go anywhere for research, maybe could do with an advance...?' She is frowning even more as she finishes.

Emma stares at Betty and Les's faces. They look acutely uncomfortable and it dawns on her that these two relative strangers, who have business troubles of their own, are offering her their assistance. She looks quickly away, touched and mortified, trying desperately to tuck in the misery that she has unwittingly left showing.

'Emma, love...' Betty takes a step towards her.

Emma looks back at her, and all she can think is she likes

it when Betty calls her 'love'. To stop the tears that threaten, Emma rushes into speech. 'I'm okay, really I am. We had savings and life assurance. And I was paid pretty well for the research I did.'

'Research?' Les queries, and Emma remembers that she didn't really tell them what she had done before – had made it sound like she had worked in admin at the university. Her CV's academic record had been pretty brief, concentrating on her languages.

'Yes, well, I'm a scientist by training. My doctorate was in enzyme genetics and—'

'Goodness me. A doctor, you say?' Betty exclaims.

Les beams at her. 'Well, fancy that.'

'It's nothing really. Most of the people I worked with were far more qualified than I am.' This is true. In her field Emma knew herself to be a junior part of a highly prestigious team. And she rarely used her title outside of work – she found too many people told her about their back or bowel problems.

'But a doctor, you say,' Betty repeats. 'Well, I still think that's an impressive achievement.' She says this like she is proud of Emma, and Emma finds herself standing a little straighter and smiling shyly down at her.

'How long has it been now?' Les changes tack, a look of concern on his face.

Emma is not really sure which event Les is referring to. 'Well, I got my doctorate about twelve years ago, and it's just over a year since Will died.'

'And you're not getting any better?' Les looks increasingly concerned.

His wife is giving him furious glances. 'Would you "get better" if I died?' Betty interjects, tartly.

Les's reaction reminds Emma of someone pretending to throw a ball for a St Bernard. His confusion is complete. Eventually, Betty takes pity on him and turns her attention to Emma. 'So you're interested in who supplied the flowers for the *Titanic*?'

'Yes, and more than that – I think there must have been a florist on board. If you think about it, all the public rooms would have needed decorating and flowers would have been ordered for some of the cabins. Someone with skill must have arranged them.' Emma can hear her voice coming out squeaky in her anxiety to persuade Betty.

'Are there records you can look up?' Betty asks.

Emma relaxes. She has said it out loud and no one has laughed at her. 'You would be amazed at the information that's available. All the crew are listed – but no mention of The Florist. I can't find her name anywhere. It's a real mystery.' She can't help herself, she is back to imagining a very specific person, The Florist. Betty nods and Emma takes this as encouragement and goes on. 'I found a quote from someone, saying that the *Titanic* was "a ship full of flowers". It was April, so there would have been lots of spring flowers to choose from. Other greenhouse varieties, too, like roses. Oh, and there were flower storage areas, so presumably she needed more flowers for things like corsages, buttonholes and bouquets during the voyage. I just think The Florist must have been on board, somewhere.'

'You've given this a lot of thought,' Betty says, pushing her glasses up.

Emma doesn't say that she has thought of little else for weeks.

'You keep saying "she". Maybe it was a man?' Les ponders.

Emma ignores this altogether; in her mind it is always The Florist. Female.

Like her?

She hurries on. 'It began when I couldn't sleep, and I ended up watching a programme about the *Titanic*. It was the night I should have... Well, I'm sorry, Les, sorry I didn't, I couldn't... Anyway, I kept thinking about the flowers and the clove carnations and the smell of them and the cigar smoke, and what had happened to The Florist.' Emma is aware she is gabbling – free wheeling – brakes off. 'I think flowers matter in some way. We fill houses – and ships with them; we use them to send messages; we grow them; we even eat them. Once you see that, you start to see flowers everywhere.' Emma glances at the roses, lilies and delphiniums lined up on the shelves of the Cabin. 'When we marry, we carry flowers; when we die...' Emma has hit a pothole. She tries to say something more, but the words stick in her mouth.

'Love, has this anything to do with your ... um ... your loss?' Betty asks, gently.

Panic forces the word out. 'No!' Emma says, emphatically. But there has been a miniscule pause, a tiny disconnect – a flaw in her perfectly reasoned case. *Is* it to do with her loss? Emma hardly knows.

'So,' Betty says slowly, sidestepping the obvious crack in the pavement, 'what can we do to help?'

Emma feels confused. 'I don't know really. I guess it's just good to tell someone about it. Say it out loud.' She doesn't add, 'I have no one else to talk to'. Instead, she offers Betty one truth, 'I think I've become a bit obsessed.'

Betty leans over and pats her arm, then starts gathering up the coffee mugs. 'Well, it's nice to hear you talking for once. You just let us know what we can do to help.'

Emma is surprised by her own shock – and she then wonders why. She knows she has been struggling to hold it together, to engage in even short conversations. As she watches Les walk to the door, she starts to wonder if she began the game of trading clichés or whether it was the other way around.

Les turns before leaving, clearly still troubled. He blows out a breath, making his beard tremble. 'So is this book going to be about the *Titanic* or about flowers?'

Emma may not be sure where this idea of a book came from but there is one thing she is certain of, 'It's about finding The Florist on the *Titanic*.'

And saving her. Emma does not say this last part out loud. She isn't even sure what it means. The thought just slips through the door at the last moment and makes itself at home in her mind.

Chapter 16

Violet

Plumbago

She watches her mother from the corner of her eye, follows her movements from under half-closed lids. If she can keep her in sight, she will keep hold of her. The reality of her mother moving around the house – folding, carrying, pulling, shifting, muttering – reassures her. She clings on to the sound of her, the feel of her steps vibrating through the wooden floor.

She has her own share of the work – more than her share. After all, she is the eldest, and at sixteen almost a woman. 'Something of a señorita,' her father had joked.

Now there are no jokes, just the serious business of packing up a house.

'Roll them – don't fold them – you will get more in.'

'Call your brothers, they need to be ready when the cart comes.'

The days of playing are over – and she must roll and fold and pack alongside her mother. Whenever possible, she tries to work near her. It is all part of keeping hold of her, making sure she doesn't leave them.

She doesn't worry about losing her four brothers, even though they can scatter like marbles over stone and be as difficult to locate. Eventually she knows they will roll back.

Nor does she have to worry about her sister. She is a new addition to their family, one who arrived just as their father fell ill. A light in the darkness. She toddles around at a surprising speed on the tips of her toes. Her sister follows her around the small house, just as she follows her mother.

She lets her sister follow her to say goodbye. Together, they gather a bunch of wildflowers, and she ties them with an old yellow ribbon that once adorned a straw hat. She holds her sister's small hand as they walk up the hill and carries her when she gets too tired. She doesn't want to be with her mother now; she thinks her mother's sadness could overwhelm them and wash them all away.

Loss has changed her, too, but she cannot put her finger on exactly how. When she tries to imagine her finger finding the spot and pressing it, like when her mother asks her to place a finger to tie a ribbon, she fears she would not be able to bear the pain of it. So she focuses on the flowers she holds in her hand.

They take their bunch of flowers and place it on a grave by the wall. The plot is marked by a trailing blue plumbago that their mother planted, the petals tiny and delicate. She hopes the plumbago will grow and flower, getting stronger each year. Maybe it will send out tendrils and wrap its arms around the two stones next to it. Graves where no one ever leaves flowers.

She knows her father will forgive them for leaving. He understood when he grew sick after the operation that there was little chance of them keeping the house. The farm had gone a few years earlier when he could not afford to keep the flock. Now there is nothing left to sell.

Her mother had talked about the Lord providing and said she knew it would work out. But she thinks nobody, not even the priest, believed her. Her father knew they would need the help of family, and their family are an ocean away.

So now they are piling everything they own into a cart and are starting on the journey. All they will leave behind in Argentina is a grave on a hillside planted with plumbago.

Chapter 17

Emma

Bearded Iris

The evening has brought more rain. Emma looks out into the garden from the kitchen window and thinks back to her conversation with Betty and Les. With the memory comes warmth, and a glimmer of something else ... anticipation? She had said she was writing a book, and maybe she will do just that. She has no idea what type of book, but it feels like it could be the start of something.

Her phone rings. It's her mother. She feels a faint headache form at her temples, but the lingering warmth gives her the confidence to answer.

'Hi, Mum, how are you?'

'Ah, you're there. Nice of you to call me back...'

Her mother lets that hang a while – an early marker that claims the space and air between them.

'... I've been thinking about my birthday,' her mother continues.

Emma does a quick mental calculation. She hasn't missed a significant one. Her mother is sixty-seven. 'That's not until October.' Her anxiety wrings the flat statement out until only questions are left. *Have I missed something, got something wrong?*

Her mother ignores her; Emma's words are mere stepping stones to what she really wants to say. 'Mathias needs to know the numbers in plenty of time. We will all be at his chateau on the Loire.'

'Mathias?'

'You know, Mathias and Lina, friends of Paul and Celia – I've mentioned them a dozen times. Mathias is insisting we have the week in the chateau with him.'

Emma has no idea who these people are. Her mother lives on her own in Paris but surrounds herself with an ever-changing circle of the 'right' people. Well, Emma corrects herself, the right *men*. Thinking back to Mathias, Emma wonders what his wife, Lina, thinks of this week in the chateau – 'with him'. Not 'them', she notices.

Her mother rattles on, 'Mathias employs over a hundred gardeners. He has a lime tree grove, a topiary maze and five thousand Oriental lilies.'

Emma does another quick calculation; fifty lilies per gardener. She doesn't imagine Mathias is a man who gets his hands dirty.

'Mum, I'm thinking of writing a book.' She doesn't know why she says this. Maybe to grab at something, to stop the slide into her mother's world?

Her mother ignores this. Did she even say it at all?

'We're going for the week, but my plan is that you should come down for the weekend. Mathias is hosting a party for me on the Saturday night. You could fix it around one of your conferences…'

Great, I'll ask the scientific world to plan an international symposium around your birthday, and, by the way, Mum, I've left work.

She is back to words that only resonate in her head. She has never told her mother about her new job, and as her mother never asks about her work, weeks pass, months pass and her mum is none the wiser about her life.

'… We will be heading down the river on M's boat on the Friday night – I haven't included you in that. You can have a night in the chateau. It's wonderful, original baroque. We can't take the children on the boat – it's not really suitable—'

What children?

'—but I said you wouldn't mind keeping an eye on them.'

Ah, so I'm the free childcare.

'You're *so* good with children.' Her mother pauses, and Emma relaxes infinitesimally.

'I always said you and Will should have had a family.'

She is winded, as though her mother has driven her fist into her guts. A compliment to make her drop her guard, and then the full-force punch.

She never confided in her mother about not being able to have children. Now she wonders if she knew anyway.

'We would have liked that, too.'

'You'll have to speak up Emma – it's no good muttering at me. It's important to get this sorted. You really need to make more of an effort.'

'I'm writing a book, Mum.' She is sweating now, wanting to get some words out about herself, her own life – something to ease the ache that has started in her abdomen and is now spreading to her heart.

'Really? Have you got a publisher?' Her mother does incredulous well.

'It's about flowers.'

'Then you'll love the chateau, Mathias has more than a hundred gardeners.'

'You said.'

And I don't give a toss. Nobody needs that many gardeners.

'You'll need an agent. It took Carrie over six years to get hers, and then she only got a deal for one book. I read it and really, I'm not surprised. She only has herself to blame. I've always thought *I* should write a book…'

As her mother talks about the many books she could have written and how successful they would have been, Emma tries to remind herself of all she has done. But her qualifications, languages, friendships and loves are nothing – just dust in the air. She tells herself that at forty she should be beyond the reach of her mother's spite. She doesn't even live in the same country. But logic and reason have no place here. All she is left with is the bare thought: if your mother cannot love you or even like you, what hope have you got. She would like to phrase this thought as a question, plant even the smallest seed of doubt, but she cannot find it. Nor can she find the tools to root out the thought.

Will was the one person who could uproot the words planted by her mother, and she has to live the rest of her life without him.

Emma is sitting at the kitchen table, staring into space, when she realises someone is knocking on the back door. A large figure stands there, rain dripping from his hood.

Les.

Emma jumps up, managing to summon a smile.

Shaking water onto the mat like a great St Bernard, drops of rain still clinging to his beard, he hands her a soggy, spindly plant. 'I was passing. Bearded Iris. Doesn't look much now but it will be good for next year. Flower is a right beauty.' He then adds, frowning, 'Doesn't live long, mind.' As if realising what he has said, he coughs loudly twice, before saying, 'Well, time will tell.'

'Thank you, Les.' Emma replies, warmly. 'Would you like a cup of tea?'

'No, no. Deliveries to do. Time waits for no man.' He looks at his feet but doesn't move. 'Emma, we just wondered, it doesn't matter but… why didn't you mention you were, well, a doctor and a scientist? Betty and I … well, Betty wanted me to ask.'

Emma can't help feeling that Les wishes his wife hadn't allotted him this task.

'Oh, Les, I'm sorry. I thought you might think I was overqualified, but not with the right stuff. I just wanted a change, I suppose.'

'You can never have too many strings to your bow,' Les responds, looking brighter.

'And I guess,' Emma continues, 'I thought focusing on the languages might make you think I would remember the plant names.'

'Now that is interesting.' Les nods. 'Always struggle with the Latin names myself.'

'Les,' Emma says, tentatively. She thinks she might not have such a good opportunity to say what she wants to him. 'I'm sorry if I seem rude sometimes—'

'No, no, not at all,' Les interrupts.

Emma pushes on. 'Sometimes I think something in my head and it comes out wrong when I say it.'

'A loose cannon?' Les suggests.

Emma laughs. 'I guess,' she admits. 'I suppose I should look before I leap.'

She thought this might make him smile, or at least respond in kind, but instead, Les is looking preoccupied. Eventually he says, 'My first boss, now he spoke a fair few languages. He always said the thing that mattered was what language you thought in – said it made all the difference to how you spoke to people. Even had a bit of Japanese, he did. Now he said they were very polite folk.'

The realisation hits Emma like a hearty blow from Tamas between her shoulder blades. She is only ever rude in English. A second startling thought follows: she may not speak Japanese but what if she thought in Spanish (her favourite language) and then replied in English? At the very least, it would buy her time.

'Well, with all those languages ... food for thought, eh?' Les casts one last look around her kitchen and turns to leave.

After she shuts the door, Emma stands on the mat looking back into the kitchen as Les had done.

It really is the most god-almighty mess. She is glad that Betty didn't come with Les – she would hate her to see this.

She puts aside thoughts of her conversation with Les and her earlier one with her mother. She has something much more pressing to do.

It takes Emma most of the evening to clear the kitchen. She starts with the table, sorting, recycling and binning the accumulation of the past months. When the mess still inhabiting the kitchen sides is thrown into stark relief, she attacks this, too. For months she has not been able to find the energy or impetus to tidy up, but now not only does she never want Betty to catch sight of this – she also wants more space to work.

As she cleans, an idea comes to her. In her old research work, it was all about looking for connections. Isn't this what she needs to do here?

By 10 p.m., she is back at the kitchen table, laptop and printer in front of her, with a pinboard propped beside her chair. Periodically, Emma adds a photograph or note to the pinboard. She has been collecting pictures of the female crew. Some photos were taken on deck; some appear to be copies from old family albums. The women vary considerably in age and beauty – some have frank, open faces, others look grim, as though life has hardened them. She will just have to keep going, with a logical, scientific approach – making connections. Did any of them have a particular interest in flowers? Did they have some background in floristry?

The one thing that hasn't changed throughout all her research, is her belief that The Florist was a woman.

Chapter 18

Violet

Painted Carnations

She had expected winter in England to be cold – and rainy. Everyone on the boat had been more than happy to discuss the weather. At first she thought they had exaggerated. This rain, which drifted rather than fell, could not be the famous London rain everybody talked about?

But weeks on, months on, she has realised the persistent power of it. While nobody was watching, this insignificant drizzle has politely robbed everything around it of colour, until all is grey and damp.

The only splash of brightness in their street is an advertisement painted on the side of a house at the end of the terrace, wet brickwork showing through the red and white painted flowers.

Carnation Milk, the milk from contented cows.

She has not seen a single cow or sheep since they arrived in England, and she wonders if they too come in tins here.

'Carnation Milk is the best in the land,
Here I sit with a can in my hand.
No tits to pull, no hay to pitch,
You just punch a hole in the son of a bitch.'

One of her brothers – whoever is nearest – might get a swipe from their mother if they reach the end-line, but it doesn't stop them singing it as they pound up the stairs to their small flat on the first floor. Her brothers have quickly adopted the songs, the sayings and the accent of London. They have learnt to dodge through the streets and alleyways, and they jump and splash through the puddles with ease. 'Right little Londoners,' their uncle calls them.

She has no idea where they are today, but she is glad to have the kitchen for just herself and her sister as they try to make something of their mother's hat ready for her interview tomorrow. She pulls gently at the brim, easing out the creases. Her sister sits close beside her, looking through a box of ribbons, proud of the fact she knows her colours.

She doesn't mind what ribbon her sister chooses as long as it isn't yellow. She wonders if the yellow ribbon bound around the flowers at her father's grave has now faded to white, fluttering and flying somewhere over the grasslands that surround the church.

Her sister is looking up at her anxiously and she realises she hasn't responded to her.

'Yes, a blue ribbon will be perfect. She'll like that.'

Her sister smiles.

The rain will probably try and rob her mother's hat of any shape, but she wants to put up a fight against the damp. She knows her mother must look her best, that they all need her to get this job. She overheard her mother and uncle discussing it. Her mother had ended up reassuring the big man as he shifted from foot to foot. She had said she knew he couldn't do more for them, she was grateful for what he and the family had done. He mustn't worry. She'd said she was happy to look for work, and if work meant she had to go away, so be it. They would manage.

After his visit, her mother was unusually quiet and had not even tried to swat at the boys when they came in singing. She just kept looking at them, saying very little.

That evening, the priest calls to talk to her mother about the boys, but she does not want to overhear that conversation. Nonetheless, sitting on the stairs with her sister, she can make out the shape of her mother's whispers if not the precise words.

While her mother's words are indistinct, the priest's are clearer. But then he is a man who would never hear a pin drop.

'It's for the best. The nuns will look after them.'

Not wanting to hear more, she takes her sister to the park at the end of the road to feed the ducks.

They at least seem to like the rain.

Chapter 19

Emma

Cowslips & Buttercups

Sleep does not come easily, and she wakes again at 2.23 a.m. Giving up, she gets out of bed and pulls an old jumper over her pyjamas, then heads for the kitchen. She puts the kettle on and sits down on the flattened cushion of her kitchen chair before reopening her laptop. She clicks on the next link in her list of female crew.

And there she is.

A photograph.

The recognition is instantaneous.

Emma sits frozen, staring at the screen. She has the sense of looking down on herself – registering her own shock, her bemusement.

Where on earth does she know her from? She can't place her exactly, but she cannot shake the feeling she has seen her before. She can't put a name to what she feels, but she acknowledges it for what it is – more than just familiarity. It is a connection.

She gazes intently at the face before her. The woman seems to be, what – twenty-three? Twenty-four? Her hair is tucked up beneath a white cap. It is a black and white photograph – what colour was her hair? Brown? Or maybe auburn? It looks like one curl is about to escape.

Emma is aware of her eyes straining, as if by looking harder she will find the answers. She wants to turn to someone and say, 'Look! Can you believe it?'

Emma reaches out and touches the face on the screen. 'We've never met before, have we, but I *know* you.'

She recalls the *Titanic* documentary and the formal tribute of lilies cast out into the Atlantic. She is not at all sure that this girl likes lilies. When she looks into her face and thinks of a rebellious curl escaping from her cap, it conjures up the delicate tangle of cowslips and buttercups. Perhaps she was a country girl at heart?

A sudden downpour makes Emma look up at the window. But now she is flushed, warmed – insulated against the rain. Why does she feel such a strong connection with this girl? Is this the connection she has been looking for?

'But I don't believe in things like this.' She says this out loud to see if it helps.

The silence presses in on her and Emma closes her eyes. Her mind goes where it always does. She opens her eyes a fraction, the kitchen barely in focus. Her tiredness and an odd light-headedness blur the edges of her vision. She thinks of all the times Will sat on the chair by the Aga, mug in hand. She doesn't want the forty-three-year-old Will, the husband who died in her arms – she thinks that would break her. She blurs her vision more and conjures up the younger man, makes him mid-thirties. Lean, almost skinny from all that exercise, but a nice face. An open, familiar face.

'Can you believe it?' she whispers.

He looks up from the article he is reading on his phone. 'Believe what?'

She almost answers – *believe in you* – but forces herself to frame a new question. 'Look, this face. I know it from somewhere.'

Will doesn't move from where she has placed him, but she knows he sees what she sees. 'Where d'you know her from?'

She almost laughs. Wants to say, 'Well, if I knew that I wouldn't be having an imaginary conversation with my dead husband.'

When he raises eyebrows at her, quizzical, grinning, she does say this.

Will's laugh is immediate, a mix between a bark and a chortle.

Emma holds her breath, as if by staying totally still she can extend the sweet anguish of this memory. She exhales and forces her next question through her tears. 'How can I possibly recognise her?'

'Well, you've been spending a hell of a lot of time reading

up about the *Titanic*. Maybe you saw her somewhere in a book or online?'

Emma shakes her head. She knows that's not it. She cannot explain why she is so sure, but her certainty is solid – tangible.

'Why have you been getting so obsessed about the *Titanic* anyway?' Will asks, putting his phone down and picking up his tea. He mutters, 'Would've been quite nice when I was alive. Never could get you to watch documentaries.'

'Maybe it's because I thought you'd be interested.' She stares at the space where Will isn't. 'Or perhaps it's about the flowers.'

'You did always love flowers.' He sighs. 'White peonies.'

'Yeah.' She can't say any more. She wants to ask him so much, demand so much from him.

'So do you think she's The Florist?'

'Yes … no…' Emma is glad she has made him change the subject.

'She's not, you know,' Will says, half grinning, picking up his phone again.

'How can you tell?'

'Just look, Ems. You're the scientist.'

She enlarges the image and the shock of disappointment makes her insides feel hollow. Of course she must already have seen it – but she'd been too focused on the face in the photograph for it to have registered.

On the front of the woman's starched white apron is a large cross. She was not The Florist. She was The Nurse. Why would The Nurse be involved with flowers?

Even as she holds tight to a slender thread of hope, Emma knows it doesn't make sense.

'Did she survive?' Will asks.

'What?' Emma is distracted by her disappointment. She reads on. 'Yes, she was rescued.' Well, that was something.

'You still think you know her?'

Will is reading her thoughts.

'What, a long lost relative?' Will laughs.

Emma doesn't.

'You really think so?'

She ignores him and reads the few sparse details. Emma has noticed that the information about the female crew is often less detailed than for the men. Perhaps society hadn't been that interested in working class women?

Once again she stares intently at the face on the screen – if the memory she is chasing doesn't come from her recent research maybe it is something in her past? Has she seen this face before in an old family album? She checks the details; The Nurse's family originally came from Ireland. There are no Irish people in her family, as far as she knows. Her father's parents were from Seville, and her mother's family? She recalls they came from Kent and going further back, France. The Nurse certainly doesn't look like her. Trim and petite, with dark eyes. But then Emma doesn't look much like her parents, or grandparents, come to that.

She looks up to ask Will what she should do next – but he is gone. She stares at the empty chair until her head aches and it feels like the band tightening around her brow will crush her.

She stands and goes to sit in his place. She rubs the arms of the chair, slowly and repeatedly.

'What should I do, Will?'

'I don't know, Ems.'

Will is not back, but she knows he is there within her, a part of her. So much time – so much love. How could it be otherwise.

'I am sorry, you know,' he says.

'I know,' she whispers, but inside her, something twists out of shape and she recognises this wringing, contorted thing as anger.

Emma stands up quickly and paces around the table. She goes round and round in circles, and it takes four laps of the kitchen for the cramp-like thing inside her to ease.

She stops on her fifth lap by the back door and opens it. She looks out into the dark tangle of garden, breathing in the scent of old roses and Doris pinks.

It is 3.56 a.m. on a late July morning, the birds are starting to stir, and Emma thinks she may finally be going mad.

Chapter 20

Violet

Flowering Beans

One of the first things she spots are the scarlet petals. There are no flowers planted in the garden but in the vegetable patch the runner-bean wigwams look like they have been painted with hundreds of red dots. She hopes this means the boys are being well fed. Vegetables. And meat maybe? Fish on a Friday.

She wonders if anyone reads to them. They are too old for fairy tales about beanstalks, but maybe they would like stories about adventures and far away countries. Perhaps she will find a book to bring them next week. She could read it to them. The nuns do not seem to be the sort of women who would curl up with a book. She wonders if they even bend.

When her mother was appointed stewardess for a shipping company, the boys went to live at the orphanage. She would be away at sea for many weeks, her mother said; it was enough that her eldest daughter had to look after her sister on her own. There had been no discussion, she wasn't given any choice in the matter. Nonetheless, she carries the burden of guilt as if she packed it herself.

No one else can see the guilt she carries; most people think she is a young mother living quietly with her daughter. She is now twenty and can pass for older, and her sister is only six, so she can see that it is an easy mistake to make. When she holds the warmth of her sister on her lap, counting out numbers on her chubby fingers, she wonders if her heart is making the same mistake, too.

Each week she visits the boys in the orphanage, reading out letters that her mother has sent. They never know when a letter will come, so sometimes she re-reads a letter two or three times, emphasising different things to reassure them.

'She is being kept busy, but the tips are good.'

'She says they saw dolphins yesterday following the ship. Imagine that.'

'Now it is only three more weeks until she's back.' She tries to decipher the date in her mother's slanting handwriting – 10th or 20th? August 1907. 'This time she'll be home for two whole weeks.'

They listen as she reads, but sometimes she catches them glancing out of the window and she wonders who she is reassuring.

She is finding it hard to adjust to the quiet. She cannot believe that she ever used to dream of a peaceful day all to herself. Her world is still filled with noise – the calls in the street, banging doors, their downstairs neighbour singing or shouting as the mood takes her – but inside she feels like someone has stuffed an onion in her ear and wrapped a big muffler around her head, as her mother used to do when she had earache. Without the boys, the flat is so still; the floorboards don't bounce as they used to. When she visits her brothers, she is struck by the unnatural quiet of them. They are washed-out versions of the boys they used to be. The nuns have achieved what their mother never could: they have become as quiet as mice.

Something else has changed, too, but she can't quite put her finger on it. Her father used to talk of the feeling and rhythm of a song; he said these were a song's heartbeat, as important as the melody. She would like to hear the boys singing again to check that their hearts still beat the same.

Even her sister is quieter now. Her presence is something she has taken for granted, like her shadow, but now her sister has made friends with girls from their street and often disappears with them into another world, leaving her alone in the silent flat.

This afternoon, she is back.

'… we were running away from a dragon with black eyes…'

She knows the dragon is the coalman who is certainly sooty but cannot, as far as she knows, fly and breath fire.

'… we hid and made a boat out of an old tree trunk and sailed away. Dragons can't swim,' her sister recites with borrowed confidence.

But they can fly, she thinks, and tries to smile.

Her sister senses sadness in the half-smile and urges her. 'You could come and play with us, too.'

But she knows she cannot follow her sister into this world. She has forgotten where the door is, and even if she could find it, she would be too tall to get through. She remembers her father *calling her, 'Something of a señorita'. She wonders when she finally grew up.*

She thinks back to Dia de Los Muertos, when the fragrance of incense and flowers mixed in the warm Argentinian air to welcome home the dead. Her mother told her that the gates of Heaven swung open on that day to let the souls slip through and visit their loved ones. First to come would be the children, welcomed by sweets and toys piled on family altars. Then it was the turn of the adults. Graves were scrubbed clean and houses filled with the smell of baking. In pride of place was the marigold – its colour so fierce, its fragrance so distinctive, that even the dead could not fail to notice it. Her mother said some of the souls might get lost and need guiding. Marigold petals strewn on the path would show them the way.

There is no one left to lay petals for her father and the sea would soon drown her path of flowers, so instead, in the quiet of the flat, she speaks to her father. She talks to him in Spanish, even though she knows he struggled with the language. Somehow she's sure he will be able to understand her, and the words that flow and spin from her remind her of when she was a little girl and ran round and round in circles just for the pleasure of it.

Chapter 21

Emma

Marigolds

Emma settles herself on the edge of the bed in the guest room. Beside her is the chest of drawers where she keeps old photographs and letters. Most of her photos are on her phone or her laptop, but she has a feeling there is a large brown envelope in here somewhere with photos of her dad's family. She cannot rid herself of the sense of connection she felt with The Nurse. It's like a memory she can't quite retrieve – something once seen in the context of her own family, flickering at the corner of her eye.

When she finds the remembered envelope, the contents are sparse and disappointing: old, black and white holiday shots from a different era (but certainly not as long ago as 1912). She is toying with the idea of looking up how to research her family tree when she spots a stack of letters lying in the drawer beside a pile of albums.

Ever since she conjured up Will in the kitchen, she has felt the need to get closer to him, even if this brings misery that she fears she will not be able to bear. Her mind drifts back to December, kneeling in the garden among the snowdrops, seven months on from Will's death. She had hoped that was the mark of something new, the beginning of some sort of recovery. But instead, came pain that left her winded and shaking.

She extracts the bundle of Will's letters. She knows he found it hard to tell her he loved her, but he whispered his fears and dreams to her in their bed. Hidden in the dark, his breath against her hair and neck, he shared who he was with her. And she loved him for it.

He also wrote to her. Emma had always enjoyed writing letters, encouraged by Granny Maria who was a great correspondent. In the early days of their relationship, Emma had left notes for Will in his overnight bag or tucked away where she knew he would find them – a childhood habit, one that she had hoped to pass on to their children. Will had collected her notes, keeping them in a neat pile in his sock drawer. And then one day, to her surprise, he started writing long letters back. The words he could not always say seemed to flow from his pen, and she treasured those early letters, tucking them away with the many letters her grandmother had sent her.

She opens a letter at random. The familiarity of Will's handwriting catches her on a new barb of pain. The pages are still creased from where they had been left folded for her, eight years ago.

Oxford. Thursday. 5 a.m.

Ems,

I'm writing this as you sleep. I've decided to leave early and drive to the airport – better than waiting for a train back when I land. The meeting in Dusseldorf may go on, but I should be home by 6 p.m. tomorrow. Pub? Or we could take some wine down to the river?

I didn't disturb you when I got in last night – it was too late. The firm's away-day of 'Strategic Energising' was as bad as I thought it would be. Questions, scenarios, role-play and then more questions. I wanted to stand up and say, 'Ask me any question and the answer is always going to be the same: "a Dr of Genetics with red hair".' That amazing hair – I'm looking at it now.

After a day of it (what has 'Strategic Energising' got to do with the law anyway?), we had an entire evening playing 'Team Togetherness' games. Just when I thought it couldn't get any worse. It was Barry's idea. God love him. I know you feel sorry for him and think he's lonely, but you try spending an evening with him. We spent a long time breaking off into pairs and finding three positive words to describe each other. Fenella started (Loud, Lazy & Likes a Liquid Lunch?), she demolished Nick with Diffident, Detailed and Dull. Loud snorty laugh from Fenella as everyone else shifted in their seats. I can't remember what Nick countered with, but it was something pleasant – but then he's a nice bloke. I lost interest at this point because I was thinking of you. So much better than dwelling on Barry, who I was paired with (don't worry, Ems, I was nice about him).

The first word I decided on for you was: Brave. You know where I'm going with this one. But, shit, she's a piece of work, your mother. I know she doesn't make you feel brave – quite the opposite. But I think it takes courage to keep going in the face of such criticism. I wish you'd just cut her loose but I know that's easier said than done. Interesting that Guy decided to live halfway round the world – just saying.

Enough of your mum. Second word: Bossy. 'What me? Bossy?' You bet. You're stealth-bomber bossy. You don't nag or shout, but how is it we end up watching the series you want on TV and my very interesting documentaries never get a look in? And where did my black jeans (which had years of life left in them) go? And as for my plan for a music room for my drums in our new house, what happened to that? I rest my case, M'Lud.

Final word? Beautiful. I'm watching your face now as you sleep. When we first met, your face had a different look. I can't quite describe it; it was like it was closed down. I never want you to feel like that again. So, yes, Beautiful. But it's not just your face, Ems, it's you – inside and out. Don't think I don't know you've been trying to set up Barry with Nicky from the estate agents.

Stay Brave, Bossy & Beautiful.

Will x

Emma puts the letter back and closes the drawer. She knows she can't read any more. She fears what is left of her will unravel.

Downstairs in the kitchen, her body is trembling as she makes herself a coffee. There was once a time when she lived a life that she had thought was reserved for others. She and Will had a social life, went to the pub, met up with friends. With Will by her side, she found courage.

She pauses, stirring her coffee. He must be the only person

in the world who ever thought her bossy. With everyone else, she rarely found the voice to say what she wanted.

Her mind skips to Barry – clumsy, earnest, eager to please, Barry. She and Will were just buying their first house together, having outgrown the tiny flat they shared after their marriage. Emma had tried to set up Barry with their estate agent. Poor Barry. Had she recognised herself in him? Had she wanted to share some of her newfound happiness? She wonders whatever happened to Barry and Nicky. They had certainly dated for a few months, but then Barry changed jobs. Had they married? Had a family? Lived happily ever after?

She clenches her hands, hard, refocusing her thoughts. She cannot let herself go where her mind is taking her.

She looks down at her taught knuckles and wonders what The Florist's hands had been like. When the ship lurched, had those hands closed hard on a wooden rail, as she looked down into the churning blackness? She has read that the sea was smooth that night, but being a poor sailor herself, Emma knows there is always movement: a sickening, swaying roll, followed by a deceptively gentle tilt as, deep below the surface, the sea thrust its fingers into the ship's wound.

Emma places her hands flat on the solid kitchen tabletop. Maybe The Florist had hidden in her cabin? Was she holding tight to the metal post of a bunk bed, breathing in the smell of new paint, sweat and salt, as the floor shifted beneath her feet?

She looks out the window towards her neighbours' house. The path to their front door is lined with rows of marigolds. A few days ago, Les told her about a programme he had seen on

National Geographic, how he'd learnt that in South America, during the festival marking the Day of the Dead, paths of marigold petals were scattered through the streets to guide the dead back to their loved ones.

Emma studies the line of marigolds, with their lollipop-orange petals. Most days she knows she would lay a path of petals hundreds of miles long to bring Will home. But there are moments when her unruly imagination sends a sudden blast of wind, when the path shifts beneath her feet and marigold petals are scattered over the Oxfordshire countryside.

In her mind's eye, she sees a landscape painted with thousands of orange teardrops, and she wonders if she really wants Will to find her.

Chapter 22

Violet

Cornflowers

Her mother picks away at the cloth on the table and she is sure she will soon be picking away at her and her sister. She wonders what they have done wrong. They have laid the table and placed a jam jar of cornflowers on the windowsill. Perhaps her mother thinks she bought them and wasted money, but they were given to her by the old man who has a garden by the station. She would like to tell her mother about how he told her the names of the flowers on the railway bank: rosebay willow herb, dog rose, enchanter's nightshade. But she is mesmerised by the picking finger.

Her sister is stood behind her chair, one small finger on her back, keeping connection with her elder sister. Her finger does not pick but taps gently as if transmitting her anxiety in morse code.

She looks around for what they have missed – they have spent the past two days washing, ironing and tidying. Is something in the wrong place?

Then it comes to her. Her mother must feel in the wrong place. Is she thinking of the ship, of the friends she made on board? Does she want to be with them? So she asks her – after all, she is the eldest – and her jealousy gives her courage. She knows her sister would never find the words and the boys are still miles away, waiting for their Sunday-afternoon visit.

'Is it strange to be home, Ma? Do you miss the ship?'

'God bless you, child, I would be glad if I never had to go to sea ever again.'

'Then what is it, Ma?' Her sister has found her voice.

Her mother looks at them both. 'You say we can't see the boys before Sunday?'

They both nod and the picking stops. Her mother draws herself up and nods back at them. 'Well, that can't be helped. Haven't you made the room look nice. All so tidy, and flowers and everything.' She smiles. 'My goodness, it is quiet without the running and stomping.'

And she realises what is troubling her mother: the boys are in the wrong place. Maybe she and her sister should have left the room messy; slammed doors and scattered the cornflowers on the wooden floor. Maybe that would have made for a happier homecoming.

Later that night, when her sister is asleep, her mother calls for her and pats the arm of her chair. She sits on it even though it makes her too tall and she can't really see her mother's face properly. Her mother touches her arm and looks down at the fire, her forehead and nose tinged pink from the glow. Away from the firelight, where her brown hair curls around her ear, her cheek is pale like uncooked dough. For the first time she notices that her mother's hair is streaked with grey.

Her mother phrases the question slowly: how would she feel about going to sea? The work is hard, but she would meet all sorts of people. She knows of a company that may be looking for crew — she could put in a word. She tells her daughter she is a good girl.

Before her mother has finished speaking, she has jumped in with worries about her sister and brothers. Her concern shocks her, like a plunge into cold water. Who will look after them? How will they manage? As she comes up for breath, she realises she is now looking at a different view, her mother's view.

'Would you stay at home then? Could the boys come back?'

Her mother puts her head on one side. 'We'd have to wait and see.'

This has always meant 'yes', in the past. She feels suddenly hopeful for the boys.

'I wasn't too well on the last trip. I'm not sure how much longer I can do the work.' She smiles up at her daughter. 'And you're such a good girl. A woman now, truth be told. Twenty-one next birthday.'

'Something of a señorita?'

Her mother looks puzzled, as if she has heard this before but can't quite place it. 'Well, what do you think?'

She thinks she will have to put her sister in her case and keep her in her cabin with her. She thinks she cannot bear to be without her. She thinks she wants to cry. She thinks she wants her father to come and save her.

She says, 'I think I could do it if you told me what to do.'

To balance the lie, she tells one truth: 'And I would like to see dolphins.'

Chapter 23

Emma

Scabious & Larkspur

'Tamas hasn't found Bealing & Son but he's come across a woman who knows a bit about them.'

Emma turns from the funeral spray she is binding together with twine. 'Really?'

Betty is looking smug. 'Yes – she makes scrapbooks of old photographs from different flower markets. Her husband's people had a stall at Covent Garden, oh my goodness, for years. They went way back. She began by sorting out photos of his family and her interest grew from there, apparently.'

'So, does she have photos of Bealing's nursery?'

'I don't know about that, love. You'll have to ask Tamas when he comes in. She's the mother of one of the growers he knows.' Betty pats her shoulder, then nods towards the small tree Emma has lifted onto the bench. 'What's with the plant?'

she enquires, a crease between her brows.

'I just need one long twig,' she says, picking up her secateurs. 'My customer and her sister were always fighting – either that or they didn't speak for months. She told me it was usually over something stupid. Sometimes she forgot what. And then – well, then it was too late.' Emma uses the twine to add an olive branch to her spray of pale pink scabious and cream larkspur.

Betty pats her shoulder again, and Emma thinks this time it might be with approval. Betty has an older sister who has 'grown very grand and now thinks she's a cut above'. This makes her think of her own mother. She called her on the way to work this morning to see if she could shed any light on relatives from around 1912 who might have some connection with the *Titanic*. Her mother was clear in her dismissal of the idea: 'Irish? *Titanic*? The Nurse? What are you on about, Emma?'

Les comes into the Cabin carrying a tray of lavender plants, letting in a stream of watery sunshine. The rain has abated, and the sun is doing its best to break through the clouds. He is shortly followed by Tamas, whose large arms are wrapped around bundles of golden rod, white veronica and long-stemmed cornflowers.

'You have heard?' Tamas says, depositing the flowers on the bench. 'You have heard?' he repeats looking at Emma and nodding his head furiously. 'I, Tamas, have found your Bealing's, like I said I would.' He then frowns and looks uncharacteristically anxious. 'I say this, but we are not there yet. You must meet this woman who I have found for you. She is the key to the puzzle – I am sure of this.' He hands Emma a piece of paper with a name and an address in Lincolnshire on it. 'She is expecting you to call and then to go and see her to talk. Her son says she is not a woman who does Zooming.' Suddenly he throws his arms wide, narrowly missing Betty. His confidence has returned. 'It is like a quest. We are the Four Amigos. I play these games on my computer at home. I am a warrior looking for treasure. I make Berta into a dragon or sometimes a troll or a pig. This I do to make her laugh.' Emma can't help noticing that Tamas is looking anxious again, and she wonders how funny Berta finds being a pig.

Betty is looking bemused, but Les smiles encouragingly at Tamas. 'You've done a great job, Tamas. I am sure Emma is very pleased.'

And she realises she hasn't thanked Tamas. Hasn't, as yet, said anything. So much for her thinking in Spanish. That's all very well, but she does actually have to open her mouth and speak.

'Tamas,' she begins.

But his attention has been caught by something outside of the window and he is off again. 'Look at that dog – that Dachshund. It is like a sausage. It is so small and fat, I could put it into bread and eat it.' With this he bangs out of the door, and Emma can see him striding towards the small dog. She presumes he is going to pat it. She just hopes he doesn't step on it. Or eat it.

'Well!' Betty says, watching him go.

'Well,' echoes Les, then he too heads for the door. 'Best get on. No rest for the wicked.'

'That's great news about Bealing's,' Betty says, before turning to collect her secateurs. 'You all right here, love? I've stuff I need to do in the polytunnel.'

And with that, she also disappears and Emma is left alone.

She may not have immediately thanked Tamas, but as she watches him through the window making a fuss of the miniature dog, she *is* grateful. In fact, she feels she has quite a lot to thank the *Titanic* for.

It first started after days of watching Betty chatting to customers. Betty would greet them and then somehow introduce all manner of subjects: the shoes they were wearing; a new film she'd heard about; an old song she loved. Before they knew it, people would tell Betty about their childhood, their families, and how they'd always wanted to play lead guitar in a band. It seemed there was nothing people weren't prepared to share with her. Emma hadn't wanted to replicate this – she still felt the need to keep a distance – but she had wanted to take a small step towards having a conversation, making a connection. And so she had begun to mention having seen a programme about the *Titanic* to customers. And it had worked. It seemed everyone had something to say about the *Titanic*.

Tamas is back – and it seems he is no exception. 'I have been thinking and reading about the *Titanic*. It was a remarkable and big ship: two-hundred and sixty-nine metres long, twenty-eight metres broad, with a height of fifty-three metres from the keel to the top of the funnels…'

Since introducing the subject into conversation, Emma has begun to recognise different *Titanic* types. Some, like Tamas, are

Numbers Nerds, with an astonishing range of facts and figures at their fingertips. Others, like Les, are Detectives, fascinated by uncovering the *real* reason behind the sinking (so far: a fire in the hold; poor grade steel; shoddy rivets). She has talked to Romantics (oh, the dresses; the Turkish baths; the only way to travel to New York), the Sympathisers (can you imagine what it was like…), the Conspiracy Theorists (it didn't sink; was never actually finished), the Morally Outraged (stokers abandoned; company cover-up), and the Unbelievers (*Titanic*? That's just a film, isn't it?). She's not quite sure where she fits in all of this. Maybe there should be a category of Recently Obsessed?

Back home in her cottage, she has also discovered there is an online community of *Titanic* devotees. Among the people she has encountered, there are two who she would like to get to know better. One is a woman in London who is curating a forthcoming V&A exhibition about life on board ocean liners – Emma has already put the date of the opening in her diary. She worried at first about going where there would likely be crowds, but when she framed it in her mind as a 'research trip', she found the prospect far less scary.

The other person she has connected with is a retired perfumier living in Paris, well known for creating a famous range of floral fragrances. His area of interest is the phials of perfume carried on the *Titanic* that were found intact on the ocean floor. They have only had a brief exchange, but Emma is keen to know more about the perfume, and she wonders if, like her, he would be interested in finding out more about the flowers on board.

She has tried to keep her research focused on the flowers and The Florist on the *Titanic*, but every now and then Emma has found herself pulling up The Nurse's photograph on her phone. She keeps staring at her face, trying to make sense of the feeling she had the first time she laid eyes on her.

Meanwhile, Tamas is still in full flow. '… and sixty-six thousand tons of water it moves ouf of the way…'

To try to stem the flow Emma throws in, 'Romania?'

He bites. 'No! You must try again!'

'Bulgaria?'

He shakes his head, and before she can make her next suggestion, he points out of the window. 'There he goes, that sausage dog. We have a dog such as that one.'

Emma knows she looks surprised.

'Yes, I see you think I would have a big dog. A wolf, as big as a horse.'

She smiles. 'Well, yes, Tamas, I suppose I would.'

'Ah, well, you are right. Mitsy is not our dog. It is the dog of our daughter, Greta.'

'Do you look after Mitsy for her, then?'

'I am supposing you would say we are adopting her dog. Greta, our daughter, she died.' Tamas slaps his arms around his body as if he is suddenly cold, and his eyes brim with tears.

Emma is shocked. She knows there is nothing she can say that will help, but she says it anyway. 'Oh, Tamas, I'm so sorry.' Then she reaches out and rubs the big man's shoulder.

'My husband died just over a year ago,' she tells him. 'He had an undiagnosed heart condition.' It is the first time she has volunteered this information to anyone. It feels like a small offering to a man who has lost his daughter – a man she didn't even thank for finding out about the Bealings.

'I am very sorry for your loss,' Tamas says.

Emma is moved by his quiet formality. It seems very unlike the man who bounds and stamps his way into the Cabin delivering their flowers.

He looks away, out of the window. Without turning around, he says, 'It is a journey you are on. Do not try to travel all of it on your own. This is what I say to Berta.' He pauses for some moments. 'I am not sure she is listening to me. I think perhaps she does not wish to travel with me.' With this he gives a shake of his head and turns and leaves.

Emma watches him striding away down the path. Then she looks under the counter for the *Back in 5 minutes* sign, hangs it on the outside of the door and goes to find Betty.

Chapter 24

Violet

Periwinkles

They are playing a waiting game. She is waiting for a letter to tell her if she can come for an interview. Her mother is waiting for the money order to be delivered for her work on board ship.

Her mother sits on the bottom step of the stairs, watching the letterbox, her toes tapping. She is humming to herself but they can't catch the tune. She and her sister sit on the top step, watching their mother watching. Her mother has always loved games and she can magic them from the air. She makes a game out of sharing and a game out of doing without – she is very good at that one. Now she is playing the waiting game. The feet tapping in time to her private song are wearing her second-best boots. They are part of the game, too.

If the money order comes, then the running will start. Her brothers are home now and ready to go; they have played this game many times before and know just what to do. They raced in the back yard to find the fastest runner, tripping and shouting as they ran up and down. She thought her mother might fall out of the window, leaning out and calling to them, clapping her hands for the winners and losers alike and blowing them all a kiss.

The fastest runner has been chosen, and when the money order comes, he must run the first leg in the game. Down the alley, past the church, up the hill to the pawnbrokers where sits a pair of handsewn boots in the window. He must take the money order with him and race back with the change – shillings and pence – and the boots, of course. Her mother will want to be wearing them when the game ends.

When the money is back, runner number two must set off for the butchers at the end of the street and runner number three to the market, dodging between the carts and horses. Runner number three is usually her youngest brother. Small and quick, he never lets anyone cheat him out of what is his due.

Runner number four, slow and strong, will go to the coal merchant, trusted to carry the weight without spilling a single lump.

Now, the boys are stomping and stamping in the yard, like young colts ready to be off. They just have to wait for the game to start.

If the postman does not come, the game will not be spoilt. Runner number one will race to the pawnbrokers with her mother's periwinkle broach, and runner number two will buy scraggy mutton rather than beef for dinner. As her mother always says, 'God never shuts one door without opening another'.

She tries to imagine God reaching out to open their front door, but the hand she sees grasping the brass door handle isn't God's but her mother's.

Chapter 25

Emma

Cerise Bougainvillea

'Now this is nice. A day out, just the two of us. Not that I don't love a bit of time with Les, but it's not the same, is it? Men. They don't always want to chat about the same things. I must say this is a very comfortable car. I had to give up my Mini when we bought the garden centre. Not practical really, although I once got a seven-foot Christmas tree in the back. I did laugh, and you should have seen Les's face. But as he said, 'Betsy, you need the right tools for the right job'. That was true, of course and the van is just the ticket. But quite hard on the backside when you've been driving for a while. I suppose it's the suspension – it doesn't have the give – not like these modern cars…'

They have only been driving for ten minutes, and Emma is already regretting asking Betty to come with her. It will be another two hours before they get to Stamford, which is where she has arranged to meet Tamas's contact, Jane. She cannot think what has got into Betty.

'Now, what music have you got here? It's nice to have a bit of music when you're driving. It's one of the few times I sing: church at Christmas, the shower and in the van. You can really belt out a song driving along on your own. When I'm coming back from my sister's, I put a bit of Elvis on. After all, there's no one to hear me and it makes the journey go in a flash. Let's have a look … um … I've never heard of them. Ah, Adele, you can't go wrong with Adele. Even Les doesn't mind me playing her in the bungalow…'

In the garden centre, Betty's conversation flows gently like a stream. Now, trapped in the car, it swirls and buffets Emma until she opens her window just to hear the rush of air passing by.

'You might want to put the window up, love – you won't feel the benefit of the air-conditioning.' Betty's newly ironed hummingbird T-shirt is starting to wilt in the heat.

As they pass Northampton, Betty moves on to firing questions at her instead, and Emma starts to miss the monologue. Betty asks about where she grew up, about her previous work. 'Fancy that, a scientist and a linguist. And you spent two years in Italy and France, you say…'

Then she progresses to family: does she have any brothers or sisters? Emma tells her about Guy in Singapore. She can sense what is coming next – parents. And sure enough, this is Betty's next question. Emma has no desire to talk about her mother, but she does tell Betty about her dad and his love of gardening.

'So you two were close, then?'

'Yes, but we didn't spend hours talking. I don't know. It just worked – if that makes any sense?' Emma knows she is not expressing herself very well, but smiles, remembering. 'When I helped him in the garden, we could go for hours without talking.'

'Well, no one could ever say that about me.'

'No, they certainly couldn't,' Emma interjects with a laugh.

The car falls silent, and Emma knows without having to look that Betty will be startled and blinking. She meant it as a friendly joke – but words that were gentle and funny in her head spewed out as bitchy. Why hadn't she paused and thought in Spanish? She glances at Betty but cannot see her face; she is turned away looking out of the passenger window.

And then, as if Emma hadn't spoken, Betty starts up again, chatting about this and that – non-stop. She thinks of apologising, but the chatter runs up and down between them like a wall. Instead, she puts Adele on softly in the background and hopes Betty knows she is sorry.

As Emma turns into the car park in Stamford, Betty falls silent, but as she opens her door she remarks quietly, 'Don't mind me, love.'

They have arranged to meet Jane in an Italian café off the High Street. Emma lingers near the door for a while, speaking a few words in Italian to the owner, and feels the enormous pleasure of stretching a much underused muscle.

On the walls are photographs of the rooftops of Florence and in the entrance to a conservatory sits a large terracotta pot containing a huge, cerise bougainvillea. Emma thinks Les would be impressed.

When Emma joins Betty at a small table in the conservatory, she is deep in conversation with a tiny woman who looks about Betty's age. Everything about her is small and neat. She has the tiniest feet Emma has ever seen. She reminds Emma of an illustration from a children's book she once read: *Mrs Pepperpot*.

Betty briefly introduces her to Jane and the two women return to discussing their families. Despite just meeting her, it seems Betty already knows all about Jane's son, who grows daffodils but is now thinking of expanding into peonies, and also his wife (teacher, but would like a change) and children (Daniel, who loves Manchester United; and Ruby, who is a minx and too knowing by half). In turn, Emma learns that Betty's mother died six months ago and that she is finding it hard without her and that Les has been tested for prostate cancer and got the all-clear, 'thanks be to God' – just getting old, the specialist said. Although he is still 'piddling like a leaky tap every few hours at night'.

Emma is appalled to find she knows so little about Betty. She had no idea Les was worried about his health – all this on top of money worries. She feels her skin growing hot and clammy as she thinks of the past two hours. She didn't ask Betty a single question about herself and smiled inwardly when she saw her hummingbird T-shirt.

'I'm sorry to hear about your mum,' Emma says, cutting across the women's conversation. 'How old was she?'

Betty looks round in surprise. 'Eighty-six, but you would never have guessed it. She was always dressed just so. Even at the end she wore nice, tailored skirts and jackets.' Betty laughs. 'I think she despaired of me,' she says, with a smile down at her hummingbird. She blinks out through her glasses at Emma. For the first time, Emma notices she has on a new pair, a special pair for their day out.

'I always think you look nice. I like your wildlife T-shirts,' Emma says, and means it.

'Well, you can't make a silk purse out of a sow's ear, and that's a fact.'

One of Les's sayings.

'I'm sure Les doesn't think that. I always get the impression he's very proud to have you by his side.' It is only as she says it that Emma recalls the sideways glances Les sometimes gives his wife.

'Now you'll make me blush,' Betty replies. 'Do you know, one New Year's Eve we played this game, and he was asked to describe me in three words. Do you know what he said? "Small, ship-shape and sexy." He'd been drinking of course.' But Betty is clearly delighted by the memory. Mrs Pepperpot laughs along with her.

Emma feels the room tilt.

'Emma, what is it, love?' Betty stretches her hand out impulsively towards her.

Oh God, how could Will have got it so wrong? Brave, Bossy

and Beautiful. How could *she* have got it so wrong?

'I, I … don't know, nothing. Nothing.'

Both women are now staring at her.

'What is it, love?' Betty repeats, softly.

Emma tries to blink her tears away and concentrate on Betty. 'No, sorry, nothing. Just a sudden memory. I know that game.'

The owner approaches the table, and Betty launches into an animated discussion with him about their order, drawing Mrs Pepperpot's attention away from Emma. By the time Betty has decided on her choice – having changed her mind three times – Emma is able to meet her eye across the table. She knows Betty has been buying her time and wonders how she could possibly have been rude to this wonderful, kind woman.

Betty pauses as if she is going to say something to her, but appears to think better of it. Instead she turns to Mrs Pepperpot, saying briskly, 'Now down to business, Jane, what can you tell Emma here about Bealing's?'

Mrs Pepperpot pulls a large brown envelope from her bag and places it on the table, her beautifully manicured nails just touching the flap.

'As I said on the phone, I've made it a bit of a hobby finding out about the families who worked at Covent Garden, like my Tony's.' Mrs Pepperpot fixes remarkably blue eyes on Emma. There is something in her look that gives her the impression Mrs Pepperpot doesn't quite approve of her.

'Since Tony died, I've had a bit more time for my scrapbooks, and the ancestry websites have been a boon. They make investigation so much easier.'

Emma nods her agreement. She has spent the last couple of evenings signing up to similar websites in an attempt to find out more about her family. It seems her research has now divided into two parts: finding The Florist; and trying to understand the connection she feels with The Nurse. Her mother's family have been easy to trace, having lived in Kent for many years and France before that. But, so far, she can find no conceivable link with the ship or The Nurse. She has yet to start on her father's family.

Mrs Pepperpot continues, 'Sometimes I start with a photograph I come across and just go from there.'

'Like a treasure hunt?' Betty suggests.

'Yes, just like that, and it's led me far and wide, discovering the history of markets and nurseries all over the country.' Mrs Pepperpot pulls a sepia photograph from the envelope.

'And this, is F.G. Bealing,' she says, laying the photograph in front of them. 'Francis George Bealing.'

Emma and Betty simultaneously let out a long breath.

The young man staring back at them has a narrow neck and broad forehead. His ears stand out slightly from his head and he has a serious look on his face.

Betty glances briefly at Emma.

'Francis, or Frank Senior, as he became known, was born in Gillingham in Dorset in 1865. By the 1890s, Frank Senior and his wife Harriet had moved from Dorset to Southampton, where they had started a plant nursery. Business was going well and they provided many of the ocean liners that docked there with plants and flowers, and as you know they supplied the

Titanic. It was very much a family business – their son, Frank Junior, worked alongside his father.'

Mrs Pepperpot reaches into the envelope and pulls out another black and white photograph showing two men standing alongside a cold frame of carnations.

'F.G. Bealing & Son,' Emma remarks.

Mrs Pepperpot just stares at her. Emma can't think for the life of her what she has done to upset the tiny woman opposite her. Surely it can't be that she is simply too big?

'By what has been written about the family I gather that Frank Senior was bit of a tough taskmaster. A driving force.' Mrs Pepperpot looks up, and says with meaning, 'Men like that aren't always easy to be with.'

Emma wonders what Mr Pepperpot had been like. Had he been a driving force? Was he a man who overruled his wife – cut across her when she was speaking? She thinks of their conversation when she sat down. She barely said hello and then interrupted Mrs Pepperpot to speak to Betty. She feels dismayed and exhausted by her continued ineptitude.

She tries to make amends. She phrases the words in Spanish in her head, then speaks in English. 'This research is so thorough, Jane. It must have taken you a lot of work and it's extremely kind of you to take the time to share everything you've learnt with us, isn't it, Betty?'

Betty joins in the praise. 'It certainly is. A real professional job – you can tell you're an old hand at this. We would never have been able to find out all of this on our own, would we, love?'

'No, never.'

Emma has the satisfaction of seeing Mrs Pepperpot's back straighten slightly. She doesn't exactly smile at Emma, but her look loses some of its frost as she says, 'Now, as I said, Frank Senior seemed very much to be the boss, but it was his grandson who recorded what went on the night before the *Titanic* sailed. He was the third generation to run the business, until Bealing's ceased trading in the 1960s. I guess they went out of business.'

'That's why you couldn't find them, Emma,' Betty comments.

Mrs Pepperpot continues. 'When the *Titanic* set off from Southampton on its maiden voyage, Frank Senior would have been forty-seven, Frank Junior twenty-two. Together they drove the cart of plants and flowers to the ship the evening before it sailed.'

'The night of the ninth of April 1912,' Emma murmurs, imagining the scrape of metal wheels over stone and the bulk of the *Titanic* looming out of the darkness.

'They took tarpaulins into the foyer and spread them out there. Then they unloaded the plants – about three to four hundred of them – plus all the flowers they would need for the journey. Then they started the job of arranging the plants around the ship. I get the feeling that the *Titanic* stewards had a say in where they went but Frank Senior was very much to the fore.'

'A driving force,' Betty mutters.

'Then they put the cut flowers into storage for later,' Mrs Pepperpot adds.

Emma pictures the father and son trundling away on the empty cart.

It seems Mrs Pepperpot is following her train of thought. 'I wonder who arranged them, then?' she says. By now she is leaning forward, a gleam in her eye.

'I've been researching stewardesses who might have had a background in floristry,' Emma tells her, 'but I haven't found anyone yet.'

'Well,' Mrs Pepperpot says slowly, 'you might want to look for anyone with a background in gardening as well. The first florists were gardeners, after all.' She looks from Betty to Emma. 'They were the ones who learnt the trade from working in the big houses, making up bouquets, buttonholes, corsages and arranging the house flowers. When the railways spread, it was gardeners who started the nurseries and provided their floristry skills as a service.' She looks intently at Emma. 'I see now what you're saying – those flowers needed arranging, and you're wondering who was the florist *on board*?'

Emma smiles to herself. Maybe a recruit to the Recently Obsessed?

The small woman sits back in her chair. 'Well, that really is fascinating. A proper mystery.' She glances at Emma, who smiles encouragingly, feeling there is more Mrs Pepperpot wants to say. She is right.

'There is one thing I found out that might interest you. The Bealings were famous for their floral buttonholes. They provided them for the first-class male passengers. They were known as "Bealing Buttonholes".'

Emma wants to say, *I know, they made them from clove carnations*, but she isn't sure *what* she thinks anymore. So much of what she has been dwelling on has been in her imagination.

She feels she has taken a big step forward in meeting Mrs Pepperpot. It has shed light on so much and made her investigation feel real. But she can't help feeling there is still someone out there, hiding in the shadows.

Or perhaps there are two people? The Florist and The Nurse.

Chapter 26

Violet

Bleached Poppies

'You seem far too young.'

She cannot tell him he is far too old. His head is shiny where his hair has grown thin, and his neck reminds her of the turkey they once had for Christmas.

If she said this, she would be travelling back home without the prospect of a job. So instead, she sits quietly as he frowns at her, and tries to look as old as she can. She drops her chin and rounds her shoulders as she has seen the pedlar woman do when the wind whips down the street trying to steal her shawl. Her skin is tissue-thin like bleached poppy petals. She is the oldest person Violet has ever seen. Violet wonders if he would like her to be as old as her.

'Most of the women we employ are sailors' widows. They seem to fit in, know a bit about the world.' He then adds, 'A better age.'

He does not tell her the secret of what this age is, so she waits and continues to try to look like the pedlar woman.

She has become used to waiting: waiting for the letter to come, waiting for the tram to take her into the heart of the city, waiting to be let into a building that is home to more stone and marble than the graveyard. Then she waited in the corridor filled with paintings of ships that did not move and people that did. Streams of them, flowing past her as she waited, some rushing so fast that the draught from them ruffled the fabric of her skirt.

But now, when she has come to rest, told her tale and tried to sell her wares like the pedlar woman, it seems she is too young. The man appears to be waiting, thinking. Maybe he is waiting for her to get older.

He swallows like an anxious bird. 'And you are far too pretty.'

She can see this worries him more than her age.

It does not worry her like it worries him. Her mother says she has no more idea than a babe born when it comes to the lads, but she has learnt a little. She knows the butcher's boy weighs her smile as an extra scoop on the scales and that the postman weaves a different path to bring their mail two streets early if she greets him and asks after his family. She sees her mother fret and shake her head at the men who straighten their backs as she passes by.

She thinks she is right to be wary of the butcher's boy, who looks as if he would like to pinch her flesh as he does the plump steak he is testing – but she knows her mother should not worry about the postman, who laughs like a man who has enjoyed the game but has long since given his boots away to another.

She now sees that she does not need to grow older as she sits on this hard office chair; she only needs to smile.

She is sure Mr Turkey was never a pincher or a man who pressed a sweaty hand into a girl's palm, but she can sense there was a time when he strutted and held his back a little straighter for the sake of a smile.

How strange it is that she has to use pretty ways to persuade him that she can make herself ugly.

Chapter 27

Emma

White Heather

In the car on the way back, Betty goes over all that Mrs Pepperpot has told them. When eventually the car falls silent, Emma almost tells Betty about the photograph of The Nurse, but she has so little to say, and the scientist in her is determined to keep the focus firmly on the project's objective: to find The Florist of the *Titanic*. The Nurse is a tangent – even if Emma keeps pulling up the woman's photograph on her phone and frowning at it.

Instead, Emma wracks her brain for something to ask Betty – she doesn't want a replay of their journey to Stamford. For a moment, her mother's words echo in her head: *If only you would make a bit more effort.*

'Betty, how did you and Les meet?'

Betty looks startled, but this time, in a good way. 'Oh, now, that's a long time ago. We both come from a small town in Derbyshire. Les was working as an apprentice builder – a good, local firm – and they were doing some work at the Town Hall where I was secretary to the buildings manager. Well, one Friday I came out of work and Les was waiting for me, and he asked if I would like to go and see a film with him the next day.'

'And you went?'

Betty starts to laugh. 'I did, and I got such a shock.'

'Why, what did he take you to see?!'

'It wasn't that, love – it was Les. I think he was the first punk I'd actually seen in the flesh. We didn't get a lot of them in Glossop.'

'Les?!'

'Well, of course, he couldn't shave his head or anything like that – his boss would have had a fit. But in the evenings and on weekends, he spent hours spiking his hair up and he had these ripped trousers with safety pins and an old leather jacket. He looked a right sight, I can tell you.' Betty is still laughing.

'But you must have liked him, if you agreed to go out with him again?'

'Well, he was Les, wasn't he? He couldn't hide that.' Betty grins. 'But it was a while before I would go anywhere but the cinema. No one could see us there in the dark. By the time I agreed to go to a disco with him, I had persuaded him to buy a nice pair of Wranglers and to stop spiking his hair. The leather jacket I always rather liked,' Betty remembers fondly.

'I'm sorry about what I said earlier, Betty.' She can't bear it if this woman thinks she was trying to be unkind to her.

'What was that, love?'

'About you ... talking.' Getting the words out is excruciating but Emma ploughs on. 'Sometimes I think something in my head and when it comes out, it sounds all wrong.'

'I wouldn't worry about that, love. We all do it.'

'Really?' Emma asks, doubtfully.

'Well, look at me rambling on about singing in the shower. As I was saying it, I was thinking, Emma doesn't want to hear all this.'

'Really?' Emma repeats, with more confidence this time. She says tentatively, 'Les gave me some interesting advice – well, he sort of made me think of it. He mentioned that one of his old bosses spoke a lot of languages and that it was what language you thought in that mattered, and so I've been trying to think in Spanish before I speak, but I'm struggling to get it right.'

'Les is good at advice,' Betty says proudly.

An image of Les as a punk comes into Emma's head, and she laughs out loud.

'What?!'

'Was Les *really* a punk?'

Betty joins in the laughter. 'He certainly was.' Her laughter stops abruptly.

It is Emma's turn to ask, 'What?'

Betty lets out a long sigh. 'I suddenly thought of Tamas.'

Emma's own laughter drains away. 'He mentioned his daughter to me – Greta?'

Betty's voice loses all of its gaiety. 'Oh, yes, dear. That was terrible for him and Berta. I'd say it was two years ago now. She died of cancer. She had only just turned twenty.' She pauses for a while, looking out of the window. 'I never really know how Tamas is getting on – we only ever see him for a few minutes here and there. But I do worry about him and Berta.' She looks back at Emma. 'I think Tamas feels he has to keep everyone's spirits up, and I imagine that can be a little wearing. On both of them.'

Emma finds herself wondering about the unknown Berta. Maybe grief has to take its own course, find its own level. She is not surprised by Betty's next question.

'How did your husband die, love?'

Emma takes in a deep breath. 'It was a heart attack.'

'That's so sad, love. What was he like?'

What can she possibly say? She uses the time it takes to negotiate a busy roundabout to order her thoughts. How can she distil all those years, emotions and memories into a few sentences? Let alone what has happened since.

In the end, she decides on one story to tell Betty.

'He was the sort of man who took the vicar out and got him drunk.'

'What?!' Betty exclaims.

Emma smiles. 'Yes, I know. Will wasn't a regular church goer, but they were both keen cyclists, and so they got to know each other a little. Will noticed that everyone dumped on the vicar. You can't say "no, I don't want to listen to your problems" if you're a vicar, and no one ever asked how he was or listened to him. So, Will would take him to London, where he didn't know anyone. He never said what they talked about – probably sport – but at least the vicar could just be a man having a drink with a mate.'

It's a good memory – it was one of the many reasons she loved her husband – but it is as much as she wants to say. So, quickly, she asks Betty another question, a question about flowers – a safe place to be.

They talk about the garden centre and flowers. Then Emma asks about Betty and Les's family and finds out they have a son, Ben, living in New Zealand. For Emma, it feels companionable, comforting. She thinks how much she likes Betty. How well it is all going.

Until.

They are on the outskirts of Oxford, passing a country pub famous for its curries. 'Oh, love, we could stop and have a drink and a bite to eat,' Betty suggests.

The faint fragrance of spices reaches them through the open windows of the car and before she can stop herself, Emma says sharply, 'NO!'

And with that, Betty is back to startled, blinking, and Emma is silenced once again.

Sitting in the kitchen that evening, Emma goes over her day. So much was good: being with Betty; some of their conversation; speaking Italian again; and eventually, Mrs Pepperpot and all she had told them.

She glances at the images of F.G. Bealing & Son, now pinned to her noticeboard.

Yet, despite all this, she still didn't manage to get it right:

speaking across Mrs Pepperpot, and that comment about Betty talking too much. Her stomach twists in shame. And then there was that 'NO!' when Betty suggested they stop for an Indian meal.

Emma lays her head on her arms that are folded on the table.

Telling Will's mother that her son had died was the hardest thing that Emma had ever done. She wouldn't let anyone else do it. And she did it straight away.

The ambulance had left; the people had eventually gone (she had insisted on that). She returned to the conservatory – a bleached wood and glass structure off the dining room, where she and Will had sat making plans for their garden only hours before.

Later, she would recall that time between everyone leaving and the phone call as a series of bizarre still-life paintings. On the table in the conservatory, rice from their takeaway lay scattered like confetti. One chair was still overturned, near a side table where a neighbour had left cups of tea that nobody had wanted. An orange bag she had never really liked hung on the back of a blue chair. The French doors were propped open with terracotta pots filled with white heather.

Sometimes she tests herself on the images, like a child playing a memory game. For some reason it seems important to remember them all.

What she can never bear to recall is the smell of that evening: the acrid odour of urine mixed with Indian spices.

The first time she smelt curry after that night, she fell to her knees and vomited onto the pavement like a dog coughing up poison.

She remembers the call, the phone heavy as a bullion bar in her hand. She wished she could have spoken the words in Italian, the language of tragedies. But all she could offer were softly spoken English words.

So, with these, she had sat on the floor between the congealing curry and spilt wine, and had quietly broken a mother's heart.

Chapter 28

Violet

Faded Roses

Her mother laughs with relief and surprise when she tells her the story of the interview and that despite her not being the age of a 'sailor's widow', she has been given the position of junior stewardess.

Then her mother sets to work.

'We'll make you a wardrobe of clothes that'll add to your years.' Then she mutters under her breath, 'and that will scare the daylights out of the bravest man.'

They put away her two pretty dresses, and she and her mother play at dressing up. Her sister joins in, too, but her heart is clearly not in the game. Her mother cries with laughter as she pulls a baggy dress over her daughter's head, but her sister cries real tears.

She cannot bring herself to look at her little sister, even though she wants to gather up every sight and sound of her. So she watches her in the wardrobe mirror. The back-to-front face is easier to bear, and she manages a wink and a smile for her when she is dressed and displayed for their inspection.

The clothes are packed away, and all she has to do now is turn her hat into the sort of thing a sailor's widow would wear. The roses that bloom on it must be put in the window to fade in the sun. Her mother tuts when she sees them there, and she asks her mother what else it is she should do. She wonders if there is something she has forgotten.

'Bless you, child, no. You will look the part.' She pauses to pinch her daughter's cheek as she passes. 'But there's no hiding the roses that bloom here.'

Chapter 29

Emma

1,190 Carnations

Betty and Les are waiting for Emma when she arrives at the Flower Cabin the following morning. She reads concern in their look, and something else: supressed excitement?

'My God, Emma, you look like you haven't slept a wink.'

Emma is pretty sure this isn't what Betty meant to say.

'I know!' Emma replies, realising she sounds like she's accepting a compliment. 'I woke up in the middle of the night and couldn't sleep, so I started searching.'

'Les, go get us all a coffee.' Betty dismisses her husband, and Emma is reminded once more of the tortoiseshell cat that lives with the big, wary dog.

A long pause. 'Right you are.'

Emma senses Les searching for the right saying about coffee.

'Right you are,' he repeats, for once defeated.

As the door bangs behind Les, Betty pulls out a stool for her. Emma glances at the boxes of flowers waiting to be unpacked in the corner – Tamas must have come early this morning. These days there are fewer and fewer boxes, and she doesn't like to think what this might mean for the business. It is not long to autumn, and she can feel Santa's Grotto looming.

'The flowers can wait five minutes,' Betty says, patting the stool. And for once, Betty doesn't say anything more. Emma wonders where the woman from yesterday has gone.

'Betty?' Emma wants to say something to her about last night, but how to say it without inviting more questions? Instead, she changes direction. 'When I got home last night, I was going to give up, move on.'

'But?'

Emma looks at Betty's butterfly T-shirt, not quite meeting her eye. 'Then I thought Mrs Pepper … Jane … wouldn't have given up.' Nor would Will, but she doesn't mention that.

Betty says nothing, waiting.

Emma hurries on. 'I thought of the stores on the *Titanic* that were full of flowers after Frank and Frank had left that night: the daffodils, roses, daisies, carnations and all the other spring flowers, standing in buckets – waiting in the dark for the ship to wake up.'

As she says this, she wonders about the fragrance that would have welcomed the person opening the store door. Could anyone ever hope to recapture that scent? She thinks briefly of Philippe, the retired perfumier who she has been emailing, the expert on floral fragrances who investigated the perfume bottles found on the ocean floor.

She continues, glancing around her, 'Betty, I can't stop thinking about the flowers in the store. Who looked after them? There were five hundred vases delivered to the ship, so someone must have arranged the flowers into them, and...'

Les kicks open the door, and it occurs to Emma that he must have run all the way from the café. 'Here we are, wake up and smell the coffee.'

He smiles slowly at his wife and the words, *small, ship-shape and sexy* come into Emma's mind.

Betty takes the proffered mug and turns back to Emma, but not before Emma catches the hint of a sideways wink. Emma takes her coffee from Les, but can read nothing in his pleasant, bovine expression.

'Where was I? The vases, right. So I tried to find more references to flowers in passenger accounts, and there are so many – the daffodils "as if fresh picked," and someone else mentioning the tables of the à la carte restaurant, "gay" with pink roses and white daisies. And then I thought about what Jane, said about the first florists being gardeners, and I wondered... Well, if there was no official florist on board – and there isn't really any record of one – maybe one of the stewards, female *or* male,' she says, glancing at Les, 'could have had a background as a florist *or* a gardener and been responsible for the flowers.' Emma realised in the night that her own – what? Obsession? – was getting in the way. She had fixated on the idea of a female florist – but why couldn't The Florist have been a man?

'Can you check something like that?' Betty asks, sipping her coffee.

'Yes – there are so many records about the crew online. I'd already checked the women for a floristry background, but I double-checked them looking for a new connection with gardening and then I started on the men. I ruled out third-class stewards, because steerage would hardly be decorated with flowers, but I included all the first and second-class stewards. All the reports say that the second class on the *Titanic* was like every other liner's first class.'

'How many stewards was that?' Betty queries.

'It ran into hundreds. I also tried to look into what their parents had done, because of course they might have learnt their trade from them.'

'And you looked at them all?' Betty sounds stunned.

Emma nods. 'It was tragic, Betty, so many times I was reading about their families and their children, and then at the bottom it just said: "Died. Body not recovered". Over and over again. Some bodies were found, and then it records who identified them – it must have been terrible for their shipmates. Sometimes they could only be identified by their possessions.'

The Flower Cabin has grown quiet, and Emma catches the sound of birds and traffic in the distance.

'Did you find a gardener?' Les asks.

'Yes and no. William Hughes and John Ransom, who were first-class stewards, both had fathers who were gardeners, but they went to sea when they were young, and there's no mention of them having worked as gardeners themselves. They probably wouldn't have had time to learn the trade. Humphrey Humphreys—' Emma catches the look on Betty's face. 'Yes, I did wonder what his parents were thinking. He was a second-class steward. He grew up in Devon, where his father was a gardener, but he died when Humphrey was eleven, so he had even less chance to learn from him.'

'Do you know what happened to them, love?'

'They all died.'

Emma wonders if Betty is also thinking of Mrs Humphreys, who lost both her husband and her son.

'I got hopeful when I found Jacob Gibbons. He was a second-class steward, and although his father started work as a labourer, he became a gardener and Jacob worked for him as his assistant.'

'And?' Les asks.

'I thought maybe Jacob was The Florist until I read that father and son worked as gardeners in the grounds of the Dorset County Lunatic Asylum. I wouldn't say they had much call for corsages or bouquets.'

Les looks genuinely disappointed, so Emma adds, 'Jacob was saved in lifeboat eleven. When he got to New York, he sent his family a cable. It read: "Saved. Well. Daddy." And it wasn't long before he came home to them.'

Les suddenly rubs his eye as if he has some dirt caught in it.

Emma recalls Betty telling her about their son in New Zealand and asks them if they think Ben will ever return to live in England. Betty has to answer for Les. 'Oh, I don't think so, love. He's in the wine trade. We keep telling him that English wine is on the up, but you know, with his wife having the new baby and their son Zac getting on so well at school…'

Emma has no idea what to say, so offers, 'Jacob went on to have a good life. It doesn't look like he ever went back to sea and he and his wife ran a guesthouse overlooking Poole Harbour. They already had a daughter, Jeannie, but they went on to have a son, Arthur. Jacob lived until he was very nearly a hundred.'

Betty shakes her head slightly. 'You really remember all those details?'

Somehow, Emma feels it is the least she can do. She thinks of the words spoken by Jacob about that night:

It has been denied by many that the band was playing, but it was doing so and the strains of 'Nearer my God to Thee' *came clearly over the water with a solemnity so awful that words cannot express it.*

'So where does that leave us?' Les asks, slowly, and Emma is warmed by the word 'us'. She thinks suddenly how very fond she is of Les.

'You know, Les, I have no idea. I keep thinking there must have been a florist, even an unofficial one. I mean, think of the buttonholes – it looks like Bealing's provided some, but surely they couldn't have prepared enough for the whole trip? If every first-class male passenger was given one every evening, that would be … depending on your source, about one hundred and seventy-three male first-class passengers.' Emma is aware she is becoming a Numbers Nerd. 'They left on the tenth April and were due in New York on the morning of the seventeenth, so let's say one hundred and seventy buttonholes, times seven nights, that's…' Emma starts reaching for her phone.

'One thousand, one hundred and ninety,' Les declares.

Betty goes to speak but closes her mouth like a trap. The St Bernard has got one over the tortoiseshell cat. Emma imagines this doesn't happen very often.

Betty is quick to recover. 'Which brings us to what we wanted to talk to you about, love.'

Emma detaches herself slightly, protecting herself from what is coming. Last time they offered help, she wanted to cry.

Betty walks over to stand by her husband. 'We have been doing our own investigating.' They both stand straighter, like a couple of magicians about to pull off their most audacious trick. Emma cannot decide if Betty is Les's assistant or his rabbit.

'I also did some thinking last night, and I decided it was a matter of working out the logistics,' Betty pronounces solemnly. 'I thought we needed some expert advice, and Les reminded me that there *is* someone you could talk to. I have a friend whose mother worked on the *QE2* as a florist, and she's done a few bits and pieces herself for a cruise ship.'

'Betty, that's amazing!'

'It was daft really, love – I should have thought of her sooner. She's a florist I've known for years, and when I needed a refresher course, when we decided to start the Flower Cabin, I went along to one of hers. Clementine really knows her stuff. Anyway, I called her last night when we got back – she'd love to talk to you. The only thing is, she moved to Cambridge, so it will mean another day out if you want to meet her in person.'

Emma jumps in, keen to make amends for yesterday. 'You'll come too, won't you? It would be fun. We could even stay the night?' Emma looks enquiringly at Les, suddenly unsure if she should be checking with the St Bernard.

'Not this time, love,' says Betty, 'but thanks for asking. I think better you see Clementine on your own.'

Emma is about to ask why, but is distracted by Les, who is looking at her with anxious expectation.

'So you think it's a good idea?'

'Of course I do, Les. It's a brilliant idea. And thank you.'

Emma is in no doubt; the magician and his assistant deserve a standing ovation.

Chapter 30

Violet

Borrowed Periwinkles

They all travel to the station with her, a jostling, whistling convoy, moving through the grey city like a procession that has mistaken the day of the carnival. She remembers the festivals that filled the streets in Argentina and she searches the air for the scent of tuberose and incense. But all she can smell is wet soot, cabbage and the sick sweetness of something that is rotting its last.

Each brother wants to hold something for her: her large case, her small cloth bag, the parcels of food her mother has packed. Her sister just wants to hold her hand. When they get to the station, she drops it as if she can no longer bear the weight of it.

At the platform, the carriage is loaded with her bags and she is loaded with advice and kisses. The boys do not kiss, but they bump up against each other and scuffle – a final display of half-hearted punches and kicks performed just for her. Her mother reaches in her pocket and pulls out her periwinkle broach, which she pins to her eldest daughter's coat before patting her cheek.

Then the train door is slammed. She wonders if the sound will always remind her of this moment.

As the train shudders, she can feel the movement, the pull of the engine taking her away. She concentrates her thoughts on the texture of the seat under her hand, bristly like a soft brush. The wave of excitement that brought her to Waterloo is now spent, and as it ebbs, she hears the distant sounds of the station like the grating of pebbles being dragged underwater.

Now she sits and strokes the seat as the world passes her by. She knows her mother would tell her to keep her hands in her lap – 'You don't know what you'll catch' – but it occurs to her she no longer has to do what her mother says. Or what she thinks she will say.

Through the sadness that descended like fog, breaks a thin gleam of watery sunshine. She is grown-up now – more than something of a señorita. She could put her boots on the wrong feet, wear her rose hat on a Tuesday, sit in the park on a damp bench and look at the flowers for as long as she cares to.

She imagines a young woman with auburn hair sitting on a bench, crossing her feet at the ankles so her boots are the right way round. She knows the young woman is lonely without the budging, shifting bodies on the seat beside her, but in her mind's eye she lets her stretch out both arms along the back of the bench, claiming all the room, making the space her own.

In the railway carriage, the man travelling to Southampton to sell typewriter ribbons wonders what the beautiful girl opposite is smiling about.

Chapter 31

Emma

Begonias

Before Emma heads for Cambridge, she makes a detour to the garden centre. She finds Les among the begonias. Begonias are far and away Les's favourite flower and Betty told Emma when she first started that, should she ever need him, the first place to look would be among the begonias.

'You've got a good day for your trip,' he comments, stretching his back and putting down the bucket he is carrying.

Emma likes this about Les, he always gives you his full attention. 'Are you taking the A421 via Bletchley? That should be the quickest route. Though I'm not sure if the road works have finished outside Buckingham – in which case you might be better to scoot down and go through Aylesbury.'

Emma doesn't admit that she leaves all this to her sat nav. 'Which would you go for?'

'Umm. Six of one, half a dozen of the other.'

'A game of two halves,' Emma responds, before realising this makes no sense whatsoever.

Les puzzles over this. In the end, he discards it, 'How did you get on planting out the lupins I gave you?' he enquires.

'Good. I've put them against the cottage wall where they'll get plenty of sun.'

Les nods his approval. 'They were battered by that recent storm, so I didn't think we could sell them, but they should recover and do well for you. After all, storms make for stronger roots.'

Emma smiles slightly. 'And a plant is known by its roots.' She can't quite see if Les is smiling behind his beard but she thinks his eyes are starting to gleam. 'And good things only need a start,' he offers.

Before Emma can find a response, Les adds, 'And don't forget, Emma, to plant a garden is to believe in tomorrow.' He coughs and suddenly becomes absorbed in uprooting a weed that is growing by the side of the path.

'Were you after Betty?' he asks, standing upright once more.

'Yes, I was hoping I might be able to persuade her to change her mind and come with me.'

'Not here I'm afraid, she's popped out for a few hours.'

'Oh.' Emma feels ridiculously disappointed. 'Les...?'

'Yerrss?' He draws the word out slowly suspiciously and glances longingly at his begonias. Emma supposes they never give him trouble like this.

'Have you met Clementine?'

'Oh, yes.' He sounds relieved, like this is a question he can easily answer.

'What's she like?'

Les is now looking like an anxious St Bernard. Eventually he says, 'Nice woman.'

Emma gets the impression Les is not used to discussing others. He surprises her by adding, 'Betsy sets great store by her.'

'In what way?'

'Well,' he says slowly, 'Betty says Clem's just one of those people who—'

They are interrupted by a harassed-looking man with a toddler in tow, needing advice about sheds.

Les brightens, clearly back on safe ground. He nods a farewell to Emma and launches into a discussion of overlapping apexes and scalloped profiles.

As Emma walks away wondering, *one of those people who* what?, she reflects that 'shed speak' is as foreign a language to her as discussing people appears to be to Les.

It is only as she is driving away that she remembers the other reason she went to the garden centre. She has been meaning to ask Les if he's ever done any research into his family tree. With his interest in history, it seems possible, and he might have some advice.

Her own research is stalling. Not only is the search for The Florist taking precedence, but she is unearthing nothing of interest in her family tree. The more she digs, the more it feels like trying to find a connection with The Nurse is just a distraction. She senses something is slipping from her, without having any idea of what it is.

As she drives, she lowers the sun visor and rummages, one-handed, in her bag for her sunglasses. She is starting to get what she now thinks of as one of her headaches. These are often accompanied by a wave of exhaustion that leaves her listless and lightheaded. Mostly she puts this down to grief – except when the headaches arrive in the middle of the night; then she starts to worry she is developing the degenerative condition she used to research. This irrational fear always dissipates with the dawn.

Chapter 32

Violet

Wax Flowers

The journey from Southampton Station to her lodgings is accompanied by unfamiliar noise and familiar rain. As water drips from the moustache of the porter beside her she wonders if he is raining, too. He has the demeanour of a cloud heavy with water and disappointment. She knows her tip is not going to alleviate his gloom. It is all she can spare, and she spends the journey imagining the moment when she will hand it over.

At the lodging house, everything is brown, and very little light seeps through the brocade drapes. The furniture is heavy and weighed down by ornaments: stuffed birds with beady eyes; wax flowers that will never drop; and picture frames encrusted with shells that can no longer hear the sea. On the floor are numerous animal skins. She wonders if the dark furniture fell on them squashing them flat, pinning them to the floor. She does not like to step on them and add to their misery so plots a path around them as if they were islands.

The landlady who greets her is as large and solid as her furniture, but when she talks her voice is bright and light, and her eyes are merry. She thinks of a nurse she once knew when she was a little girl.

Her landlady sits her at the table and pours her cups of steaming tea as the men who lodge with her come and go. Some are old – tanned as dark as the brown furniture. Others are young and walk as if they are still rolling the deck of a ship. Her landlady explains that she likes to accommodate sailors, her late husband having been a man of the sea. Some sit for a while and smoke a pipe, sharing stories as the smoke gently drifts through the air. Her landlady tells her that the sailors' favourite tobacco is called Faithful Lover.

All the men are respectful and kind to the new lodger, and she begins to see that her landlady's house is like the earth of the old man's garden by the station: dark and heavy in which good things grow.

The following day she sends her luggage on, then leaves the lodgings, holding tight to the bag containing her letter of introduction. When she reaches the docks, the cranes rising out of the gloom remind her of the vultures she once saw in Argentina, long necks straining downwards to pluck at the inside of a carcass.

As she gets closer, the ships appear to draw themselves up to tower over her. She feels herself shrinking, afraid she might be crushed beneath their enormous hulls. She cannot measure their enormity on any scale she knows and so as she walks, she focuses on the smaller details: the face of a porter, a newspaper seller, her hand in her new glove – things she can fit into her mind.

Her eyes follow a cart loaded with crates of she knows not what, drawn by a horse that restlessly shakes his head as if he too is worried about being crushed. As she steps aside to let the cart pass, she catches the scent of the sea mixed with a pungent oily tang and she knows this is the fishmonger's horse. Then the scent of Faithful Lover breaks through the fishy smell, and the familiar smokiness calms her.

Only when she finds her ship does she raise her eyes to take in the full size of it – and although she does not smile, she does not cry either. Her vessel is the smaller sister of the ships that are moored around it. This gives her comfort, and she draws the letter from her bag.

On the front of the envelope, Mr Turkey has written:

Orinoco: Steamer Class.

Destination: West Indies.

Chapter 33

Emma

Sunflowers

Clementine's flower shop is in an alleyway off Magdalene Street, close to the river. Two large, double doors are thrown open onto the passageway, and flowers are lined up in baskets around the entrance, creating a path leading into the shop. Next to the door, bunches of flowering mint and lemon snapdragons are wrapped in brown paper. In front of these are wooden crates full of crimson and candy-pink geraniums.

Emma can't help smiling as she walks into the shade of the shop. More flowers are arranged here around an enormous cotton sunshade. The fabric of the shade is a mixture of cobalt blue and gold. Lime-green tassels hang from its outer edge. Underneath the umbrella, in large, turquoise jugs, are dozens of sunflowers. The air smells so similar to the Flower Cabin that Emma immediately feels at home. She wonders if all flower shops smell the same, and whether it would ever be possible to bottle this fragrance. She thinks of Philippe, the retired perfumier in Paris – if anyone would know, he would.

Clementine comes out from the back of the shop and Emma introduces herself.

'Oh, please call me Clem,' the woman says smiling at her. 'Everyone does.'

Clem looks to be in her late fifties; her black braids, flecked with grey, are tied back from her face with what appears to be the same material as the umbrella. She wears a sundress of lime-green and purple flowers.

Clem calls for her assistant to come and meet Emma.

'Gilly's got it all under control, so we can go and sit out the back and talk.'

Clem leads the way through a kitchen to a small, courtyard garden. The flowers growing up against walls are even more colourful than those in the shop; pink lilies and orange crocosmia are planted alongside purple agapanthus. In terracotta pots, lime-green alchemilla cast feathery shade over scarlet begonias. Emma thinks how much Les would enjoy seeing them.

Clem motions for Emma to sit at a table piled with books and plant pots, then disappears back into the kitchen. As Emma sits down on the bright orange canvas chair, she wishes she had worn something other than a plain navy dress. She feels like a dark splodge on a vibrant palette.

Clem returns with two enormous glasses of white wine. She hands one to Emma before sitting down with a sigh.

'How's the lovely Betty?' she asks.

'She's good and sends her love. Have you known her long?'

It occurs to Emma that she is not feeling nervous. Perhaps it's being in Cambridge; she spent three years in the city as an undergraduate, and being reminded of her academic past and her friends, the Glory Girls, puts her at ease. The warmth radiating from the woman beside her, helps, too. She thinks momentarily of the smiley, friendly girl in the library.

Clem tilts her head up towards the sun, eyes narrowed. 'We met when we shared a stand at a local garden festival – you know, one of those plant and flower stalls. My partner and I used to live just outside Oxford. I don't think Betty and I stopped talking or laughing all afternoon. Betty says you're now working as a florist at the garden centre?'

Emma then admits what she has been tempted to say to every customer she has ever served: 'I'm not really a florist.'

Clem opens both eyes wide and turns to her. 'I've trained a few florists in my time, honey, and I think it's either in your blood or not. Some of the fanciest florists I've met have no soul when it comes to flowers.'

Emma thinks of Les saying good morning to his begonias. One day she followed the yellow snake the wrong way and she nearly bumped into him. She swiftly retreated but not before she had overheard him greeting his plants.

'I've always loved flowers,' Emma continues, picturing her dad in his garden, 'but I think I'm a bit out of my depth. Has Betty told you about our search for The Florist on the *Titanic*?'

As Clem nods, it dawns on Emma that a few weeks ago

she would not have shared this. Perhaps Tamas was right – it was better to travel with others. She realises Clem is looking at her thoughtfully, and for a moment she is reminded of Les's comment: '… just one of those people who…' Who *what*?

Emma takes a sip from her glass of wine. She is glad she decided to stay overnight in Cambridge and that her car is already parked at the hotel. 'How long have you been a florist?' she asks.

Clem smiles. 'Ever since I left school – it's all I ever wanted to do. My mother was a florist, too.'

'Betty said she worked on the *QE2*?'

'Yes. I once did the flowers for the *Oriana*, just before her maiden voyage, but Ma, she was the expert. When she was young, she did six transatlantic crossings and two round the world trips. She loved those trips.'

'Did they need a lot of flowers on board?'

'For sure – masses of them. They used to take on new flowers for the shop when they did their stopovers. Ma said when they docked in the West Indies, they brought on board the flowers she'd known as a girl. She came to Britain from Jamaica as a teenager, and I think she missed those flowers. Well, you would, wouldn't you?' Clem stretches out in her chair, green and purple flowers rippling.

'Wow! So they had an actual flower shop on board,' Emma remarks.

She settles back with her wine and begins to tell Clem what they have discovered about the Bealings and how the cut flowers were stored on the *Titanic* the night before they sailed.

And that, despite all this, and the passenger accounts about flowers, there was no record of a florist sailing in the crew of the ship.

'We could work out what was involved, you know,' Clem eventually offers.

'How do you mean?'

'Well, the number of days at sea, how many people. I bet I could make a good guess about what they needed to do.'

Emma sits up straighter in her chair. 'Well, for a start, Les already worked out that they would have needed 1,190 buttonholes.'

Clem raises her eyebrows. 'There we go. And what else? First question, how many passengers? Do you know?'

Emma makes a grab for the notebook in her backpack, 'There could have been around 2,500 passengers, but there were 1,317 on board for the maiden voyage, plus the crew.'

'That's a big ship,' Clem acknowledges. 'I know they're building some liners that will take, oh, five thousand and more, but the QE2 was still a world of a ship and that took around two thousand passengers. And how full the ship is doesn't matter as much as how full it could be. You've still got to have everywhere looking its best.'

A ship full of flowers.

'Now, the work would depend on how long they were going to be at sea.'

Emma is already on it. 'From leaving Southampton, it was due to take about seven days to New York, via Cherbourg and Queenstown.'

Clem chews on her thumbnail. 'You'd have to change the flowers at *least* the once. The thing is they'd want the ship to be looking good when they got to New York. Ma, she said they did tours of the Q*E2* when they got to America – you know, VIPs and such like coming to have a poke around.'

Emma stretches her legs out, luxuriating in the warmth of the sunshine and the absorbing conversation. She remembers a piece she'd read during her research and turns eagerly towards Clem. 'The *Olympic* had eight thousand visitors when it first docked in New York.'

'The *Olympic*?'

'It was the *Titanic*'s sister ship; they were built alongside each other, but the *Olympic* was launched a year earlier. It was basically the same ship, but when it came to finishing the *Titanic*, they made some changes, like closing in one of the decks and turning one of the promenades into more cabins and a French-style café. It wasn't that the *Titanic* was so much bigger than the *Olympic*, in fact it was only three inches longer – it was just heavier – and that's how it came to be known as the largest ship in the world.'

It amazes Emma how much she now knows about the *Titanic*.

Clem nods and puts her wine glass down. 'So, where were we? Your florist would have to change the flowers at least the once.' Clem looks thoughtful for a moment. 'Do you know whether they were getting telegrams on board?'

Emma looks up. 'Yes, they were. In fact, there were so many messages to do with the passengers that they weren't following the shipping news and weather – that was all part of the problem. Somebody in the *Titanic*'s radio room actually sent a message saying, "Shut up, I'm busy"!'

Clem shakes her head, adding, 'Well, that's more flowers for you. People sending their loved ones flowers on board.'

'So, you think there really would have been a florist?' Emma asks, trying hard not to plead.

'Look, I can only go by my mother's work, but I know she was often rushed off her feet. I'd say the *Titanic* would need someone on board, someone who had a gift with flowers.' She looks pensive for a moment. 'But without a shop to manage, they might be working at other stuff, too. That's my guess.'

Not The Florist, then, but a stewardess (or steward) who had a gift with flowers – Emma rather likes that thought. She thanks Clem and tells her to wait while she goes next door to a delicatessen and buys a bottle of Prosecco and three cakes. She lets Clem's assistant, Gilly, choose the first cake and pours some Prosecco into her mug, before returning to the garden.

Clem looks as though she is asleep, but she opens an eye when she hears the glug and fizz of the wine. 'It's a shame Betty couldn't come,' Clem says, raising her glass in a toast to her.

'I know.' Emma pauses. 'When we went to Stamford together, I think she enjoyed it…'

'But?' Clem looks at her over her wine glass.

Emma doesn't say anything.

Clem laughs. 'Did she talk a lot?'

Emma gasps in relief. 'She never stopped.'

'She does that when she's nervous – doesn't pause for a single breath. It's quite something.'

'Nervous? You think so? I thought she was really looking forward to it.'

'Doesn't mean she wasn't nervous,' Clem says, leaning forward and choosing a cake.

'I'd not thought of that.'

'And you, well…' Clem is studying Emma.

'What?' she asks, defensively.

Clem smiles at her. 'Well, honey, let's face it. I bet you scare the hell out of Betty!' She starts to really laugh this time.

Emma is incredulous. 'What?'

Clem just keeps on grinning at her. 'You have to look at it from her point of view. You're a scientist, a doctor, Betty tells me. You speak, what is it – four languages?'

Emma nods, embarrassed.

'And she told me you picked up the floristry work like you'd been born to it. Hell, you *are* impressive.' Clem is still smiling at her.

'I don't feel impressive,' Emma admits, looking back at her. 'Most of the time I can't seem to…'

Is this what Les had meant? That Clementine was the sort of person who you ended up confiding in? Emma might not be able to finish her sentence, but she is surprised she has said this much.

White peonies come to her mind: fresh from market, petals stuck so tight, like round pebbles on the end of the stem. But they opened, didn't they? Eventually.

'Betty told me about your husband…'

'Will.' Emma looks up. She wants Clem to know his name.

'I know Betty is happy to help you if she can. And between you and me, I think what Betty needs just now is to have someone to keep an eye on. You know, since her mum died. She loved her but, boy, was she a handful. I think she led Betty a right dance towards the end. Now with her gone, I don't think she likes to admit it, but she's at a bit of a loss…'

'My mother's difficult, too,' Emma says. 'I don't think she's a very nice woman, and I worry a lot that I'm like her.'

Emma cannot believe she has spoken the words, finally voiced the fear. She has never told anyone this before, not even Will, but she has always worried that her struggle to fit in is somehow rooted in selfishness. And there is no one more selfish than her mother. Like mother, like daughter?

'Then don't be like her,' Clem says briskly, pouring them both more Prosecco. Emma blinks. Can it really be that easy? Is it simply a matter of choice?

She shakes her head. 'Do all your friends come to you for advice?'

Clem just sits back, closes her eyes and smiles up at the sun, not saying anything. Emma decides to follow suit.

Maybe this is why Betty didn't come; maybe she hoped her friend Clementine would talk to Emma, realised that sometimes it is easier to open up to a stranger.

With eyes closed, Emma listens to the buzz of conversation from the shop and the ring of a doorbell nearby. From the distance comes the sound of a voice talking loudly above the traffic.

She isn't sure if she's been asleep, if she's been dreaming, but she suddenly knows there is something else she wants to ask Clem.

'What I suppose I'm trying to find out … what part of this is about,' she says, picking up her wine glass and waving it expansively in the air, 'is why flowers? *Why* do flowers matter?'

Clem's laugh is a snort this time. 'You don't ask for much, do you, honey?' She hugs her arms about her and looks sideways at Emma. 'I can tell you this, flowers are everywhere. Not just for weddings and funerals but for christenings, birthdays, new homes, thank yous – for just about everything. I've been into people's homes, gardens, offices – where they eat, party and pray – and in all these places, flowers are welcomed like friends.' Clem leans over and clinks her glass with Emma's. 'And another thing – most flowers are sent from women to women. Not for the grand occasion or as a big showy gesture.' She grins. 'That's what some men think we want. Ha! They're fools.' She continues, reflectively, 'Flowers are about women reaching out when their friends are celebrating or when they're sad or sick or grieving. Flowers say, "I will always love you, my friend".'

Emma finds she cannot speak.

When she can control her voice, she checks if Clem sends her flowers to addresses outside of Cambridge. Then she orders a hand-tied bouquet to be delivered to a curly-haired woman who lives in a small bungalow behind a garden centre in Oxford.

Chapter 34

Violet

Forget-me-nots

The Big Barbadian who is the Smoking Room steward crosses the rising deck as if he is taking a summer walk. The rougher the seas, the broader his smile. She wonders, as he leans his body weight into his large feet, whether he is pushing the ship into the waves.

He is the kindest person she has met on board, and he passes her hints and advice like a man feeding a kitten he has grown fond of. He makes up for her cabinmate who looks like a woman who would put kittens into a sack and drown them.

When she first found her cabin, she thought two women were already living there and that she had made a mistake. Then she realised her companion had simply spread her possessions onto every surface like a child refusing to share. Not that she can imagine her cabinmate ever having been a little girl. Rather, she thinks she was born angular and irritable and old.

Her cabinmate offers no help, only resentment, and this she dishes out like it is harvest time and she has cut it fresh herself. On top of the lashings of resentment, she has one piece of advice, which she hands out like a slap:

'The youngest has to do more of the work, it's only fair.'

It doesn't seem fair to her, but she soon finds out it is true. It feels like she never stops moving. She runs to help her passengers; she spins to clean and clear; she jumps when spoken to. Everything is rushing and bobbing – the ship and her on it.

She does not know which is worse: the seasickness or the homesickness. The seasickness leaves her white and sweating. Until now, she never knew you could sweat with cold. She tries to lean into the waves like her large friend and concentrates hard on not being sick, especially when she is being bullied by the over-perfumed woman with bad teeth in Stateroom Four. She wonders what would happen if she were sick all over her and her Pekinese, in its puce satin bed. Would she be thrown overboard? She doubts if even the kindly Big Barbadian would dive in to save her.

Her homesickness comes in waves like the seasickness. It can start with the sound of feet pounding on the wooden deck or the sight of blue flowers embroidered on a handkerchief. The memory of her sister wearing a forget-me-not crown she has woven for her – a prelude to pain.

The homesickness and the seasickness are things that must be borne, and when the sea calms and the temperature rises, she finds both are easier to endure. As the sun comes out, painting the ship in brighter colours, so the passengers seem to unfurl like flowers. They smile at her and think to praise her for an extraordinary service, like fetching a shawl, then a book, then a parasol. Their memories improve, too, as the sun bakes their hat-covered heads and soon they can recall her name and remember they are meant to tip her.

The sun does not reach into her companion's part of the cabin – which includes the entire floor, all the surfaces, every drawer and most of the hanging space in the cupboard. Here it is still winter.

Sometimes she escapes the chill, and up on the deck, hidden behind the lifeboat winch, the sun warms her shoulders and arms until they are the temperature of freshly baked bread. There are precious minutes here, moments when she can watch the world of water.

And it is from here she spies her first dolphin.

Chapter 35

Emma

Brass Flowers

As Emma emerges from Clem's flower shop, she thinks she will never tire of visiting Cambridge. She loves the arched gateways that lead into the colleges and the secret worlds within, and the soaring, cathedral-like buildings that appear around each corner.

She walks along, thinking about Betty and Les, and about what an amazing woman Clem turned out to be. She is now confident that there *was* a florist of some sort on board the *Titanic* – maybe not *The Florist*, but someone who had a gift with flowers. She still does not have the least idea how she is going to find this person but she is sure something will come to her.

She smiles at strangers, knowing this is not what her mother would do, and she touches the top of her head to feel where the sun has warmed it. What was it Clem said? *Don't be like her.* Simple as that.

She runs her fingers through her hair making it bigger, wilder.

On the corner of the street, she stops to stare at the dipping rays lighting the buildings around her. She gazes at the golden stone, the herringbone brickwork and the intricate patterns created by the shadows. Looking down, she sees with surprise that the streets are paved with flowers. Beneath her foot is a small brass, flower head set into a paving stone. A bit further ahead is another and then another.

She follows the flower path, stepping carefully from one paving stone to the next, toes touching the flowers but never the lines on the street. In all her years in Cambridge, she has never noticed these flowers before.

When she comes across the scarlet door of a tapas bar, Emma realises how hungry she is. She opens the door and is met with a wall of conversation and laughter, and catches two waiters exchanging remarks in Spanish. She has the pleasant sensation that this bar is everything she hoped it would be. One of the waiters shows her to a tall stool in front of a broad slab of mottled wood that stretches across the full length of the bar. It reminds her of a natural history programme about the Baobab tree that Will once insisted they watch together.

When the waiter returns, she looks up confidently, knowing her Spanish is good. And, as her father had once commented, her accent improves in proportion to the amount she has drunk.

She orders several plates of tapas and, in memory of him, a chilled red wine. At the last minute, she decides to order just one glass rather than the full carafe. She also adds a large bottle of sparkling water to her order and congratulates herself on how sensible she is being.

The waiter brings her bread and cutlery and Emma asks him if he knows why there are flowers on the pavement outside. The young man shakes his head. 'I'll get my dad – this is his bar. He always knows stuff like that.'

The short, balding man he beckons over looks to be in his sixties; he wears his white apron long, coming down almost to the ground. It strikes Emma that it might look comical on anyone else but this small, rotund, neat man wears the mark of his trade with confidence and authority.

His son says something to him in Spanish, and when he looks confused, Emma adds her explanation, also in Spanish. The older man beams at her and compliments her on her accent.

'The flowers are an art project for the city; each of the brass heads represents a flower found in the architecture of the colleges surrounding us.' He raises his hand and sweeps it in an arc around him, like a conductor motioning his thanks to his orchestra. 'The flower path runs for a mile through the city. I believe each flower has a meaning, a significance, for the college it represents.'

'A path of flowers,' Emma murmurs, to no one in particular. 'I was so right to come to Cambridge.'

'Indeed you were, señora,' the owner agrees, smiling at her. He tells her that his name is Roberto and introduces his son as Antonio. Roberto presses Emma to call him if she needs anything during the evening. 'I will personally look after you,' he promises.

Emma turns her attention to her food and then to the people around her. At the other end of what she thinks of as her Baobab tree sit a young couple. The boy reaches out and tucks a stray curl behind his girlfriend's ear. It sparks an echoing memory in Emma, and she drinks more deeply from her plum-coloured wine.

Roberto is as good as his word and keeps a careful eye on her, appearing from the kitchen every now and then with an extra plate of something special he thinks she might like to try, talking to her in a stream of eager Spanish.

'I think that's you… Excuse me, Emma, I think that's you.'

Antonio is nodding at her phone, which is facedown on the Baobab tree alongside her notebook. She grabs it, and in her haste answers without looking. She scrambles from her stool to find a quieter spot at the back of the bar.

'Hi! Hi! Give me a moment. I'll go somewhere where I can hear you.'

As she passes Roberto, he calls her back and holds the fire-exit open so that she can step into the alleyway running along the side of the building.

'Hi! Sorry about that.' Emma is suddenly conscious she is bellowing into the phone.

'Emma?' Her mother's voice is thin and tinny in her ear. 'Why are you shouting? And why haven't you got back to me?'

This is not what she needs, especially on top of the wine. 'Did you call earlier? I'm sorry, I didn't know.' She hates that she is already trying to placate her mother.

'No, I emailed you. I'm sure I did. Mathias certainly seemed to think it had gone.'

She leans her head against the brickwork of the alley wall. A headache is lurking behind her eyes. 'What did the email say?'

'It gave you all the details you need for my birthday. You have to book it now.'

'Book what?'

'Your flight, and you need to pay for your accommodation.' Her mother is talking to her like she is a simpleton.

She tries to gather her thoughts. 'Didn't you say somebody or other was hosting it?'

'*Mathias* – his name is Mathias. And you cannot expect him to pay for everything. The upkeep on the chateau is enormous.'

'How much are we talking about?'

'Your share is just for the weekend, so it will only be seven hundred euros.'

'You're kidding?!' The words are out before she can stop them. And for once, she doesn't want to put them back.

'I don't know what you're making such a fuss about. This is a prestigious private chateau, not some B&B.'

She can hear that her mother is still trying to keep a lid on her temper, trying to persuade her.

'It's not like you're short of money.'

That old chestnut. Emma has never told her mother the

amount of life assurance she received when Will died, and her mother never tires of trying to find out.

'It would be good for you to meet some new people.'

Emma is surprised her mother's new friends even know she has a daughter.

'People will think it is most odd if you're not here for my big party.'

Not as odd as my mother not coming to my husband's funeral.

'Look, Emma, I haven't got time for this – for goodness' sake, it will be wonderful. You'd think I was asking you to go to the dentist.'

You didn't even come to Will's funeral.

The repetition of this thought keeps her strangely calm. Normally, as her mother's voice becomes more persistent, she caves in, knowing what can come next. A habit ingrained over years, over decades, one she cannot seem to break.

But now she thinks of the cloying, heady scent of Madonna lilies and she says, 'I'm not coming, Mum.'

The phone goes quiet, and thoughts flash through Emma's mind as she concentrates on the pinpoint of unnatural silence in her ear. How has she finally found it possible to defy her mother? Was it the time spent with Clem, the woman who told her she did not have to be like her? Is it the drink talking? Maybe it was speaking Spanish again and thinking of her father?

Precise words pierce the silence. 'You *are* coming. Don't be so bloody selfish.'

'I'm not coming.'

'Oh, *you're* coming,' her mother repeats. 'I have told everyone you will look after the children.'

God! What is this woman like?

'You'll have to find someone else.'

Emma hears a sharp intake of breath. She's not sure if it is from her mother, or herself – instinctively preparing for what comes next.

'Oh, I know what this is.' Her mother's voice is slow and precise. She takes her time to deliver the blows. 'Not having children and being on your own has brought out the worst of you, Emma. You've always been selfish – never able to fit in with others. You just *have* to be different.'

Emma tries to think of Clem's advice earlier, of sitting in the courtyard garden in the sun. She tries to keep hold of her belief in herself.

But her mother hasn't finished. 'Maybe if you'd had a family you would be less self-obsessed, might think about others more... You never put Will first ... it was always about you... I'm surprised he...'

As her mother talks, her words worm their way deep inside Emma, into a place that will never hold a baby, safe and secure. They burrow into the core of her where she keeps her secrets, hidden so deep that no one else will ever know.

When she can bear it no longer, she hangs up and turns her phone off.

To ease her head and stop the shaking, she concentrates on her breathing. Short breath in, long breath out. As a scientist, she knows this tricks the brain into releasing calming chemicals that fight adrenalin. In through her nose: one, two. Out through her mouth: one, two, three, four. Quietly, slowly – no one must notice.

The last time she used this, she was kneeling in the freezing mud with snowdrops clutched in her clenched fist: she had rocked and breathed.

Emma looks down at the Baobab tree as it swims in front of her. She has no idea how she got back to the bar. Her breathing is ragged. When she holds her hands out in front of her to see if they are shaking, she cannot tell through her tears.

She places her palms flat on the wood, as if, in some way, this will save her from falling further. It doesn't. Emma feels the tears running down her face and the snot dribbling from her nose, and she finds that all she can do is remember to breathe.

Her sobs when they come rack her chest and tear at her body. She cries for the husband she has lost and the baby she can never have, and despite everything, despite all she knows, she cries for what Will has missed out on, and she weeps in misery and fear because she knows she is lost.

Emma can hear voices but doesn't understand what they are saying. She is vaguely aware of someone touching her back and holding her arm. All she can do is cry. She watches her tears splash the Baobab tree and this makes her cry even more. It strikes her that she never cries like this and for the briefest of moments she thinks about trying to pull herself together, but the relief of her anguish is too great.

She sinks into it with a feeling of letting go after a very long journey.

When Emma finally returns to some sense of herself, she is sitting at a small Formica table in an alcove off the kitchen, hidden from the main body of the room. She vaguely remembers Roberto guiding her here, his hand on her elbow, his arm about her waist, talking to her quietly in Spanish. She recalls thinking he would make a good ballroom dancer, guiding you firmly and safely around a room.

She looks up to see him looking at her anxiously.

'I'm sorry,' she manages to say, automatically using the language her father taught her.

'Don't be so English. Do not apologise,' Roberto replies, also in Spanish.

Emma is touched and surprised by Roberto's obvious anger. She tries to smile, but all she wants to do is sleep or cry. She cannot imagine she will ever want to do anything else again.

Roberto pushes a cup of inky, black coffee towards her. He loads her coffee with sugar and hands her a small paper serviette for her face. Emma wonders if this is where Roberto has his morning coffee and plans his menus.

He passes her a small, sweet, almond biscuit. 'You should eat this.'

Emma stares down at the butter-coloured biscuit in her hand and at the grains of sugar gathering on her fingertips.

'Why didn't he love me, like I loved him?'

Roberto shakes his head and half stretches out his hand.

'Why wasn't I enough?'

Roberto says nothing. As Emma knows all too well, there is nothing he can say.

She smiles sadly. 'I try and hold on to the good in him, and there was lots of good, so much that I loved.' She looks up. 'But it's not enough.'

She drinks her coffee and eats her biscuit as Roberto gently fusses. Can he call someone? Where is she staying? When Emma says she just wants to be alone, he hangs his long, white apron over his chair and escorts her in silence back to her hotel.

On the front step, he kisses both her cheeks like her father would have done, and Emma thinks her heart has finally broken.

Chapter 36

Violet

Grassland Flowers

She is dreaming of her father. He is walking through a grassland scattered with flowers, surrounded by a flock that is the size of an ocean. Or is it a sky? The sheep populate the endless landscape like miniature cream clouds. She can feel the woolly fleeces scratchy against her legs. She is trying to get to him but cannot reach him. Her legs are slow and heavy, each step almost more effort than she can make.

Then, just when she thinks she will never find him again, he turns and smiles at her, waving his old brown hat in great circles in the sky.

Waking, there is a glimmer of her father nestling in her mind, and this momentarily eases the chill of remembered death as she breaks the surface of the dawn.

And then come thoughts of the daughter he never really knew.

She thinks of the plump snug softness of her sister's hand in hers, and she turns her head away from her cabinmate's inquisitive gaze. She will not show her tears to another.

As she shivers into her dress, she wonders if it is more painful to mourn the dead or the living.

PART 2

Chapter 37

Emma

Grey Tulips

From where she lies on her hotel bed, she can tell that the light has changed. The previous night she pulled one curtain, but it had been too great an effort to reach for the second.

Her performance downstairs had taken every last bit of her strength. She had mounted the steps to the hotel, talked to the receptionist, booked her room for a few more nights, explained she would be working and would not wish to be disturbed. She had even smiled.

Closing the curtains on her one-woman show was just beyond her.

She knows it is early – 6 a.m., perhaps. She has no idea where her phone is and no interest in finding it. She cannot see the glass of the window from where she lies curled under the covers, just the muted light of an overcast day falling on the linen curtains. Their pattern of grey and white tulips seems smudged and lifeless.

She closes her eyes and goes back to sleep.

When the evening streetlights turn the tulips to pale orange, she gets up and runs a bath, moving slowly, carefully, each step an effort. She lies in the bath and looks at her legs and wonders what they will be like when she is an old woman. Her skin still looks young, flushed from the previous day's sun and the warm water surrounding her, but her bones feel like they belong to another, prehistoric age. She would like to curl up and sleep in the bath, but the cooling water and hard edges drive her back to bed.

She wakes looking at the same curtains in the same grey light and wonders if the previous day was a dream. Her head is aching, but then so is everything, and she doesn't think paracetamol or any doctor is going to help her.

She orders breakfast she doesn't want, to stop the staff from speculating and possibly calling her room or the police. She feeds her croissant to the pigeons on the windowsill but drinks her coffee with a vague feeling that half reminds her of pleasure. Her phone has run out of battery and she makes no attempt to find her charger. She does not want to know what time it is or to move beyond the limbo she now finds herself in. She has thought in circles for days and weeks and months and she has been through every emotion from disbelief to rage, from despair to misery, and it has always led her back, totally exhausted, to where she started:

Why did Will have an affair?

There was a time when she would have bet the happiness of her marriage on the certainty that she would have known. Or that, at the very least, looking back, she would appreciate there had been signs. Now she cannot believe her naivety.

But they *had* been happy, hadn't they?

Emma stops the thought before it can nudge others like it to the cliff edge. The only way from there is down. Did she bring it on herself? Had she neglected Will? Was there something wrong with her – something intrinsically unlovable? Was her mother right?

Instead of letting loose these thoughts, Emma sits by the open window and pushes her fingers deep into her hair, thumbs pressing into her aching neck.

She returns to the bed, curled up like a question mark. When a sudden downpour drums against the window, the sound brings some comfort, but then comes the drifting metallic scent of the rain, and she is taken back to a late December garden, the day she found out about Will's affair. Kneeling in the mud in the freezing rain, clutching at snowdrops she had ripped from the earth.

On the third day, the ringing of the hotel phone breaks in upon her like a pneumatic drill. She sits up in bed, hugging her knees, and stares at it. A few minutes later there is a gentle knock. When a piece of paper is pushed under the door, she realises she has been holding her breath. The note is from Roberto, asking if she's all right. He has included his mobile number.

Emma turns the television on just to raise the volume

of sound in the room. If the phone rings again, she has no intention of answering it, but she wants some background noise to cushion its impact.

It is Agatha Christie season on ITV3 and Emma settles down with crisps and a small bottle of red wine. She has only just discovered the minibar in the wardrobe and she thinks she might work her way through it. It seems preferable to talking to someone about room service. She banks the pillows around her and pulls all the cushions off the bedroom chair so she is cocooned in a little pod in her bed. She wonders what Agatha Christie thought about when she ran away from the world and hid in a hotel in Harrogate.

Miss Marple knows better than most that flowers can kill you. Her friend, Dolly Bantry, might have missed the clues, but Jane Marple spots that the sage leaves picked to stuff the duck have been swapped with foxglove leaves which contain the poison digitalis. Sir Ambrose might think he has got away with it. But Miss Marple and Emma know what he's done.

The knocking is more persistent this time.

'Emma, are you in there?'

She recognises the voice immediately and after a second presses 'mute' on the television.

'Emma?' The voice sounds anxious.

Fighting the almost overwhelming urge to keep quiet, Emma throws back the covers.

Betty is standing in the hallway, her glasses misted from the sudden change in temperature. She has a maroon anorak on and Emma finds herself wondering what animal jumper is underneath. She is carrying the kind of old-fashioned suitcase that, up until now, Emma thought only existed in Agatha Christie films.

'Emma, love, are you ill? Les and I were so worried when you didn't turn up yesterday and then again today. I said, "It's not like her" and Les agreed, he said, "She's always here ahead of time. An early bird catching the worm, that's our Emma". And then the flowers came, and they were so pretty, love, and oh, how they smelt, and they look just perfect on the dresser with the blue and white china. I can't remember the last time someone sent me flowers. But there was no mention in your message of not coming back, so I gave Clem a call, and she said she hadn't seen you since you visited her but she remembered the hotel you were staying in, but when she phoned there was no answer, although they did say you were still here. And you're not answering your mobile, although I expect you know that without me standing here like a fool telling you. So Les suggested I come myself, because we wondered if you'd had an accident or were ill. Because there's no denying something is up…' Betty changes her suitcase into her other hand.

Emma starts to say something, but Betty interrupts.

'… and you can tell me to mind my own business, but a fool can see you have the weight of the world on your shoulders, and as Les said, "Betsy, a trouble shared is a trouble halved", and I thought, you know what, he's right. He may not say a lot, my Les, but he has the knack of putting his finger on it…"

Emma takes hold of the handle of the suitcase and pulls it,

with Betty, into the room, closing the door behind them. Betty blinks in surprise, then puts the case down. She continues with barely a pause.

'… So anyway, I didn't like to take the van as Les was due to deliver some slabs, an acer and a nice lemon clematis to the other side of town, so I worked out the trains and buses and it really wasn't that difficult at all once I'd got my bearings and with a couple of magazines to pass the time the journey was a bit of treat in its way. Although I have to say I've been that worried, love …'

Emma sits down suddenly on the bed. 'It's okay, Betty,' she says, knowing it isn't but wanting to reassure her, to calm her, to stem the flow. 'I don't know what I was … I'm so sorry … I should have sent a text … I didn't mean you to … and Les, too …'

If she could laugh she would. A woman who can't stop talking and a woman who can't start. Emma knows Betty deserves better from her, but reserve, embarrassment and reluctance still drag at her legs, hobbling her every effort.

Betty sits down beside her and grabs both of Emma's hands. 'Just tell me what it is, love. Just *say* it.'

And then she finds a way.

The Spanish words start like a rumble of thunder in the distance. Then they bank and flow, cascading into the room. As Emma spread her words out in front of her, she pulls her hands from Betty's and with gesture and inflection she lifts the words and throws them at the walls. Angry Italian words explode over Betty's head and words riddled with bitterness hit the window and drip down the glass as if they were rain. Softer French words curl around the legs of the furniture like smoke and cry and die there. For her finale, Emma returns to her first love, Spanish, and she lifts her head and howls her words like a she-wolf.

Betty looks down at her hands, no longer holding Emma's. They are still held flung outwards, like a child waiting for an inspection after washing.

She looks up. 'Now tell me so I know,' is all she says.

This time, Emma finds the words in the language of moderation and common sense. The plain, no-nonsense English words.

'Back in December, seven months after Will died, I found out he'd had an affair. It was somebody at his work. I haven't told anyone about it. I can't share it with my best friends because, despite it all, I feel it would be disloyal. They really liked Will and I want to hold on to that. Stupid, I know, but I don't want them to think badly of him. So now I rarely contact them and I miss them. And I miss Will and I miss us.

'But I don't trust the memories of us anymore. All I thought I had has been torn apart. Every day I walk and think in circles until I don't know where I am or who I am – or who he was. And all I can do is keep getting up, getting dressed, saying stupid things and fixating on this research, this florist. And sometimes it feels ridiculous and pointless, even mad, but it's all I can hang on to. Sometimes it's the only thing that makes sense. And everything hurts, Betty. My head, my heart, my bones hurt, and there never seems to be an end to it. And I don't know what to do anymore.'

'Oh, you poor love,' is all Betty says, but the four words are too much for Emma. She thought that after the night in the tapas bar, she had no more tears. It seems she was wrong.

Betty wraps her arms around as much of her as she can hold, and Emma leans into her and sobs on her shoulder, smearing old mascara and tears across Betty's maroon anorak.

Chapter 38

Violet

A Single Rose Petal

She worries she will not be able to find comfort in a world that feels this big. All she can see, day after day, is the sweeping breadth of the ocean moving all around her. It is like waking up in the story her father used to tell her, a tale filled with giants. She doesn't think she has ever felt so small.

At home, the boys used to fight over who was the biggest, squabbling and pushing over inches and half inches. Sometimes an indrawn breath could make all the difference. Now she wonders how to measure the vast world she has come to inhabit.

She has crossed an ocean before, of course, on the journey from Argentina to England, but she cannot recall ever thinking about the distance she was travelling. Then, her world was fenced by her mother's expectations; 'Take your sister and show her where the bathroom is'; 'Keep the boys away from that lady's cat'; 'Don't wander too far'. Her world is still restricted by certain rules – where the stewardesses can and can't go – but it feels for the first time in her life that she is walking with her head held up, taking in everything around her.

But how to measure it? In miles? Or by the number of waves in the ocean? Or maybe the number of dolphins?

When she stands on the deck at night, she wonders how she is ever going to count the stars that fill the enormous expanse above her.

The Big Barbadian offers her some words to help her. He tells her that an ocean is only a number of drops of water, like the raindrops that drip down the portholes some mornings. Without these drops, there is no ocean. She thinks of the day she found her way onto the ship, when she concentrated on the small details, the ones she could fit into her mind. She thinks the Big Barbadian may be right, so she looks around the ship, her head still held up, but with a new eye. Without the thousands of small iron rivets, the massive hull cannot exist. Without each single petal, there is no golden bowl overflowing with roses to decorate the captain's table. And without each silken stitch, the passengers could not gaze at the thirty-foot tapestry that cascades from above the grand staircase.

It comforts her to think that such small things matter. For if this is the case, then maybe she has a place in this new world after all.

Chapter 39

Emma

Loosestrife & Valerian

They don't talk much more about Will. Once Emma has recovered herself, Betty looks at her closely and says, 'All of that can wait.' She then suggests Emma has 'a nice soak in the bath', while she tidies the room, makes her bed and orders her some food.

As she does this, Betty brings her up to date with news from the garden centre. She seems particularly pleased that she was able to persuade her sister to come in and help while she's away.

'Well, let's face it, she's got nothing better to do. It'll do her good to get her hands mucky for a change.' She sounds almost gleeful.

When Emma comes back from her bath, Betty's anorak is off, and Emma sees she is wearing a yellow rabbit jumper.

As Betty once told her that rabbits are designated springwear, she realises Betty must have been unusually preoccupied when she dressed this morning. Emma finds herself apologising again for worrying her.

As Betty fusses and chats, Emma supposes this is what it feels like to have a mother looking after you. She wants to say something to reassure Betty that she would like her as a friend, not as a substitute mother, but as Betty hangs up her clothes and collects the used glasses, she realises she is overwhelmingly grateful to have both.

At around 8 p.m., Betty departs for Clem's flat, where she is staying. 'I'll be back tomorrow,' she says. 'Be ready at 10 a.m.'

Emma looks at her enquiringly, but Betty will say nothing more.

Whatever Emma expected, it was not that Betty would decide to take a boat trip.

The rain has stopped and the sun is trying to shine. The maroon anorak has been put aside in the bottom of their little rowing boat, and Betty adjusts the sleeves of her swallows in flight sweatshirt as she sets about positioning the oars. Betty tells her to sit still and that she knows what she's doing. To Emma's admitted surprise, she does. Betty handles the oars with minimal fuss and maximum effect.

As they move further from the busiest part of the city, the fields begin to stretch out between the gaps in the buildings. The riverbank is a mass of purple loosestrife and white valerian, and from where Emma sits it looks like the cows in the meadows are walking knee deep in wildflowers. The air that moves in a gentle breeze across the water carries a hint of something floral mixed with verdant notes. She thinks of the fragrance of flower shops and wonders again if a perfume could ever hope to capture it.

'Where did you learn to row like this?' Emma asks, breathing in deeply and trailing a hand in the water.

'My first boyfriend moved to Derbyshire from North Wales and he missed the sea, so we used to go out rowing on the reservoir. He taught me. My goodness, that's some time ago now. The thing is, love, there weren't many places you could go in those days if you didn't have much money. He couldn't afford the pictures and I didn't fancy hanging out in the bus shelter or down by the railway embankment. Taking a boat out was cheap and you could get a bit of privacy. He taught me how to row, among other things.'

Emma looks up quickly.

'He taught me how to roll a baccy cigarette and blow smoke rings,' Betty says, raising her eyebrows in response to Emma's look.

Watching Betty row reminds her of something she read, late one evening. 'There was a stewardess on the *Titanic*,' she tells Betty. 'I forget her name now, but she was from the Murray River in Australia. She'd spent some time with a farming family there who taught her to row. She managed to get into one of the lifeboats. Anyway, she must have done some of the rowing, because when she got to America the first thing she did was travel back to Australia to thank the family that taught her.

She said that knowing how to row saved her life.'

'Are you still going to write your book?' Betty asks, lifting the oars and letting the boat drift forward on its own.

Emma finds she can't answer this one. She doesn't even have a clear idea of what type of book she might write.

'I just wondered,' Betty continues tentatively, 'whether this started because you needed … I don't know quite what, but when I think of all the stuff you've been bottling up and what that must have felt like – well, it's no surprise you turned to something else, and really is it any wonder? Not that it isn't interesting, and as for you saying last night that this quest, or whatever Tamas likes to call it, is ridiculous, well, I have to take issue with you there…'

Emma is losing the thread and is glad when Betty retraces her steps and asks: 'You said you haven't told anyone about Will in all this time?'

Emma shakes her head.

'Not even your mum? I remember you saying she was still alive.'

'Oh, you haven't met my mother,' Emma screws up her face. 'I don't think we've got long enough to talk about her.'

'Another day?' Betty suggests.

'Another day,' Emma agrees. She notices that Betty is steering towards the bank and it occurs to her she may be tired. 'Shall we stop for a while, or if you want me to row, I'll give it a go.'

'No, let's just pull up for a bit,' Betty says as the boat bumps up against the bank close to a willow tree.

Emma leans out and grabs a root, pulling them closer in.

Betty stows the oars and reaches for her anorak. From the inside pocket she pulls out a thermos flask and starts unscrewing the top.

Emma looks at Betty and finds herself wanting to talk, to spill the thoughts that come to her at 4 a.m., the fears that burrow deep into her brain when she can't sleep. She would like to speak in Italian, but as she looks at Betty with her curly hair, old-fashioned glasses and ironed jeans, she knows she has to force herself to say it in English.

'Sometimes, I think if I'd known about the affair, I might have been able to save Will. I did CPR when he had the heart attack, and… Well, maybe I could have worked at his chest harder, forced his heart to start beating. They say rage makes you stronger. I think I might have brought him back to life, pulled him back to me, so that I could ask him why.' After a pause she whispers, 'I worry I didn't do enough, Betty.'

Betty tuts. 'I'm sure you did all that you could. You know I'm our first-aid responder at the garden centre, and on all the courses, they say it's worth doing CPR but the thing that makes the biggest difference is getting the defibrillator there.'

'They did come quickly, and they had all the equipment.'

'Then there was nothing you could have done differently.'

Emma nods. So, she really couldn't have saved her husband. Her knees feel weak and she is glad she is sitting down. She wonders why she's never had this simple conversation with anyone else.

'How did you find out about the affair?' Betty asks, handing her a coffee.

'His work sent home a box of his things from his office after he died. I kept putting off looking at it, but after Christmas I decided I would go through everything.' Emma looks up at the sky. 'You know, I think I wanted to do something practical because I'd been avoiding so much stuff and I felt guilty.' Emma shakes her head. She holds out her thumb and forefinger. 'I was this close, *this* close to just throwing all the work stuff in the bin. Then I thought Will would want me to sort any paper or card into the recycling.' She watches the clouds pass overhead. She has relived this moment and the choice she made a thousand times.

'What was in the box?' Betty asks.

'A second phone. I thought it was someone else's, so I turned it on just to find out a name so I could return it. That's when I found the text messages between him and one of his colleagues.'

Words, a jumble of words, written words. The realisation as they came together. Phrases she carries like brands on her skin.

'Did you know her?'

Emma shakes her head. 'She came to his funeral. Blonde, good-looking in a pale, posh kind of way. I remember thinking it was nice his colleagues cared so much about him.' Emma gives a small snort. 'She was being comforted by one of the other partners. I wonder if they knew, if they all knew,' she mutters.

'Or maybe she was just moving on to the next one,' Betty says, and Emma loves her for her spite.

'Was the affair still going on when…?' Betty can't finish.

'No, it ended about eighteen months before he died.'

'How long had it gone on for?' Betty asks. 'Did you ever know?'

Emma swallows. 'I went to see her.'

Betty looks surprised.

'One day, when I couldn't bear the speculating, all the different scenarios that were going on in my head, I thought, why don't I just ask her?'

'And she saw you?'

'I actually think she was relieved. She said she'd been expecting me to ring for months.'

'What happened?' Betty asks.

'We met for coffee in Starbucks. It felt so … ordinary. I kept looking around, thinking there must be people here who are having affairs.' She sighs. 'It was all so predictable. She was maybe ten years younger than Will – an associate in his team. So boringly obvious. And I sat there thinking, I'm in Starbucks on a Wednesday morning and I want to kill someone. Quite ordinary really.'

'I think you were very brave to meet her,' Betty says, gesturing towards the coffee that Emma holds untasted in her hand. 'Go on love, it will warm you up.'

Emma hadn't realised she was shivering. She takes a small sip. 'Was I brave or a total fool?' She sighs, remembering the blonde girl with pale eyes. 'She was more nervous than I was and that made her seem even younger.' Emma sees again the girl's poise cracking in front of her. 'So I started to feel sorry for the woman I wanted to kill. Just my luck.' Emma tries to laugh and she sees Betty try to smile.

'How long had it gone on?'

'Five months or so. They'd been at a conference together. *So* predictable.' Emma's voice is harsh and she can feel her throat aching. 'She said I should know that Will had put an end to it, and she went on about how Will loved me very much.' Emma feels the old rage and thinks of the snowdrops she ripped from the rain-sodden garden. 'That's the point when, if I'd had a knife on the table, rather than one of those stupid wooden, stirry things, I would have stabbed her.' Emma's body shakes in earnest now. 'He had talked to her about me, told *her* about us.'

She wants to try and explain to Betty how this betrayal was far worse than her husband screwing another woman. 'Being with Will changed everything for me, Betty. It was like, here was this world that other people lived in and if I just trusted him I could go there too.' She looks up at Betty, 'And it *was* different. I began to think he was right. We did things like other couples, had friends, went out for walks, for dinner. I was brave when I was with Will. Everything seemed possible – if I just believed in us…' She cannot go on but manages to whisper, gratefully, 'It's so good to say these things. I think I've been going out of my mind.'

'Well, I'm not bloody surprised.' Betty's anger fills the boat and spills over into the water.

Maybe it is the surprise at Betty's fury, or the warmth emanating from it, but something eases in Emma, and she can feel Betty's sympathy seeping into the dry, tightly packed layers she has wrapped around her greatest pain.

She reaches out and holds on to the sides of the boat to steady herself. 'I think about that girl sometimes, Betty, and I wonder, if he'd left me for her, would they have had a baby? Would there be a small boy with sticking-out ears and black, black hair who would have Will's blood rushing through his veins. Would I have recognised him if I saw him in the park or riding his bike?' She can almost picture the little boy, pedalling away like crazy. 'Would he tell bad jokes like his dad, want to learn the drums even though he was crap at it? Would he run like Will did, staring at the horizon like he really believed he could get there?'

Betty tries to say something, but Emma stops her, wanting to get this last part out. 'I can't have children, Betty, and Will would have made such a beautiful dad. He would have raced and jumped, sure-footed into fatherhood. I know that. And it just seems so unfair that there's nothing left of him. And sometimes I can't make sense of that, so I just look at the flowers and watch them grow and fade and reflower. Even the simplest daisy. If they can do it, why can't I?'

'Oh, love.' Betty's voice cracks and Emma can tell she is crying. 'You mustn't think like that. You have this life, and look what you've done with it, all the things you have achieved. And I'm sure your husband loved you.' She reaches out and pats her hand. 'Of course he did. Men can be *such* fools.' Again, Betty sounds furious. It is so unlike her, and Emma is reminded of Roberto's anger at the tapas bar. 'And look what you're doing now – you've become a florist and then there's the book you're going to write…'

'You really think I can do that? I've not really thought it through, and I can't even find the person I'm looking for.' She almost says 'people', and the image of The Nurse and a blurry figure hidden behind flowers come into her mind. Who exactly is she looking for? Who does she want to find?

Betty pours them both another coffee and then rows them slowly back to the boathouse. Soon, Betty has clearly had enough of silence. Question follows question, and the journey back begins to remind Emma of their drive to Stamford.

To start with, Emma finds it hard – Betty's only area of interest appears to be her life with Will. But her enquires are gentle, focused on the smaller details of their life together: what books he'd liked; where they'd gone on holiday; the kinds of meals they'd shared. As Emma retrieves these small isolated memories, jigsaw pieces of their life together, she finds comfort in examining the disparate fragments. Taken individually, each tiny part makes sense to her in a way that the huge truth of Will's infidelity doesn't.

She looks at the woman rowing opposite her and thinks about how much she underestimated Betty when they first met. She recalls the interview when she spoke in clichés – and she smiles slightly; perhaps Les picked her for the job.

So, she keeps answering Betty's questions. She doesn't think these enquiries about Will are magically turning a key, but maybe they are oiling a lock.

As they approach the boathouse, Emma leans across to her friend. 'I don't make you nervous, do I, Betty? Not now, surely?'

'No,' Betty tells her, 'I don't think you ever really did, love, but sometimes you can be very reserved, and I'm not always good with silences.'

'What does Les say?' Emma suddenly wants to know.

'Oh, you know Les…' Betty pauses for a moment. 'He says, "still waters run deep".'

They look at each other and both start to laugh until the boat rocks beneath them.

Chapter 40

Violet

Lily

The varnish on the ship's rail is blistered from the sun. The decks are bleached like driftwood. The night's breeze is soft and warm, but the stars above her look cold and hard as ice. She wonders if they have names or are too tiny and numerous to be christened.

Her mother believes in christening all God's creations, however small they are. She suspects her mother would name the stars after the saints, although she thinks even her mother would run out of saints before naming them all.

She wonders if she will ever have a child of her own to name. She would like a little girl, she thinks, but maybe that is because she misses the weight of her sister on her lap, the feel of her cheek against hers. She does not want to replace her sister and does not think she could love her own child more, but she feels deep inside her a yeaning that sometimes catches her unawares, like when a wave appears from nowhere out of the calm ocean. Then something shifts inside, a sudden longing at the heart of her.

If she were to have a baby girl, she thinks she would name her after a flower, however much her mother would line up the saints in front of her for inspection. She might even be brave enough to turn down the blessed Virgin's name (her mother's ace). She does not want to hold a 'Mary' in her arms. Instead she thinks of 'Rose' or possibly 'Daisy'. Her choice of name changes like the seasons: 'Primrose' appearing in the spring, 'Lavender' in the summer and 'Marigold' when the fields ripen to gold.

Standing on the deck, the latent heat radiating from the wood beneath her hand, she thinks of a little girl in a white dress, called Lily.

Chapter 41

Emma

Sweet Peas

That evening Emma and Betty walk past the scarlet door of the tapas bar. She's glad Betty said she fancied Italian so she doesn't have to feel guilty about not eating at Roberto's bar. She intends to call in and thank Roberto, but she doesn't think she can face it just yet. She doesn't know if she could ever look at the Baobab tree again, much less sit at it.

She asked if Clem wanted to join them, but Betty says it's her wedding anniversary, and she and her husband have gone away for a few days.

Betty's ringtone breaks in on their conversation and they slow down as Betty fumbles for her phone. Emma feels a jolt of concern – Betty rarely ever uses her mobile.

Betty frowns as she answers it, mouthing at Emma, 'Les.'

'Hello, love. Is everything okay?... Oh, I see ... well that *is* odd ... have you phoned the ... Oh, I see.' A longer pause. 'Ah, well maybe that's it ... No, that's the only number I've got. Everything else okay? No ... try not to worry, love. Bye then.'

Emma looks expectantly at Betty. 'Is Les okay?'

'Yes, he's fine, but Tamas didn't turn up today.'

'Oh.' Emma thinks of Greta, and pushes away an image of Tamas holed up in some hotel room as she has been, lost in waves of grief. 'He's probably just ill,' she says, not sure whether she is reassuring Betty or herself.

'Les phoned the wholesale market and a few florists, and it looks like Tamas delivered some flowers this morning but then just disappeared.'

'He's not answering his phone?'

'Apparently not. Les is a bit worried in case he's had an accident. He wondered if I had a home number for Tamas, but I only have his mobile.'

Emma frowns. 'Maybe his van broke down?'

'Maybe,' Betty says slowly and doubtfully, 'but why wouldn't he answer his phone?'

Because he doesn't want to be found, thinks Emma, looking back on her past few days. She's being foolish, of course; Tamas is nothing like her. There's probably a normal explanation. 'Is Les worried?' she asks.

'Um, I think he is, poor love.'

Emma is worried, too, and she can tell Betty feels the same. They walk along in silence for a moment.

'You'll need to get back to Les soon, I expect,' Emma says. She tries to keep her voice neutral. She isn't sure she will ever be able to let Betty go. Emma is looking forward to being back in the garden centre but she has enjoyed this time alone with Betty.

'I can spare another day – perhaps we could have a look around some of the colleges? It's very quiet in the garden centre this time of year.'

Emma doesn't say what she's thinking – *isn't summer your busiest time?* Instead she asks, 'Are you and Les worried about the business?'

Betty pauses as she looks up at the street name and starts searching for the restaurant Clem has recommended.

It is only when they are sat down with menus, wine and olives in front of them that Betty eventually answers. 'It's just the number of people coming in. That dratted ring road. Things had been tootling along very nicely before that. I can't deny it, it's a worry, love. In fact…'

Oh God, Emma thinks, *she's going to fire me.* Then she can't decide which would be worse: being let go or being kept on through pity.

'… it's no harm you having some days off now and then if you want to go on with your research – in fact it helps us, if that's okay with you?' Betty doesn't wait for Emma to answer. 'And I've talked it over with Les…'

Here it comes.

'… and in the autumn, we might have to drop you to two days a week.'

Emma is weak with relief. 'You know, I could start to take photos of our funeral work. We have one funeral director on side, but there wouldn't be any harm in me going to call on a few more.' Betty is looking at her oddly, and she wonders if she has overstepped the mark. 'I'd do that in my own time. I wouldn't expect you to pay me for it.'

Betty shakes her head, as if this isn't the issue. 'Clem thinks you have the makings of a very good florist, you know,' she says eventually.

'How on earth can she tell? She's never even seen me work.'

'I know, but she said something about the flowers you chose for the bouquet she sent. And understanding a message? I have to say, she lost me.'

Emma grins, feeling like she has been awarded a prize from a favourite teacher. 'Clem said something about people having a feeling for flowers, a connection. Well, look at Les and his begonias.'

'Oh, he proper loves them,' Betty says, grinning back at Emma.

'Why begonias? Why not roses or petunias?'

'Well, his dad, Big Les, was a prize grower.'

Emma can't help wondering how tall Les's father was; Les himself stands well over six feet. 'And he grew begonias?'

'Begonias and sweet peas. He won prizes for them all over the county. My Les went with him, carrying the plants and helping his dad keep the displays tidy.'

'It's funny though, love,' Betty goes on. 'Les can't abide the smell of sweet peas. Won't have them in the house. Says they remind him too much of his dad. They make him too sad.'

There it is again: fragrance. Emma thinks of the smell of flower shops and of the lilies her mum sent to Will's funeral, and how the smell of burning leaves and Jasmine always brings her father back. With Will it was sandalwood. Something else occurs to her. 'I was reading that one passenger said being on the *Titanic* was like being on the Riviera, because of the fragrance from the flowers.'

Betty looks up. 'My goodness, I imagine that was wonderful.' She pauses. 'It really is interesting, this research of yours. It feels like you have discovered something special.'

Emma shrugs. 'I don't really know what I'm doing… Even if I did write a book, I'm not sure what angle I would take. But I know what you mean about the flowers – it brings the *Titanic* to life somehow.' She thinks of Guy's comment about how it changed how he imagined the ship. Perhaps the title of Les's talk would even fit: *Secrets of the* Titanic? After all, the scent and sight of a ship full of flowers was a secret known only to those who had been on board.

Betty interrupts her thoughts. 'Emma, love, don't go all quiet on me again.'

She looks up at Betty. Thinking of Guy takes her back to her family, to her mother. 'Betty, do you think we can choose who we are?'

Betty looks confused.

'It was just something Clem said.'

Betty laughs. 'Well, I can't choose to be a blonde with legs up to my armpits.' She pauses and twirls her wine glass in her hand. 'But I can choose not to be a stuck-up madam who looks down on her family.'

Emma doesn't say, 'like your sister?'; instead she asks, 'So you think we *can* choose?'

'Oh, love, I think most of us can. Not all the time perhaps, and maybe not those poor souls, children and the like, who've had it so bad they don't even know they've got a choice. But the rest of us? Well, as Les says, "You can't go much wrong, Betsy, if you always treat others as you'd like to be treated".'

Not for the first time, Emma thinks that Les is a very wise man. It makes her sad to think that he and Betty are so worried about the garden centre.

'Look, thinking about the business, Christmas is coming – we could do door wreaths and arrangements? Surely that's a busy time?' She tries to keep her mind on this rather than Santa's Grotto.

'Well, maybe. Yes, yes, I'm sure things will pick up.'

Clearly, Betty doesn't want to dwell on the garden centre, so Emma leaves it at that – for the time being, at least. Instead, she tells her what Clem concluded about the florist on board.

'I see,' Betty responds with interest. 'A part-time florist who worked on other things as well. Now that is fascinating. I'm glad Clem was of some help, love.'

'Oh, she was,' Emma replies, thinking – *in more ways than one*. 'She certainly gave me lots to think about.'

Betty doesn't ask any more, but there is a degree of understanding in her look.

The meal is good, and Betty decides to finish with a coffee.

'I don't normally drink coffee this late, love, but that was such a nice meal, and I suppose I am on holiday, really. You know I haven't been able to go away for a while, what with Mum and everything. This has been such a treat.'

They finish their coffee and Emma insists on accompanying Betty back to Clem's flat. As they walk, they speculate on what might have happened to Tamas, both admitting to being uneasy, and then the conversation turns back to Will. Betty asks, 'Did you ever suspect he was having an affair?'

Emma knows the answer to this one. 'No.'

'Or understand why it happened?'

Emma has shredded this one until there is nothing left of it, trying to find reasons, blame – alternately with Will, the associate or herself. 'I don't know... I've thought about how absorbed I could get in my work and about the fact we couldn't have children, but I don't honestly think it was because of either of those. The only thing – and it's just a vague feeling – is I think Will found it hard when he turned forty. He was such an active man – I mean he still ran and everything like that – but I wonder if maybe he was anxious about getting older. I know it sounds ridiculous me saying this, but Will just wasn't the sort of man who had affairs.'

They have reached the door to Clem's flat, so Emma wishes Betty goodnight and walks away, dwelling on her and Les.

There is no way around it: whichever way she views it, she still can't believe Les used to be a punk.

Chapter 42

Violet

Frangipani

The time passes like the weather. Sometimes it races like a great North Easterly – the blast of harsh early mornings the prelude to days of rushing and carrying. Other times, the hours seem to hang like a still, grey day. The work is slower, but the passengers' demands are never-ending, like the vast sky that sweeps above them. Then there are a few precious times when the weather is perfect and the languorous days are there to be stepped into like a warm bath. She remembers when her first ship arrived in the West Indies and the Big Barbadian took her to meet his family. They sat at a long table by the beach, the air rich with a fragrance his mother told her was from the frangipani flower. They ate food she had never dreamt of and drank a heady, caramel punch that gave her dreams of home.

Since then, she has returned home a few times, made her way onto different ships and finally found her sea legs. She is a proper sailor now – if she smoked a pipe, she would pack it with Faithful Lover. She has discovered other crew members who are friendly, like the Big Barbadian. Some are too friendly; she knows her mother would shake her fist at them. She has learnt to step and sidestep, twist her waist to avoid an arm, duck her head to dodge a kiss. Sometimes she hums a tune in her head as she does this, as if it is a private dance.

She has met no one else like her first cabinmate, who would have shut the door on life just for the pleasure of keeping it waiting in the cold. Most people are like her – they have their good ways and their bad ways – and the majority of transgressions are easy to ignore. Like when the soup chef spits Italian curses if he feels a storm is brewing, or the potboy takes more than his share of milk for the kitten everyone knows he keeps under his bed. Or when the cashier pretends she has made a mistake so that the restaurant manager will lean over her shoulder to examine her exquisite figure work.

As she moves around the ship – rushing to fetch and carry, pausing to take orders, hovering on the ball of a foot to exchange a glance, a smile, a raised eyebrow – she tries to hold fast to her mother's favourite maxim: love thy neighbour as thy self. It is easier with some neighbours than others. But then her mother had never told her that life was easy.

There is a rhythm to her days that she has come to accept, if not love. She sometimes imagines she is sat on a fairground ride; the people around her look happy or sick or frightened, but her own face is blank. In her mind's eye, she watches a man in a leather *waistcoat and mustard scarf turning the handle of the ride. Only he knows how fast they will spin or where they will go. She does not know many people who run their own rides – most people are like her, sitting, waiting, making the best of it.*

She knows she is better off than the stewardesses who leave their children behind each time they go to sea, the sailors' widows who Mr Turkey spoke so highly of. She still does not know their ages, and she thinks it would be hard to guess, because leaving their children has lined their faces just like the years have done.

Sometimes she wonders if the faint line between her brows has been drawn there by her sister's finger.

Chapter 43

Emma

Red Carnation

On the way back to her hotel, Emma makes a detour to the
tapas bar. Roberto is just ushering out the last of his customers
when he sees her approaching.

'Ah, Emma, please come in – I have been hoping I might see
you again.'

He greets her in Spanish and politely bows her in, the long
white apron wrapped about his neat, plump figure still pristine,
even after an evening of service.

The tapas bar is dimly lit, and Roberto settles her at a
candlelit table at the back. He cuts short her thanks for his
kindness, instead pressing a nightcap on her. Emma chooses a
glass of chilled red wine, in memory of her father, and for the
next hour they talk in Spanish about families and friendship.
Roberto wants to know all about her father – his language and

his hometown. His manner of speech is slow and formal, and he chooses his expressions carefully. In some ways, he reminds her of Les – well, a miniature, Spanish Les.

As he pours them both a second drink, their talk turns to what brought her to Cambridge. She explains her interest in the *Titanic* and her investigation into the flowers on board.

'And you are being helped by a woman who herself worked onboard ship?' he queries.

'Yes and no,' Emma explains. 'She's helping, but it was her mother who actually ran a flower shop on board the *QE2*.'

Roberto sips his small glass of port, toying with the petals of a red carnation that stands in a narrow vase on the table. 'This is a most unusual project. And yet, I know that after all these years the *Titanic* still has a lot of international interest.'

Emma nods. 'I guess it's because it was such a catastrophic event at the time, the sinking of the unsinkable ship, and so many different nationalities were involved.'

'Were there many Spanish people sailing on the *Titanic*, do you know?'

'Ten,' Emma replies with the certainty of the Recently Obsessed. 'Nine were passengers and one was a member of staff. Most of them survived.'

He nods grimly. 'Where do you go next in your quest?'

Emma is reminded of Tamas and, for a moment, is side-tracked by a nagging worry.

Without waiting for an answer, Roberto continues, 'You must continue, you know – I have a feeling it is part of your recovery.'

They have not talked about Will, but Emma is in no doubt that Roberto has a good idea of what she is struggling with. After breaking down in his bar, her normal defences have collapsed – but somehow, she doesn't want to rebuild them. It's a relief and a pleasure to be at ease with Roberto.

And maybe the Spanish is helping, too. Talking to him in her father's language brings a huge measure of comfort.

'I'm going to keep going, I think.'

'Well, I am very interested in history myself, so you must tell me how you get on, and if I can help in any way, let me know.'

Emma feels a warm wave of gratitude. 'I can't believe how helpful everyone is being.'

'Myself, I am not surprised,' Roberto replies.

'Really?'

'No – not at all. In my experience, if you ask people for specific help and it is within their capacity to provide it, almost everyone is happy to give that gift.' Roberto nods thoughtfully. 'Most people say vaguely, "If there is anything I can do to help, please ask". It was like that when my wife died.'

'I'm sorry,' Emma responds, studying Roberto's face.

'Ah, it was many years ago now. I was quite a young man, if you can imagine that.' He smiles.

'My husband passed away last year,' Emma says. It feels easier to speak the words in Spanish.

'I'm sorry to hear it,' says Roberto. He sips his own glass of wine, as though he knows she doesn't want to say more. 'What I have discovered over the years is that most people do wish to help – it is just they do not always know what to do. So you have to be clear about what you need, and if it is something they can accomplish, most are generous.' He sits back in his chair. 'So, no, I am not surprised that you have people helping you.'

'People do often run towards a disaster,' Emma muses.

Roberto shakes his head, smiling. 'You are not a disaster, señora.'

Emma returns his smile. 'No, I mean – well, it can take a huge shock, like a disaster, to get people to overcome their reluctance to push themselves forward. As you say, people often don't know what to do. But I think you're right, if you say what you really need and someone can help, people are amazing.' Which makes her wonder why she hasn't simply asked for more help over the past year.

Emma starts to collect her things and rises to leave. At the door, Roberto bows slightly and hands her the red carnation from the table. Emma thanks him for his kindness and wishes him goodnight.

'But not goodbye, I hope,' he responds.

She leans forward and kisses him on both cheeks, just like her father would have done.

Chapter 44

Violet

Embroidered Flowers

Today, she decides not to think of goodbyes; she will think of reunions instead. She is leaving her shipmates, some of whom are now her friends, but she is going home, too; she will see her family again.

It is the prelude to the bank holiday weekend, and the train from Southampton to Waterloo is packed. She sits on her case until a young man with a smart Malacca cane offers her his seat. She does not know whether he needs the cane to walk or holds it just because he likes the feel and swish of it in his hand. But her knees are aching, so she takes the seat. He tells her he is going to stay with his sister in Putney, that they will be a gay party of ten, including his mother who makes the best summer pudding anyone has ever tasted. She knows this is not true about his mother, but when she sees him limp away from the train she is glad she did not tell him.

The best summer-pudding cook is waiting for her with the boys and her sister in an archway at the station. The boys are taller than she remembers but do their best to hide it by thrusting their hands deep in their pockets and looking at their boots. As they look down, her little sister stretches up as if checking she has remembered the position of every freckle on her face correctly. And so they stand until their mother grabs them and hugs them, knocking them against each other until they are jostled and bumped into the right size and mix once more.

Then the talking starts, and the words follow them through the streets, past boys selling newspapers, between carriages with gleaming, shifting horses and over the river that now seems like a stream compared to the seas she has crossed.

Once they are home, there are changes to exclaim over: a new lamp, a larger table, and a blue and white plate piled with fresh baked scones. There are presents to unpack from her case and a package to unwrap from her sister – a sampler sewn in colourful threads, welcoming her home, her name nestled in a bed of embroidered petals.

Chapter 45

Emma

Night Stock

Back in Oxford, Emma heads to work. When she opens the door to the Flower Cabin, Betty is in full flow: '… so many places she knew of and short cuts into the colleges. And it was a treat to hear her speaking in, oh, I don't know how many languages.' She pauses. 'Oh, hello, love. I've just been telling Les a bit more about our time in Cambridge.'

'Has anyone heard from Tamas?' Emma has been worrying about him all night.

Both look at her, faces full of concern.

'No word yet, love, but Les is going to give the wholesale market another ring in a bit. He doesn't want to make too much of a fuss.'

'Mountain out of a molehill,' Les agrees, nodding.

Emma remembers her conversation with Roberto – people

wanting to help but not wanting to push themselves forward. She is about to say something more when the door swings open with a bang.

Tamas stands there, flower boxes on his shoulder, smiling at them. He has the most magnificent black eye that Emma has ever seen.

'Ah, Les, there you are. They have been telling me you have been ringing. You are a good man. But here, you see I am returned!'

'But your eye,' Betty says faintly.

'Ah, that is nothing. You should have seen my face when my cow stamped on it.'

'But what happened?' Emma asks, ushering him in and helping him unload the flower boxes.

Tamas becomes overly preoccupied sorting the boxes. 'It was nothing... I may have missed my turn and made a mistake... My van well it will need some work. But I tell the farmer I will replant his tree, and he is a man who knows how it can be.' He glances at them, looking like a guilty schoolboy.

'My goodness!' Betty exclaims. 'Berta must have been worried sick.'

'I called her from the farm phone. But my mobile, the screen it is cracked so it is the only call I make.'

'Ah, so that's how it was,' Les declares. 'All's well that ends well.'

But Emma is not so sure they have heard the whole of it. She is all the more convinced that Tamas is holding something back when he changes the subject.

'You have not won our game yet!'

Not knowing how to voice her misgivings, Emma resigns herself to the inevitable. 'Hungary?'

'No!'

'Slovakia?'

'Ha! No, that is not it.'

'Poland?'

'You people say we are all Polish. This is not true.'

Emma thinks this is a bit unfair; she has listed most of Europe before getting to Poland.

'I give up!' she says.

Tamas stamps his large feet on the floorboards, making the buckets of flowers dance. 'I am from Moldova!'

Emma feels a surge of laughter and lets go of her worries. Tamas is back being Tamas. They are all looking at her expectantly, so she says the first thing that comes into her head (thinking it in Spanish first). 'I've read they make very good wine in Moldova.'

Tamas is delighted. More stamping, more dancing buckets. 'This is true! Berta's family, they are famous for the wine they make.' He stops suddenly, looking down at his big boots. His shoulders slump.

The cabin falls silent, and Emma is reminded of films where everything stops, characters frozen, mid-action on the screen. From the corner of her eye, she sees dust motes hanging in the air, caught in the sunlight streaming through the window.

Still Tamas looks at his boots. Still they all stand waiting.

The large man in front of them seems to visibly crumble.

He doesn't fall, but every part of him appears to sag as if in defeat. 'I think Berta is leaving me.'

The spell is broken. Betty and Les spring into action. 'Come over here, Tamas,' Betty says, touching his arm. 'You come and take the weight off your feet and Les will get us all a coffee.'

Les is already halfway to the door. 'I'll bring us some cake too,' he says looking towards Betty, who nods encouragingly at him. 'Be back in a jiffy.'

Emma steps out of his way and pulls out a stool for Tamas to sit on. He hasn't said a word since his announcement, and again she imagines him as a large overgrown schoolboy: awkward, lost and, unexpectedly, painfully shy.

'Oh Tamas,' she says, stepping forward and rubbing his shoulder. 'I'm so sorry. Is it … is that why you crashed?'

She doesn't think he would have done it on purpose, but concerns about Berta might easily have affected his concentration while driving.

He shrugs his shoulders, helplessly.

Betty and Emma exchange a look behind his back.

Tamas stays slumped and silent, then his shoulders start to shake, and he gulps at the air as he sobs. He looks up at Emma and then towards Betty. His eyes are now streaming with tears, his face crumpled like an old cloth. He gulps again and wipes his nose on the back of his sleeve.

Betty pats his shoulder a few times in rapid succession and then walks briskly to the door to hang up the *Back in 5 Minutes* sign. 'There we go – no one will disturb us now.' As she says this, Les reappears carrying a tray of mugs and slices of fruitcake.

They settle around Tamas, seated on an array of wooden crates and an upturned dustbin, and hand around the cake and coffee. Tamas blows his nose on some kitchen roll that Betty has handed him.

'Now tell us what's happened since we last saw you, Tamas,' Betty says, patting his knee.

'It is about Greta. I know this. I have tried, but it is hard.' He looks around at them, frowning and puzzled. 'My Berta says I do not understand. But I do.' He studies the fruitcake in his hand, as though he might find the answer there among the raisins and dried apricots. 'I want to make her smile, and she says I forget our Greta.' His left hand clenches and he thumps his chest. 'This is like saying I forget to breathe. She thinks I have no heart. But my heart is too big. How can I tell her these things?'

'Do you talk to her about Greta?' Betty asks.

'I try, but it is making us so sad that I stop.'

'Have you tried to tell Berta that? Can you explain how you feel to her?' Betty suggests.

Tamas glances towards Les, and Emma sees an unspoken exchange between the two men – *these women, what do they want from us? We would do it if we could.*

'Could you write to her?' Emma hears her voice before she realises she has spoken. They all look at her. She continues, embarrassed, but determined. 'It's just sometimes it's easier to write things than say them.'

And for a moment it is almost as if Will has pulled up an old crate and joined the circle. She would not be surprised to hear the scrape of the wood against the floorboards. They continue to watch her, expectantly.

'My husband, Will—' she wants to say his name, acknowledge his presence '—Will, he couldn't always put things into words. He was a lawyer, so maybe that was odd, but he was … well, he couldn't always say and sometimes the things…' She listens harder, strains her ears, not for the sound of the wooden crate shifting on the floor, but for the low sound of Will's laughter as she struggles to get the words out. 'We used to write to each other,' she says, trying to free her mind of her husband, and looking directly at Tamas. 'He would leave letters under my pillow, and when I read them, I understood.'

Her mind flinches at the next thought – would she have understood if he had written that he was having an affair? She stands up suddenly and then sits down again, dismissing the unwelcome thought of Will's affair. The movement makes her feel light-headed, but it helps, as though she has tipped the thought from her lap. Still, they watch her, three startled faces. 'Could you write to Berta?' she asks Tamas again.

He seems to consider this for a moment. 'When we were young, and I first see her riding through our village on the back of her father's cart, I follow her on my bicycle. She says she does not notice me, but I see her looking over her shoulder. I find where she is living and though it is far bigger than our house, I know her cook. She is a cross woman who is a friend of my mother, so I am careful. I tell her I look for work, but I find out Berta's name. That is when I write to her.'

Tamas's face relaxes as he talks, and Betty reaches out and

catches the fruitcake as the plate becomes slack in his grip. He does not seem to notice as she plucks it from his hand.

'She does not write back to me, not until much later. But I keep writing to her. I find out what books she is borrowing from the library, and I read these books. And one day I write out a poem for her from one of the foreign writers that she likes so much. Now when I see her on the cart, she smiles at me, and I know.'

He looks around as if he had forgotten they were there with him. 'With Berta I always knew.'

'Oh, love. you should definitely write to her. Tell her how you feel.' Betty's words exhale softly. 'Are you certain she's leaving?'

'She is not gone today, but I think she plans it. I see the cases – they were in the attic, but she has now put them under the bed.'

'You need to strike while the iron's hot,' Les says, firmly, 'No time like the present…' It seems that he is going to say more, but at that moment, the door to the Cabin opens and a young woman in a bright yellow dress stands in the doorway, 'I'm sorry, are you open? Or should I come back later?'

As one, the four of them rise, and stools, crates and dustbin are pushed aside as they busy themselves clearing a space for the customer.

Later that afternoon, Betty and Emma sit alone on the bench outside the Cabin. The afternoon sun warms their faces, though the breeze is cool as it ripples through the magenta and cream

234

stock planted in pots at their feet. 'It was a very nice thought you shared with Tamas, love. You know, about the letters.'

'Pillow post,' Emma says dreamily, looking at the puckered petals of the stock, breathing in their scent.

'Is that what you call it?'

'I guess. It's just something that started with my dad, or maybe thinking about it, his mum – I'm not sure where the idea came from. But it was something we shared, and it helped. My mum wasn't always…' Emma leaves it there; it is enough to sit among the flowers with Betty and think of her dad.

'I might tell Ben about that. They're having a few problems with their eldest – it seems he hasn't taken to his baby sister. Wants her to go back where she came from.' Betty laughs. 'Maybe his dad could write to him. He's very good with his reading and writing is our grandson, Zac,' she says, proudly. 'Pillow post, you say?'

Emma nods. 'I've been thinking, Betty – I'm going to go to London to visit the woman I've been emailing at the V&A museum. The preview is next week. Am I all right to take Wednesday off?'

'Of course. What preview's that, love?'

There is still so much she hasn't told Betty and Les – about the V&A exhibition, about the perfumier she has been emailing in Paris. Or the photo on her phone of The Nurse – she has not mentioned her to Betty and Les, either, or her feeling that she is connected to her somehow. Or, come to that, her search online through her family tree.

She glances at Betty and can see she is waiting, expectant.

'Oh, the V&A. Well, there's an exhibition coming up about life on board ocean liners. I've been emailing one of the curators, and she's got me an invite to the preview night. She's putting me in touch with a historian who has a particular interest in the *Titanic*, and he's agreed to meet me there.'

'Well, that's wonderful, love. And you say that's on next Wednesday?'

Emma would love to ask Betty to come with her, but she only has the one invitation and feels it would be cheeky to ask for another. She starts to explain this, but Betty cuts her short.

'Oh, no, love. You go to that – but maybe we could meet up afterwards? Les could book that nice French bistro near the station, and you could fill us in on what you find out. Maybe we could ask Tamas, as well. I think the poor man could do with something to look forward to.'

'Should we invite Berta?'

Betty looks doubtful. 'Who knows if she will still be around. And I can't imagine she would want to meet a bunch of strangers – can you, love?'

'So just the Four Amigos?' Emma says, with the ghost of a smile.

'Yes, which is probably more than enough to being getting on with,' Betty agrees wryly.

As she drives home that evening, Emma finds herself dwelling on Tamas and Berta, then on Betty and Les. It seems their first instinct is always to help other people – but who is helping them? Their business seems to be struggling, and while they don't talk about it, she can tell that they are both worried. What was it her old professor used to say about her? She was a scientist who had an instinct for getting to the root of the problem?

Perhaps she should spend more time thinking about Betty and Les's problems and less time poring over her own troubles. She has thought a bit about the garden centre, but maybe she should be more specific: research what other garden centres are doing; look for ideas in other sectors; think how the Flower Cabin could attract more customers?

When she gets home, she takes these thoughts and a glass of wine up to the top field to watch the sun go down.

Chapter 46

Tamas

Yellow Zinnia

My Berta,

I call you this, even though I think that you may leave me. Like Greta is still our very own girl no matter what the doctors, the illness or God decided. I have no say in these things. My heart tells me how it must be.

You wonder that I laugh at the funny men on the television or can smile at the sunset at the back of our house. I see you look at me, and you do not understand, and I cannot explain. Still I cannot find the right words. I have been sitting here very late, and I have been reading your books. These are the books that I think give you comfort. Sometimes when I cannot find you in the house, I think I will find you folded within the pages, thin and delicate like the paper. You have always been dainty – I think that is the word – but now you are so thin and sad. I think if I touch you, I will tear you. Then I think you are broken already and perhaps I should hold you to try and put you back together. But my hands are large and clumsy and maybe I will only break you some more. I can lift you – I could always lift you into the big tree in your parents' garden. Do you remember that? I would lift you now, but I do not think this is what you want.

I used to write to you, didn't I? I found the writers you loved, and I borrowed their words, having none of my own. I have been with your books tonight and this is what I can find to try to tell you why I laugh at silly jokes and smile when I see the bright yellow zinnia in the garden.

They are words from the Romanian poet that you like so much.

Laughter has no memory.
Time flows on,
And we slip, like a pebble
Between the inhale and the exhale.

I laugh, Berta, because then I can stop time. It stops for as long as it takes for me to breathe in the air and force the laughter out. Then time restarts and all I can do is think of our beautiful girl and feel the never-ending pain of losing her.

I do not want you to leave me, Berta. I am nothing without you. My life began when I saw you sitting on the cart in the sunshine wearing your blue dress with a red scarf in your hair. I know you may have to go, and if this is what you need,

I will bear it. And people will hear me laugh and stamp about the place. They will shake their heads and wonder if I miss you at all.

Your Tamas

Chapter 47

Violet

Carved Flowers

The new White Star liner, the Olympic, is a ship like no other.

She has a friend who sails with the Cunard Line and all the talk there is about being the first, being the fastest. But for her money – if she had any – she would always sail with the White Star Line. The crew she works with look down on the ships of the Cunard Line, rushing hither and thither, trying to push their way in where they don't belong.

She does not say this to her friend.

What the White Star Line promises is luxury – perhaps not in the small cabin she shares with another stewardess but in first class and even in second class, the opulence is enough to take your breath away. On the Olympic, the staircases sweep, the glass sparkles and the carvings of flowers in the pale oak panelling are so realistic she almost believes that the wooden butterflies nestled there might fly away as she approaches.

The corridors of the Olympic are a new map that has to be learnt by heart, with shortcuts to negotiate and navigate. But around her are the faces of old friends and acquaintances – familiar outcrops in an unfamiliar landscape. They greet each other, share a word about their new home, and time allowing, swap gossip like waiters exchanging plates as they pass.

And presiding over it all, making sure that these exchanges do not cause the steps to falter, the pace to slow, is The Purser. He may not wish to serve on the Cunard Line either, but she suspects he wants his staff to be the fastest moving beings on the seas. Sometimes she thinks that when she gets home she should challenge her brothers to a race. If The Purser were watching her, she would certainly win.

She is in her cabin looking for a clean apron. Lost in thought, she has forgotten for a moment what she came in here for. She unhooks the sampler hung over the bed. Since her sister gave it to her, she has taken it on every voyage, a reminder of home and the small fingers that sewed it. At night before she goes to sleep, she sometimes counts the stitches that make up the petals of the flowers and the letters of her name.

She does not do this to help her sleep. The thought makes her smile – no stewardess would ever need to count sheep or stitches. At the end of a sixteen-hour day, sleep is always waiting, hat on, bag packed.

No, she counts the stitches to rid her mind of the clutter – the lists, the irritations and the gossip – clearing it to leave space to think of her family and especially of her sister. She wonders how she is managing at home and allows herself the small sin (three Hail Marys) of hoping she is missing her, too.

Chapter 48

Emma

Dog Roses

There is a crowd gathering at the entrance to the V&A, and Emma shuffles into the queue feeling like an imposter. People are hailing others in the line and, as they creep forward, she feels a familiar dread rising inside her. Then she hears a couple, some several metres ahead of her, talking in Spanish, and she turns to the stranger next to her and, smiling, asks if she has come far. As she says it, she marvels at how far she has come – although in quite a different way.

When she reaches the entrance to the museum, she is handed an envelope from the curator who had put her name on the guest list. She says goodbye to her new acquaintance and opens the note.

It is an apology for not being able to meet her in person – *You can imagine how crazy today has been* – but it explains that she has been in touch with her historian friend, Alistair, and that Emma should contact him: *He'll be here somewhere. He's a* Titanic *nut*. Emma steps aside and texts the number on the note.

It transpires Alistair is already halfway through the exhibition and he suggests that they meet at the end. His final message says he is wearing an orange top and has a nose she cannot miss.

Emma puts her phone away and steps on board.

From the first display, she is mesmerised. The exhibits bring to life how ocean liners became the showcase for the best in interior design, decoration and furniture from around the world. Every detail was considered, from the glassware to the smallest match holder. She gazes at maple and silver-bronze tables from the *Queen Mary*; exclusively designed dishes from Wedgewood for the Orient Line; and huge gold panels depicting godlike athletes from the French ship, the *Normandie*. Company competed against company and country against country, each aspiring to the pinnacle of taste and modernity. Black-and-white footage shows movie stars posing on deck and a replica 'Grand Staircase' illustrates how passengers sought new and more extravagant backdrops for their haute couture. When competition was fierce, a company might choose a particular claim to champion: the Cunard Line was all about being the fastest, while the White Star Line wanted its ships, the *Olympic*, the *Titanic* and the *Britannic*, to be the most luxurious ocean liners in the world.

Emma is so anxious not to keep Alistair waiting that she almost misses the final exhibit: a large plinth on which is projected the rocking, undulating water of a grey ocean. In the centre of the display, is a panel of pale, sand-coloured wood – it looks like it is floating there. It is intricately carved with musical instruments, ribbons and flowers.

She stands transfixed. This is a panel from the *Titanic*. This carved panel, which she can almost reach out and touch, was part of the first-class lounge. Frank Senior and Frank Junior had probably walked past it carrying armfuls of plants.

She studies the carving, trying to take in every detail. The flowers look like wild dog roses. Did another flower lover – a florist of sorts – ever look at the these and try to decide if they were roses?

Putting aside the strange connection she feels with The Nurse, she feels a parallel pull to the idea of an unofficial florist being on board. She has established there *were* flowers – a ship full of them – and Clem supports her view that someone must have been providing a floristry service.

Emma studies the carved petals of the dog rose. She feels as if she is in touching distance of this fellow flower lover. She wonders, not for the first time, why it matters to her so much, and why she still keeps thinking of this flower lover as 'her'. Maybe as a florist herself (she decides she likes this title), she doesn't want the *Titanic*'s (unofficial) florist to be overlooked and forgotten by history?

You want to save her.

Emma doesn't know what to do with this final thought, so instead she looks around her for a historian called Alistair.

He really does have a beak of a nose. He also has an angular, attractive face and a very good haircut. She spots him first by his bright orange jumper. He wears a bag slung across his chest and everything about him – his face, his clothes, his shoes – are a lot younger looking than Emma was expecting. He doesn't look much above twenty-five. Somehow, she thought a historian with an interest in the *Titanic* would be an ageing professor.

She introduces herself, and he shakes her outstretched hand, suggesting as he does, that they go to the members' room where they can get a coffee. As they walk, he explains that he is a maritime historian with an interest in the social impact of shipping and shipbuilding, particularly around the First World War era. As he speaks about his fascination with the *Titanic*, Emma recognises the same deep-seated passion that fires many of the scientists she has worked with. She breathes out.

They sit down at a table, 'All I've gathered so far is you've been looking into the florist on the *Titanic*.' He leans towards her, smiling, 'So tell me more…'

Chapter 49

Violet

Remembered Honeysuckle

Somebody once told her that The Purser spent several years training to be a priest. She can hear it sometimes in the pitch of his voice when he instructs a gathering of stewards: he is a man who can read a list like it is liturgy. She has heard some of the restaurant staff call him The Purser Priest behind his back. She knows no one would say this to his face – not because they are frightened of him, but because he is a man who everyone knows is straight and true, like the creases he likes pressed into his trousers. The only time she has heard him shout was when the baggage steward swore at the bellboy. The Purser Priest is not a man who allows the Lord's name to be taken in vain.

She wonders what he would have been like as a priest. She thinks he would have worn the vestments well and imagines a determined flick of his cassock as he turns to mount the pulpit.

The eyes that she sees emerging over the top of the gilded bible bring her daydream to an end. His eyes are not like those of the priests she has known. The priests of her childhood had a different look altogether – one had eyes like a greedy hawk, while another had a watery eye that seemed to be gazing through a film of the Virgin's tears. And there was one who looked at the children as if he would have liked to taste their tears.

The Purser is like none of these. He has eyes that shift from side to side – checking, checking – but when they land on you (and if you are not found wanting), his eyes invite you to share something with him. She thinks that as a small boy he might have kept toffee and string and beetles in his pockets. She suspects he was a boy who liked to share a joke.

It is while she is thinking this (and carrying a plate of scones to a woman who herself looks like a plump cake) that she is approached by a woman in a pale, lemon dress.

'You will excuse me for asking you,' she says, uncertainly, 'but you remind me so much of a child I once nursed in Buenos Aires.' She smiles, apologetically, but her eyes are merry – and for a moment she is taken back to a hospital bed in a garden and a blanket of honeysuckle.

The woman turns to the tall, dark-haired man who has joined them, and she wants to ask him if he has brought a snail's shell in his handkerchief as a gift.

Dr and Mrs Merry Eyes are delighted to find that the young girl they looked after all those years ago did not die.

The doctor looks at her in wonder. 'I remember you so well. I must say, I call this a miracle. We had so little hope – indeed, no hope.' He shakes his head, but he is smiling at her.

She decides not to tell him that her mother calls it a miracle, too, or that he should have prescribed honeysuckle.

The doctor tells her that it was he who insisted she was moved into the garden, because he heard she loved the smell of freesia. As she was dying anyway, he saw no harm in it.

She lingers a little while, not dying but talking.

But she cannot wait long, the cream in the scones is melting and she must hurry on. She does not want The Purser's eye to land on her and find her wanting.

Chapter 50

Emma

American Beauty

Emma gives Alistair a potted history of her investigation and thanks him profusely for meeting her. As he swats away her thanks, she notices that the freckles on his hands run all the way down his long fingers to his neat fingernails.

Emma concludes, 'So, I'm pretty certain there was an unofficial florist on board, possibly working part-time on the flowers, but there's no record of who arranged the flowers on the *Titanic*. It's a total mystery.'

Alistair grins. 'And I expect you've discovered they had everyone else on board.'

Emma nods, reaching for her coffee. 'I know. I wonder why, if they recorded people's jobs in so much detail, they didn't show The Florist.'

'I'll tell you what I think, for what it's worth. I bet it was because it was a woman.'

Emma wants to reach out and hug him.

'In 1912, a man's profession was what mattered – women were mothers and housewives. Although, actually, this was a load of shit and lower-class women were working their arses off to keep families fed. But it's not what the Victorians or Edwardians wanted us to believe. So when it came to recording a woman's job, they were hardly likely to go into a lot of detail. The women didn't matter as much as the men as far as they were concerned. You can bet if it was a man looking after the flowers, they'd have given him a proper title.'

For the first time, Emma can imagine Alistair teaching in a lecture theatre, gesticulating enthusiastically as he spoke.

'Knowing I was meeting you, I looked up a few things about other ships and I found that the *Aquitania*, which was launched a year later, *did* have a record of a gardener on board. A man.'

Emma leans forward. 'Well, the first florists were gardeners, so that makes sense.'

Since meeting Mrs Pepperpot, she has looked into the Bealings in more detail and found that in the 1881 census, Frank Bealing's occupation was recorded as 'Gardener' but by 1891 he was described as 'Florist'. She starts to explain to Alistair about the Bealings and their buttonholes. She then tries to articulate what she'd thought as she went through the exhibition. 'These ships were showcases, right?'

Alistair nods.

'No detail was overlooked. So it makes sense that the flowers were part of it.'

'Emma, you're pushing an open door. Hey, the White Star Line built a seventy-metre tender, the *Nomadic* – real bit of class – and filled it with Champagne, just to take passengers the half-hour journey from the quayside at Cherbourg to the *Titanic* waiting at the mouth of the harbour. Of course they would have filled the *Titanic* with flowers.'

Buoyed by his enthusiasm, Emma continues. 'I've looked at what flowers were in fashion in 1912. So, take American Beauty – that was a deep pink rose. It was popular with high-end customers and might well have been one of the flowers on board. It was a favourite of one of the passengers, Madeleine Astor. And there's lily of the valley, too. When Lady Duff Gordon boarded the *Titanic* at Cherbourg there was a huge fuss about the lily of the valley that was delivered for her stateroom. She was a very fashionable dress designer, so I bet it mattered to her to have the right flowers. When the *Titanic* sank, people gathered outside the flower shop that sent them, waiting for news of her.'

'This is great stuff.' Alistair rubs his long fingers together. 'You know, I could do a whole module on this: "Rearranging the Flowers on the Titanic".'

Emma thinks that wouldn't be a bad title for her book either. Alistair's animation intrigues her. 'How come you got so interested in the *Titanic*?'

'Well, it certainly wasn't the film. Leo and Kate? Give it a rest. No, it was my grandad. He used to take me down the docks at Southampton when I was small. He'd been a porter there when he was young. He kept scrapbooks on the *Titanic* – it was a bit of a hobby of his. We'd sit by the fire on a Sunday, going over them with a cup of tea. Well, I got a glass of milk and I'm now pretty sure Grandad drank whisky.'

There it is again: family following family. Just like Les and his begonias.

Alistair looks around for a waiter. 'Do you fancy another coffee?'

Emma shakes her head as Alistair orders himself another espresso. 'Okay, so where were we?' Alistair asks.

'Well, we think it's likely to be a woman, right? But I've been through all of the stewardesses' backgrounds and so far, nothing.'

'Let's look at it a different way,' Alistair says. 'You're thinking of the *Titanic* as one whole world. But there were countries within it. Continents, even.'

'What do you mean?'

'Well, think of the variation between steerage and the other passengers – that would be like completely different continents. Steerage accounted for over half the passengers. No flowers there I'd say.'

Emma nods. She has thought of this, although it now occurs to her that Clem and she had based their calculations on the whole of the ship, which makes her uneasy.

Alistair continues, 'Then, with the rest of the ship there were different sections and different people in charge of them. Different countries. Take the first-class à la carte restaurant – it was run by a guy, Luigi, and he owned that space. It may have been White Star Line property, but he employed the staff there, not them. That was his kingdom.'

Emma frowns; she is not sure she likes where this is leading. 'But I've looked at Luigi and there's not a florist on his team.'

'Doesn't mean one of the team didn't arrange the flowers. No, the more I think about it, the more I think, that's how it would have been handled. Different areas of the ship, different people. Not one florist, at all, but a number of individuals with flowers just being part of their job. Instead of looking for one florist, I think you could be looking for several people.'

Emma is reminded of the time she made an error at the start of her PhD – a simple slip that left her feeling sick and glaringly exposed. Now, not only has she probably overestimated the work involved she has not considered how the ship was organised.

Meanwhile, Alistair repeats slowly, 'Yes, different countries.' He is smiling at her like she should be pleased.

She is left hanging, one hand still holding on to the tail end of hope. She cannot move in case she falls. She cannot say anything in case she cries. What had she been thinking? How could she have been so stupid, so naïve?

She thought she could solve the mystery of The Florist on the *Titanic* – really thought she would uncover something historians had missed.

What if there was no one special person with the gift of flowers?

She should have acted like a scientist and let the evidence lead her. Instead, she has fixated on one idea, without even undertaking a rudimentary background check on the organisation of the ship. She flushes with shame. She thinks of Betty, Les and Tamas who have arranged to meet her for lunch tomorrow to hear her news from this evening.

Her image of The Florist is dissolving in front of her eyes, and all she is left with is a photo on her phone of The Nurse, who in reality is probably nothing more than a woman who reminds her of someone she used to know.

And now she wants to cry in earnest, put her head on the table and say, 'That's it, I give in. I give up'. She concentrates on Alistair's bag on the chair beside them, counting and recounting the stiches in the leather.

Something in her stillness seems to percolate through Alistair's absorbed abstraction. 'Don't look so worried,' he says. 'I think we're getting somewhere.' He sounds almost jolly.

She turns away, keeping a wall of red curls between them, watching the rest of the room as if absorbed in the people she finds there.

'Emma?' He sounds uncertain.

When she doesn't reply, he hesitates for a few moments, then continues, more slowly this time. 'Look, let's assume the folk in the restaurants sorted their own stuff out and provided a list of what they would need to someone who did the flower ordering. That still leaves the flowers for the passengers, their cabins, and … well, what else is there?'

Eventually the silence forces her to turn back.

'Jeez, Emma. Are you okay?' He sounds concerned, confused.

She hadn't realised her face would give her away so

completely. The thought of trying to explain pushes her down the only other path open to her – just keep going. 'Buttonholes, corsages, flowers sent as gifts to the passengers, and arrangements for the first-class lounges,' she rattles this off, not quite looking him in the eye.

'There you go then,' he says encouragingly, as if reassuring a child. From the bemused look on his face, Emma can tell he has no clue what just went on.

'Now, flowers for passengers would have definitely come under the purser,' Alistair continues, still watching her closely. 'I've always reckoned he was the one person on board I would've liked to meet. No one seemed to have a bad word to say about the guy. He had a table in the restaurant like the captain did, for a few chosen guests: the purser's table. Everyone wanted to be on his table, and apparently Captain Smith would give him the most difficult passengers because he could always bring them round. Just sad he went down with the ship, like the captain…'

As he talks, Emma feels a flicker of hope. Alistair seemed to think there is something worth pursuing – and after all, isn't he the expert here? He talked of 'worlds', but the purser would still have been overseeing what would be a large 'country' – a country that needed to be filled with flowers. She thinks back to the description of the *Titanic* scented with fragrance 'like the Riviera'.

Alistair grins. 'And another thing I can tell you about our friend the purser – he was the bloke in charge of the stewardesses.' He sits back, an expectant look on his face.

'So, you think stewardesses were working for the purser on the flowers?'

He nods.

Okay, not The Florist, but three or four stewardesses who arranged the flowers. Emma considers this. It couldn't have been just anyone. After all, it wasn't as simple as that – not everyone has a gift with flowers. Her mother, for instance, was terrible at arranging flowers. This thought dawns on her with an immense feeling of pleasure.

She looks at Alistair and manages a smile.

'Look, Emma, I think we could both really do with a drink. Do you fancy getting out of here? I know a great cocktail bar nearby.'

She pauses – thinking of her train – but it is still early.

'Go on, Em. You know you want to.' He grins at her. And she realises he is quite right.

Chapter 51

Violet

Stephanotis

She reviews the list The Purser has given her and wonders how she will manage to get it all done. The Olympic has just set sail and she still has so many tasks to complete. She would like to ask The Purser why it is that the youngest stewardesses get more of the work – this is something that has never varied, whatever ship she is on – but she thinks she would need the safety of a confessional, with a screen between her and those flicking eyes to ask him such a question. She does not want The Purser's eyes to rest on her and find her wanting, so she picks up speed and rushes on, like the hull beneath her feet.

When she stumbles, she thinks at first she has forgotten to tie her bootlaces or that her mother's prophecy has finally come true: 'One of these days you'll rush so much you'll meet yourself coming back and trip yourself up.' Then she realises the stumble is just the first step in a drunken dance, and she is lurching, feet staggering, arms flung out, side-stepping towards the wall.

And then she is falling.

And she is not the only thing to fall; the lamp and ashtray have joined her on the floor. She is glad the White Star Line always insist on the best quality wool carpets for their staterooms.

A box containing powder has flown from the dressing table, coating the carpet around her in a layer of lavender scented dust. She can see spots, like spilt icing sugar against the black of her skirt. The lavender cloud is still settling when she notices the stephanotis scattered around her. The vase rolls back and forward on the dressing table and the water flows and drips onto the carpet, leaving darker splashes in the lavender powder.

Her mind skips to finding a bucket, tidying up, saving the flowers – and it is only then comes the thought, which she understands should have been her first thought: why did the ship stumble in the first place?

It occurs to her that she is in a bucket herself – a bucket floating in water.

She hears people rushing past the door and overhead comes the scraping of chairs and feet. And still she sits on the floor like an indecisive doll.

The door opens abruptly – not with the cough, gentle tap and murmur that The Purser has taught them but with a swish and a clang.

'You want to get out of here, girl.'

And then the steward with the red hair and bandy legs is gone. She pulls herself up and heads to the door. She peers into the corridor and watches the barrelling bandy legs hurrying away. She can hear her mother's voice: 'Just look at that. He wouldn't stop a pig in a passage.' It dawns on her that the legs (that wouldn't stop a pig) are moving at considerable speed.

So she closes the door behind her, leaving the powder to settle and the water to drip, and follows the bandy legs along the passageway to the stairs, running as fast as she can.

Chapter 52

Emma

Fuchsia

The bar is dimly lit and decorated in shades of plum and faded gold. The shelves behind the counter are a beacon of light in the gloom, glistening with coloured bottles and polished glasses. Two barmen in white coats look up as they enter. There are several small tables around the edge of the narrow room, but Alistair heads to the tall stools at the counter at the back of the bar. The walk through Kensington has done much to dissolve any constraint between them. Alistair didn't ask why she was so upset earlier, but he told her about his family, who now live in Edinburgh and about his four older sisters who are forever trying to organise his life for him. He told her his favourite sister is also called Emma and that he always calls her 'Em'.

As they sit down, one of the barmen comes up and introduces himself as Jan. Emma guesses Jan is in his late twenties; he has short brown hair, a slight beard and hazel eyes. He wears his white barman's coat neatly rolled to just below the elbow. and Emma cannot help but watch his hands and arms as he puts out small, square serviettes on the bar and offers them each a cocktail menu.

'Let me know when you're ready.'

Jan speaks with a slight accent. Emma, the linguist, isn't sure where it is from and, quite frankly, she couldn't care less. Just looking at Jan is enough for her.

As Jan walks away, Alistair catches her look and gives a small snort of laughter. 'Your face!'

Jan has moved to the front of the bar to serve new customers, and Emma is suddenly very aware that her slim-fitting, navy skirt is riding up above her knees. 'I know!' she says, trying to simultaneously read the cocktail menu, pull her hem down and stop herself from laughing. 'But he's gorgeous.'

'Not my type,' Alistair says, looking at Jan critically.

'Oh, God, I'm not being serious – it's just he took me unawares.'

'You wish,' Alistair mutters, laughing.

She puts her head down, pretending to read, shoulders shaking. Eventually she draws a deep breath. 'I think I'll see what Jan recommends.'

Alistair says nothing but raises both eyebrows.

Jan is back. 'Come to a decision yet, or would you like a recommendation?'

Alistair speaks for both of them, which is just as well, because Emma's tongue seems to have become stuck to the roof of her mouth. 'Yes, we do need your help, Jan. Do you have anything that has a floral twist to it?'

'Floral,' he says slowly. 'I think I can do that. Do you fancy something that has a sour note, or would you like to start with some bubbles?'

'Oh, bubbles, I think,' Alistair says.

Emma makes a huge effort to get hold of herself. 'I know that sounds like an odd request, but I'm doing research for a book that's all about flowers.' Emma hopes her voice is a nice blend of scientist and schoolteacher.

'That's a first, for sure. Leave it with me.' Jan looks at her and smiles, and Emma knows she has never felt less like a schoolteacher in her life. She tries to ignore Alistair, who is now silently laughing beside her.

The first cocktail Jan suggests is a Parisian Rose. 'This has a base of Grey Goose vodka, flower shop tincture,' he explains.

Emma looks at him in disbelief. 'Flower shop tincture?'

'Better believe it,' Jan says, looking up briefly from constructing their drinks. 'Grey Goose is a French vodka – then I'm adding a little lemon juice and syrup, and topping it up with pink Champagne.' He places the tall, fluted glasses in front of them. 'Now for some extra flowers,' he says, sprinkling the tops with pale-pink, sugared rose petals.

'It's *so* pretty,' she enthuses.

'And do the bubbles go up your nose?' Alistair asks innocently.

Emma kicks him on the ankle.

Jan is soon away, serving some hard-drinking Russians further down the bar.

'This is exhausting,' Emma exhales. 'I'd forgotten what it's like to fancy someone.'

'Do you want to go somewhere else?' Alistair asks.

'No, this is fun.' Emma sips her Parisian Rose. 'Do you have someone in your life?' she asks, then immediately worries that she sounds like a women's magazine.

'Did have – didn't work. Left me for his personal trainer.'

'I'm sorry.'

'No, you're all right. It's getting easier. Think I might even get back out there. What's not to love about a lanky historian with a fanatical interest in the *Titanic*?'

Emma wonders if this is why she has slipped so easily into Alistair's company – their shared obsession? Sharing an interest does seem to pull people together – she thinks of the Glory Girls – and it occurs to her that maybe people with a shared connection like helping each other.

'How about you?' Alistair asks.

Emma is saved from answering by the reappearance of Jan, who asks them what drinks they want next.

'We're in your hands,' Alistair says, draining his drink.

Next on Jan's list is a blackberry and elderflower martini. He serves this with a small purple and pink fuchsia head hanging on the side of the glass.

'It's the arms,' Emma whispers, sipping her martini, the fuchsia resting in the curls she has tucked behind her ear. She is staring down the bar, watching Jan work.

'I only ever consider personality,' Alistair says, then laughs at Emma's startled look. 'Nah, legs,' he confesses. He tips his head sideways towards Jan. 'He likes you,' he declares.

'No! No, far too young,' Emma exclaims – but a little wistfully.

Alistair grins. 'So?'

As they drink their martinis, Emma tells Alistair about the people who have helped her with her research: Les, with his interest in the historical society; Guy and his realisation about the photographs of the *Titanic*; the smiling girl who helped her in the library; Tamas finding the flower nursery; Mrs Pepperpot pulling together the photos of the Bealings; Betty and her never-ending encouragement; Clem with her insight into how much work there was for a florist on board. 'She was *really* helpful,' she concludes.

'Bit like myself then.' Alistair nudges her shoulder with his, and picking up the cocktail menu, says, 'I tell you what – I'd like to try a cocktail they'd have drunk on the *Titanic*. We should toast your florist, or florists,' he says, 'whoever they are.'

Emma glances at him sideways.

'What is it?'

Emma breathes in. She can feel the alcohol loosening her tongue, 'You know, I thought I was here to save her.'

'You've lost me there.'

'I… My husband died a year or so ago, and … well, it's complicated.'

Alistair reaches out and touches her arm. 'Jeez, Em, I'm so sorry.'

She doesn't want to talk about Will, really, not because she feels she can't confide in Alistair, but because she is enjoying herself. And for the first time in months feeling good feels normal.

'You don't have to talk about it if you don't want to, Em.'

She thinks of the people who called her 'love' and 'honey' and now 'Em', and she is glad. So she tries to find the words, fleetingly wondering if Alistair speaks French or Spanish.

'A few weeks ago, when I started wondering if there was a florist on the *Titanic*, I couldn't let the idea of finding her go. It's become an obsession, I guess – I think partly to stop me dwelling on other stuff to do with my husband.' She looks at Alistair to see if he's with her.

'Go on.'

'I got it into my head that if I could find her and prove she'd survived, I would have saved her, and that would make a difference, somehow.' She glances at him. 'Mad, I know, but I wasn't exactly thinking straight.' She smiles. 'I've spent quite a lot of time lately not sleeping, not talking and in fact, not doing much of anything.'

'Been there, would have got the T-shirt but couldn't be arsed.'

Emma laughs. Then she tries to put into words what has just come to her. 'I guess what I'm trying to say … not very well … is that it's just struck me that maybe I wasn't there to save her – I think she was there to save me. To stop me from drowning.'

Alistair turns his whole body towards Emma and half smiles. 'Who knows? As they say Em, "stranger things happen at sea".'

It is just what Les would say.

'Look, I've been thinking, Em – I know you were disappointed when I said that thing back there about the *Titanic* being made up of different countries—'

'No, it's—' she begins.

'Em, you looked like a puppy who'd been kicked. But think of it this way: you wouldn't have come this far without all those other people you mentioned. It's turning out to be a team effort, right?'

She nods.

'Well, I think the flowers on the *Titanic* were the same – different people doing their bit. And maybe there wasn't one maestro, one top dog, but that doesn't mean the efforts of the people who helped aren't worth celebrating, from the Bealings to a few florists of sorts on board. All those small contributions matter.'

Emma imagines all the people who have helped her meeting up. She'd like to put a big table in her garden near the apple trees and cook lunch for them all. She would serve chilled red wine and lamb or maybe paella, something her father would have liked.

Alistair calls Jan over. 'So, Jan, we're going to need all your skill – we have a challenge for you. We need a cocktail that they would have drunk on the *Titanic*…'

A few minutes later, he and Emma are holding two cut-glass tumblers. They toast The Florist (or more likely Florists) and sip their Manhattans.

While they are finishing these cocktails, Emma reaches into

her bag for her phone. She opens up the photos and holds the image she has been obsessing over out for Alistair to see.

'I want to ask you about her.'

'Oh, I know her,' Alistair says slowly, smiling at the serious young face staring up at him.

'The thing is, I keep coming back to her. I know she can't be The Florist on board because she was The Nurse, but—'

Alistair grins. 'No, she wasn't.'

'But…' Emma frowns, pointing to the cross on the starched white apron. 'What about the nurse's uniform?'

'That's a First World War uniform,' says the First World War historian, confidently. 'When she was on the *Titanic* in 1912, she was a common or garden stewardess – or not so common as it turned out. You know her name, right?'

'Violet.'

'Yep,' Alistair says, 'This here is Violet Jessop. Famous to us *Titanic* nuts because she survived three collisions on White Star liners – the *Olympic*, the *Titanic* and the *Britannic*.'

'Wow, I didn't realise it was all three,' Emma queries.

Alistair nods, 'She nearly died when the *Britannic* went down. It was used as a hospital ship during the First World War and hit a mine. This is when this photo would have been taken. Violet was in the water for some time and she couldn't swim. Can't quite remember how she made it.' Alistair shakes his head. 'You'd think by the end no one would have sailed with her.'

'She must have been very lucky – or unlucky, I suppose, thinking about it a different way.' Emma frowns. 'Why had I got it into my head that she was a nurse on the *Titanic*?'

'That's cos of the photograph. They always use it on any article to do with the *Titanic*, but it was taken a few years later.'

Emma stares at the screen. Violet Jessop – a stewardess who *became* a nurse. She feels the old, tugging undertow of recognition, and a new thought strikes her: she wonders if Violet Jessop liked flowers.

'Out with it,' Alistair demands, staring at her. 'What's Violet got to do with it all?'

'It's just a feeling. I know it sounds stupid, but when I saw her I thought I recognised her.' She is blushing now. 'I felt a connection – something to do with my family. I just can't place it.'

He is laughing. 'A long-lost relative?'

She wants to say, *Yes. Maybe*, but feels it would sound stupid.

'Do you know if you have any relations who were involved with the *Titanic*?' he asks.

'I've been looking into my family tree – nothing on my mother's side and my dad's family are Spanish so that's harder going. But nothing so far.'

Alistair grins at her. 'You want Violet Jessop to be your florist, don't you?'

Emma's mind is racing. She has been thinking of her research as two parallel lines: The Florist and The Nurse; but now the two strands twist. An image of a DNA helix forms in her mind, two parallel lines close together and spinning in unison, and she says, on instinct, 'Of course I do', and laughs, thinking how unscientific she is being.

Alistair takes pity on her. 'Look, I could have a dig into her past if you like – you've got me hooked now, too. Everyone just talks about the fact she was on all three ships; I don't know how much is written about her work and if she knew anything about flowers. But at least her name's gotta be a good sign. Think about it – her parents probably liked flowers, if they called her Violet, so maybe they passed that onto her.' He leans forward suddenly. 'Hey, Em, are you crying? Violet was saved – she was okay. She survived. Oh, Em, please don't. You'll start me off.'

She smiles at him through her tears. 'I'm not really crying,' she says, half laughing and half crying.

'Yeah, looks like it,' Alistair says, grabbing some serviettes off the bar and handing them to her.

'It's just feels like something has come together. I can't explain it more than that.'

'Look, we don't know that much about her yet. But she did survive – she wasn't drowned. Come on, cheer up. Surely that's got to be worth another cocktail?'

When they eventually leave the bar, Jan presents Emma with a cocktail menu. He has written his number on the back.

She puts it in her bag, not because she has any intention of ringing him, but because it is always nice to be asked.

Chapter 53

Violet

Crumpled Daisy

She is leaning over the rail, along with most of the passengers and many of the crew. They are heading in a straight course away from Southampton and out to sea, but no one is studying the dappled horizon; all are focused on the British warship drawing closer and yet closer, as if an all-prevailing undertow is dragging it towards the Olympic's *bow.*

Can't the warship steer away? Have they lost control?

The sudden turning of the Olympic *that tipped her off balance earlier, must have been their attempt to avoid a collision, but it doesn't seem to have been enough.*

She hears the intake of breath around her like a theatre audience gasping in unison.

And then the warship rams them.

The grinding and screeching reverberates through the air

and through her. The crowd exhales and their screams and cries infiltrate the metallic cacophony, creating a far more frightening living sound. They surge with the shuddering of the ship, and there is a second crippling groan of metal.

Out of the corner of her eye she sees people stumble and watches her friend who works in second class crumple on the deck. The next instant, a large man in a fur-collared coat crashes against her, taking her feet from under her. Her mind acknowledges the inevitable even while feet and arms flail.

Then her elbow is clutched in a firm grip. The Purser has caught her.

The Purser is close to forty and holds himself like a captain. He is the kind of man who makes you feel safe. For an instant, it reminds her of her father, and of how he used to catch her when she stumbled as a little girl.

He places her hands back on the rail and they both look down at the devastated hull of the warship and the yawning gash that has been torn in their own hull.

'Now then. Nothing to worry about,' The Purser declares.

She is not sure if she has thrown him a look of disbelief. She wonders if she dares. But he adds, 'This is the safest ship ever built – watertight doors in each section will be closed by now. There is no fear of sinking.' He looks towards the warship, which is in far worse shape than they are, figures swarming on deck. He averts his eyes. 'Built to last, designed by the best engineers in the world.' He is not talking about the warship: The Purser is a White Star Line man through and through.

She wonders if The Purser, like her, prayed to God the moment the great crash came. She thinks how lucky the White Star Line are to have The Purser Priest on their side.

He is proved right. No one is hurt; two watertight doors closed fast and saved them all. Everyone proclaims that it was a miracle no passengers were in their cabins when HMS Hawke tore a hole through the walls, crushing furniture and panelling like matchsticks.

It is of no note that a stewardess left one of those cabins only minutes before the collision – but she remembers the red-headed steward with bandy legs in her prayers.

Chapter 54

Emma

Hollyhocks

The walk up the hill to the field, plus a large mug of strong coffee has made little impression on her hangover. She descends to the garden, wondering if a bacon sandwich might help. She is meeting Betty, Les and Tamas at one o'clock, and she doesn't want to be feeling like this when she sees them.

And how is she feeling? The nagging thought sits behind her headache, a question that has been there before and has nothing to do with the number of cocktails she drank last night.

Her headache is now coming in waves. She wonders if she is 'going down with something'. She repeats this in her head the way Granny Maria would have said it, a reassuring voice keeping greater concerns at bay – worries about serious illness that worm their way in. Since Will's death, these are more frequent visitors. She pushes against the panic. Everyone tells you that grief is exhausting.

Anyway, this morning isn't a day for dwelling on headaches; the sun is shining and her garden is, quite frankly, looking good. The honeysuckle is beginning to wrap green tendrils around the top of the new arch she has installed by the back door, and the hollyhocks, either side of it, are standing tall and proud – no flowers yet, but there are buds of cherry and peach tucked in between the broad, green leaves. She walks to the back door, the lavender bushes that border the path like a series of rolling waves, washing her legs in scent as she passes.

A bacon sandwich and two paracetamols later, she breathes more easily and pulls up the notes she has been making on her laptop. There is now a folder on her desktop entitled: *Garden Centre Research*. In it are examples taken from all over the country of success stories, new approaches. She has also looked at other industries, what trends are emerging, and she has explored the Instagram and Facebook posts of florists around the country. At least she has approached *this* research like the competent scientist she once was. She just hopes Betty and Les won't mind if she makes a few suggestions – won't think she is sticking her nose in.

She spots Betty and Les sitting at a table by double doors flung open onto the street. There is no sign of Tamas.

'Tamas called and says he's sorry he can't make it,' Betty tells Emma as she sits down. 'He and Berta are going to have a day out.'

Les leans forward. 'We think that may be a good sign.' He nods a few times. 'Anyway, Emma, tell us all about it. What did you find out?'

She looks at their expectant faces, and her nerves are back. She doesn't want to let them down. She notices that Betty is wearing her best glasses and has a dragonfly shirt on that she hasn't seen before. Her palms start to sweat.

Betty interrupts before she has a chance to start. 'I must say, love, I like that top. The colour really suits you. You should wear turquoise more often.'

'Oh, I … I thought a change…' She takes a deep breath, 'Thank you,' she says. After a pause, she adds, 'I have a lot to tell you, I just … I just don't want you to be disappointed.'

'Oh, I don't think you need to worry about that, love,' says Betty. 'Spit it out.'

'Would you mind if we found out there wasn't a florist? Or not one main florist anyhow – just different people who had a way with flowers, each doing their bit?' And she goes on to explain about Alistair and his view that the *Titanic* was a series of countries within the ship. As she finishes, she can't stop herself adding, 'I hate the thought of letting you down after everything you've done to help.'

'Now, listen, love,' Betty says, 'we are in this together and half the fun is the searching. When we were first married, Les and I used to go on treasure hunts – we would squeeze into our old Morris Minor and off we'd go. We won once, and we were cock-a-hoop.' She smiles at her husband. 'But my favourite night was when we passed a restaurant Les knew I had a fancy for – dead expensive it was – and he'd booked a table. Even put my favourite dress in the boot.'

Les reaches out and takes Betty's hand. 'Pale green it was – I'll never forget.'

Betty laughs. 'You forgot the shoes and tights, though, didn't you?' When she sees Les's face fall, she adds, reassuringly, 'It didn't matter a bit. I put the dress on, and we had a lovely time. And no one could see my Hush Puppies under the table.' She turns to Emma. 'Anyway, love, what I'm trying to say is that we didn't find a single clue that night and it was the best treasure hunt we ever went on.'

Les pats his wife's hand, then turns to the waiter who has arrived to take their order. It's no good. Emma still can't see Les as a punk.

Over lunch, Emma tells them all about Violet Jessop. She feels now is not the time for secrets, and wonders fleetingly if Betty has told Les about Will's affair. She hopes she has.

When she shows them the photograph of Violet, Betty and Les study it for some time.

'She's a pretty lass, isn't she?' Betty says. 'There certainly is something about her. You know she reminds me of someone… maybe it's my old maths teacher. You would see all the dads lining up for a chat with *her* at parents' evenings.'

'And you recognised her?' Les asks, rubbing his beard. 'You think you might be related to her?'

'I really don't know what I think anymore, Les – I just can't help feeling it's something to do with my family. Anyway, Alistair said he'll have a look into her background for me.

For us,' she corrects. 'Violet surviving the three shipwrecks is what tends to get written about, so I really don't know if he's going to find anything that might link her to flowers. Or me.' She shrugs. 'But it seems a shame to stop now. I've also been looking into my family tree. So far I can't find any link to anyone on the *Titanic* or any Irish blood – Violet's family were originally from Ireland. But you never know…'

Les asks her in detail about the sites she has been using. It seems that most of the Historical Society members have been busy exploring their ancestry – some going as far back as the Norman conquest. Les's family, it appears, were originally Cornish fisherman. This she can certainly imagine (much more than him ever being a punk).

As they are getting ready to leave, Betty rummages in her bag for her phone. 'I wanted to show you something, love,' she says, and she starts to scroll through her photos. 'Ah, there it is.' She turns the screen towards Emma. 'I told our son Ben about your pillow post and he's been trying it out with our grandson, Zac. It seems he is not at all convinced that having a baby sister is a good thing, but Ben said the letters are really helping. I think it makes Zac feel he's doing something his sister can't. This is a picture of the last thing he left under his dad's pillow.'

On the screen is a photo of a piece of pale blue paper. All around the edges are drawings of … dinosaurs? Birds? Emma is not quite sure. In the centre of the page in a bigger drawing, two figures are riding on a surfboard, one larger and one smaller. There are massive waves around the board and a bright yellow sun above it. An arrow drawn from the surfboard lists a maker's name.

Seeing Emma studying it, Betty declares, 'I think that might be a bit of a hint. Zac's after a proper surfboard.' She smiles. 'But don't you see?'

Emma knows she must look confused.

'That's his sister on the back of the board with him.'

Emma smiles. 'Ah.'

'Well, it just shows you it's working,' Betty says with satisfaction. 'Usually Zac draws her being eaten by a shark.'

As Emma walks away from the bistro, she realises she forgot to show Betty and Les the notes she brought with her in her bag. A document headed: *Ideas for the Garden Centre*.

These will just have to wait for another day.

Chapter 55

Violet

Lilac

She pulls her suitcase from under her bed and starts to pack. After her shoes and clothes are arranged ('roll, don't fold'), she pauses before adding the three magazines that one of her American passengers gave her. She believes she has earned every one of the colourful pages.

The American languished her way to New York, calling for her favourite stewardess to bear her company. She explained it was not seasickness she was suffering from – goodness, hadn't they sailed every summer in Maine since she was a girl? – no, it was neglect of the cruellest kind that was draining her spirit. She could not say more.

But she insisted her favourite stewardess return for each instalment, sometimes requiring her to sit with her late into the night. She was charming in her requests and tearful in her thanks, a handkerchief scented with lilac pressed to her lips. Her tears traced pale lines in the powder on her exquisite face. She begged her friend to visit her in New York and personally put into her hands the magazines she had no use for.

Finding herself near to the American's home one afternoon during shore leave in New York, she decided to visit. Curiosity and sentiment stifled her mother's voice whispering in her ear: 'No good wlll come of it.'

As usual, her mother was right.

She was ushered into a room filled with guests, the pale, thick carpets softening the sound of conversation and laughter like a fresh fall of snow. The American was as charming as ever and moved forward with the graceful gestures she remembered from the hours they had spent together. Her voice rose in gentle enquiry, and as she turned to introduce her dear friend to the others, her favourite stewardess knew for certain that she had no idea who she was.

She would like to throw away the magazines that smell of lilac, but she knows her mother and sister would like to look at them and will enjoy seeing how much she is valued by her passengers.

Finally, she places the bundle of well-read letters from home into her case. It is good to think she will soon be returning to the address written on the top right-hand corner of each. She frowns, thinking of the last letter. Her mother wrote to urge her to take up the new post she has been offered, and she is not sure whether to follow her advice. She likes the Olympic; she is used to it. Still, at least she would not be alone. Friends here with her on the Olympic are to change to the new ship, and they say they would like to sail with her again.

She packs the last of her belongings and reflects that her reluctance is unlikely to tip the scales when weighed against a mother who is always right. Perhaps, as her mother says, it will be an opportunity.

And, at the very least, it would mean serving on the most splendid ship the world has ever seen: the Titanic.

Chapter 56

Emma

A Bed of Roses

'Do you have five minutes? There are some ideas I'd like to run past you both about the garden centre. I'm not trying to interfere – I just hoped I might be able to help a little.'

They are back in the Flower Cabin, sheltering from a thunderstorm, sharing coffee and a lemon cake that Emma brought in with her this morning – a better attempt than the cake she tried to make weeks ago, after she missed Les's *Titanic* talk.

It occurs to her that maybe Betty hasn't told Les she has discussed their business problems with her, and perhaps he will mind.

But Les appears to be smiling behind his beard. 'Well, I always say, two heads are better than one.' Then, glancing out towards the rain, he says, 'There's no time like the present. Just let me get something to sit on.' He reaches behind him for a large crate, which he places beside Betty's stool.

Despite Les's encouragement and Betty's smile, Emma's voice wavers as she starts. 'Betty explained that the main problem is the drop in numbers since the ring road was built.'

Both nod solemnly at her.

'I was wondering … well, instead of thinking of your location as a problem, it could be a real bonus for us.' She hopes they don't mind her saying 'us'. 'Every other garden centre in the area is on a very boring industrial estate or in a shopping complex – whereas we have the most beautiful backdrop.' She thinks of the mornings when she has sat on the bench looking across the allotments to the downs that rise up behind the garden centre. 'The only problem is, just that: it's the backdrop. Everything faces the wrong way. The café windows look out on to the front and the car park. I just wondered – could we turn it all around?'

Les rubs his beard. 'You mean open up the back?'

Betty chimes in. 'It's only the wooden storage sheds behind the back wall.'

'Exactly,' Emma rushes on. 'If you could take out some of the end section and put in French windows, the whole café would look out over the garden centre *and* the downs. Who wouldn't want to look at that over coffee and cake? The café could be a venue for events too – for parties. perhaps evening classes. We could even start a book club for those interested in nature and gardens.'

'Now, that I would really like,' Betty exclaims.

'You could even move the flower shop near the café, Betty – people always like to watch as we make up bouquets. It's a bit like seeing someone cook.' She doesn't add that she would like to make their posies less formal. Slowly, slowly – one step at a time. 'And we often have flowers we can't sell but still have some life left in them, so rather than throw them away, we could make up posies for the tables, and this would remind people we sell cut flowers as well as plants. And if we do events in the café, we can always suggest that we supply the flowers for those.' She glances down at the notes in her hand. 'I've also been researching other industries, and it seems to be all about developing things people will talk to their friends about. I think a lot of it is about creating a bit of theatre. I was reading about an interior design show where they covered unexpected things in fabric – like the outside of a bath, or a beach hut. We could do it the other way round – take a sofa and instead of cushions, have flowers planted out in it. Anything that makes people stop and look.'

'A bed of roses,' Les says, slowly.

'Perfect.' Emma beams at him. 'The other thing I know from being new to gardening is that people really need ideas. So maybe we could take some small plots – and I mean very small – plant them up and then have a display behind it selling what's in that patch. We could have different colour themes…'

'Or gardens that attract bees and butterflies,' says Betty, with a glance down at her Red Admiral T-shirt.

'Exactly. And we could support all of this kind of thing through social media.'

She is tempted to say more but decides to leave it at that.

'Well, Emma, you've given us a lot of food for thought.' Les glances at Betty, who smiles encouragingly. 'And you would be happy to help us with this?'

'Of course – I'd love to. For example, I could set up an Instagram account for us and run it.'

Both Les and Betty are nodding now.

'Well, you leave it with us to mull over,' Les says. 'I need to get on now and see to the begonias – they won't be liking this downpour. Give us some time to think it through.'

Emma nods, but she can already tell that they like her ideas. Maybe it's not just about asking for the help you need; sometimes it's also about being prepared to offer specific help. She was worried about interfering, but this doesn't feel like that.

The moment Les steps out into the rain, Tamas comes running full pelt into the Flower Cabin, flower boxes held over his head. Tamas puts the boxes down and then stamps and shakes like a very large dog. Emma notices that both she and Betty are looking at him expectantly.

'This is the weather the ducks like, I think,' he booms, taking the towel Betty is offering him. He rubs it vigorously over his bald head.

He emerges from under the towel and, seeing them both still looking at him, laughs. 'I see you look at me. You women, you always want to know. But I am not going to say anything.' But he continues to smile.

'You had a nice time with Berta though, love?' Betty asks a little anxiously.

'I think that my Greta would say to her dad that he is not always such an old fool as he appears.' He laughs again. 'She used to say this about her dad, he is not *always* a fool – often, but not always.' With that, he hands the delivery note to Betty with a nod. Then he turns abruptly and takes Emma's hand in his and with slow formality bends from the waist and kisses it. 'This is for you, for reminding me that words should sometimes be written down.'

She is left astonished but smiling, hand still held out. He turns and, forgetting to pick up the empty flower boxes, throws open the door and runs back out into the storm.

Emma and Betty watch as he splashes down the path, leaping over flowerpots and making tidal waves in the puddles as he lands.

Betty gives a deep sigh. 'Well, love, that looks very promising, I do have to say – a lot better than I had been expecting.' She chuckles. 'And not one mention of you looking like his cow.' She pauses as she opens up the first flower box. 'Now, what about you, love? What's next for you?'

It's not a question Emma can answer.

She is still thinking about it as she draws up outside her cottage later. Alistair said he would be in touch soon, but she really has no idea how long that will be. A few days? A week? A month? And then what?

She can't help feeling she should go and see her mother. Not for the party – God forbid – but she has all the old family photos and documents, stretching way back. She wants to get her hands on these.

But it is not just the photos. Emma hasn't spoken to her mother since her breakdown in Cambridge, but she increasingly feels that she needs to talk to her properly – not on the phone but face-to-face. She knows she doesn't want to, but sometime soon, she thinks she will have to.

A trip to Paris?

Paris is where Philippe, the retired perfumier, lives, so she could kill two birds with one stone (as Les would say).

Another thought brings a genuine smile to her face: maybe Betty would like to come with her?

Chapter 57

Violet

Golden Tulips

Her friend, the bar steward, is unloading the glasses in preparation for their maiden voyage. He has asked her to tell him what she thinks of their new ship, the Titanic. *He is waiting for her to answer.*

How can she say that it makes her feel drunk, like the time he made her take a second brandy against the cold? Then she had tried to get into her cabin but the handle seemed to have been moved to the wrong side of the door and she was left foolishly rubbing her hands all over the metal painted surface to find it.

It is the same all over the Titanic. *It is a ship so like the* Olympic *that it is almost a familiar old friend. She knows its virtues and its idiosyncrasies – but things have been moved, details changed. She expects to find a certain something around a corner only to discover it has vanished. And then she bangs her knee against a table that shouldn't be there.*

Her friend is still waiting patiently, rubbing the crystal glasses with a white cloth so new it looks like stiff card in his hands.

She remembers a trick she has learnt from her brothers, boys so full of questions they rarely have time to answer what is asked of them.

'I would be interested to hear what you think of her?' she says.

She diverts him as easily as the boys distract the priest when they ask him a question about the scriptures. He picks up another Champagne glass to polish while he considers the question.

'I told my wife that we are making history. It will be something to tell the lad that his dad was on the maiden voyage of the Titanic.*'*

Her friend and his wife have just had their first child, and the experience is so fresh he still looks at everything through the eyes of a new father. The ice buckets are large enough 'to bathe a baby in', and the linen of the napkins 'fine enough for a christening gown'.

'So you prefer her to the Olympic?*'*

'I'm not saying the Olympic *wasn't a grand ship, but this, well, this is…' He pauses as he searches for the words. '… This is majestic.'*

He's right: the smart new robes of the Titanic *are fine enough for a Queen. The ship may still feel like an impersonator, but she is a mimic in a splendid new cloak. Staircases sweep with gleaming banisters; etched glass partitions sparkle and shine; and the tiles of the Turkish baths shimmer in shades of turquoise and green, like jewels from under the sea.*

But she thinks it is the fabrics within the ship that impress her most: the golden and red tulips woven into the first-class chairs, the softness of the wool carpets. And she has never seen lacework like the covers on the beds in the staterooms – lace so delicate it could be made from, well … from babies' hair.

She smiles at the thought and promises her friend she will come back and see him when she next has the chance. She still has half her cabins to prepare before the passengers arrive, and time is sailing on.

Chapter 58

Emma

Gardenia & Wisteria

They catch the Eurostar with a minute to spare. Emma had forgotten how long security could take, the thought of simply boarding a train lulling her into a false sense of having plenty of time. Betty picked up on Emma's growing anxiety as they waited to get their bags screened and as a consequence hasn't stopped talking since.

'... and here we are and no bones broken,' she finishes as the train pulls out.

Emma is in urgent need of a coffee. She also thinks she had better call her mother. She has avoided making this call – better to ring when she's on her way and there is no way of backing out. Beyond asking to see old photo albums and documents, she really has no clear idea what she wants to say to her mother – she just has a vague feeling it will come to her when they meet. She does her best to ignore a small voice in her head that keeps whispering: 'Forty years of not saying how you really feel and *now* you think it's going to be different?'

She WhatsApps the information on the small hotel she has booked for them to Betty and leaves her studying this as she goes to find a quiet spot to make her call.

Her mother picks up on the second ring.

'Mum, I'm on my way to Paris. I'm hoping we can catch up over supper tomorrow or the next day. Or lunch, or maybe breakfast if you're busy.' She has at least got the words out but despairs that her voice has already taken on a conciliatory tone.

'What are you talking about, Emma? Paris?'

'I said, I'm on my way. I'm on the Eurostar,' she declares, feeling foolish.

'But what on earth were you thinking?'

'I'm coming to Paris for a few days,' Emma repeats. Is it really that hard to grasp? Or is her mother punishing her for their last call?

'But you can't.'

So, she *is* still angry she won't come to the chateau in October.

'Well I am,' she says boldly, bravely.

'But *no one* is in Paris in August.'

Emma stands by the baggage rack of the swaying train and closes her eyes. How can she have forgotten?

'Emma, are you still there? Paris in *August*?'

Emma can hear her mother turning to someone else, and a

muffled, 'Emma's going to Paris – I have no idea what's got into to her.'

Her voice comes back more clearly into Emma's ear. '*No one* is in Paris in August.' She says this as though to suggest otherwise would be a personal affront.

'Well, I will be,' and Emma starts to laugh, 'Oh, and Betty will be too.'

'Betty? What are you talking about, Emma? You know I always go to Antibes in August.' Her mother's voice grows querulous, then muffled once more, 'Mathias, I have no idea what she's talking about.'

Emma is still laughing when she sits back down opposite Betty. Her overwhelming feeling is one of relief. She is going to Paris, and she doesn't have to see her mother. The decision to face her has been taken out of her hands. She knows the concierge at her mother's apartment building will let her in to collect the old photographs and papers, and before ending their call, her bemused mother agreed that she could borrow them. Besides, she has received an email from Philippe (who *is* still in Paris), saying that he would be delighted to meet her. She has no idea what she hopes to achieve by this visit, but he had encouraged her to reach out if she were ever in Paris, and he is certainly a man who knows a lot about scent and flowers.

With this in mind, she is still grinning to herself when Betty says, 'I've ordered us two glasses of Champagne, as my treat.' Then she adds, 'So your mum won't be there?'

'Nope.'

'And you don't mind?' Betty sounds confused.

'Nope.' Emma grins. 'I know I should – it's half of why we're going – but I don't.'

'But I thought you had things you wanted to talk to her about?'

Instead of answering a question that is likely to tie them up in knots for hours, she asks, 'What was your mum like, Betty?'

Betty settles back in her seat. 'Oh, she was a wonder – so talented. She'd been a seamstress for the designer Norman Hartnell in London and worked her way up to be an embroiderer. My mum once showed me a photo of a white evening dress they had made for the late Queen – it was covered in the tiniest, hand-embroidered gardenias. My mum was working there when she met my dad. He was an accountant—'

'So was mine!' Emma smiles. 'Well, that's how he started – he ended up in the City. He had one of those brains that see patterns in figures.'

'A bit like mine,' says Betty. 'Well, my dad ended up in Glossop and that didn't suit my mum at all. But what could she do? In those days, a wife had to go with her husband.' Betty sips her Champagne.

'Did your mum keep working when they moved?'

'Yes, first in a dress shop and then she took on some private customers making their clothes. But, well, it wouldn't have been the same, would it?'

'Was she very disappointed?'

'You could say that.' Betty sounds uncharacteristically sarcastic.

She waits, feeling Betty might want to say more.

'I think *Disappointed Woman* just about sums up my mum. I think her job, her neighbours, her house and her husband all disappointed her. Although she was pleased my sister married well – she perked up a bit then.'

Betty stares out of the window, and Emma can tell she is miles away.

'And you and your mum?'

'Well, what do you think, love? Look at me.'

Emma looks at the small, neat, rounded woman in front of her, with her curly hair, old-fashioned glasses and sequined, butterfly sweatshirt, and she thinks she is a beautiful sight to behold.

'I would say that if she could raise a woman like you, she had done something right with her life and should be very proud.'

Betty blinks several times and Emma thinks her friend might cry. She thinks she might, too.

Betty smiles slowly. 'Well, towards the end, she did soften a bit, and that was a blessing.'

'Did you … make your peace with her before she died?'

Betty chuckles. 'I don't know if I'd go that far, love.' She looks thoughtful. 'But it was okay. Yes, it was better. What about you and your mum?'

Where should she start? It occurs to her that Betty and she have more in common than just a love of flowers and fathers who were accountants. She had once read about an experiment in which people from all sorts of backgrounds gathered in a room without speaking. They were asked to go up to people they instinctively felt comfortable with. It turned out that twins gravitated towards twins, only children to only children and so on. She wonders if she would have found Betty in that room.

She draws in a deep breath. 'My mum was extraordinarily beautiful when she was young. I've seen photos of her, and she really was incredible. She's not bad now at sixty-seven.' Emma thinks of Mathias. 'Men still notice her, and she's used to people doing things for her because of her looks.' She wonders how much her dad minded that. Had he gone to the garden because of her mother's stream of 'friends', or had the 'friends' come because he was in the garden?

Emma sighs. 'She's very elegant, loves beautiful things...'

'And?'

'And she's not a kind woman.'

Emma remembers Granny Maria saying that the most important thing to look for in the person you married was kindness. The adolescent, romantic Emma thought this disappointingly mundane, but for the first time, she wonders if her grandmother had been thinking about her mother. The importance of kindness strikes her now, more than ever. After all, it is helping lift her, little by little, from the depths of her despair. Tamas going to such lengths to find the Bealings; that helpful, smiling girl in the library; Mrs Pepperpot giving up her time to meet them; Clem sharing her wisdom and wine; Roberto taking care of her in Cambridge; Alistair with his knowledge and the research he is doing for her; all these kind, kind people. And that is before she even considers Betty and Les.

She looks at Betty, who is screwing up her nose as she sips

tentatively at her Champagne – she must be the kindest person she has ever met.

'What? Why are you smiling at me like that?' Betty puts down her glass. 'Tell me more about your mum. You said there were things you needed to say to her?'

Emma immediately stops smiling. 'I try to fight it, Betty, but however much I tell myself I'm forty and recite my CV in my head, when I see my mum it's like I am five years old again and I feel like I did when she used to scream at me.'

Betty tuts. 'Well, that's no way to treat a child.'

'It wasn't all that often. I wasn't abused, nothing like that.' How can she describe it? 'It was the lack of kindness rather than unkindness,' she says, although she wonders if that is really true. Wasn't her childhood littered with small acts of unkindness? Didn't the effect of these build like the layers of ice packed around a snowball?

'But you got on well with your dad, I remember you saying?'

Emma is happy to be diverted. 'Yes, he was a sweet man, very gentle, and he would always try his best to protect me. We spent a lot of time in the garden together. But he wasn't there all the time.'

'Do you know what you want to say to your mum?'

Emma just shakes her head. Instead, she asks her own, simpler question, 'Shall we have another glass of Champagne?'

'Oh yes, let's, love.'

After Emma has ordered, Betty asks, 'What did your mum think of Will?'

'Well, he was a good-looking corporate lawyer from an okay family, so she approved.'

'And she liked him?'

'I have no idea. I don't know if she ever really knew him.' Emma pictures her mother on their wedding day, beautiful in a white silk suit and enormous hat. No woman could have held a candle to her – certainly not the bride. Emma had expected such a display and didn't really mind – but then she had Will. He was all she thought about, that and knowing her dad would walk with her down the aisle. She wonders now if her father had already known he had cancer. He died less than a year later.

Betty is slowly turning her glass in her hand, 'Is it getting any easier, love?' She pauses. 'Will?'

Emma feels her defences rise, bracing herself for the pain. The wave washes over her, but this time does not knock her off her feet. All she can think to say is, 'Yes.'

Betty waits, but Emma cannot find any more words.

'Do you think you have forgiven him, love?'

'No.'

What else is there to say but the truth?

Emma books them into their hotel in Montmartre and from there takes Betty up the steep steps to Sacré Coeur. She wants her to be able to get her bearings and to see the expanse of Paris laid out below her. The sun has turned the underside of the clouds pink and the rooftops orange. Betty points excitedly to the Eiffel Tower in the distance, her curls gleaming tortoiseshell in the late afternoon light.

Over supper in a restaurant near their hotel, they discuss Emma's suggestions for the garden centre.

'I think you've gee'd Les up no end,' Betty says, as she nibbles away at the French bread. 'I heard him singing this morning while watering the plants. He hasn't done that in I don't know how long.'

'Does he think it would be easy to renovate the café?'

'Oh, that doesn't faze him at all, love. He's even talking of extending it to give it a veranda looking out over the downs and of growing a wisteria along it. He's always had a soft spot for wisteria. And just before I left, he said he had a few ideas of his own and would tell me about them when I got home.'

Emma feels a stab of longing to be back in the garden centre in the early morning, to hear Les singing to his begonias. Perhaps after a few days in Paris, it will be time to go home, to continue rebuilding her life, bedding in a new kind of normal.

As they walk back to the hotel, Emma checks her phone for the umpteenth time. There is still no news from Alistair.

Chapter 59

Violet

Primroses

Fat, burgundy snowflakes are falling from the sky. She stands at the porthole, craning her neck to peer upwards. A loud cheer goes up from the deck above and a few more flowers fall. Clove carnations are being tossed into the water where they float and spin in the waves. They bob for a final encore and are then sucked under by the churning water. A stray handkerchief joins them, floating through the air then crumpling like a broken kite. They are leaving Southampton, and the passengers are marking the occasion in the traditional way.

Normally a ship like the Titanic *would be accompanied by a flotilla of boats, tooting, piping and blasting their good wishes in a language all of their own. The coal strike has put pay to that and the water is strangely silent – but this only makes the cheers seem louder than normal, more distinct.*

She wonders if The Purser Priest, who has also transferred to the Titanic, *knew the men might throw their buttonholes into the air when the massive ship pulled away from the dockside. She feels sure he must have done. He is not a man who leaves things to chance; he is a man who understands that small details matter. She imagines he ensured that buttonholes were delivered to staterooms early in the day, rather than in the evening as was normal, just so they could be thrown.*

It seems a shame that the flowers have been consigned to a watery grave so soon. She would like to rescue one carnation and keep it in her cabin, but she would never be able to reach out far enough to catch one as it falls.

She is pleased to be sailing once more with The Purser, who is becoming her friend. There have been snatched conversations spread over many evenings, many journeys – a few minutes here, a few minutes there – in which she has talked of her sister, he of his wife.

Occasionally they have shared their plans for their gardens. The Purser's garden runs down to the canal at the back of his house and includes a rose garden, of which he is very proud. Her garden exists only in her imagination. They both know this, but it does not stop him asking how her dahlias have done this year, anxious to know whether the colours were as glorious as last. And it does not stop her replying.

She considers for a moment going up on deck. She has never been on deck for the start of a voyage and she would like to see the people lining the rail of the ship, waving to strangers and loved ones alike. But her place is below, unpacking and unfolding.

She thinks of that day many years ago, when her job was to pack and fold, when she helped fit her family's life into a number of small suitcases and baskets. Now she is pulling what seems to be a never-ending stream of silk and satin dresses from a large trunk. She feels like a conjuror as she shakes out the yards of material. She imagines a dove flying out from one of the case's many compartments, like she once saw with her sister in a theatre off Leicester Square.

As she lifts out an evening gown, a pretty blonde maid appears in the cabin, carrying a large vanity case made of dark green leather. Shaking out the dress, she can smell the fragrance of a lingering perfume emerging from the folds of silk. There is also the acrid smell of stale sweat and she wonders how well this maid knows her job. The young maid thanks her for her help and says she will take charge of the dresses. The maid is nervous and flushed. Perhaps it is her first post.

In the next cabin, she must tidy up the scattered possessions that have been thrown onto the bed, chairs and desk. She watched these passengers arrive, a couple of newly-weds who moved cautiously around each other, not yet used to the other's rhythm. Trapped together in the cabin they both faltered, movements quick and nervous. When he suggested they go up on deck to watch the ship depart, they both threw their possessions down in relief and headed swiftly for the open space. On deck they can stroll arm in arm as they did when they were courting.

She picks up a hat decorated with a scattering of lemon primroses. She would like to try it on – and privately thinks it would suit her better than the pale bride, who she feels should be decked out in warmer, blushing pinks. But her mother has always had very strict views on the subject of envy, and she is sure she would have something to say about coveting thy neighbour's hat. So instead, as she clears and tidies the space around her, she thinks of her own new hat, decorated with sweet peas. It is the prettiest hat she has ever owned. The only thing that would make it the perfect hat is if the sweet peas were real and she could breathe in their fragrance as she walked.

As the ship begins to move, she glances again at the primrose hat and allows herself one thought, which she does not think her mother would begrudge her: her sweet pea hat would not suit the new bride either.

Chapter 60

Emma

Jasmine

After ensuring Betty is safely aboard a sightseeing bus, Emma takes a train to the suburb where Philippe Hanchard lives. She turns down a leafy avenue leading away from the station. Despite the heat that is visibly rising from the tarmac in the road, the air is less oppressive here than in the city. She hopes the change in atmosphere will help with the headache taking up residence just behind her eyes. She pushes hair off her clammy forehead and steps deeper into the shade.

She finds the house halfway up the street, behind a set of large green, wooden gates. She can see very little from the road, only treetops and part of a roof. Philippe Hanchard buzzes her in through a small door set into the wall. A cobbled path leads away from the door, under an arch of purple bougainvillea, and along the side of a single-storey stone building.

As she turns the corner, she realises this is the back of a summerhouse. At the front, a series of double doors open on to a rectangular swimming pool. White, wooden loungers are arranged around it, and on a round table is a pile of navy and white striped towels. The pool shimmers turquoise in the sunshine and in the corner she can see lemon hibiscus heads turning lazy circles in the water.

Reluctantly, she leaves the pool and follows the path past lawns edged with rosemary, and terraces planted with golden rudbeckia and scarlet verbena. She can hear a sprinkler going somewhere in the distance. She approaches the house through an avenue of ceramic urns planted with marguerites. It is a low, rambling building: part Baroque and part curved modern extensions of smoke-coloured wood and glass. In front of the main door, up a short flight of stone steps, stands Philippe Hanchard, his long arms open.

'Welcome,' he says.

Emma follows Philippe across a pale, flagstone hallway into the kitchen.

'I'm rather presuming you would like a coffee?' he says, over his shoulder, as he approaches an electric-blue coffee machine.

'Yes please.'

'Good, I'll make these and then we can go into my study.'

They both speak in French, and Emma feels that the language suits such an elegant setting. She watches Philippe as he works. He is a tall, thin man with short grey hair cropped close to his head. In another era he could be a beautifully ageing Hollywood star – either that, or an elegant monk. She imagines he must be nearing seventy. He is extremely well dressed, but from his hands it looks like he does his own gardening. They emerge from his crisp white cuffs, brown from the sun, his knuckles like knotted wood.

'Your garden is beautiful,' Emma comments.

Philippe sighs contentedly. 'Now I'm retired, I spend most of my time there. My wife prefers to make our home a beautiful space, but for me it is always the garden.' He loads a tray with their coffees and a plate of honey-coloured macaroons and directs her to his study.

The study glows the colour of rosewood – the floor, the bookshelves and the desk are pale gold warmed with a hint of red. Three tall windows are shielded by muslin blinds, softening the bright August light that floods the room.

A door to the side of the desk appears to lead into a small, modern laboratory. She catches the glint of glass test tubes and bottles within. There is also an open wooden box on Philippe's desk containing four neat rows of glass phials. He explains that the day-to-day running of the business is undertaken in the South of France and in central Paris, but that he still likes to keep his hand – or rather, his nose – in.

Philippe gestures to two chairs by a low table. He sits down and hands her a coffee, before leaning back and crossing one long leg elegantly over the other.

'Thank you so much for meeting me,' Emma says.

'It's my pleasure. It sounds like an intriguing project,' Philippe comments. 'Tell me, have you found your florist on the *Titanic* yet?'

She puts her coffee cup down and tells Philippe about their

investigation and what she has concluded, although out of shyness she stops short of mentioning her feeling of connection with Violet. Her thoughts flit to Alistair, and she glances down at her phone, before continuing. 'I was fascinated by what you wrote about the phials of perfumes from the *Titanic*.' She looks around the room, smiling. 'I'm surprised you don't have flowers in here.' She knows Philippe is a world expert on floral fragrances.

'I keep flowers away from this room – indeed, anything that might interfere with my ability to smell the fragrances I'm studying. I shouldn't really be drinking coffee, but…' He shrugs. It is the type of shrug Parisians are famous for, but which you hardly ever see.

She draws a deep breath, unsure what to ask next, half fearing the debilitating shyness of old will resurface.

But she needn't have worried, Philippe dives into the subject that has been his lifelong passion. 'I think from the moment we started making perfumes, flowers were vital because they were the most obvious source of natural fragrance. In ancient times, it was through fragrance people spoke to the gods. And sometimes,' Philippe smiles, 'when I smell an exquisite floral fragrance, I believe the gods are speaking to me.'

Emma feels herself relax. 'So you think flowers are part of sending messages?'

'Yes – even if it is simply the message you want to convey about yourself by the perfume you wear.'

'Do you have a favourite floral fragrance?' she asks.

Philippe gets up and walks over to a large cupboard. He pulls open the doors to reveal rows of shallow drawers. As he slides one towards him, Emma can see they are divided into sections, each one containing a perfume bottle. He selects one.

Then Philippe talks at length about his own journey through fragrance, what inspired him and how he built his business. Their conversation delves into the chemistry of perfume making, and this, and his gentle charm, puts Emma completely at her ease. It is some time later that she remembers why she came here in the first place. She puts down the perfume bottle she is holding.

'How did you find out about the perfume phials on the *Titanic*?' she asks.

'A journalist came to me – he had heard about them being brought to the surface.'

'What were they doing aboard in the first place?'

'A German perfume maker, Adolph Saalfeld, was travelling to New York in the hope of making his name in the American market. The phials belonged to him.'

'And they lay intact for all those years?'

'Some were broken of course, but they eventually rescued three leather satchels containing, I believe, twenty phials.'

'And you have seen them?'

Just by his smile, she knows that he has.

'You could still actually smell the perfume?'

'Yes, but it was so much more than just a perfume. I am not sure the journalist I was talking to really understood that. It was Adolph Saalfeld's work – the hopes this man had for the future. It was the *Titanic*, an era encapsulated in a scent.'

'They say the flowers on board the *Titanic* filled the rooms with a fragrance so beautiful that it reminded passengers of the Riviera,' she tells him.

'Ah, that is fascinating. Now that would really be the true fragrance of the *Titanic*.' His eyes gleam, and she wonders if he would like to recreate that fragrance. 'Can you tell me more about the flowers they used?'

She takes him through the flowers she knows about and those she imagines would be on board based on the season and what was available and fashionable in 1912. He makes notes in a small black book with a slim silver pencil.

As he writes, it occurs to her that Roberto was right: people like to be asked for their help, especially – she's thinking of Alistair – when they share a common interest.

Emma looks down at the time on her phone. 'I am so sorry, Philippe – I've kept you for hours.'

'Not at all. It has been thoroughly enjoyable. Please, will you join me for something to eat and drink?'

Emma doesn't even try to put up a fight.

They sit under an umbrella at the poolside table, drinking white wine and sharing a goat's cheese salad. After lunch is over, Emma takes off her shoes and settles by the side of the pool with her feet dangling in the water. Philippe has been telling her about his daughter, Juliette, who now runs their family business. It is obvious he is enormously proud of her. As he speaks, she wonders if Philippe could be persuaded to join them all for her lunch under the apple trees in her garden. The picture forms once more in her mind: all the people who have helped her, gathered together in one place.

He stands up and passes her a fresh glass of wine. 'Do you have children, Emma?'

'No, my husband Will and I couldn't have children.' She is staring at the water, as she continues. 'My husband died just over a year ago. It's been hard. I found out, seven months after he died, that he'd had an affair…' She doesn't know why she adds this last part. Maybe the effect of the heat and the wine? Maybe because Phillippe is a stranger, and she's far from home? She wonders if by saying it out loud, it somehow lessens the power it has over her.

Philippe looks thoughtfully at her for a moment. 'Stay there,' he says, before disappearing towards the house. He reappears five minutes later carrying coffee cups balanced on top of the wooden box of phials Emma saw on his desk earlier.

'Did you know,' he says, as he unloads the coffee, 'that our sense of smell is the only sense that has a direct connection to the two areas of the brain most strongly associated with memory and emotion, the hippocampus and amygdala? That is why, when we come across familiar smells, we are transported back to the place we smelt them and how we felt.'

She nods, thinking of how the metallic scent of rain takes her back to that December day in the garden, seven months after Will died.

'Come up here,' Philippe beckons, putting the box aside and handing a towel to Emma. 'We are going to use fragrances as a way to consider the painful memories you carry. It is something my daughter and I have done together occasionally.' For a moment, a cloud passes over his face. 'There was a time when we did not speak for almost a year.'

He waits until Emma is settled and has her coffee in front of her, then asks, 'Is there a fragrance you particularly associate with your husband?'

Emma immediately answers, 'Sandalwood,' and he draws a phial from the box and hands it to her.

She opens the stopper and a spicy aroma drifts into the warm air. A memory threads its way towards her, as if summoned by the scent. She looks at Philippe trying to articulate her feelings. 'The first time I sat down beside him…' She passes a hand over her eyes. 'It was an old-fashioned smell for someone of our age and I remember thinking that was sweet, unexpected. But it was also unnerving.'

'How long were you together?' Philippe asks.

'We would have been married ten years last month.'

'I'm not going to ask you about his infidelity Emma – that would not be fair. But have you been able to forgive him?'

Emma so wants to say she has, but she shakes her head.

'It takes time,' Philippe says. It was a statement of fact. 'It took my wife two years and two weeks to forgive me.'

She looks sharply at Philippe.

'It took my daughter longer,' he adds.

Emma lets out a long breath.

'Were you unhappy with your wife?' She has to ask.

'No.'

Emma stares at him helplessly. 'Then, *why?*'

It is a long time before Philippe answers. 'Some people have affairs as a matter of course. Some believe they have connected with someone new in a profound way – that may or may not be true, of course. I had an affair for fun. Therein lies the depth of my vanity and my stupidity.' Philippe holds her eye for a second then frowns and turns away.

Emma watches the hibiscus flowers twirling slowly in the shimmering water at the side of the pool. 'Will wasn't the sort of man who had affairs. And I thought we were connected … but I wonder now if we had lost sight of each other.' She glances back at Philippe. 'He wasn't a vain man, but when he turned forty, maybe he felt something had changed. I don't think I got it, because he was very fit for his age. But maybe that was it – "for his age".'

She has been over this so many times in her mind since talking to Betty. Had Will been restless? Slightly distracted? Had he known at some subliminal level that there was something wrong, that the body he had always been able to rely upon was going to let him down? It is a knot she cannot undo.

'Loss and betrayal are a powerful combination to overcome.' Philippe turns back to her. 'Tell me Emma, can you think of a time when you have been really happy, on your own – without Will?'

She smiles crookedly at Philippe. 'Do I have to?'

'You know you do.'

Emma tears herself away from Will and the scent of sandalwood and searches for a memory. Her eyes start to gleam with a smile, before she is even aware of it.

'Tell me,' Philippe prompts, immediately noticing the change.

'I am in the Flower Cabin – that's the flower shop I work in. The people there with me are all helping search for The Florist on the *Titanic*.' She can picture Les sitting on an upturned dustbin, Betty beside him, Tamas leaning on the counter. 'I'm telling them about my research.'

'Close your eyes and tell me what you can smell in this Flower Cabin of yours.'

Emma holds her face up to the sun, and for a moment she thinks of Clem and the scent of her shop – do all flower shops smell the same?

'There are the lilies. They are the first to greet you when you open the door – they are big, pushy flowers, and their scent is heady and rich, full of importance.' She smiles, eyes still closed. 'Then when you step in, there is the sweet, powdery scent from the stock.' She pictures the dark-green enamel buckets filled with their plump, frilly heads – magenta, white, and peach. 'As you get closer, that's when you catch the scent from the more modest flowers. The roses are there: some cream, some pale lemon and a vase of tall roses the pink of cherry blossom. Their fragrance is subtle and understated, but if you lean your face close to theirs, you can catch the scent of an English garden in the summer.'

In her mind, she is now standing in front of the banks of flowers, searching for other fragrances – there is the smell of the wooden floor, and what else? She turns towards the counter.

'If we are lucky, we have some sweet peas in. We put them by the till, and usually the first people to see them buy them. No one can resist their scent.' She opens her eyes and looks at Philippe. 'And behind the smell of the flowers, there is a greenness, I don't really know how to describe it, but it's an important part of it all. Maybe it ... balances it?' She half laughs. 'I'm not really sure what I'm talking about.'

'You're doing splendidly,' Philippe assures her, turning to his box and busily searching through the phials. Eventually, he selects four and opens them. With his gardener's hands, he wafts the scent towards her.

'Oh yes,' Emma says. 'That's the beginning of it, for sure. That's how it smells when you first open the door.' With the fragrance comes the thought of Les, Betty and Tamas waiting for her behind the half-open door. She smiles, wondering if her perfect fragrance should have the smell of fresh coffee mixed in with it, too.

Philippe frowns slightly. 'I can tell this is a complex fragrance. It will be the middle notes that will speak to the heart of you. I wish we had more time…' He glances back to the house, and Emma can't help feeling he would like to be in his laboratory, experimenting.

'Jasmine,' Emma hears herself say suddenly.

'And what does Jasmine make you think of?'

'My father.' Emma can feel something shift within her. 'He died ten years ago. Four months after we got married.'

Philippe returns to the wooden box, then hands her a phial.

'Oh, that's my dad,' she says, opening it. 'Definitely. In his shed, which was really an old-fashioned greenhouse – part potting shed. On the wall at the back, he grew jasmine. I think it reminded him of Spain.'

She pictures the green wooden door with its peeling paint, sticking slightly as she pushes it open. She hears the door scraping on stone and then, then, the warm air is filled with the scent of jasmine. Sunlight falls through ancient glass, and in that mottled brightness, her father looks up and smiles at her.

She breathes in the scent from the phial once more. 'He loved his garden like you do – your hands are a bit like his.' Emma looks down at her own hands. It is so hard to describe her father; he is more of a feeling than a place or occasion. 'He didn't always say much, but it was the certainty of him… It was like having a hand in the small of your back that you can barely feel, but you know the hand will not let you fall.'

She inhales the jasmine and closes her eyes, fighting the tears. 'I never got to say goodbye.'

'Did he die suddenly?' Philippe asks, taking the phial gently out of her hand.

'Yes and no – he'd just started cancer treatment. We knew it wasn't good news. I'd been there at the weekend and was due back the following week, but he suddenly went downhill.'

Philippe stands up. Taking a pristine linen handkerchief from his pocket, he hands it to Emma, holding her hand for a moment as he does so. He glances towards the house and then nods as if reaching a decision.

'I am going to make you a perfume, English Emma. It is going to have deep within it a foundation of sandalwood blended with jasmine. But that will not be at the very heart of it. The heart will be the modest flowers that sit waiting for you in the flower shop, the flowers that tell a tale of an English garden. The top notes…' Philippe looks towards the house once more. 'I do not yet know what the top notes will be, but they will add a balance, a greenness to your perfume.' He smiles. 'I can tell you this though, Emma – it will be a perfume for your future.'

Chapter 61

Violet

Lily of the Valley

Everywhere she looks, there are boxes: boxes filled with liquor, chocolate boxes tied with sky-blue ribbons, cases stamped with the crest of great Champagne houses, squat boxes containing she knows not what – and in there, somewhere, are the boxes she must rescue.

This is the resting place of the latecomers, the last packages to be taken on board the Titanic. *They must be scooped up and ushered to their rightful places, like tardy children loitering outside school. They have just set sail, and this square space must be returned to normal as soon as possible. People will come and go, dresses sweeping the tiled floor like desultory maids. Then the voices will lift and fall in undulating conversation. But for now, the voices are loud and urgent, words tossed across the boxes.*

'Bring the one to your right. No! the box of brandy by your foot.'

'How many did you say were for Stateroom Six?'

'How in damnation can I see who it's for if they won't address it properly!'

'More chocolates for the family in Stateroom Three, sure they'll be as sick as pigs if they eat all this lot.'

She stands back to avoid being crushed by a man with enormous arms carrying what looks like a tea chest. She hears him mutter as he staggers by, 'What in God's name can they want with this?'

She is glad The Purser Priest is not around to hear it. She saw him earlier today as dawn was breaking and they were scurrying up onto the upper decks – ants heading for work. He nodded at her as she passed and said, 'Be so kind as to come and see me in my office when you've finished arranging your cabins.' He is a polite man, even at his busiest. Then he turned and was off, issuing more instructions, to the left and to the right. She could not see his face but imagined his eyes shifting, flicking, checking.

From where she is stood, her back to the wooden panelling, she catches the scent of something – not sweat this time, or Faithful Lover, or new paint, but something sweeter, more delicate. A fragrance is sneaking towards her through the piles of boxes.

She has only once seen lily of the valley growing wild. It was underneath a tree in the grounds of the orphanage where the boys lived for a time. The nuns were not women who lovingly tended flowers – if they had been, she thinks they would have known better how to care for the boys they grew. She remembers kneeling *on the grass by the flowers and burying her face in their petals and leaves. If the nuns came, she planned to look them straight in the eye and say she was praying; she would say the water on her cheeks was dew from the leaves. She remembers the delicate white flowers tickling her face and the scent, so green and clean and sweet.*

And now it is calling to her again across a field of boxes.

Chapter 62

Emma

Flowers of the Coral Tree

Both Emma and Betty are tired when they meet back at the hotel, so they decide to eat just around the corner in a bistro Emma spotted earlier. Betty has been to see many of Paris's famous landmarks and is clearly delighted with herself. She even managed a few French phrases when she stopped for lunch.

Over supper, Emma tells Betty about Philippe and the perfume he is planning to create for her.

'What a wonderful thing to do, love – he sounds like a very special man.'

A special man who had an affair, Emma thinks. She wonders if Betty is thinking the same.

When Emma tells her about using fragrance as a way to explore memories, Betty is particularly taken with this. 'So that explains why Les can't abide the smell of sweet peas,' she comments. 'I remember they filled the church with them when Big Les died.'

They are walking back to the hotel when Emma's text alert sounds.

'It's Alistair!' Emma glances briefly at the message. 'He wants to know if I'm free for a Zoom call.'

'Now this should be interesting,' Betty responds, picking up her pace.

Emma asks Alistair to give her ten minutes and hurries after the accelerating Betty.

They find a spot in the hotel library, a small room that serves as a coffee shop during the day but is currently deserted. Through the frosted glass doors at one end of the room, they can see glowing lights and hear laughter from the bar.

Emma has her tablet up on the table in front of them when Alistair calls. First, she introduces Betty and then she leaps in. 'So what have you found?' She meant to ask Alistair how he is – his face is inscrutable, and yet…

'Wait and see,' he says, raising a glass of wine in salute to her and Betty.

Alistair is sitting on a grey sofa, in what appears to be a plainly furnished sitting room. He has a black and white cat curled on his lap.

He leans forward and adjusts his screen before starting. 'Violet did write about her life – looks like it was in the 1930s when she decided to attempt her memoirs. She didn't have much success getting any interest in them, but a *Titanic* historian took them up, oh, years later, and you can read her extracts along with his analysis.' He pats the pile of books beside him on the sofa. 'I get the impression from reading his notes that he thinks some things are well recalled and some … less so. Maybe things shifted in her mind over the years. Also, there are some big gaps.' He takes a sip of his wine. 'For instance, she doesn't go into what actual work she did in a huge amount of detail. So I have to admit, at first I thought we'd drawn a blank.'

He leaves a long pause, and Emma and Betty glance worriedly at each other.

'But then I read the memoirs again, and the thing that began to strike me is that flowers featured throughout her life. I don't mean as window dressing, but as something with real significance for her. So, take her childhood – she grew up in Argentina, although her parents were Irish. She had four brothers and then a much younger sister, who I get the impression she was very close to. Violet was the eldest. Anyway, when Violet was writing about her childhood – and remember, she would have been really small – she was noticing the wildflowers on the Pampas, the flowers in the cities and also the flowers of the coral tree. I looked that one up,' Alistair adds proudly. 'It's Argentina's national flower.' He continues. 'She also has strong memories surrounding a death in the family. She wrote about a grave planted with … plumbago, I think it was?' He pauses. 'Have I said that right?'

'Yes, it's a trailing plant,' Emma says. 'It has small, baby-blue flowers.'

Alistair nods and pauses as his cat stretches out beside him, the tip of its tail waving across the bottom of the screen as if in lazy salute. 'Anyway, Violet also wrote about decorating her mother's hat with roses and – this is an amazing bit – when she was little and really ill in hospital, they moved her bed out into the garden so she could be among the flowers. At that point, they all thought she was going to die. She wrote that the doctor did it because they knew how much she loved flowers. Anyway, she's there in the garden supposedly dying and someone, I think her mum, brings her a huge bunch of honeysuckle which she knew Violet loved, and the smell of it revived her.'

'That's lovely. What was wrong with her?' Betty asks.

'I can't remember exactly – something to do with her lungs.'

'But she recovered?'

'Yes, thanks to the honeysuckle.' He grins, but then his face becomes serious. 'Sometime after that, her dad died and the family had to move to England.'

'So Violet would have spoken Spanish and English.' Emma finds this thought comforting.

'Anyway, they ended up near relatives in London, and that's when Violet's mum went to sea.'

'She was a stewardess?' Emma feels somehow vindicated – family following family.

'That's right. She went off and Violet was left at home in charge of her sister. Her little brothers went into an orphanage.'

'Oh, now that must have been tough,' Betty says.

Alistair nods. 'But not uncommon, sadly. In the end, her mum wasn't up to the work, and that's when Violet went to sea.'

'And the brothers?' Betty asks, looking worried.

Alistair smiles at her. 'Yes, Betty, the boys came home to mum.'

'Oh, love, that is good.'

Emma smiles, too, but she can't help thinking of Violet and her sister – that must have been a terrible parting.

They pause while Alistair gets up to refill his wine glass.

As he sits back down, Emma says, 'It's great of you Alistair to do all this.'

'Are you kidding? I'm really thinking of writing a module around this. It's fantastic stuff. You wouldn't mind, would you?'

Emma shakes her head.

'Were you serious about writing a book?' he asks.

'I don't know.'

'You should. Would you make it non-fiction or weave it into a novel?'

'Oh, I'm not sure. I just think there's a story in there … something about the stories that flowers have to tell. And,' she adds, slowly, 'something about family. How we follow our parents, and grandparents.' She smiles thinking of Alistair's tea-drinking Grandad.

'What is it, Em? There's something you're not saying.'

'I can't help wondering: why the *Titanic*? And more particularly, why I felt so drawn to Violet.'

'Kindred spirits?'

When she doesn't answer, Alistair continues, 'So, back to your kindred spirit. She went to sea and worked on a number of different ships, including the *Olympic* and then the *Titanic*.

324

Oh, and another great part of the story – you remember the doctor who got her bed put out into the garden? Well, this doctor had a bit of a thing for one of the nurses and Violet was a go-between for their love letters. They left the hospital before she got better, but years later, they bumped into Violet on board ship and were amazed to find she had survived and was then working as a stewardess. As I said, she didn't write that much about her work, so what she *did* write has special significance.'

'And?'

Alistair pauses, his expression impossible to read.

Chapter 63

Violet

Crimson Roses

She wraps the skirt of her new uniform tightly round her legs to slide through a small alleyway formed by wine cases. There is no point in collecting more dust, more work. She moves like the crab she once saw in the West Indies – a crab following a scent. And then she finds them: box upon box of flowers.

On the top, wrapped in muslin, are the lily of the valley. Beside them, dark and pungent, are bunches of violets tied with ribbon and lying in a basket. Beneath these are the boxes she must lift and sort.

First, she tweaks the corner of the top one. She tells herself this is just to check, but really it is because she cannot resist looking. Inside, she glimpses perfect rose heads, lying like crimson silk against the straw.

The steward with the large arms has returned, and she cajoles

326

him into helping her. He is busy: he has his own work to do; The Purser will be after him. But she knows she has him at the first smile. Sometimes, it is like offering a kitten a piece of wool; they cannot resist it. She knows that with his help, she will be able to move the flowers to the pantry in one trip.

She carefully unpacks the boxes, laying the flowers side by side, keeping the cards and messages in order. 'Bon Voyage', with the translucent white lilies; 'I love you, my Darling', with the rich roses; 'Bonne chance à New York', with the pale pink carnations; 'Safe journey, Dearest', with the violets. There is no message with the lily of the valley.

She finds other flowers like this – no message, just a name, sometimes a cabin number: the bronze orchids, the creamy white daisies and the tall yellow roses.

No one has ever sent her flowers, but if they did, she thinks she would like a card to come with them, handwritten with a message of love. She cannot imagine the words, but she thinks of dark ink and of curling handwriting against the white of paper.

She smiles a little as she trims the roses, flicking the thorns off the stems into the straw with her thumb. She is a hard worker, a busy young woman, and except in the worst storms, she is calm and efficient. She is also someone who tries to find the good in every situation. In this, she knows she is her mother's daughter. She thinks that her friends and family know this about her, but she is certain they do not know that she traces her finger wistfully over the cards that say, 'I love you'.

Before she begins to move the bouquets she has arranged into her passengers' cabins, she stands still, surrounded by dozens of flowers – glorious fresh blooms, their fragrances mixing into a unique perfume just for her. For a few minutes, these are her flowers. No other passenger on the ship will have the joy of such abundance or hold so many kind and loving messages in their hand.

Chapter 64

Emma

Anemones

Alistair is still silent (and Emma and Betty are holding their breath) when he suddenly grins, declaring, 'Violet *did* arrange the flowers on the *Titanic*.'

'Really?!' Emma is aware of having squawked. 'Really?'

'Oh, my goodness!' Betty exclaims simultaneously.

Alistair laughs. 'I was trying to keep a straight face – couldn't do it. But yes – she did. On board, she had a number of passengers to look after, and she wrote about arranging their flowers. Apparently, boxes and boxes of flowers arrived for the voyage as gifts, and she struggled to get enough vases for them all.'

'Amazing,' Emma says, sitting up in her chair.

'She wrote about those roses you told me about.'

'What? American Beauty?'

'Yes, those boys.' He frowns slightly. 'She doesn't mention

doing flowers around the ship,' he sounds regretful, 'but that's not to say she didn't. The way I figure it is, the young stewardesses got more than their share of the work, so she would have been one of the first the purser asked to help with the flowers. And he knew Violet from their time together on the *Olympic* – they were friends, apparently.'

'Yes, and if she had been able to decorate her mother's hat with fresh roses, I bet she could have made a corsage and buttonholes.' Emma smiles to herself: a girl with the gift of flowers. But something is bothering her – a memory of something she has read but can't quite recall.

'What's up, Em?'

'I'm just trying to remember … no, hang on, it might be in my notebook.' She darts up from her seat, returning a few minutes later, by which time Alistair and Betty are deep in conversation. It appears Betty has found out all about Alistair's sisters and the rest of his family, too.

Emma sits back down and flicks through her notebook. After a few minutes, she lets out a triumphant yelp, 'Got you!'

Betty looks at her expectantly.

'And?' Alistair prompts.

'*And* the purser of the *Titanic*, Hugh McElroy, was a man who liked flowers and understood the importance of them.' She knew it was there somewhere.

'How do you make that out, love?' Betty asks.

'The night before the *Titanic* sailed, he took his wife to the ballet.' Emma is momentarily sidetracked. 'That's so sad – that would have been the last time she saw him.'

'Flowers, Em,' Alistair urges.

'Right, yes – it was a famous Danish ballerina who was dancing, and Hugh McElroy organised flowers to be sent to her dressing room after the performance. He chose a special bouquet in her national colours, including red and white anemones. Now *that* is a man who thinks about flowers – *that* is a man who would have wanted his passengers to have beautiful flowers around them. You say he was friends with Violet? Then he must have known she loved flowers, too, and that she had the skill to arrange them. So surely she would have been the obvious choice for helping with flowers for the public rooms and for special bouquets for passengers.' She looks expectantly at Alistair, desperate for him to agree.

'I'll buy that.'

She laughs, shakily. 'You *do* think I'm right, don't you?'

'Yes, Em,' he says patiently.

'I certainly do,' says Betty.

The three of them sit quietly for a moment. There is a burst of laughter from the adjoining bar.

'So how do you feel now?' Alistair breaks the silence.

'On one hand, still confused as to why I think I recognise Violet, yet on the other I'm pleased and I suppose proud to think we've found a florist on the *Titanic* – even if it's not the traditional florist I was envisaging at the start. And I think you were right in what you said in London – you shouldn't ignore someone's contribution just because it's only a small part of a bigger team.' She smiles at Betty.

'That's history for you, Em,' Alistair says, ruefully, 'I should know. People think it's about finding one big truth – something no one else knows. But it doesn't really happen like that. In fact, a lot of egos have crashed and burned chasing after one spectacular historical find. Most of the time it's small discoveries, tiny triumphs. When you add your bit to the mix you're fitting into a much bigger picture. Then when you stand back and look at it, you don't really see your bit anymore, but you do notice the other people standing beside you gazing at the same view…'

'And?' Emma prompts.

'And then, if you have any sense, you all go to the bar and have a few drinks.'

Emma smiles at him. The three of them are looking at the same view now. It's like her scientific work. Terrible genetic conditions, diseases, viruses – only ever beaten when people worked together.

Her mind drifts to her home and her garden. Her plan to gather together all the people who have helped her returns – she will mow the lawn under the apple trees and cook lunch for them all. She could serve butternut-squash ravioli to start and then slow roasted lamb, and maybe hang some lights from the branches above the table.

Her thoughts are interrupted by Alistair. 'Look, I've got to head out now, but I wanted to catch you before I went. There's more stuff to do with what happened to Violet in later in life, but I'll email you all that.'

'Fantastic,' Emma says, gratefully. She is feeling lightheaded with all they have learnt and wonders if Betty feels the same.

She seems unusually quiet and thoughtful.

'Look, before I go, there's one other thing I did want to show you. I'm going to hold it up the screen so you can read it for yourself.'

She leans forward.

There, on the screen is an extract that Alistair has highlighted – words written by Violet Jessop, stewardess of the *Titanic*: *I myself could not live without flowers.*

'Oh! There you go, love,' Betty enthuses, losing her air of self-absorption.

As Alistair's screen goes blank, Emma finds she is lost for words. She links her arm with Betty's and squeezes it tight. Her mind cannot seem to take in all they have found out and how far they have come. She feels exhausted and giddy, but also exhilarated. She doesn't know quite what to do with herself. She turns to Betty, and it strikes her that she looks tired. 'What now—?' she starts, thinking perhaps they should head for bed.

But it seems Betty has other ideas.

'I rather liked Alistair's idea of all those historians getting together and sharing a drink. I do feel we ought to celebrate.' She glances towards the warm glow of the bar. 'Do you know, love, I have never had a Champagne cocktail and I rather think I would like to try one.'

Emma grins and pulls her friend to her feet, dismissing the ache that is now working its way down her neck to her back.

'Then that is exactly what we'll do,' she proclaims as she leads the way to the bar.

Chapter 65

Violet

Daisies

She stands just inside the doorway for two, three seconds, watching. The Purser is writing at his desk, his fountain pen flicking across the page, bold but neat, in the manner of the man. She thinks of the handwritten letters of love attached to the bouquets she has arranged. She does not wish for this man to write to her – he is a married man and some years older than her – but she would not mind if she met someone who grew into such a man. When she thinks of the word 'Gentleman', The Purser is who she thinks of.

She knows there are men who have been born to this title, and she has met many such men on board ship. Some are considerate men who remember her name – but most would not think to help her if she dropped something or struggled to open a door while carrying a loaded tray. Sometimes she wonders if they even see her at all. She thinks maybe these men have had the title of Gentleman for so long they have worn it thin, like an old shirt.

'Ah, Violet.' The Purser looks up. 'Come in.' He checks his watch. 'Do you have everything you need?'

This is his way of asking if everything is just so. She assures him all is well, happy that she will not be found wanting. She is rewarded by a smile.

'Well then, sit awhile – a few moments' peace will harm no one.'

She sits down on the chair by his desk but does not let her back ease into it. If she gave in to this comfort, she fears she would never get up again.

They talk of the time they spent with their families before boarding the ship. He remembers to ask after her sister, and she hopes that his wife is well. He tells her they had a grand send-off with a night at the ballet and supper afterwards. He says his wife looked very fine in a new dress.

'And what do you think of our great ship, the Titanic*?' he asks.*

She tells him she thinks it a shame that the passengers must be on board.

When he laughs, she tries to explain.

'It will never again look as it does on its maiden voyage. Everything is so beautiful and new. Everything is in the right place.' Despite herself, she is warming to the imposter.

'Ah, but even a beautiful stage is nothing without the players.'

She wonders if he is thinking of the ballet, and she knows the passengers are lucky to have such a man looking after them. If she were The Purser, she might be tempted to pull up the gangplanks and sail away without them.

He picks up his fountain pen, and he is back to the business of the ship. 'I have been looking through your passenger list and have made a note here.' He indicates the name of a gentleman, a rising man in the world. 'His man sent instructions. He is particular about the buttonhole he wears and requires a white rose each evening. You will see to it?'

He is kind enough to phrase it as a question, but she knows that there is only one answer. She nods, but he does not notice. He is back to the list. He points to another name. It is a woman she knows of old from other voyages, other ships. She can hear her mother's voice: 'That woman has a tongue that could clip a hedge'. For some reason, she is not frightened of this woman, perhaps because she has learnt that her very lack of fear infuriates the Hedge Clipper so.

The Purser catches her eye. 'Precisely,' he says. It is enough.

He hands her a telegram. In it are instructions for flowers for her stateroom – a gift from her son. When her other son finds out about this, as no doubt he will from his mother, she suspects there will be more flowers to follow. The Hedge Clipper appears to delight in dangling her two sons like puppets, as they dance a jig for her favour and their expected inheritance. She has learnt this from her maid who is a watchful woman, known to be generous with her observations when she takes her nightly inch of whisky. After the second inch she sometimes prophesies, 'She should be careful. One day they will get together and bury her in her garden and that will be the end of that'.

The Purser continues. 'I will leave the choice of flowers to you. I know I can rely on your good taste.'

This is high praise from The Purser, who likes flowers almost as much as she does.

She suggests a seasonal mix of spring flowers. She has already been to check the flowers in the store and is on nodding terms with the daffodils and narcissi. She also found a container brimming with lily of the valley, but she does not think the Hedge Clipper deserves these.

'Have you been to see the Ritz?' he asks suddenly.

This is the nickname of the à la carte restaurant on board. She is unsure if he will mind that she has already explored the ship with her cabinmate. Certainly, he would not approve of their riding the elevator with the lift steward and bellboy for three trips.

She is relieved when he does not wait for an answer.

'The tables are decorated with roses and daisies. They do look … just so…'

The Purser is a Christian, but she knows he still does not like to be outdone by the manager of the Ritz.

'I think we should have some flowers arranged in the first-class lounge for the passengers,' he remarks.

'Bowls of roses and lily of the valley would be pretty,' she suggests, 'and the scent would be very welcoming.'

He smiles. 'Ah, lily of the valley, one of my wife's favourites.'

The Purser Priest is not a card player or a gambler, but they both know that lily of the valley trumps daisies.

'You will see to it?' he asks, and this time it is a question. He smiles like a little boy who once enjoyed toffees and beetles and jokes.

'I will indeed, sir.'

At the door he calls her back. 'Violet…' His face is expressionless, but his eyes are gleaming still, 'Bealing's brought a particularly fine delivery of flowers for our maiden voyage.'

She knows this. The scent as she opened the flower store door was so beautiful it made her cry. She does not tell The Purser this. She just waits, interested to hear what is coming next from the man with the gleaming eyes.

'We should not forget that God's creations should be appreciated in their abundant glory.'

And so, The Purser Priest has given her his instructions. She should not stint in her endeavours – as a Bible reader, she knows this is the equivalent of being told to use her talents.

Much as The Purser does not like to be outshone by the manager of the Ritz, so she does not like to be cast in the shade by the other stewardesses helping arrange the flowers on the Titanic, even though some of them are her friends. She will happily follow The Purser's instructions to the letter: nothing will compare with the flower displays in the first-class lounge.

Later some might even say that the fragrance from the flowers reminded them of the Riviera and that, without a doubt, it appeared that the Titanic was a ship full of flowers.

Chapter 66

Emma

Silk Amaryllis

In the bar, Betty is sipping her second Champagne cocktail. Emma feels exhausted and would have gladly gone to bed after the first, but she hasn't wanted to spoil Betty's fun.

Betty has been talking about how much they have to tell Les, Tamas and Clementine. Emma mentally adds Guy, Mrs Pepperpot, Roberto and Philippe to the list. Perhaps she will go back to the library and seek out the friendly, smiley assistant who helped her right at the start.

Betty is looking thoughtful now, and Emma is reminded of her sudden silence when talking to Alistair earlier. 'What's up?' she asks.

'Oh, nothing really, love. It's just I wonder what happened to Violet the night the *Titanic* sank.'

'She definitely lived,' Emma reassures her.

'Yes, I know – I remember you telling us about her surviving three shipwrecks.' Betty smiles. 'It's just that I feel I've got to know her a bit now, and I was wondering how she managed to survive.'

Emma nods. 'I know what you mean. Alistair said he was sending some more information – maybe we'll find something in there.'

Betty nods. 'What else do you want to do while we're in Paris?' she asks.

Emma studies the cocktail glass in her hand. 'I thought tomorrow I'd go to Mum's apartment and dig out all the old family photos and documents.' She shrugs. 'You never know.'

Betty pats her knee. 'Indeed you don't. And there's your family tree to look into, too – I remember you said you were getting somewhere with the Spanish side of the family.'

Emma nods. This is true. Through a few Spanish websites, she has pieced together more on her dad's family. But as yet, there is nothing that could possibly link her to Violet Jessop.

Betty insists on paying for their drinks, despite Emma's protestations. As Betty heads to the counter, Emma stands up and crosses the bar, slipping into the ladies' toilets.

At first, she thinks the crash is someone dropping a colossal pan in the kitchen. Then she sees her phone, spinning towards the bathroom's outer swing doors, and she realises her legs have gone from under her.

As her head smashes into the sink and she hits the floor, she has no sense of the rest of her body, just the sickening sound of her cheekbone and temple hitting the marble.

There is no pain, just sound.

From where she lies, she watches the door fly open and Betty appears, her face as white as the marble she is stood upon.

Emma watches as a large metal planter rocks back and forward on its side, amaryllis scattered around it. She knows they are too orange to be real. She wants to tell Betty this but finds she cannot speak.

She can only watch as scarlet blood seeps towards the flowers along the grey veins in the marble. She wants to say: *Now that's the colour red they should be.*

She comes to as they ease her onto a stretcher. She cannot see Betty anymore, just a man and woman in uniform. There is now no sound, but the pain is crushing her head, eating into her skull, and she tries not to cry out. As she is carried through, drinkers from the bar move aside, hands together, heads bowed as if at a funeral. She sees another man in uniform by the door, relaxed, casual, chatting to the girl from behind the bar. He fancies her, she thinks – and then someone puts a mask over her face, and Emma sinks into the darkness.

Chapter 67

Violet

Hyacinths

It is cold on deck, and she regrets not bringing her winter coat on this trip. Her mind had been set on New York in the spring: the avenues, the parks, the blossom and sunshine that on some days can make it feel like an English summer.

Despite the cold, she likes to come out on deck each evening. She stands back, making room on the promenade for the young men who are heading for a night cap – or three. She has seen that look before – the night is young and so are they. She is young, too, but she feels a hundred years older than the sleek-headed men who walk like they own this deck. Older, yes, but not necessarily wiser. She imagines these men have winter coats in their cabins.

A young woman steps out of a doorway on the arm of an elderly man. She holds the door open for them, and the woman nods at her as she passes by. She leaves behind a fragrance in her wake –

an unfamiliar perfume, intense and sweet. But among the mix of scents, there is something she recognises: she is transported back home to the bowl of hyacinths that her sister gave their mother for a birthday present.

She walks past the windows of the first-class lounge and looks in. She smiles to see the banks of flowers, the droplets of water on the petals sparkling like crystals in the light. It pleases her to think that The Purser's flicking eyes will have alighted on them. She can imagine his smile as he thinks of the daisies at the Ritz. She allows herself a smile, too.

In the glow from the lamps, she can see the gowns she has brushed and hung now filled with flesh and bone. Some women spill from the tops of their dresses, arms plump and white, while others look like the dressmaker has sent them a size too large. Her mother would want to give these women a good meal – whether they wanted it or not. Then there are the women who wear their gowns like a glorious second skin – you cannot see where the shimmering cloth ends and the milk white shoulder begins. They are luminous creatures that turn and glisten in the light, diamonds sparkling as brightly as the stars above her head. These beautiful women walk like they own the world, not just the deck beneath their satined feet. She thinks maybe they are right.

She turns her face to the sea and walks over to the rail. The wooden varnish is smooth under a hand that she knows is rough from stripping roses. The air is so sharp that she only takes in small gentle breaths, not wanting to fill her lungs all at once with the icy air. She once fell into a stream as a little girl, and the cold reminds her of this. The water was not high, but then neither was she.

As her father strode in and pulled her up into his arms, the cold had made her heart pound so much she could not drag in a breath.

She has still not learnt to swim, but few she has met on board have. They prefer to spend their time on shore sitting with friends and family, swapping stories and smoking Faithful Lover. If it came to it, they say it will be up to God, and they would prefer a quicker ending.

In the years that follow she sometimes returns to the memory of this moment, looking out into the icy darkness. Did she feel a premonition of tragedy? Did a feeling of unease seep into her like the icy air? She can never quite decide.

Chapter 68

Emma

No Flowers

Emma can hear voices but cannot open her eyes. It seems like something is pressed over them. She thinks she hears Betty's voice, but it can't be her. This woman is trying to say something in French. She knows Betty is in the garden centre with Les, where they only speak English.

She is swimming upwards but cannot break the surface. Voices bubble through the water that seems to fill her ears. She tries to listen to the words, focus on each one in turn. The more she listens, the more the words take shape and she can string them together to make something of them in her mind.

The man is speaking in English with a French accent. She thinks of Philippe and of striped towels by a swimming pool.

'Your friend has an injury to her head and her blood pressure is not good. That could be to do with the fall, but we are wondering why she fell in the first place. Do you know if she has any health problems?'

Emma wonders who this man is talking about. She thinks she should find out but nothing seems worth that much effort.

Betty answers, which strikes her as odd. 'As far as I know, she's fine. She has been under quite a lot of strain. She is…' Hours seem to pass. 'I have noticed she's been looking very pale and dark-eyed over the past few weeks.'

'Any allergies?' someone says.

'I don't think so,' Betty replies, 'but I can't be sure.'

'Well, there is nothing more we can do now. We are going to monitor her progress and we will be running tests in the morning. We wondered if she may have an underlying heart condition – do you know if there is any history in the family?'

'Her husband died of a heart attack… No, no, I'm sorry, that's hardly…'

An image of Will walking away floats before Emma's eyes.

'Her father died of cancer – I believe it was lung cancer. Her mother is still alive. Leave it with me. Oh, goodness… I'll have to try to contact her mother.'

Emma wants to tell Betty that she is doing really well. She sounds so worried. But no words come.

'That would be helpful,' the man says. 'Right, we have your details – we will call you if there is any change.'

'I'm not leaving. I don't have to leave, do I?'

'No, of course not. It won't be me you will see again, but another doctor will be in in the morning.'

'What time is it?' Betty sounds bewildered.

'3.15 a.m. Try and get some sleep.'

Emma does as Betty is told.

Emma knows she is lying on a bed and that the glow from the light in the corner of the room is blue. She supposes it is night for no other reason than because there is no sunshine.

She can see the outline of a person asleep in a chair beside her bed. She tries to turn her head towards them, but the pain makes her gasp. She can just see the top of a curly head and the door to her room that stands half open.

She watches as people walk past the door: some are strangers – doctors she supposes. She knows that much. Sometimes people from her youth pass by; her old Spanish teacher; a friend from college; and then, Roberto in his long white apron. None of these people come in.

She feels no surprise at seeing them, but the people she most wants to see – Will and her father – do not pass by.

Someone is asking where she comes from. She hears Betty answer, so maybe they aren't talking to her. Betty says something about Oxford and the person asks if that is near London.

Later, she hears Betty telling someone where Oxford is. 'Yes, quite close to London.'

Later. 'No, it's not in London, but not far away.'

Years later she hears Betty again. She is saying, yes, she lives in London. Emma wonders why she is lying.

She swims in and out of time. When she is submerged, there is nothing; when she breaks the surface, there is heat. Through half-closed lids she can see the open door and the blue light.

Once she wakes in a capsule, machinery all around her.

Sometimes people circle her bed and move her – an arm lifted, a body rolled.

Afterwards, she settles back into the heat, watching the half-open door through lashes that blur her vision. When she sees her mother walk through the door, she knows she must be dreaming.

So she sinks back and lets the darkness take her.

Hours pass; it may be years. She tries to think the sheets off her burning legs, keep their weight away from her body. Nothing moves but the heat pulsing in time with her breathing. Breaths so loud she struggles to catch the doctor's words.

Someone is crying.

Betty.

It is a soft and plaintive sound and makes something within her ache.

She thinks it is the sound of sorrow.

She cannot find Betty to comfort her; she cannot tell her it is all going to be all right.

For she remembers she is woman who no longer believes in happy endings.

Chapter 69

Violet

Scattered Orchids

She wonders if it is God or her father watching over her when she is called to one of the last lifeboats simply because she speaks Spanish. They need someone to help those who are struggling to understand English.

She hands the passengers into the swaying boat, but in truth, she needs their hands to steady her on the tilting deck as much as they need hers to guide them. There is a delicate, cool, scented hand, a plump hand that clutches hers too tightly, a manicured masculine hand that pulls away from her as if scalded by the shame of needing assistance – or maybe he knows he should be giving way to others. In among them is a firmer, broader hand, more calloused than the rest. And for a moment she thinks it is her father's hand in hers, guiding her. When she looks to see who it belongs to, there is nothing but the backs of dark wool overcoats and the merging of fur wraps and worsted stoles.

When at last she joins the lifeboat, they hang suspended alongside the ship and she is caught between a world of warmth and light, and a world of chilling blackness. Despite the push and the shove of it, the warm world is yet enticing. She recalls the Olympic, *The Purser's assurance that the watertight doors would hold firm. The deep, still blackness holds no assurances – no moon to bring comfort, just high above, the brilliant, unblinking stare of thousands of indifferent stars.*

She wraps the eiderdown she has borrowed off a stateroom bed more tightly around her. Her friend the second-class steward found her in her cabin and urged her to dress in her warmest clothes. Only as his normally respectful hands plucked garments from her wardrobe did she finally register his fear. When he brought forth her sweet pea hat from the cupboard, she took it gently from his grasp, telling him that it was not the hat to wear to a shipwreck.

He held her hands for a long moment and said softly, 'You must wrap up warm.' In that whisper, she heard her mother, the woman who is always right.

With her mother's voice chivvying in her head, she made a detour into one of the staterooms. She thought how strange it was that she should be able to have her pick of these. All the doors were open, and clothes, shoes, cases, flowers, even jewels lay scattered on the carpet beneath her lurching feet. She stepped over a scattering of orchids and plucked an eiderdown from the bed. With no winter coat, she hoped no one would begrudge her this.

Now, suspended in the lifeboat between the contrast of light and dark, she imperceptibly leans towards the comfort of the light.

A woman next to her rises and, shaking free of her companion, scrambles out of the boat – the light has won. The woman is swallowed by the swarm of bodies that swirl on deck. There are cries and shouts but there is also laughter. She thinks of the young men. She wonders if they had another nightcap; perhaps they think it will give them protection against the cold.

She feels the lifeboat sway beneath her. This way? That way? Then she sees the steward of the sweet pea hat rush by, and she remembers the persistent pressure of his hands. He is followed by The Purser.

She has never seen The Purser Priest run before.

And it is then that she knows she must stay where her father's hand led her.

The winch beside them screeches, and a young engineer pushes them away from the side, shouting instructions to those behind him. Another figure appears close to her left shoulder; her head is now level with his knees. He reaches down – he clearly knows her, but she cannot see his face, and afterwards can never recall his name.

'Here, you, Miss Jessop, take care of this.'

The urgency of his voice causes her to stretch her arms upwards. Into these he half pushes, half drops a bundle wrapped in a blanket. Instinctively she clutches it to her. She hopes he hasn't stolen something from the scattered possessions and that she will be taken up as a thief.

As she pulls back the edge of the blanket she feels the lifeboat start to drop.

Chapter 70

Emma

Violet

All is quiet except for the gentle hum of the blue light. Emma teeters on the edge, her body poised as if for a drop. She listens.

'You can tell a lot about a person by the flowers they send to a funeral.'

Emma looks at the young woman standing by her bed. 'Did I say that or did you?' she asks.

'Maybe you thought it,' the girl replies. She has auburn hair tucked into a white cap, and blue-grey eyes. Emma knows her but can't remember from where. She pauses, looking down at Emma. 'What flowers would you like? Do you have a favourite flower?'

'Peonies – it would have to be white peonies. And…' Emma has lost the word, but she knows she could find it if she could smell it. The flowers have a distinct fragrance, headily perfumed

352

but delicate. Then it comes to her. 'Jasmine. How about you?'

'My mother thought honeysuckle was my favourite, but really I've always loved roses the best.'

She seems so familiar. How does she know her? The answer seems just out of reach.

'Can I have two choices?' the girl asks. 'You had two.'

'Of course – it's your funeral.'

The girl smiles, and Emma thinks she does, too.

'Roses and lily of the valley.'

'Good choices,' Emma agrees.

The young woman sits on a chair that she hadn't noticed before by the side of her bed. She has on a black dress and a white apron.

'Are you a nurse?'

'Not yet.'

The girl isn't making sense, but she doesn't want her to go.

'If I'd had a daughter, I think I would have called her Rose. Or possibly Lily,' the girl says. 'I never had any children.'

'Do you regret that?' As Emma asks this, she hears a bell ring. Somewhere in the distance a little boy with black hair and sticking-out ears flicks a bell as he pedals furiously away on a bicycle.

'Oh, I regret a lot of things, but as my mother said … no, it's gone … something about another door opening, I think.' She smiles a little wistfully. 'She also said that children could be a gift even if you weren't a mother.' The girl tucks a stray curl back into her cap and says more matter-of-factly, 'I tell you what I *do* regret. Not taking my toothbrush with me that last night. It's a small thing, but you have no idea how much you can miss a thing like that. Yes…' She pauses. 'I've found that it's always the small things that end up meaning the most. You don't realise it at the time.' The girl looks round, as if to check no one is listening. 'I did once think about the jewels, though. It was only once mind, when the roof needed mending. In the end, the boys came to visit, all the way from Australia, and had it fixed in a trice. I never really would have taken the jewels, you know.'

'What jewels?'

'It was when I went into that stateroom and fetched the eiderdown. There they were, scattered like chicken feed on the bed and floor. Only, it was diamonds and rubies instead of corn.'

'Did you think about picking them up?'

'It never so much as crossed my mind – only much later did it occur to me I could have done. At the time, all I thought was, there you go, Purser – I told you the passengers would mess up your beautiful ship.'

'What was he like?'

'The Purser? A real gentleman. His great-nephew came to see me, you know. Sweet boy, he'd just bought a new car. He was that proud. And didn't he have the look of The Purser Priest. It was uncanny.'

The room falls silent. Nothing moves in the corridor beyond the half-open door, and all Emma can hear is the faint buzz of the blue light.

Then she hears another sound, a rasping sound, and she realises it is coming from deep within her. Words are becoming an effort, but there is something she wants to tell this girl.

'You know I've been looking for you?'

The girl looks down at her. 'Maybe I've been looking for you. Have you thought of that?'

'Then you *do* know me?' As Emma whispers this, it sounds all wrong. Surely she wants to know how she knows this girl, not the other way around? There does not seem to be enough time to untangle the words, so instead she asks, 'Will you sit with me for a bit?'

'As long as you like.'

'I don't want to be on my own.'

'You haven't been on your own for some time now, but I think you know that already.'

She does.

'Is dying difficult?' Emma asks.

'Oh, not at all. It's living that takes some getting used to.'

Chapter 71

Violet

Baby's Breath

She unwraps the makeshift blanket parcel and stares in amazement at the baby in her arms. The surprise soon turns to concern.

She wraps the eiderdown she has borrowed to keep her warm around its tiny form. She wonders where the baby's parents are. She looks around the boat as if expecting to find the baby's mother or father there, and is surprised to see they have already launched and are rowing away from the ship.

All night as they drift, helpless in the cold, the tiny baby in her arms is her anchor. When the Titanic gives out a rending moan, splits and sinks, she soothes the baby as she cries.

She carries the baby close to her heart, tucking her hands around her tiny fingers. She sings an old song her mother taught her, the words muddled, her voice a whisper – but it helps to dampen the sounds that wash with the waves towards their boat.

As the night progresses and an awful silence settles, she and the sea rock the baby, and sometimes the baby sleeps. Then she holds her face close to hers, breathing in the scent of the baby's head. She remembers holding her baby sister like this, and the thought brings her closer to her.

She reaches into the pocket of her skirt and runs her fingers over the stiches of the sampler she has tucked there. A precious gift – just like the baby in her arms.

Chapter 72

Emma

Funeral Flowers

She feels the movement of the bed and watches the ceiling tiles flitting overhead. They seem to have positioned her like a doll, tucked with both arms outside of the sheets – or maybe this is how they lay you out for a funeral?

But as they wheel her through the corridor, it is definitely Betty beside her. She doesn't think Betty would be with her if she was already dead, although she is quite prepared to believe that Betty might be an angel.

The figure accompanying her doesn't look like Betty – she looks tired and is wearing a plain blue shirt – but Emma can tell it is her, because she hasn't stopped talking.

'... So you'll be in surgery for a few hours – they've given you something to relax you now, but I'll be with you until they take you in and they say I can be with you when you wake up.'

Emma tries to say something, but her mouth is so dry it seems cemented shut.

'They thought at first it was your heart, and I was that worried, love, I felt sick. And anyway, I got hold of your mum in the South of France, and by the time she got here – it took her a day or two, but come she did – they had run more tests, and, love, you are so anaemic they said it was a miracle that you were still standing. That didn't seem to worry them too much and they gave you a blood transfusion – really, they have been very good. They ran all sorts of tests, and at first they thought you were fine, that you would just need some iron pills and so forth, once you'd come round from the bump on the head, but when they scanned your head they found there was a fragment of bone loose from where your eye socket cracked and they were a bit worried about it causing a blockage if it travelled into your brain, so they're going to sort it out. They've had to shave some of your hair away, but it will grow back as good as new, and short hair is very fashionable these days. And some have a bit of short and a bit of long, and everyone seems to like that. So now the infection is under control … did I tell you that? They think you may have got it when your head hit the floor. They've done an amazing job at getting rid of that – you were completely away with the fairies, love. Oh my goodness, yes. But as I was telling you, they think they can operate now and sort you out. They're *sure* they can operate.'

Betty stops suddenly. Emma can hear the bed wheels clicking as they turn. Then Betty says in a quiet voice, 'It will be okay, love. I know it will.'

She knew from the talking that Betty was nervous. Now, the abnormal quiet tells her she is truly frightened.

As the wheels keep turning, she thinks of Will. Would he be waiting for her? She thinks he might be. Or maybe she will catch a glimpse of him again, running – eyes on the horizon like he believes he can get there.

She wants to tell Betty that she must not worry, that if he is there, it will be okay – she will be where she is meant to be. She wants to tell Betty that she has already chosen her funeral flowers.

But no words come.

Chapter 73

Violet

Dahlias

If walking among the flowers of the Pampas is her beginning, she hopes walking among the flowers of her own small garden will mark her ending.

She is an old woman now. Her hair is grey, and she feels the wear and tear from years of fetching and carrying deep in her joints. She likes to think she has lived a full life, rich with travel, friendship and family – even if she did not have her own children to care for, nearby she has her sister and her nieces and nephews.

Over the years, unwanted memories have stalked her. She has learnt that she cannot outrun these but she can move more erratically than they can. She can spin on a heel and dodge into a distracting thought or pinch her weary limbs and force them into action – get up, turn the radio on, make a cup of tea, walk in the garden to greet the dawn.

Sometimes the memory of The Purser comes, unbidden, on these early morning walks. He asks her how her flowers are doing, and she invites him to follow her to see how glorious the dahlias are this year. The thought of flowers helps divert her from the sadness that, in the early years, felt like it might tear her in two.

Sometimes, the memories get tired of playing the stalking game, and they lie in wait to ambush her. Like the night when she was poised on the top step of the stairs down into the London underground. The air-raid warning was sounding and she was holding on to the handrail, jostled by those pushing past her. She was paralysed by fear. Should she go down below or stay up in the freezing night air? This way? That way?

She stood there, a middle-aged woman, terrified, unable to move, not knowing which decision would save her – which would kill her.

She watched a mother carrying a toddler in a clumsy embrace, dragging another child by the arm of his coat. Their gas masks were bouncing against the older child's head as they descended, and he let out a whine of protest. They were a bumping bundle of old wool coats and trailing mittens, but the mother's legs were solid and steady; she did not rush the steps but took them one at a time.

She felt her own mother in that noisy, measured progress, and her limbs unlocked and she took the first step down.

A young man – really only a boy – knocked her elbow, and for a brief moment he turned his face to hers in apology. His girl was by his side – dark hair swept up, holding tight to his arm. Her scented fragrance drifted through the cold night air – floral and exotic, reminiscent of an abundance of flowers.

Then she saw them: her friend the bar steward sitting alone on a deckchair, staring down at the packet of cigarettes in his hand, no doubt thinking of his new baby; the bellboy kicking at some ice on the deck, running, hands aloft as if he had scored a goal; one of the boys from the band saluting her as he passed, earnestly, studiously carefree; her friend with a sweet pea hat in his hand, his face white and taut – just a boy's face, really.

What was going to happen to the young man who passed her on the steps? Would he live to be an old man, doing the football pools, working his allotment, married to his girl, playing with their grandchildren? Or would he be caught in an air raid or be wounded on some battlefield, calling for his mother as he died? She knew even old men cried for their mothers.

She sank down until she was sitting on the steps to the underground, her face wet with tears.

At times, she has found herself repeating certain words in her head: we didn't know, we didn't understand.

Once, standing alone in a field near her sister's house, she shouted the words out loud. She was thinking of the lifeboats swinging away from the deck only half full, of those same boats pulling away from dark shapes in the water.

We didn't know, we didn't understand. *The words are not enough.*

She is grateful her lifeboat was almost full, but there is still guilt.

She knows you cannot choose the time you die. Death takes the young and the old.

But still there is her own guilt. The guilt of simply living.

Over the years she has found her way with the living and with the dead. When the worst memories invade her dreams and she wakes up sweating, there is one memory she reaches for. It is a talisman against the darkest of the horror. She remembers the warmth of a small body held close to her and the powdery scent of a downy head against her cheek. As usual, her mother had been right: children could be a precious gift.

She never knew the baby's name. When they at last reached the Carpathia and her feet were firmly upon the deck, a woman rushed forward and grabbed the baby from her. Afterwards, she thought it was odd that the woman did not thank her. Later, when the nightmares came, she thought it was odd she did not thank the baby's mother.

Now she rises from her chair and walks across her kitchen. It is time to water her roses, and she hopes there will be some new sweet peas to pick. She may be an old lady – she may move slowly as she unlatches the door and reaches for her battered sun hat – but in her mind she is still a young woman, still the age she was when she first stepped aboard the most magnificent ocean liner the world had ever seen.

Chapter 74

Emma

The Gardener

She hovers somewhere above her bed. Her body is not speaking to her in a coordinated way. It is a language of indeterminate senses: the feel of her neck tipped back on a pillow; the smell of something metallic – not rain; the itch in her leg; something white obscuring the vision in one eye.

She thinks of playing the memory game of images from the night Will died, but she cannot recall any of them.

She is moving. She knows that. Is she still heading to theatre for surgery? Or is all of that over?

She looks for Betty. She is not able to move her heavy head, but her eyes are flicking, checking, searching.

She finds her – Betty is walking by her side. She is not speaking, and Emma cannot see her face.

Ahead of them, double doors swing open, and her vision

clears to show an empty trolley being wheeled through. They move to the side, and she watches it as it passes. She wonders who was on the trolley and where they are now.

She hears the doors clang a second time and looks towards the sound.

Les is walking through the doors towards them. His stride lengthens, and then he is running, large feet pounding the vinyl flooring.

Betty stops stock-still and then, as she takes one step towards him, he reaches her. He lifts her off her feet, and she is clinging to him, burying her head in his shoulder, sobbing.

Emma can hear Les's deep voice, muffled by Betty's curls. 'It's all right, Betsy. I'm here, Betsy, I'm here.'

Betty is struggling to get the words out. 'I told you not to come. I said I would be all right.'

'I know you did, but what was I to do, my love, when I thought you needed me.'

Emma can feel tears trickling down the side of her head into her ears.

'Oh, my little love,' Les murmurs as Betty sobs.

'She … they…' Betty is trying to get the words out. 'She was in there for hours, Les, and they've just told me…'

Betty cannot speak for crying.

She waits.

Les waits.

'It was so tough, but in the end they got all the bone fragments out. She's going to be all right.'

And then Betty breaks down completely, and she clings to

Les like her life, her happiness, her existence depends upon him. Which Emma thinks it might well do.

Then Les is looming over her, his large gardener's hand covering hers.

'Better late than never,' he says, squeezing her hand.

'And better the devil you know,' she whispers back through cracked lips.

Betty is now holding her other hand, and between sniffs, she adds, glancing up at her husband, 'And you have to give the devil his due.'

'Oh, I do, Betty,' Emma whispers. And somewhere deep inside of her is laughter. She can't quite bring it to the surface, but she thinks it will sit there and wait for her. And as Les would say: laughter is the best medicine.

PART 3

Chapter 75

Emma

Red & White Geraniums

When Emma wakes, Betty is sat in the chair beside her. She is wearing a shirt covered in red ladybirds, and Emma immediately knows that all is right with the world. Betty has her nose in a book, but she turns as Emma stirs.

'Betty, did I dream it or did my mother come to see me?'

'Yes, she did, love. It took me a while to find her number and to start with, I don't think she realised how serious it all was – she just kept saying you shouldn't have come to Paris in August.' Betty sniffs. 'As if that has anything to do with the price of fish.'

Emma half smiles. 'Is she coming back?'

Emma's phone got smashed when she collapsed and like Tamas's after the crash, her screen is now cracked and her phone unusable.

'Well, love, it seems there was something she needed to get back for, and so once she knew you were all right,' Betty sniffs again, 'well, she went off to visit these friends, but she's coming back at the weekend.'

'Good of her,' Emma observes.

Betty gives her a long look and returns to her book.

As Emma lies, half drifting in and out of sleep, she thinks of Violet. She wonders if she will ever dream of her again, but something tells her she never will. Each time she thinks of the dream, her memory of it becomes more faded. Perhaps one night all that will be left are the words: 'Then you *do* know me?' Although even now, Emma wishes she had asked the question the other way round: 'How do I know you?'

Most of her thoughts are of Will. Something has shifted, she can tell that. There is less pain. Occasionally, she tries to recapture the former agony as a way to reach him, but it is somehow elusive. All she finds is an aching emptiness rather than the searing pain of old, and she knows she has to say goodbye.

She first realised it with Philippe by his swimming pool – breathing in the scent of sandalwood. She wonders if, from now on, she will always associate the smell of sandalwood with the smell of chlorine.

The weekend arrives and with it comes a visit from Philippe and from the hotel manager, who wants to see how she is doing. There is no sign of her mother, just a delivery of a vast bouquet of Madonna lilies with a note wishing her daughter a speedy recovery and assuring her she will be back in the week to see her.

Emma asks Betty to give the lilies to one of the nurses and returns to emailing Guy on her tablet. She is still waiting on a new phone, but Betty has brought her bag into the hospital with clothes and other things she might need.

By Monday, there is talk of her being allowed to 'go home' to the hotel – and by Tuesday, Betty has arranged for them to have adjoining rooms on the ground floor, despite Emma insisting she is perfectly capable of walking up the stairs.

Les helps her organise this 'homecoming', before returning to Oxford and the garden centre. They are to follow three days later.

Les bids Emma a warm farewell, adding, 'And as for the future … well … you may not know what you want, but you know how to get it.'

This makes an odd sort of sense to Emma, although it is certainly not one of Les's usual sayings. She smiles, asking, 'Where's that from, Les?'

He rubs his beard, 'The Sex Pistols.'

Breakfast has finished and Emma has secured herself a table by the window in the hotel's dining room. The hotel is much the same – busy with summer visitors – but for Emma it has the feeling of a seaside hotel at the end of the season. The red and white geraniums in the window box beside her are looking parched and leggy.

She is wearing a simple dressing rather than a bandage, and with a scarf around her head, she is able to hide where her head has been shaved and make it look like she has swept her hair up to one side. She still feels fragile and a bit sore, but there is no doubt that the blood transfusion and iron pills have made a big difference. She has not had a headache for days and she is no longer swamped by the lethargic light-headedness she had grown so used to. Despite the fragility, she feels like a new woman.

She has even managed a trip to her mother's apartment to collect the suitcase of family photos and documents her mother kept there. That was not a pleasant trip. The stark elegance of the echoing apartment was a reminder of her childhood – not that there was anything in the décor or ornaments that Emma could remember. It seemed as though, since her father's death, her mother had whitewashed her family out of her life.

Still, she did find the documents and photo albums and although she hasn't felt ready to delve into these yet, they are safely stored under her hotel bed.

For now, Emma's laptop is open on a table by the window, and she has just had an email from Alistair. Since their Zoom call he has emailed her more information about Violet's later life: how she had married briefly but it hadn't worked out; how she had never had children; how, when she retired after a life at sea, she moved to Suffolk to be near her sister, happily tending her garden until she died.

She is partway through typing a reply to Alistair when Betty joins her, carrying a pot of coffee.

'Everything good with you?' Emma asks, already knowing the answer. Les and Betty have decided to come back to Paris in the autumn to celebrate their fortieth wedding anniversary.

'More than good, love,' Betty says, sitting down. 'Do you

remember I said Les had some ideas for the garden centre? Well, he told me on the phone last night that the deal he's been working on is ready to go through. And, if I agree, we'll be selling a small parcel of our land.'

'Really?' Emma tries to sound positive, but she knows it comes out as worried.

Betty smiles, reassuringly. 'He says you gave him the idea when you talked about what you could do with a small plot – you remember, to give people some inspiration? Well, it gave him the notion that maybe we didn't need quite so much land and could manage with a bit less. It will give us money to do the renovations and it will mean we won't be worrying. Plus we can visit New Zealand each year – we thought January would be a good time to go.'

'Who are you selling the land to?'

'Well, that's the great part, love. The council is keen to provide more allotments in the area, and so they're offering a very good price. In the long run it saves them money if they can add to an existing site rather than start new allotments from scratch.'

'Perfect,' Emma says, thinking of the gardeners she has watched from the bench at the back of the garden centre.

'Les has been talking to the bloke at the council, and we may be able to run a market in the summer to sell surplus produce from the allotments. Les already knows a few of the gardeners and they're very taken with his idea. That should bring a few more people in, along with the new café.'

'That all sounds brilliant.'

'Now, what about you. Are you okay, love?'

'Yes, I am,' says Emma, and she means it. 'I think I understand and accept a lot more than I did. You know, Betty, when I was in hospital, I thought a lot about my life and my childhood, and it struck me that you can't hold other people responsible for how you feel.'

'You mean your mum?' Betty asks.

'Yes, but it's more than that.' Emma pauses. 'I think Will made such a difference to me that I thought all my happiness was wrapped up in him. In some ways, being with him made me more confident, more outgoing, but a huge part of me just sat back and relied on him to make our life happy.'

'Do you think he resented that?'

'Not exactly. I think, most of the time, we *were* genuinely happy. And when we hit tough stuff, we went through it together.'

'Not being able to have a baby?'

Emma nods. 'I just think, looking back, maybe the balance wasn't always quite right. Maybe I depended on him too much.'

'And your mum?' Betty asks again.

'I think my mother's the other side of the coin. You can't let someone who has treated you badly define you.' It strikes her that there is something liberating about saying this out loud. 'You can't hold them responsible for how you feel.'

'No one can make you feel inferior without your permission,' Betty says thoughtfully.

Emma darts a glance at her. 'That's very wise, Betty.'

Betty laughs. 'Oh, I've borrowed that one, love – I had quite a bit of time while you were out cold in the hospital. It was difficult to find books in English. I think that quote comes from a book I found about famous women. I can't remember who said it – I think, maybe, it was Eleanor Roosevelt.' She adds, in a resigned voice, 'I must admit when I read it, I thought of my sister. I know she looks down on me, but maybe I shouldn't let it get to me so much.'

'And she's been helping in the garden centre while you've been away – that's got to be a good thing,' Emma suggests.

Betty snorts. 'Well, it will be interesting to see how many plants are left when she's through. I know she's planning on redoing her garden, and I bet she's been loading up her 4x4 each night.' Betty pauses, then changes the subject. 'And Will? Have you been able to forgive him yet, love?'

Emma sighs. 'I can't, Betty – I just can't. And you have no idea how much I want to.'

When Betty heads out to do some shopping ('I suppose I ought to bring my sister something back from Paris'), Emma decides to tackle the suitcase that has been sitting under her hotel bed.

Her first thought on reviewing it properly is that there is disappointingly little to see: a photo album and a small bundle of documents. The album is of her father's family – subjects staring out at her in their Sunday best. As she turns the pages, the shots become less formal and she follows her father from when he was a little boy up until he was a student in the late sixties. Emma recognises Granny Maria's handwriting in the white lettering annotating the black pages. She looks for older relatives in the photos, and thanks to Granny Maria's careful notation she is able to identify many of them. The names all tally with her trawl through the Spanish ancestry sites – now she can put faces to some of the names.

She looks at the people in the photos and thinks of the list of professions she has uncovered, everything from dentists to dressmakers. But nobody has a link to shipping or service onboard ship.

Next, she tackles the documents, laying them out on the bed so that they form a patchwork quilt of births and marriages. She sits back against the headboard. She is definitely filling in some gaps, but she seems to be moving further away from the answer she has been secretly hoping for. As far as she can see, there is no conceivable connection between herself and a woman called Violet Jessop.

As Emma looks down at the documents and photographs spread out before her, she notices something new. It is lopsided – all the information she has leads her in one direction. Granny Maria's family is covered in considerable detail, but there are big gaps on her husband Pedro's side of the family.

In fact, as Emma sorts through the images and certificates, there is very little evidence that her grandfather's family existed at all. There is one photo of Grandpa Pedro (a man who died when Emma was a little girl) but there is no clear path she can trace back from there.

She calls her mother to ask if there are any other family albums in the flat, but it goes to voicemail.

Chapter 76

Emma

Jardinera

The next day, Emma is sitting in the small hotel library when Betty walks in.

'Come and join me,' Emma says. 'Mum's coming to see me before she heads back to the South of France.'

Emma did eventually manage to get hold of her mother on the phone, and she was adamant that there was no other information on her husband's family. All she would say was that her husband's father came from a distinguished family of wine growers.

So that was it – a dead end. Still, she can't help feeling there's something her mother isn't telling her.

Betty breaks in on her thoughts. 'Don't you want to see her on your own?'

'Not really. In fact, definitely not,' Emma says, pulling out a chair. 'I used to think I had something I needed to say to her. A conversation that would – oh, not make things good between us – but resolve some things, particularly to do with Dad.'

'But now?' Betty prompts.

'There is no conversation.'

'No conversation that would make it right, you mean?'

'No, it's simpler than that. My mother and I have *no* conversation. We don't connect in any way I can think of. You might think we'd share a love of my father, but thinking about it, I'm not sure she even liked him.' She pauses. 'What did you think of her when you met her?'

'Well, I wouldn't say I actually *met* her,' Betty says, evasively.

Emma looks at her in surprise. 'But you must have seen her when she came to the hospital?'

'Oh, I don't know… I mean, it was very brief…'

'But surely you spoke to her?'

'I'm not sure she really knew who I was or how I fitted in… I think, to start with, she thought I was a hospital cleaner.'

Emma looks horrified.

But Betty starts to laugh. 'I think your mum would get on well with my sister.'

Before Emma can answer, the staccato tap of her mother's heels announces her arrival. She pauses in the doorway – an elegant woman of indeterminate age: sleek, ash bob, precision cut; oval face with the perfect coral mouth; alabaster ankles in nude heels; a charcoal linen skirt with no hint of a crease; an immaculate cream silk shirt. She pulls large sunglasses down to look around the room, pauses a few seconds longer, confident that the room will now be looking back at her.

Then she moves across to their table.

Emma notices that her mother's face has a new, tighter look and a peerless sheen, and she fleetingly wonders if Mathias is a surgeon.

'Ah, there you are, Emma.' She frowns at her daughter, although her face does not move. 'I must say you're looking better than in that horrible hospital – although why you decided to come to Paris in August I'll never understand.' She air-kisses Emma and sits down. She ignores Betty. 'Now, I can't be too long as I have a taxi booked and I still have some shopping to do.'

'How long are you going to be away?' Emma asks.

Her mother looks sideways at her, distracted. 'Really, Emma, cerise pink, with that hair. If you can't get it right, at least keep it simp—'

'Cheerful?' Emma interrupts.

Her mother looks confused. 'No, I was going to say—'

But again Emma interrupts. 'So, you're getting the train South this afternoon?'

'What? Well, yes.' Then, still frowning at Emma's cerise sundress, her mother embarks on a long description of who she will be staying with, where they might go next and who will be there if they do. The names are all new to Emma, but she is barely listening.

As her mother talks and the waiter brings their coffees, she crosses her legs, the soft folds of her new dress settling around her. She can just see the tips of her new lime-green pumps peeping at her from under the table edge.

'Did you like Will?' Emma asks suddenly. The question has come to her from nowhere, and she sees Betty look up from her coffee in surprise.

'I beg your pardon?' her mother says, startled.

Emma waits.

'Well, yes of course I did. I thought he was very good for you. It's not every man… Yes, you were lucky to have him.'

Emma steps over the insult (in her new colourful shoes). 'It's just you never talk about him or ask about him.'

Her mother looks confused. 'Well … it's hardly appropriate… I mean, he's dead.'

There is a long silence. Emma thinks of all the things she has wanted to say over the past months: *You didn't even come to his funeral; Of course I need to talk about him; What sort of mother are you?*

The silence stretches on. Emma can see Betty sitting back as far as she can in her chair.

She draws a breath and hears herself ask a different question. 'What about Dad – did you like Dad?'

'Where is all this coming from, Emma? It is hardly the time or place.'

'But did you *like* him?' she persists.

Emma's mother glances at Betty and then looks quickly away. 'That was between me and your father. We were married for over thirty years.'

'But he was a lovely man, and you never seemed to *like* him. I don't understand that.' It is almost as if she is talking to herself. She is vaguely surprised that, for once, she is saying the words in her head out loud.

'That's private – it has *nothing* to do with you.'

'I do get that,' Emma says thoughtfully, 'but when I look back, I can't work out why you two stayed together.'

'Well, it's what you did in our family.'

'And I can't understand,' Emma continues, in the same thoughtful tone, 'why you ever got together in the first place.'

There is a 'crack' as Emma's mother puts her espresso cup down hard on the marble tabletop, and Emma knows she has succeeded in making her mother angry. She waits for the familiar feeling of dread to flood her, but nothing happens. She still feels remarkably calm.

She glances at Betty, who is watching her with a look of intense concentration on her face.

Her mother draws in a sharp breath, and as she starts to speak, Emma realises that her mother wants to hurt her. She is surprised she hasn't realised and recognised this before. 'You think you knew your father – well, you didn't. Oh yes, he was good-looking all right – the strong, silent type, I thought.' She gives a brittle laugh. 'But underneath it all he was a *common* little man.' Emma's mother is like an angry wasp – two sharp bits of colour stand out on her cheeks. 'I made him what he was – he had a good head for figures, but he had no idea how to get on. I didn't have the choices you had, so I made the best of what I did have and I made the best of him.'

'I knew,' was all Emma says.

'Knew what?' her mother asks angrily.

'That you didn't like him,' she replies.

Her mother shoots her a look of dislike, disappointment and something else.

And then Emma sees it. How could she not have recognised it before? Her mother is jealous of her.

And with that blinding insight, she sees what makes her mother so very angry – furious in fact. Her mother cannot understand how Emma's success – and she *was* successful in her way: in her academic studies, her languages, her career and in her marriage – how all that could have come to someone so lacking in the attributes her mother prizes: looks, figure, poise and social standing.

Emma laughs, and her mother just stares at her.

'What the hell is so funny?' she hisses.

'I was just thinking you got the daughter you deserved.'

But maybe, she thinks sadly, *I didn't get the mother I deserved*.

Her mother's voice cuts in. She hasn't finished. 'You think your father was so bloody marvellous. His parents sent him to a good school to help him try and fit in, but his father was just an ignorant peasant. There you go with your family tree, digging into the past. But you won't like what you find there, I can tell you. I said his father came from a family of wine growers, but I *lied*. They weren't even farmers. Your father came from a long line of jobbing gardeners. That's why I hated him working in the garden so much. But he just wouldn't let it go – he had to be grubbing around in the mud. It's a shame you didn't take after *my* side of the family more.'

Emma watches her mother struggle to try and gain control

of herself. How could she possibly think that being like her father would be a *bad* thing? She hears the creaking in her mother's voice, a voice that once screamed pure and high, and she realises her mother is losing her furious battle with age. How much energy has she wasted on such a one-sided war – the creams, dyes, surgery and the stream of men? What a total waste.

She wonders how she was ever frightened of this sad woman.

'I haven't got time for this!' her mother states, suddenly rising. 'And don't think for a moment that I will want you at the chateau for my birthday. Quite frankly,' she says, sweeping a look over Emma, 'you wouldn't fit in.'

Emma almost reminds her mother that it will, in fact, be her sixty-eighth birthday, and that this is very close to seventy, but she finds she has lost all urge to score points over this woman. She sits staring after her as the angry clack of her heels disappears into the distance.

Then she turns and smiles radiantly at Betty.

'I'm a gardener,' she says. And the word comes to her in Spanish too: *jardinera*.

It feels as though a scientific equation she has been struggling with has finally balanced. A new connection – the *right* connection – has been made. If they were a family of poor gardeners, of course they wouldn't have had photos. So that was it. She isn't related to Violet Jessop, but – Emma smiles at the thought – she *is* descended from a long line of gardeners. Family following family.

Is it enough? Not to be a descendent of a stewardess on the

Titanic but one in a long line of gardeners?

Yes, Emma decides; it undoubtedly is.

Betty lets a long breath out and starts to laugh. 'So much for not talking to your mother.'

'Would you like to go to Seville?' Emma asks.

As Betty hesitates, Emma knows this last journey is one she will be making on her own. It is time for Betty to go home to Les.

Chapter 77

Emma

Lotus Flowers

The Seville sunshine glows with a warmth and intensity that reminds Emma of rich food. She remembers Roberto and thinks how good it would be to drink chilled Manzanilla and eat tapas with him here.

After booking into her hotel, she sets out for the *Reales Alcázares*. There have been gardens in the palace grounds since it was built by Moorish, Muslim kings in the eleventh century. She has no clear idea of what she will do there, but she has a longing to be on her own and think about her father in a beautiful Spanish garden.

She steps from the coolness of the sumptuous palace into the shaded calm of the formal gardens. There are green, tranquil pools set in courtyards tiled with intricate patterns of emerald, ochre and indigo. The water is flecked with fallen petals of pink and purple, with an occasional liquid tangerine flash of a fish. Sunken gardens are planted with symmetrical lines of trees, and purple sky flower and powder blue plumbago cascade over terracotta walls.

As she walks on, sandy paths lead her further from the backdrop of the magnificent palace into gardens bordered by hedges interspersed with scarlet roses and wilder, looser greenery she can't identify. Above her, the tallest palm trees Emma has ever seen reach up into an azure-blue sky.

After an hour of walking, Emma pauses by a bank of deep orange canna lilies. The opulent flowers are now beginning to fade, the petals turning from burnt orange to a deep brown that is almost maroon. For a moment it depresses her that death is reaching into this garden, too, and then she sees above the flowers the canopy of green formed by a line of orange trees. The oranges are there, hidden in the leaves; in this season, they are solid green spheres, but come the winter they will ripen to a glorious orange. So life goes on. As one thing fades, another blooms.

Then it comes to her, a thread of sweetness mixing with the verdant greenness.

Jasmine.

She follows the scent to a small courtyard banked on all sides by walls of greenery – clusters of delicate white flowers scattered among the dark leaves. She finds a bench tucked away by a low wall, looking out onto a shallow, circular pool with a fountain. Around it, on the tiled floor, stand large pale terracotta pots planted with rosemary – rosemary for remembrance.

The still, warm air is heavy with the mingled scent of herbs and Jasmine. Emma breathes in the fragrance and, very quietly – which feels appropriate for the humble man she loved so much – she says goodbye to her father.

People drift past her – families laughing, some arguing, an elderly couple strolling hand in hand. That is how she had envisaged herself and Will growing old together – still wanting to touch and hold each other.

The courtyard clears again, the only person left is a gardener working his way up one of the flowerbeds. He is working in the shade and she cannot see his face.

When he comes closer, moving through the bed, weeding and raking, with a practised rhythm, she sees he is much older than she initially thought – a man nearing fifty. He looks up and seeing her watching him, smiles.

'It's a hot day for work,' she starts, but is caught by a half-laugh before she has finished the words.

He looks enquiringly at her.

'I'm sorry – it's just that I was congratulating myself on speaking in Spanish and then realised I was being typically English and talking about the weather.'

He straightens up. 'It is an international trait, especially among gardeners.'

She smiles. 'Have you worked here long?'

'About six years now.'

'My father's family was originally from Seville, and his grandfather was a gardener here.'

'Here in the palace?'

'No, I'm not sure exactly where but somewhere in the city. I wanted to come – I've read so much about the gardens. And, well, my father died a few years ago, but I wanted to…' She isn't quite sure how to explain it.

He pauses by the low wall next to her. 'A pilgrimage?'

'Yes,' she says, gratefully, 'I suppose you could call it that.'

'Has it helped?'

'Yes, yes it has.'

For a moment, the gardener stands staring at his feet. 'My own father died last year,' he says. 'I garden in his shoes. That is how I remember my father. Everyday.'

She glances down at his ancient boots and smiles. The first thing she is going to do when she gets home is to dig out her father's old secateurs, their handles worn where his fingers had held them.

'You like this courtyard?' the gardener asks.

'It's perfect,' she says, her eyes settling on the jasmine.

'Ah, not perfect.' When she looks confused, he goes on, nodding towards the tiles on the floor: 'You have to look at the flowers.'

She looks down at the faded tiles surrounding the fountain. Each has a dusty pink and green lotus flower in the centre. Each tile is a pattern in its own right, and together they form a much larger pattern.

'Do you know why those are flowers but not flowers?' he asks her.

She shakes her head.

'Because only Allah can create living things,' he says, 'in each tile you will find a tiny flaw.'

390

Emma remembers something that her brother, Guy, once told her about Islamic art as he took her around his gallery. Each artist had to include one mistake in their work. 'So, only God can create perfection?'

The gardener nods and bends to collect his tools.

She doesn't see him leave as she sits staring down at the tiles. She kicks off her sandals so she can feel the tiles and brickwork of the courtyard beneath the soles of her feet. So, only God could ever hope to create perfection. *The rest of us are imperfect – we are only human.*

She looks out across the sunny courtyard to the banks of perfect, white Jasmine flowers and at the pots of rosemary that stand on the beautiful but imperfect, tiled floor.

Emma is not sure whether she believes in God, but she hears the message from the garden, loud and clear: *we are only human.*

'Everyone makes mistakes,' she says aloud.

She stretches out her legs, feeling the sun warm her skin as she thinks about the man she loved most in the world. She remembers her first meeting with Will, the way he looked and smelt and laughed.

And she knows she will always remember this moment in a Spanish courtyard as the time she says goodbye, and the moment she finally forgives him.

Later that evening, Emma sits alone in a rooftop bar, gazing across the city to the ancient and ornate cathedral. She holds her chilled glass of Aperol spritz up to the light and sips it. She feels that she is marking the end of something. Or maybe it's a beginning.

She looks back on the journey she has been on since starting work in the garden centre, and thinks again of gathering all the people who have helped her together in her garden, serving lunch on a table covered in flowers. She would put Philippe to her right, Clem at his side. She can imagine them discussing the meaning of flowers and fragrances. On Clem's other side, Tamas. She is sure they would get on. She would put Betty next to Tamas, and then Mrs Pepperpot – comfortable in Betty's company. Next, Les and Alistair, sharing their love of history, and finally, Roberto and herself. She wonders for a moment if she could find the smiley friendly girl from the library.

Emma doesn't think she believes in ghosts, but maybe in the long grass where the willow tree roots curl into the stone wall, she could put a second, smaller table, with four chairs around it. The Purser's table. A place for him and for three guests: Will, her father and of course, Violet. There would be flowers on this table, too. A jam jar filled with roses, lily of the valley, jasmine and peonies.

Emma looks up into the golden sky and watches a swift soaring high above her. The truth is she will never really know exactly who it was who arranged and rearranged all the flowers on the *Titanic*. And that, she thinks, is the point: understanding there are some things in life that you will never truly know – and being at peace with that.

She loved her husband very much, and she knows Will loved her. But he still had an affair. After a journey that has taken her from Oxfordshire to Paris to Seville, she realises that she will never truly understand why Will was unfaithful – and she accepts this, too.

Emma looks around at the flowers intertwined with the rooftop and thinks of all the flowers she has seen over the past few weeks: in her garden, the garden centre, in Clem's shop, on the riverbanks in Cambridge, in the flowerbeds of Paris and Seville. The cosmos that smell of chocolate, the sunny-faced gerberas, the feathery lavender and velvety lupins, the bold, happy sunflowers and the old English roses scented with summer.

As the flowers bloom and fade they speak to her of the fragility of life – there one moment and gone the next. But each delicate petal, each fragrant flower has also reminded her of something else, something she has been in danger of forgetting.

That life is beautiful.

Emma takes one last look across the glowing city and calls for the bill. It is time to go home.

She has a book to write, a garden to tend and a lunch to host.

Nine months later, Emma will have achieved one of these three things.

PART 4

Chapter 78

Emma

Oxford

Emma lies under the apple trees, her fingers brushing a few long blades of grass that she missed when she mowed the lawn earlier. She had been asleep and had been dreaming in Spanish. She stretches her arms out wide, looking up at the sky through the branches. It is a clear May day, two years and two days since Will died.

She turns her head towards the greenhouse, where she can glimpse the tops of her young plantlings: blush-coloured hollyhocks, magenta poppies and lupins the colour of ice cream.

It has taken her longer than she imagined to find a date that everyone could make for lunch, but tomorrow is the day, and she is just about ready. She has been cooking for two days solid and all the crockery, tablecloths, glasses and cutlery are piled up in the utility room. Beside her, under the apple trees, the table and chairs are lined up ready. All she really has left to do is arrange the flowers for the tables and make up the spare room bed.

She sits up and looks out at her garden. Early white and purple aquilegia are standing guard by the gate and the peonies that line the drive look about to burst into life. Under the trees and in the (now tidy) flowerbeds, the last of the bluebells and cowslips bloom. Behind them, standing tall and proud, the foxgloves have returned.

Emma smiles at her garden – and she likes to think it smiles back at her. She couldn't have done it all without Les's advice and occasional manual labour, but she is a quick learner. After all, she comes from a long line of gardeners.

Les wouldn't accept any payment for his help or for the many plants he has given her, so instead, she has been giving him and Betty French conversation lessons over supper in her kitchen. They are planning another trip to Paris to celebrate their forty-first wedding anniversary. As Betty put it, 'At our age, love, you can't hang around waiting for someone to ask you to dance'.

In addition to French, Emma now runs Italian and Spanish conversation classes at the garden centre, the new café being a perfect space for people to gather. On warmer evenings, they throw open the doors so they can have lessons on the veranda looking out over the downs.

Since returning from Seville, her time has been taken up with her garden, her three days a week in the garden centre and her burgeoning language classes. And the book idea has changed into something else. In the end, Emma decided to follow one of the lessons she learnt the previous summer: small contributions are worthwhile, too. So instead of writing a book, she ended up collaborating with Alistair on an academic paper exploring the flowers on the *Titanic*. The paper referenced the work of what they had concluded was a band of stewardesses – the florists on the *Titanic* – but it was dedicated to one in particular: Violet Jessop.

Alistair will be staying with her after the lunch tomorrow, while Clem will stay with Betty and Les, as will Mrs Pepperpot. Roberto and Philippe have organised accommodation in Oxford with friends and relatives. Tamas will be getting a taxi over.

Emma invited Berta, too – a shy but determined woman whom Emma has now met a few times – but she politely declined. She and Tamas are now spending more and more time with Betty and Les at the garden centre, and together they are drawing up plans for Tamas and Berta to take over some of the day-to-day management of the centre, freeing up time for Betty and Les to visit their son and for Les to concentrate on growing begonias and sweet peas for the local flower shows. Berta also has ideas for extending the market linked to the allotments, and she has enlisted her father's help to work up plans to make English wine.

Emma has finally tracked down the smiley girl from the library – who she now knows is called Ellie – and while she cannot join them for lunch she is going to call in for a drink (and pudding) in the afternoon. Her only slight sadness is that it is impractical for Guy to fly over for the lunch.

When Emma heads inside to tidy the spare room, she visits her own bedroom on the way, pausing by the perfume Phillipe sent her a few months ago. As she sprays it on her wrist, the fragrance fills the room with the promise of summer, with a hint of something that stirs old memories.

Once the spare room is prepared, Emma sits for a while on the edge of the bed, enjoying the satisfaction that everything is now ready. Absentmindedly, she pulls a drawer open in the chest beside her.

She glances at Will's old love letters, bundled up alongside the letters Granny Maria sent her over the years. Can she bear to look at them? Emma glances out of the window to the garden that she has come to love so much, and thinks, now, she can.

She pulls a pile of letters from the drawer and sits cross-legged on the floor, back propped against the bed. She unties the ribbon, takes a deep breath and starts to read.

There are the remembered phrases and endearments, written in small, rounded handwriting, which always made her think of Will, the little boy, sent away to boarding school at eight. There are lines from songs that reminded him of her; lyrics that take her back to evenings spent together shuffling through tracks on his iPod, squabbling over each other's taste in music, until they fell silent over one song they both loved.

One of the final letters she opens is still creased from where it lay under her pillow. There are the three words he chose for her: Brave, Bossy and Beautiful. She smiles as she reads on and cries afresh as she runs her fingertip over where Will signed his name.

He *did* love her. And she loved him.

When she can no longer see the pages for her tears, she puts the bundle away, and starts to read Granny Maria's letters instead.

Granny Maria wrote sometimes in English, sometimes in Spanish, but always in a big loopy scrawl. The letters have been stored in no particular order and there seem to be hundreds of them. She finds advice to her twelve-year-old self about friends at school. Her grandmother's suggestions were centred around kindness, but with a sting in the tail: *If they make you cry again*, mi niña, *I will come and beat them with my big stick.*

Another letter clearly sent to a much younger Emma includes a copy of a Spanish poem about a goat trying to find its way to the sea. Next is a fatter envelope, on the outside of which her grandmother added an afterthought in English, *Ask your Papa to read this to you, I wrote it in a hurry in Spanish.*

Emma pulls the letter out, and with it comes a photograph slipped between the sheets of a second piece of paper.

She stops breathing.

She is looking at a black and white photograph of four figures on the deck of a ship. She recognises the couple from old photo albums as her great-grandparents. The man holds the hand of a child who must be Granny Maria – her eyes were always so merry. The little girl is staring up at a young woman, her hand held in hers.

The young woman is Violet Jessop.

There is no mistaking her. She is in a stewardess's uniform and is smiling at the camera. She has one hand up, shielding her eyes against the sun.

Emma gulps in a huge breath of air. She turns the photo over and sees the date – yes, Granny Maria would have been about three. There is a handwritten note on the back, too. It isn't her grandmother's handwriting – she knows that. Was it her great-grandmother who wrote this?

The girl who shared the secret of pillow post with us. What a surprise! We thought she had died.

Pillow post? Emma has so long associated pillow post with her father that she had half forgotten Granny Maria used it, too, leaving letters under her pillow when she came to stay. She had called it pillow post, too, always using the English translation – maybe liking the sound of the language? Perhaps phrasing it the way it had been said to her?

Emma opens the letter and starts reading her grandmother's letter:

Dearest Emma,

You asked me in your last letter what I was like when I was little, so I thought you would like to see this photo . Here I am! And what a lot of hair I had, don't you think? I am in the picture with my parents, your great-grandparents. My father was a doctor and my mother a nurse. They met when their families spent a year in Argentina (ask your father to look that up in the Atlas for you).

The other person in the photograph is a stewardess who worked on the ship we were sailing on. My parents had a big surprise when they saw her, because they had known her a long time ago. They had last seen her when she was a little girl and was very ill in hospital. They had always thought she had not got better.

Emma smiles as she reads this, knowing Granny Maria hadn't wanted to write that the girl might have died.

But she did get better and when they saw her again, they asked if they could take a photograph of her. And here it is.

When she was ill in hospital as a little girl, she told my parents about pillow post. She said it was a game, that they could hide letters to each other under her pillow. They did, and guess what? They fell in love!

I must go now, *mi niña*, and get to the post, but I send you lots of love.

Emma stares at the photo and letter in her hands. What was it Alistair had said about Violet as a little girl? That she had been ill and hidden love letters between a doctor and nurse.

The paper of Granny Maria's letter feels brittle in her fingers. She cannot remember this letter, at all. She looks at the date at the top of the letter. She would have been seven when she received it so perhaps that wasn't surprising. But something about that photograph must have stayed with her. She *had* recognised Violet when she saw her.

'Oh, Violet, I *did* know you,' Emma says out loud, smiling at the young woman in the picture.

She reaches out and gently touches her grandmother's hand where it held Violet's. All these years she has been using pillow post, and telling others about it, she never thought about where the idea came from. She was looking for a connection to Violet through blood and genes, and yet it was there all the time in an idea passed on from her, as she has passed it on to others.

She thinks of Will, of Tamas, and Betty's son, Ben – writing to his son, Zac, a little boy confused and upset by the arrival of a baby sister. Hadn't these people been helped by the spread of a simple idea – the idea of how to communicate with someone you loved when it felt like the spoken word wasn't enough, or when you just couldn't say those words. An idea passed on to her great-grandparents by Violet Jessop.

She wonders how far and wide that simple idea has been spread by others in their turn. She knows from her scientific work how viruses and disease could spread, but couldn't good things spread, too?

Her mind buzzing, Emma absentmindedly picks up the thin piece of paper that was wrapped around the photograph. It is still marked by the creases made by a little girl's hospital pillow.

Dr Paulo Garcia

Buenos Aires. 12th August 1898

My love, Christina,

This will be my last letter to you. I cannot stay any longer in a place where you are promised to another and our families are lined up against us like an armed band. I do not blame them – your fiancé can offer riches and status that I will never possess. My father believes that by continuing to visit you, I dishonour our family name.

I write this in the garden and the scent of the freesias distracts me. I could never mistake that clean, sweetness for any other flower. I will always recognise it, as my heart recognised you when I first saw you.

I see our go-between in her bed under the trees. She is so sick, that little one – I see her fading, disappearing. One day, with the flutter of a white sheet, she will be gone. Do you think I was wrong to move her bed into the garden among the flowers?

When I visit her, I know I am wrong to think so much of you and to look for you by her bedside or hope for a letter under her pillow.

I will be at the train station at three o'clock tomorrow. I know I ask a lot of you. I wonder I can dare, but without you there is nothing, so my fear makes me brave. Please do not come and say goodbye. I believe that would destroy me, or worse still, shatter my resolve and make me stay. Only come if you mean to travel with me.

I have little to offer except my profession, my enduring love and freesias for your bridal flowers.

Ever yours, Paulo

Paulo, her great-grandfather; Christina, her great-grandmother.

Emma gazes at the words on the tissue-thin paper and imagines a young woman rushing along a hot, crowded platform to catch a train.

She thinks of the friends who will be joining her tomorrow for lunch under the apple trees. The thought of sharing these letters with them warms her like a shot of the plum vodka Berta and Tamas gave her for Christmas. She smiles at the photograph and the letters she holds in her hands.

Her only tiny regret is that she cannot deliver this news by pillow post.

Epilogue

In Toronto, a small boy leaves a letter under his sister's pillow to say he is sorry that he teased her when she named her new rabbit 'Bunny'. He writes that it is a good name, and tells her he will collect dandelion leaves for Bunny with her tomorrow.

In a suburb of Leiden, a young man watches the face of his flatmate as she sits on the sofa emailing her mother. They have been best friends all the way through university and both now have new jobs in the city. When she goes to bed tonight, she will find a letter for her under her pillow telling her that he has loved her from the first moment he saw her.

In Galway, a mother leaves a letter and a new notebook under her daughter's pillow. On the front of the notebook is written, *She believed she could, so she did*. The mother hopes the ideas her daughter writes there will help her make sense of a world that she herself often finds overwhelming.

In Rosario, Argentina, an old man leaves a love letter under his wife's pillow. It is their anniversary tomorrow and they will have been married for fifty-seven years.

In Auckland, New Zealand, a father leaves a note and a leaflet for a fishtail surfboard under the pillow of his eight-year-old son, Zac.

Author's Note

Several years ago, while working on another flower-related project, I decided to look up who the florist was on the Titanic. *It was meant to be an anecdote to illustrate a point about the cultural and social significance of flowers. Three hours later, I was still searching online. I could not believe the amount that had been compiled and written about the* Titanic. *Yet I still couldn't find the florist.*

From there, everyday life intervened. My flower project had to be put aside as I needed work that would pay the mortgage, but the question still remained: who had arranged the flowers on the Titanic?

I returned to this question years later. It was a mystery that appealed to me as the basis for a novel, particularly as I have such an abiding interest in flowers. In my twenties, I ran a flower shop in London and later went on to photograph and write a series of books about flower shops. It was while I was compiling these that I discovered some of the secrets my character, Clementine, knows:

that flower shops are a unique window into a community, following life, from birth to bereavement; and that it is usually women who nurture and celebrate friendship through the sending of flowers.

Once I was back hunting in earnest for my florist, I not only returned to online resources but read many of the excellent books that have been written about the Titanic (see Bibliography). I visited the V&A museum's exhibition on ocean liners, the National Maritime Museum at Greenwich, the Southampton Seacity Museum and the Titanic Experience in Belfast and in Cobh. I also trawled my memory of my time at university, when I had studied social history and written my dissertation on Edwardian women.

I combined this research with what I knew as a florist and with what I had gleaned from other florist friends over the years. This included Kim, who had worked on flowers for the Oriana, and Trish, who had worked at the Ritz (who told me that a florist carrying a bouquet can go anywhere – a trick she used when someone famous was staying at the Ritz and wanted to see what they looked like!). I also drew on my experience of visiting the QE2 in Hong Kong many years earlier; a friend of a friend was running the Harrods shop on board and gave me a guided tour of the ship.

The locations I have used are mostly drawn from real life, although I have taken liberties here and there – for example, adding a flower shop to a Cambridge alleyway. The garden centre and Emma's cottage are pure figments of my imagination, which is a shame as I would rather like to pop in to see the renovations to the café and check how Les's begonias are doing.

Emma's story is entirely fictitious, as is her character and the characters she meets. However, wherever possible, I have tried to base Violet's story on events that took place, including her being given a baby to mind when she was sat in the lifeboat and her telling a steward friend that a sweet-pea hat was not the thing to wear to a shipwreck. In this, I was helped enormously by her memoirs (edited by John Maxtone-Graham). These were written some years after the disaster, so in expanding on them, I have had to imagine what the younger Violet might have felt at that time. This will inevitably be my personal interpretation, and I have taken a degree of artistic licence; another person reading her words and reading between the lines might come away with a different view. I have also taken the liberty of stringing out Emma's discovery of Violet's story. I am sure she could have found out about The Nurse and Violet's past a lot quicker than she did – but then it would have been a very short book! I hope readers will forgive me.

Violet meeting up again with the doctor and nurse she had known in Argentina (whose love letters she hid under her pillow) is recorded in her memoirs, although, of course, these people were not related to my fictitious Emma. I do wonder, though, if someone did take a photograph of such an unexpected meeting and if in some old suitcase this image is sitting quietly gathering dust. It is also true that Violet's mum believed the miracle of honeysuckle saved her daughter's life.

Hugh McElroy, who was The Purser, was by all accounts a good man who had studied for some time to be a priest before changing his mind and going to sea. He had worked for the White Star Line for many years and did indeed give the dancer Adeline Genée flowers in her national colours the night before he sailed. However in terms of his character as depicted in this book, it is based on my *imagination rather than any detailed study of the man.*

So was Violet Jessop the florist on the Titanic? *I believe she was certainly one of the people who arranged the flowers, and there is clear evidence to support this. But when* The Purser *talks to her about the flowers for her passengers and the first-class lounge, this is an educated guess from me at what might have been. I like to think it is plausible, based on the other evidence. It certainly seems true that they shared a love of flowers and that they held each other in high regard. The Purser's great-nephew wrote as much after he visited Violet when she was an old lady.*

The final thing I would like to add is about the power of coincidences. There have been times when I almost gave up writing this book – then some coincidence would pop up and I'd take encouragement from it.

When I found the blogger, Lynn Heiden, who, like the fictitious Mrs Pepperpot, used an old photograph of Frank Bealing's grandson to start an investigation into his background, I was delighted. I was then stunned when she discovered that Frank Senior had been born in the small Dorset town where I was then living and writing. I have stood in the church where Frank Senior was christened and I have decorated the pew ends with wedding flowers where his family would have sat.

As my daughter said, 'Mum, it's a sign'.

Bibliography

Many thanks to the authors who have gone before me and for their excellent research.

Every Man for Himself by Beryl Bainbridge

Among the Icebergs by Mark Brown and Roger Simmons

Maiden Voyages and Magnificent Ocean Liners and the Women Who Travelled and Worked Aboard Them by Sian Evans

Ocean Liners by Daniel Finamore and Ghislaine Wood

Titanic Voices by Hannah Holman

Titanic: Voices from the Disaster by Deborah Hopkinson

Titanic Voices by Donald Hyslop, Alistair Forsyth, Sheila Jemima

A Night to Remember by Walter Lord

Titanic Tragedy: A New Look at the Lost Liner by John Maxtone-Graham

Titanic Survivor by Violet Jessop and John Maxtone-Graham

Titanic: Minute by Minute by Jonathan Mayo

Titanic Unseen by Senan Molony with Steve Raffield

Titanic: True Stories of her Passengers, Crew and Legacy by Nicola Pierce

The Crew of the RMS Titanic by Brian J Ticehurst

Voices from the Titanic (Brief Histories) by Geoff Tibballs

Shadow of The Titanic by Andrew Wilson

Acknowledgements

Although *The Secrets of Flowers* was published in 2024 and is my third novel, it started its life several years ago in 2018. Tanera Simons read an early manuscript of the book and took a chance on me, becoming my agent. She then stuck with me through the many, different edited versions. We are delighted that it has finally found its way into the world. I know it has a special place in both our hearts. Thank you Tanera, for keeping the faith! Based on this experience, I would say to any would-be writer who is struggling – just keep going. And to the readers who have made it possible for me to now have three books published – thank you from the bottom of my heart.

I would also like to thank those who bore with me as I talked endlessly about this book in the early days, particularly my daughters, Alex and Libby. I am sorry for going on so much! And thank you to those who provided encouragement and advice as it got closer to publication, in particular Annie, Fiona,

Sonja, Anne and Judith. Also my Dad and Sally, who are no longer with us, but whose enthusiasm and kindness will always be remembered. In addition, I wish to thank Nigel, who seems to have taken the strange world of writing in his long stride and who brings such joy to the journey.

The Secrets of Flowers is dedicated to my friends Pippa and Peter Bell. Pip is my best friend, and I think has read everything I have ever written. Plus, she and her husband, Peter, took me 'sailing' on the *Olympic*, the *Queen Mary* and the *Royal Yacht Britannia*. The *Olympic* was the sister ship to the *Titanic* and in many ways it was identical. In a small hotel in Alnwick, Northumberland there is a dining room which is fitted out with panelling, mirrors and windows that were salvaged from the *Olympic*. As a surprise, Pip and Peter took me there for supper and it was amazing to see and touch such history. I would also like to mention my friend Michael who shares my interest in the *Olympic*. His family sailed on her – and, he tells me, so did George Gershwin (Michael is a keen pianist).

In researching the background to the story, I turned to many sources (see Bibliography), but I would particularly like to thank John Maxtone-Graham who edited Violet's memoirs. I hope I have kept close to her story and likely experience. Also the blogger, Lynn Heiden, whose research enabled me to connect with Frank Bealing's story.

Research and imagination may have been the start of this book in 2018, but I am well aware it is HarperCollins who helped get it over the line! Thank you to the team at HarperFiction and for all you do to support me. Editorially,

Belinda Toor, with amazing assistance from Katie Lumsden. Also Dushi Horti and Meg Le Huquet. Thank you to Vicky Joss and Libby Haddock in marketing and PR; and in sales, Holly Martin and Emily Scorer. Once again, Ellie Game, take a bow: you always create such beautiful covers.

This is a book all about flowers and it is inspired by my love of them. I would like to thank the many florists I have been privileged to know. You work so hard, often in cramped and cold conditions, yet you bring such beauty to people's lives. Thank you to those who I have worked with: Kim, Trish, Ted, Jennifer, Sarah, Katie and Jenny. Those I have met along the way: including, Leentje, Marc, Keith, Simone, Rachel, Jan, Nicki, Marcelle, Becky, Claire, Jason, Alex, Carl and Matthew. And finally, those who I haven't met – thank you for all you do, often unacknowledged in the background.

If you enjoyed *The Secrets of Flowers*,
you will also love *The Book of Beginnings*!

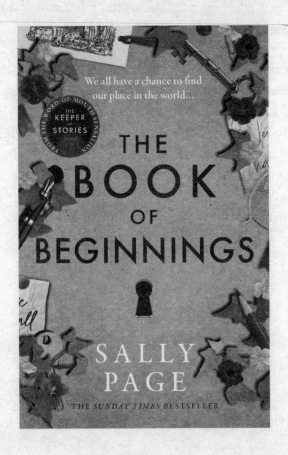

AVAILABLE NOW
Read on for an extract …

Prologue

Sometimes a heartbeat is all the time it takes to reach a decision. It may not even feel like a considered choice. Just the veering away from the prospect of more misery – a final spur to movement. The room remains unmoved. A silent witness. But loyal in its way to the woman who has just left it. The chair pushed out from the table tells no tales. The plate of half-eaten roll and cheddar (extra mature) with leftover Christmas pickle (eight months old, but still going strong) lies in mute defiance. The man calls her name, and without pausing to be invited in, pushes open the door that leads from the hall into the kitchen. And why would he pause? He has already let himself in the front door without asking.

He huffs and puffs his way around the kitchen, opening the fridge, flicking through the diary left open on the table.

The diary doesn't give her away either. Its record of parish meetings, choir practice and a planned visit to a local garden with her curate; a testament to a seemingly blameless life. Maybe there is something in the handwriting? A neatly formed hand, precise and clear, apart from a kink in the S's that look as if they would like to escape from the regularity of the line. Opposite him, the back door to the garden (which always requires a doorstop) for once stands half open, half closed. Stilled, as if in anticipation, like the rest of the room.

Then, very slowly, it swings on its hinges and quietly clicks shut.

Ninety miles away, off an alleyway in North London, another door is pushed open. A different woman, a different life. The mail piled up in the entrance slithers aside and the broken bell clinks its tinny welcome. First across the threshold is a solitary leaf. A twist of orange, sent spiralling by a late August wind that holds within its warmth the piquant tang of autumn. The woman watches the leaf's spinning progress into the quiet darkness of the shop within. For her, autumn has always been a season of beginnings; punctuated, in her childhood, by the anticipatory thrill of new shoes, crayons and pencil cases.

Now she only thinks of endings.

1

Out of place

Jo stoops to retrieve the post and, as she does so, she picks up the stray leaf. It lies in her open palm like a coloured-paper 'mood fish' that as children they would hold in their hands to tell their fortune. The leaf trembles and then is still. She wants to ask it, does this mean that one day she will be happy? She wants the orange leaf 'fish' to tell her, if when she is thinking about James, is he ever thinking of her? During all those minutes that stretch into hours, she wants to believe that if at some point he is missing her, this would constitute a connection between them. A thread of hope that she could twist around her little finger and gently pull on. Jo closes her hand around the fragile substance of the leaf, cocooning it in the hollow of her hand, and tucking the post under her arm, she pushes the door wider.

Stepping inside, her suitcase wheels rumble in rhythm over the tiles that mark the entrance to her Uncle Wilbur's shop. Taylor's Supplies is a premises not much bigger than an elongated cupboard, selling a mixture of hardware and stationery. This has been her uncle's business and home for the past fifty-two years.

Looking around, it is much as Jo remembers it. From the front of the narrow premises, one aisle leads away from the door, turning left at the back of the shop (where there is an archway to a small kitchen, a toilet, and stairs to the upstairs flat). A second narrow aisle returns back to where Jo is now standing. This is all there is to her uncle's shop, apart from the small area at the front where a glass-topped cabinet sits, set at a right angle to the window. This old-fashioned oak cabinet (which, in a former life, Jo imagines, had displayed handkerchiefs or gloves) comprises of a top shelf given over to fountain pens and, underneath, a series of broad drawers containing the larger sheets of paper that Uncle Wilbur sells.

A place for everything and everything in its place.

Jo can hear Uncle Wilbur's voice echoing in her head; and studying the shop, she can see that he has held true to his favourite maxim. The shelves may be more sparsely stocked than in previous years, but everything is neat, everything is in its place.

Apart from her uncle, she thinks, who is miles away from here.

And apart from her.

Jo glances at the gap between the counter and the wall. Here, suspended by string on a wooden pole, hang the brown paper bags. Bags that, miraculously, seemed to accommodate everything Uncle Wilbur sold, from a few screws and nails (bag twisted at the top to secure them) to a long metal saw with gleaming teeth.

And here is where Jo played 'post offices' as a child, tucked away in her secret spot. (*A place for everything and everything in its place.*) Standing behind the counter, shielding her from sight, her uncle appreciated that a busy postmistress needed a ready supply of stationery. As a little girl, one of her greatest joys had been when her uncle had beckoned her over and presented her with a brown paper bag bulging with some intriguing shape. Inside might be a notebook with its cover missing or a receipt book with a scrape in the carbon paper. Uncle Wilbur had told her (and more importantly, Mrs Watson-Toft, his bookkeeper with the basilisk's stare) that he only ever gave away 'damaged goods'. But when she was older, Jo began to suspect that when Uncle Wilbur had seen her younger self gazing covetously at a new batch of receipt books, he had run his broad, flat fingernail over the carbon paper on purpose.

Looking up, Jo notices a small, square calendar pinned to the large noticeboard on the wall behind the counter. This is all that is displayed there. The month is now August, but it still shows July's date. Fleetingly she wonders what her Uncle Wilbur used to use this noticeboard for – she can't recall it being here on her visits to the shop as a child.

Leaving the post and the leaf on the counter, Jo takes her suitcase to the back of the shop and mounts the stairs. From the first-floor landing, a half-glazed door opens into a small entrance hall. A low bench sits under a row of coat hooks, on which her uncle's dark grey winter coat still hangs.

Off the hall is a bathroom. This has an ancient suite in brilliant white, and is heated by a small, ineffective blow-heater. Jo is not looking forward to using this room. She knows from experience that even when the bath is full of hot water, the outer edge is still ice-cold to the touch.

The hallway opens up into a living room, beyond which is the kitchen. Both have long sash windows overlooking the alleyway. Opposite the first window are two doors to bedrooms. Jo wavers for a moment, undecided whether to use her uncle's room or the box room she slept in as a child when she visited for a few weeks each summer. She opens the door to the smaller of the rooms and is soon unzipping her case. Most of the clothes she flings onto a chair. What she is looking for is at the bottom of her bag.

She pulls out the dark-blue denim dungarees, their fabric stiff in her hands, like card. Jo stares down at them, unsure why it was so important for her to bring them with her. Her best friend, Lucy, left them in her cottage after staying over one evening – oh, it would have been months ago now – vintage Fifties, high-waisted, wide-legged dungarees. Lucy is a lover of all things vintage. As a teenager, and still now, as a 38-year-old woman, she wears the dresses that she begged off their grandmothers. Jo sees her own passion for stationery as an echo of her friend's quirky connection with the past, and clings to her love of newly sharpened pencils, knowing it makes her feel closer to Lucy. Even at primary school, the two of them were attuned and in step – without fail and without effort, winning the annual three-legged race at the school's sports day.

Jo sits on the bed, holding the dungarees to her. And now? Now she thinks that even if someone tied her and Lucy's legs together, they would not be able to keep in rhythm. She has never felt more out of step with her best friend, and she cannot clarify in her mind exactly why. She knows there are probably many reasons, but whichever way she stacks and rearranges these reasons – her point of view; her perception of Lucy's point of view – it never gives her a sense of truly understanding what has gone wrong between them. They rarely text each other now; and when they do something jars, and Jo can't put her finger on what or why. She just knows that if she and Lucy were to try a three-legged race now, rather than emerging as the natural victors, they would both fall flat on their faces.

Jo's far-off gaze gradually refocuses on the precise tidiness of the small room. She should really put her things away in the chest of drawers. (*A place for everything and everything in its place.*) It doesn't take long. Less than ten minutes later her possessions are stowed away and her empty suitcase is stored under the single bed.

There is just one thing she doesn't have to unpack, or to put away. There is no need. It is not something that she can hide away at the back of a drawer. However much she would like to.

Jo knows she has no option but to carry her broken heart around with her, wherever she goes. James saw to that when he left her four months ago.